Ball

of

Lies

JAMES DAYBOCH

PAGE PUBLISHING, INC.
Conneaut Lake, PA

This book is a fictional representation of a true story. All private
dialogues contained herein are conjecture. Although extensive research,
interviews, and analysis led the author to conclude that all or most of
the conversations contained herein took place, the actual occurrence
of many of these conversations is not known with certainty. Further,
the locations of such dialogues and/or meetings, exact timing, involved
parties, topics, and words to convey thoughts and associated philosophical
positions are based on the author's and other outside authorities'
opinions; and often rely on the accuracy of news articles or other
documents which, in most instances, were produced at or near the time
of the event and/or discussions. All such conclusions are believed by the
author to be the result of examining relevant, competent evidence.

Notwithstanding, the author believes the detailed facts presented
and the overall conclusions reached within this novel represent
an accurate accounting of what truly happened and why. As
such, the author looks forward to hosting future discussions
and entertaining questions from the informed reader.

First originally published by Page Publishing 2021

ISBN 978-1-6624-2582-0 (pbk)
ISBN 978-1-6624-2584-4 (hc)
ISBN 978-1-6624-2583-7 (digital)

Printed in the United States of America

CONTENTS

Never allow the fear of striking out
keep you from playing the game.

—Babe Ruth

CHAPTER 1

The Ballplayer

July 4, 1863—Rockford, Illinois

Perhaps the turning point of the American Civil War occurred during a forty-eight-hour period that began on July 3, 1863. On that day, President Lincoln's troops declared victory at the Battle of Gettysburg, Pennsylvania. On National Independence Day, Union regiments would defeat the Confederate forces at Vicksburg, Mississippi. In doing so, the North would finally regain strategic and logistical control of the Mississippi River. Boats carrying troops and supplies could once again pass freely through the Southern sector down to the Gulf of Mexico. Conversely, the Confederacy would no longer have access to the river, and the South was now effectively split into two pieces—a basic tactic in warfare. Although these battles were monumental Union victories, the war would continue to wreak havoc on the people of this nation for another two years.

Despite the thousand miles that buffered Illinoisans from the places where the battles were tearing apart the South, Northern communities were by no means spared from the ravages and loss of life that came with war. Union enlistees from Illinois would soon number two million brave lads, thus becoming the North's fourth-highest-ranking state contributing young men to the war effort. Funeral processions for the area's fallen sons were frequent, visible, and accepted as routine to the less affected. Events of the war reported by area newspapers appeared on a regular basis. Although to a lesser extent than in the South, severe shortages of supplies caused by support of the war effort were evident during every meal and most daily activities. Nonetheless, citizens of Rockford infrequently gave an outward appearance of grief from the loss of their vibrant young friends and close family members. To the untrained eye, Rockford was a peaceful industrial community. The sounds, smells, movement, and sights of everyday life remained nearly as it had always been. Regardless, such times would leave a noticeable and lasting impression on everyone's mind for the remainder of their lives. The most long-ranging effects would be the toll these circumstances had on the minds of local youth—especially those not quite old enough to serve yet mature enough to understand. Albert Goodwill Spalding was one of those young men that came of age in this place at that time.

It was not yet close to lunchtime—rather what was more commonly hailed as *dinnertime* in Rockford. The lad of thirteen years was sitting in a rocking chair positioned in the morning light and serenity of the comfortable parlor at the home where he and his aunt lived. The teen was lost in thoughts of his own issues and aspirations, largely blocking out the realities of those elsewhere fighting and dying in a seemingly distant war. Master Spalding rocked back and forth gently, with a soft pedaling of his feet, when the boy's aunt entered the home through the screen door of the kitchen out back. She had returned from her morning visit to the commercial part of town. Upon setting down some provisions and the day's issue of the *Republic Register* on the kitchen table, the aunt stepped into the parlor.

"Albert Goodwill Spalding," exclaimed the aunt. "Why are you sitting in the dark on this of all days? It's Independence Day! And such a glorious day it is!"

Albert responded, "This isn't like any Fourth of July I ever remember! You said it yourself. No one is doing any celebrating this year."

"This isn't like any Fourth of July anyone I know remembers either," commented the aunt. "Never been anything like this in my lifetime. Sometimes, I guess, it's good to reflect. A lot of good boys are dying to the south of here. Many families—people we know—are in pain. It's difficult to celebrate. It wouldn't be right. Not in the usual sense."

"It's an empty holiday today," Albert reflected.

"I disagree," his aunt replied. "It's anything but an empty holiday."

"All I know," Albert added, "is that school is in recess, and there's nothing to do. I miss being home. I miss Mom."

"Your mother loves you with all her heart," consoled the aunt.

"Why did he have to die?" inquired Spalding. "Why did my father die?"

Albert's aunt sat down on the sofa beside the chair where the adolescent was seated and leaned toward him.

Placing her hand on his knee, Albert's aunt consoled, "Praise the Lord, his illness could have been longer than it was. Everything changed for you and your family the day your father's life passed. Your dear mother now sees your future in a place like Rockford, not Byron, Illinois."

"I miss Byron. I miss my friends. I miss my family!"

"Byron is not far from here," assured the aunt. "And you can always return there. You need to have some patience. Your mother will be right along—as soon as she settles her affairs. In the meantime, I want you to spend time with the friends you've made, or at the very least, go to the common where the other boys are playing ball."

"I don't know anyone here except for you and my teacher, and that doesn't count."

"Albert," the aunt replied, "you are a tall, strong boy. I can't understand why you haven't been making friends! You must have made some acquaintances at school."

"No. I haven't," Spalding retorted. "I'm new. They have no need for another friend. Besides, I don't know them and wouldn't know what to talk about anyway!"

"You need to overcome your shyness. On my walk home this morning, I saw a bunch of boys having a good time playing a spirited game of ball on the common. You watch them sometimes. You talk about ball most every night at dinner. I know you'd be good at it."

Spalding responded, "I sit and watch them play, and no one has invited me to play with 'em!"

"If you're waiting for an engraved invitation," stated the aunt, "you'll wind up like Methuselah with nothing to show for it. You need to get over there and tell them you want to play! They'll let you in. Mark my words!"

After briefly sitting motionless, Spalding began to rock in the chair again. The aunt stood upright, took Spalding by the hand, and helped him to rise from his chair. She led him into the kitchen.

The aunt ordered, "Go on, Albert. The fresh air and sunshine will do you good. You going outside will do the both of us good. Now, go on and show the other boys how to play that game!"

His aunt then walked over to the back door, opened it, and stood holding the door open while gesturing for him to leave.

"Now go, Albert."

The sulking youth walked slowly out the door.

"Have fun, dear," said the aunt. "When you return, you can thank me for the splendid time you'll have had."

As his aunt went inside, young Spalding began his slow pace on the short walk to the city common. Albert decided to take a round-about way to the common as he sometimes did. Along his walk, he looked up the street to his left and saw a clearing where he heard some black people were going to build a large funeral home. He couldn't imagine where those people would come up with the money to do that, but when the white funeral homes refuse you and your kind, something needs to be done. Some said, with embalming and all, it would be the first of its kind in the nation. Strange that such a savage war would be going on in the South under the banner of equality while another opposite attitude would be going on where he lived. Of course, that's just the way things were. Spalding saw three kids casually throwing around a ball that looked like a baseball. The fact was, there were separate schools for white and black kids—when there were schools—and Albert wasn't aware that the young people ever played together. It was just the way things were. In all likelihood, he thought, *They* probably didn't want to be sociable any more than *we* cared to be.

Upon arriving at the park, he was intimidated to see the sight of several boys playing a game of baseball. In his book, *America's National Game*, Spalding recalled that defining moment years later:

> On this particular day, I was occupying my usual place, far out beyond center field, when one of the boys hit the ball square on the nose and it came soaring in my direction. Talk about special Providence! That ball came for me straight as an arrow. Impulsively I sprang to my feet, reached out for it with my right hand, held it for a moment, and then threw it home on an air-line to the catcher.
>
> When the game was over, one of the boys came to me and said, "Say, that was a great catch you made. Wouldn't you like to play tomorrow?"
>
> Blushing, I managed to stammer that I would; and I did, and from that day, when sides were chosen, I was usually among the first to have a place. And this was my real introduction to the game.

Spalding soon established his prowess as a talented amateur baseball pitcher. At the time, playing ball as a professional was considered uncouth by the general public. Those participating on the diamond of play were thought of as noble young men that followed established rules in the pursuit of fair competition. Men from all walks of life would join in to play ball with others, sharing a common goal of victory in athleticism, with a comradery of sharing team spirit. It was a time of lofty philosophical values that would usher in the Victorian era. It was a time when the presence of women spectators had become welcome. It was socially acceptable to be a genteel onlooker, regardless of one's station in life. Spalding would later write of his beginnings as a serious ballplayer during these days when baseball embodied the highest of American ideals in what was, in appearance, pure amateur competition. In his writings, Spalding vividly reflected on his so-called *amateur* beginnings at the onset of his fourteen-year march toward athletic immortality.

> [I began my employment]…with a Chicago wholesale grocery, where I was to receive $40 a week as bill clerk, with the understanding that I was to pitch for the Excelsiors during the [baseball] season. I was told by the proprietor not to mention the amount of my salary to fellow clerks. I hadn't been at work but a few days when a son of Frank Parmalee—of Chicago Transfer fame—who had his desk near mine, asked the leading question: "How much do you get?" I answered, "I don't know; my first payday hasn't arrived." He told me that he got $10 a week, and I suppose he ranked me as about *a fiver*.

After receiving but one paycheck, the grocery joined a litany of businesses that failed that year. Spalding needed to find another job.

> I returned to Rockford and obtained employment as bookkeeper in the Rockford Register office, also doing similar work for Mr. A. N. Nicholds, agent for the Charter Oaks Life Insurance Co., with the understanding that I was to pitch for the Forest Citys.

Yes, it was deceitful for a business owner to pay excessive wage for the sole purpose of playing ball with a local club in a manner that, in essence, falsely maintained an aura of amateur status. It might similarly seem inappropriate that Spalding would accept such an offer. To Spalding, however, it was a harmless deception, and no laws had been broken. Besides, who ever heard of a job applicant turning down an offer of employment because the prospective employer wished to pay too much money to start? This was a lesson in the American way of life, and Spalding was doing what he loved. He was playing ball!

Regardless of whether the impressionable youth had a bead on what the future held in store for him, playing along with the established system of American principles, or lack thereof, enabled him to focus on honing his pitching skills for the next two years by playing as an *amateur* with the Forest City nine. Moreover, the teen was on the cusp of a destiny that would transition his status from that of a ballplayer with local notoriety to becoming a person of national prominence.

July 9, 1867—the White Lot, Washington, DC

Four years prior to the construction of Washington, DC's, Olympic Grounds ballpark, the incomparable Washington Nationals Base Ball Club played on a less elaborate setting. Nevertheless, their temporary ball field was not without its own charm.

The old field where the Nationals played, known as *the White Lot*, had an unusual whitewash fence in the outfield. Then, too, placement of the grounds was unique to the nation's capital city. Imposing office buildings of the federal government were nearby, and with the slope of the surrounding land, the panorama provided the batter and spectators with a dramatic view when looking beyond the white of the outfield barrier. One of the more significant sights that could easily be seen was the property at 1600 Pennsylvania Avenue where the backyard of the White House was adjacent to the field where the Nationals and other teams played.

Reciprocally, the ball field could be seen by the White House occupants. The *White Lot* was on a piece of land that would later become known as the Ellipse. The ball field had been placed in that location as a convenience for federal government employees who desired to participate in or otherwise observe a good game of baseball. In addition to government employees, residents and guests of the White House often took advantage of the location. President Lincoln and son, Tad, would occasionally come out from behind the white walls of their residence to watch a game of ball. Lincoln's successor and current president, Andrew Johnson, would attend baseball contests, most visibly over the next seven months that preceded the commencement of his impeachment hearings. During an era when seating was not offered to spectators at ball fields, save a few simple benches, President Johnson authorized the placement of slant-back chairs along the first baseline so that federal employees and other visitors could enjoy a good game of ball in comfort. Home field for the Washington Nationals and other area baseball clubs was a memorable place to play the game.

It was Tuesday morning, and with most people at their place of employment, the field was motionless—save one man sitting on a team bench, accompanied by the presence of a few ravens, pigeons, and seagulls serving as onlookers. The smart fit of the man's suit coat, buttoned to the top, showed off his athletic physique. With his back to the field of play, his steely eyes glared northward toward the White House grounds. The person on the bench was Frank Jones, president of the Washington Nationals club.

As a man in his thirties, Jones was youngish in appearance for a team president of such a prestigious club, yet he was well-seasoned for his position. Born in Massachusetts, Jones later relocated during the Civil War to New York. There, he joined the New York Infantry of the 131st Union Regiment. From the time his unit left the state for assignment in and around the Washington area, Jones was trained as adjutant to his commanding officer. With his unit weathering nineteen battles that began at the ferocious Battle of Manassas, Jones gained firsthand knowledge in the art of executive decision making, high-level administration, and complex logistics. This experience, in combination with his days as a ballplayer, enabled Jones to take the helm of the Nationals club and, in this, his first year as club president, transform the ball club from one of mediocrity to having the best roster in the game. Although listed as "clerk" for a federal agency, Jones had been previously discharged as a colonel and was able to secure all the time needed to properly tend to his club's matters.

While gazing at the landscape centered on the highest office in the land, Jones spotted a familiar figure walking toward him.

The thirtyish character had a distinctive, well-manicured beard. His name was Henry Chadwick. Despite not yet being of middle age, Chadwick had already established himself as a pioneer in reporting on baseball games, an innovator by, among other things, inventing the modern-day *box score* and, for the past seven years, served as editor of *Beadle Dime Base-ball Player Guides*, the first and premier baseball publication. In his Sunday best, Chadwick carried a leather bag under his arm as he neared the bench where Jones sat.

As Jones arose, Chadwick came up to Jones and commented, "Good morning, Colonel! Your office said I'd find you here."

Jones nodded. "Thinking about the tour. Many details to go over."

"I can imagine," replied Chadwick. "It's a big trip you have planned, and incidentally, I want to thank you, once again, for inviting me to come along for the ride."

"It's an honor to have you aboard, Mr. Chadwick. You'll serve the club's purposes well."

Chadwick responded, "So long as the National's purposes are in the best interest of baseball, I will guarantee it. And now that you speak of 'loose ends,' I have a few questions of my own regarding matters in need of my attention prior to our departure. Might we sit in some of those chairs, if you have a moment, so that I may make a few notes? Having played a round of cricket the other day, my hindside is informing me that those nearby chairs will be less painful to sit on than this bench."

The two men walked a few steps to the chairs along the first baseline and sat down. Chadwick took some papers out of his portfolio and inquired, "First, is everything still on schedule?"

"The train leaves the station Thursday at 4:00 PM," replied Jones. "And, as far as I know, all trains and boats along our pilgrimage remain true to the stated times of departure."

"All right," mumbled Chadwick as he looked over the notes he had already prepared. "Here's what I have. I'll read the schedule, and please, stop me if you question whether my notes are accurate. Upon your approval, I'll feed the information to the newspapers."

"I expect to know the answers to this line of questioning like the back of my hand," responded Jones. "Lay on, Macduff."

Chadwick read his list, pausing after each city and date he named, "Saturday, the Columbus Capital Club. Sunday and Monday at the Union Grounds in Cincinnati. We'll face the Red Stockings on Sunday and the Buckeyes on Monday. From the Union Grounds, we head to Dexter Park in Chicago town with games against the Forest City BBC on July 25, the Excelsiors on the twenty-seventh, and the Chicago Atlantics two days after that."

Jones quipped, "Paraphrasing the ancient, Cassells, *by Jove, I think you've got it!*"

Accentuating his native English accent, Chadwick retorted, "Try as you may, sir, you'll never pass for an Englishman!"

Jones sighed, saying sarcastically, "I'll simply have to get over it."

Chadwick continued, "As a point of order, why do we have a day off in Chicago between when you play the Forest City and Excelsior teams? Is it a matter of taking in the sights of Chicago or preparing for the Excelsiors?"

"We'll take in some sights and relax while the team recovers from the first postgame banquet. We don't need time to prepare for the Excelsiors. We'll do that by taking batting practice with the Forest City schoolboys! We know how Forest City plays, and they've been consistently beaten badly by their rivals."

"You never know, Frank. I understand that Forest City has a couple of good ballplayers and, like they say, *on any given day…*"

"I see you're an underdogger," retorted Jones teasingly. "What other questions do you have, Henry?"

"I have your original roster assignments," Chadwick replied. "Of those players you were hoping to have along for the journey, how many of the Nationals squad could you round up for the trip and yank them away from their day jobs?"

"All of them," Jones boasted.

"All of them, eh," exclaimed Chadwick. "That's a neat trick!"

"Not really," replied Jones. "There's a couple of college students plus one other, and the remainder are all federal employees."

"It must be nice," commented Chadwick, "being a war hero with the government in your hip pocket."

"Everyone does it," replied Jones. "Despite the daily issues falling out from the post-Civil War *Reconstruction*, people in these parts remain appreciative for the efforts of former Union soldiers. Besides, there isn't a quality city team in the country who doesn't get the support of prominent local businesses. The only difference is that government is the business of Washington."

Chadwick then inquired, "May I assume *the one other* player you referred to is none other than George Wright?"

"One and the same," Jones responded.

"Well, then, he must be a government employee also," stated Chadwick.

"Why do you say that?"

Chadwick replied, "It's quite a coup to get the best second baseman in the game, and when I looked up George's stated employer, I discovered the address of the company he works for is nothing more than an empty lot overgrown with weeds."

"My dear Henry, I relish your company along our impending travels. I very much look forward to your accompaniment but more so for your learned wit and ability to capture the moment in writing, rather than to serve as an investigative reporter."

"Have no fear, Colonel. My questions are more of a sportswriter. That and curiosity rather than discerning what is amateur sport and that which is not."

"Your assurance is appreciated," Jones replied.

As Chadwick finished making a few notes, he began placing his papers back into his leather portfolio. Chadwick looked up and inquired, "If I may, Colonel, how much will this trip cost?"

"Five thousand [dollars], more or less."

"Five thousand dollars! That's a pretty penny! How much of that do you expect to be offset by gate receipts?"

"I've agreed not to take one penny from the hosts' collections," responded Jones.

"No gate receipts? Out of idle curiosity, where does this generosity emanate?"

"In part," Jones confided, "Maryland Representative Pue has a lot to do with it. I don't know what his political aspirations are, but I am aware that he has been getting chummy with President Johnson as of late. Somewhere in that rat's nest lies the answer."

"Given speculation of impeachment against the president, I'm not certain whether Congressman Pue himself might know where his aspirations will lead him. Regardless, it's good to have him on your side or—at least for now."

Jones stood as Chadwick arose. With a wide smile, Jones said, "And *now*, Mr. Chadwick, it's time to finalize plans and pack our bags. We only have forty-eight hours in which to do so."

The two men began walking across the field together as they headed off in a spirited gait. Within moments, they began to blend into the hubbub of the capital city beyond the serenity of the *White Lot*. As Jones and Chadwick walked, they told one another a few lighthearted stories of baseball and other reminiscences with intermittent laughs. They continued to disappear out of sight from where they had concluded their discussion. Expectations were high that the excursion would be both noteworthy and fun!

* * *

On the day of the trip's departure, friends, fans, and the press ensured an auspicious beginning to the Midwest Base Ball Tourney. Sadly, the Nationals' first game on July 13 in Columbus, Ohio, was poorly attended due to a publicity error in the scheduled date and time. Aside from the box scores and usual statistics, the sarcastic retraction in the local newspaper, the *Daily Ohio Statesman*, in its entirety, appeared as follows:

> THE BASE BALL MATCH.—The National Club of Washington, D.C., and the Capital Club of this city, played a match game on the grounds of the latter club, below Stewart's Grove, on Saturday morning. We announced that the game would be played in the afternoon, and were thus

informed by members of the club, and, we suppose, because of our limited circulation (about
five times greater than that of the *Journal*) the
Capitals did not deem it necessary to inform us
of the change.

So as not to rely on the competency of local clubs to spread the
word for future games, Colonel Jones, assisted by Chadwick, took
the initiative to ensure there would be no more mix-ups. As for the
outcome of the game, the final result was Nationals, 91–Capitals, 10.

Despite the disappointment of having such a small crowd on
hand to witness the glorious beating, members of the Nationals club
took solace in the final score and the fellowship that followed.

The Washington troupe soon departed Ohio's capital city for
Cincinnati, Ohio. The group arrived in town on Sunday, July 14,
to "a full day of hospitality." The contest between the Cincinnati
Red Stockings and the Nationals occurred the next day, and the
Nationals would not be as hospitable to the Ohio teams as the city of
Cincinnati had been to the Washington contingent. This time, the
game was properly advertised in the local newspapers with zeal, and
a large crowd witnessed the event. The final score of the first match,
not unexpectedly, was Nationals, 53–Cincinnati, 10.

In the July 16 edition of *The Cincinnati Enquirer* published on
the day following the match, the news article began as follows:

The Great Base-ball Game
Great Enthusiasm and Excitement
FOUR THOUSAND SPECTATORS

No game of base-ball or cricket has ever excited
such interest as the match played yesterday by the
Cincinnati and Washington clubs.

On the next day, the Nationals played the Cincinnati Buckeyes.
The result, ending after six innings, was Nationals, 88–Buckeyes, 12.

Bidding farewell to Cincinnati, the next stop on the tour was Louisville. On July 17, the day following their arrival in Kentucky, the Nationals played the Louisville club. The final score of the game was a familiar one: Nationals, 82–Louisville, 21.

The touring group's next stop was at Indianapolis, Indiana. The final score of this contest was Nationals, 106–Indianapolis, 21.

The Nationals team and its touring contingent would subsequently depart for the largest city on the tour: St. Louis, Missouri. Two games were scheduled to be played at the infamous Union Grounds. Reasonable competition was anticipated in this city where the sport was supported by a population of a quarter million people, for this, the nation's fourth-largest city. Indeed, St. Louis' population was nearly triple that of Washington, DC. Despite the imposing size of this important Mississippi River port, the colonel knew the abilities of his players and was only mildly concerned. The two matches were played on July 22 and 23, and the outcomes to the contests would be similar to what had been experienced on the Western Tour thus far held.

In the first of two games, the match yielded the following result: Nationals, 113–Union Club, 26.

The outcome of the second match, ending after six innings, was Nationals, 53–Empire, 26.

Dexter Race Park in Chicago would be the next and final stop on the tour. Chicago was nearly as large as St. Louis and also had two premier teams. In Chicago, the two teams with the best win/loss records were the Excelsiors and the Atlantics. Prior to playing a game with either team, there would be one game with a young club hailing from the interior of the state: the Forest City Base Ball Club of Rockford, Illinois.

As the train carrying the traveling baseball show began to near its destination of Great Central Station located in downtown Chicago, Chadwick saw Jones sitting by himself looking out the window.

The cagey Chadwick, seizing the moment, walked up to where the young club president was seated. "Mind if I join you, sir?"

Spotting Chadwick as he turned his head, Jones smiled and said, "Not at all, Henry! Take a load off your feet."

"Thank you. I'll take but only a moment of your time," Chadwick responded. "I have some items that may be of interest to you."

"What do you have, my friend?"

Chadwick replied, "Two news clippings from the *Chicago Tribune* that may be of interest to you. The first article covers the city's preparations for the games. As you are aware, the city's race park has a large flat area, and the City of Chicago committed to creating a baseball field on those grounds in which to play our matches."

"Dexter Park," Jones responded. "I'm hopeful the landscaping of the ball diamond and outfield will be complete and in fine order."

"As you well know," replied Chadwick, "Chicago and, indeed the entire Midwest, is *a mecca* for the game. Based on what I read here, and of no surprise, preparations were largely finished weeks ago. The ball diamond in the center of the park and the outfield are well in place and reported to be in fine condition. Chair seating has also been installed along the entire right field line."

Jones was enthusiastic. "Beautiful. Well done!"

Chadwick handed Jones the second clipped newspaper extract and said, "Yes. That's good news. This article I now hand you is of a different topic. I picked it up at a newsstand earlier in our trip. It describes a baseball tournament that recently took place in Chicago when we were starting off our tour."

"I take it," Jones quipped, "this is more of a strategic nature?"

"It is," replied Chadwick. "The excerpt describes the results of a baseball tournament held a couple of weeks ago."

Before looking at the article, Jones asked, "May I inquire as to your synopsis from reading this?"

"Nothing too earth-shattering," Chadwick said, "but rather a matter of note." As Jones stared at Chadwick, the journalist continued. "The small city kids from Rockford that we'll be facing first, they played both the Atlantics and the Excelsiors. The Forest Citys lost both games as one would expect."

Jones inquired, "And?"

"Both games were extremely close," replied Chadwick. "We've been traveling, playing games, and participating in each city's hospitality at a nonstop clip. The Forest City boys are full of youth and will be well-rested. As I believe you know, we play that team on day one."

"Williams will be pitching for us," commented Jones. "Do you not think Williams will be up for the task?"

Chadwick stood up, leaving the news article with Jones. "I would expect he will be. Regardless, I thought you might want to know."

Chadwick nodded goodbye to Jones and began walking toward the front of the passenger car in the direction of where his bags were placed, trudging and wobbling left and right in the thin aisle while the passenger car rocked from side to side as the train neared the route's final stop.

Wednesday, July 24, 1867

With the anticipation and enthusiasm the Nationals' visit had generated, in combination with the typically high levels of midweek activity from commerce and tourism during the summer months, all downtown hotels were *packed to the gills*. The largest hotel in downtown and in close proximity to Dexter Park was the Briggs House. The five-story structure of Italian ornate design formerly served as headquarters to presidential candidate Lincoln's campaign shortly after the building had opened to the public. It was no secret that the Nationals would be staying at this establishment with a maximum occupancy of 500. Many other teams of prominence that came to Chicago would also stay here so that they could witness the athleticism of the capital's club.

On the day before the first game, the Nationals received a steady stream of newsmen and other guests throughout the afternoon and well into the evening. Newspeople were fighting to have a brief interview with George Wright, yet every player for the Nationals' was deluged by the media. Once other teams began making appearances throughout the hotel and despite Jones's and Chadwick's efforts for an orderly means of getting across their message, it was a chaotic scene. It was no wonder that after but a brief period that seemed lengthy to the participants and despite an awareness of the inclement weather outside, the ballplayers were anxious to get to the field of play to begin preliminaries for the first contest.

Thursday, game day #1, July 25, 1867

A continuous rain fell throughout the morning hours, and the roads leading to Dexter Park were filled with mud. Horse hooves and the wheels from the constant parade of carriages, carts, and wagons making the pilgrimage to the park created deep ruts in the roads. Traveling to the park by such means became a navigational nightmare for the heartiest of horse teams drawing the vehicles and riders. Fortunately, the city had train service that neared the park, and the vast majority of spectators arrived in densely filled railcars one after the other.

By 2:00 PM when the honorary selection of umpire was made, despite the challenges of the commute for all would-be spectators, a crowd of more than 5,000 had assembled. Many of the guests in attendance, despite the rainy conditions, were finely attired ladies. From the field of play, all the umbrellas along the slope had the likeness of a densely populated field of mushrooms. Although the first game was to be played by the club from Rockford rather than one of the Chicago powerhouses, the crowd was the largest ever assembled in this town for such an event. In the open space behind the home plate, a tightly woven line of carriages and wagons formed a large arc extending from beyond first base passing behind home plate to the area nearest third base.

Most of the onlookers sat or stood in the open, five to ten people in depth, along the lengths of the right and left field lines. Several people made the ninety-mile trek from Rockford to the game, and Spalding could recognize a few of them. Some friends of the family, the Churchills, brought their two oldest of five daughters. The oldest, Fannie, was two years younger than Albert. Still, she had provided good company during his more recent lonely times. The next oldest was Elizabeth. Little Lizzie was only eleven, but Albert knew she was enamored with him, and as a lad of seventeen, he had fun with that. He had no idea, of course, how their paths would one day cross.

Immediately prior to game time, a flip of the coin determined that the Forest City club would bat first, and the Nationals would take the field to begin the match. Williams took the mound for the Nationals.

Years later, Spalding recalled how he and his fellow Rockford teammates felt moments before the game was to begin:

> I was the pitcher…and, as a lad of seventeen, experienced a severe case of stage fright… The great reputations of the Eastern players…caused me to shudder at the contemplation of the punishment my pitching was about to receive. A great lump arose in my throat, and my heart beat so like a trip-hammer that I imagined it could be heard by everyone…
>
> I knew, also, that every player on the Rockford nine had an idea that their kid pitcher would surely become rattled and go to pieces as soon as the strong batters of the Nationals had opportunity to fall upon his delivery. They had good grounds for that fear. Every member of the team cautioned me to take my time and keep cool; but I…recognized that every one of them was so scared that none could speak above a whisper. The fact is, we were all nearly frightened to death…

The contest began in a relatively slow start, and the Nationals led after the first inning by a score of 3 to 2. At the end of five innings, the score was Rockford–16, Nationals–11.

As the match progressed, the Rockford squad was clutching on to a dwindling lead, and the Rockford bats produced no runs in their half of the seventh inning. As the Nationals came to bat in the bottom of the seventh, a heavy downpour commenced, and play was halted. Seeing this as an opportunity to ensure a fairytale victory, the coach of the Rockford team made a plea in earnest for the umpire to call the game due to rain. The umpire refused to do so. After a time, the rain stopped, and play was resumed.

At the end of eight innings, the game was still up for grabs. Rockford led the Washingtonians by a score of 25 to 21. It was Rockford's final turn at bat. In the top of the ninth inning, the last scheduled inning, King came to the plate for Rockford. He swung and hit a pop-up in foul territory, and the ball was caught by Berthrong of the Nationals for the first out. Stearns next came to bat and made it to first base on an infield hit fielded by the third baseman. Next, Spalding and Barker each hit singles to left field. By the time the top of the ninth was over, the Forest City club had scored four important runs on five hits and led by 8 points going into the bottom of the ninth inning—what would likely be the final at bat for the Nationals.

In the eight previous games of the road trip, Washington averaged 11 runs per inning, and in this instance, they were only down by 8 tallies. An article in the *Chicago Tribune* theorized the mindset of the Rockford nine in the moment:

> When it is considered that the National nine are recognized as being one of the best and strongest clubs; their record for many seasons has been a highly successful one; that throughout an extended tour in the West they defeated by odds varying from two to five to one every nine which they met, it may be presumed that no thought was entertained by any of the [Rockford] nine; which were to be pitted against them on their arrival here of vanquishing them. Indeed it was generally believed that they would rest contented could they make even a fair scorse as contrasted with the over-weening game of their victorious opponents. No one had an idea that the Forest City nine—a club coming from a town in the interior of the state—would change places with their opponents and wrest from them the palm of victory. All

thoughts were centered upon the [next] match on Saturday, when the formidable Excelsiors should meet the Nationals, as the one in which Western muscle and skill should vie most closely with these Eastern veterans… The vast crowd watched the game with no sort of feeling that the playing of the Forest City Club was going to last.

The thoughts of the crowd watching the game was described thusly:

> Not until the…closing innings did that multitude view the game with bated breath and straining gaze, watching with increasing anxiety every part of the game…

Except for an occasional shout of encouragement from the sidelines to the Forest City boys, the crowd was remarkably quiet as Fletcher of the Nationals club came to bat in the bottom of the ninth. Spalding had pitched the previous eight innings, and whereas a starting pitcher in those days was required to complete the game to avoid default, he remained in the pitcher's box. As the lower half of the inning began, Spalding wound up and delivered a good pitch toward home. Fletcher swung his bat and hit a ground ball toward second base. Rockford's Addy fielded the ball and threw to Stearns at first base in time to quickly make the first of three badly desired outs.

The Nationals' speedy shortstop, Smith, was batting in the seventh position and next came to the plate. Spalding pitched the ball, and Smith hit a ground ball to third base and beat out the throw to safely reach first base. Berthrong next came to bat and hit a fly ball toward Rockford's Barker in short center field, and running hard, Barker could not hold the ball. Runners were safe at second and third base, and any hope for a double play was no longer in order.

Norton, the Nationals catcher, next stepped into the batter's box. Upon Spalding entering into his windup, Spalding made an "illegal" motion of his shoulder, and the umpire called a balk. This allowed

Berthrong to advance to third base and Smith to advance from third base, thus handing the Nationals the first run in the bottom of the ninth inning. On Spalding's next pitch, Norton swung his bat and hit a ground ball to second base. The capable Addy fielded the ball and threw out Norton for out number two as Berthrong came home for a second run. There were two runs in, two outs, and no one was on base; however, the top of the Nationals' batting order would now have their at bat. The best of the nation's best were coming to the plate.

Parker was slotted at the top of the Nationals' batting order. Spalding took his windup and delivered the pitch. Parker swung his bat and hit a ground ball to shortstop that was "muffed" by Barnes, allowing Parker to safely reach first base. The powerful Williams next stepped up to the plate. Upon the nervous Spalding commencing his windup, the umpire called yet another balk on the young pitcher's motion, and Parker was allowed to freely advance from first to second base. Spalding maintained his composure and subsequently delivered a good pitch. Williams swung his bat and hit a hard ground ball toward first base. Stearns fielded the ball cleanly, ran to first base, and stepped on the bag for the final out of the game.

The ensuing scene was described in the next day's *Tribune* article:

> The game was over, and the Forest City had won. The invincibles were defeated. For a moment the crowd and players stood, almost doubting the record. Then, as they comprehended what the result had been, one grand rush was made for the winning nine, and they were borne off the field on the shoulders of their enthusiastic friends, while the cheering that arose was a very tumult in its noisy confusion.

The reporter side of Chadwick knew that a seventeen-year-old beating the Nationals was big news, and deserting his travel-mates, he walked over to the center of the crowd where an elated Spalding was standing.

"Mr. Spalding, my name is Henry Chadwick, and I would like to have—"

Spalding interrupted, "Mr. Chadwick, I heard you were making the trip. This is a real honor, sir!"

"It is my honor to meet you," Chadwick replied. "May we perhaps have a few words—away from your avid followers?"

Spalding replied, "I'd like that very much, but I should tell my manager. He's the one who usually talks to reporters."

"Son," Chadwick chuckled, "your manager may *talk* to the news, but, you sir, *are* the news! He won't have a problem, and if he does, you tell him that I told you to let me know so that, in turn, I may contact him of my own volition should he take exception to our talking. From this day forward into the foreseeable future, my lad, my office will be open to you at all times."

"If you're really willing to defend me," Spalding expressed, "I'll come with you this second!"

Chadwick could not hold back a short burst of genuine laughter. "Are you staying at the Briggs House, by chance?"

"Not so fortunate, sir," Spalding replied. "Why do you ask?"

Chadwick began leading Spalding out of the center of the crowd that surrounded them and a few of the Rockford players. Chadwick said to Spalding, "It might have been a good place to meet, but that's immaterial." Pointing to the nearest side of the park, the forty-three-year-old newsman said, "Lets commandeer a couple of those chairs over there. It's easier for me to take notes."

Spalding timidly repeated, "Notes?"

The smiling Chadwick replied, "Didn't you know? Under the United States Constitution, all reporters are required to take notes without exception. Fear not, Mr. Spalding. I just wish to talk to a talented athlete who has his entire future to contend with."

The two men walked over to some secluded chairs and sat down as Chadwick pulled out of his suit pocket a pencil and a notepad.

Chadwick suggested, "Let's get rid of the formalities. Shall we? I want you to call me *Henry*."

"I'm Al or AG, sir."

The two men belatedly shook hands—vigorously.

"So tell me," Chadwick began, "how long have you been throwing that ball? It appears like you've been doing that thing since you were throwing rattles out of the playpen."

The beaming Spalding replied, "Not hardly! I first played ball four Independence Days ago."

"I like that answer," remarked Chadwick. "This could make one h——, one heck of a patriotic story! So where's home? Rockford?"

"Byron, Illinois, sir," Spalding replied, "by way of Rockford."

Chadwick asked, "Are you looking forward to living in a big city, or does it scare you?"

Spalding was young but learning. "You'll have to put that pad of paper away before I fumble for an answer to that question."

"Can't do that," jousted Chadwick. "I don't want to make your forefathers angry."

Spalding politely inquired, "Mr. Ch——, Henry, may I ask you one question?"

"When a story makes a request," Chadwick commented, "I will always elatedly comply. What is your question, Al?"

Spalding vociferated, "What made you invent the box score?"

"Oh, that little thing," Chadwick mildly boasted. "I've always been big on numbers. They help me to understand better what's happening at the time. If you put together even a few numbers just right, they paint a vivid picture. I figured there may be other sports followers out there that feel the same way I do. Back in England, the news reports games of cricket in something of a similar manner. I simply decided to reformat the cricket method and customize it to baseball. Is it my turn for questions?"

"Of course," Spalding declared. "My mother says, 'In Illinois, we always conform to our guests' wishes.'"

"Please tell your dear mother that Henry Chadwick appreciates her teachings," Chadwick requested. "I'll leave the tidbits for other reporters, at least for the moment. Albert, here's my final question: Where do you see yourself in five years from today?"

"What do you mean," Spalding asked, "by *see yourself?*"

"That's for you to decide," Chadwick responded.

Spalding pondered the question. "I can't answer your question at the moment. I'd need some time to figure that one out. Sorry if I can't give you an answer."

"Don't be sorry," Chadwick said. "You gave the best answer! Now, it's time for you to rejoin your team."

"I should get back to them," Spalding acknowledged. "My manager will be looking for me."

"It strikes me that the most important reason to return to your team is to savor the comradery with your teammates during victory. Have fun with this. Soon enough, it will all become business."

"That sounds good, Henry."

Handing Spalding his contact information, Chadwick stated, "Here's my business card, Albert. It's your turn to seek me out. If you want a great job, regardless of what that may be, write me. I can't get that for you, but I know people who will. Tallyho."

After shaking hands, Chadwick began walking toward his hotel. Spalding saw that his team was still entertaining a good-sized group of spectators milling around on the far side of the field. He quickly melted into the enthused crowd.

* * *

Washington's winning ways resumed two days later when they defeated the mighty Excelsiors by a score of 49 to 9. Two days after that, the Chicago area's powerhouse Atlantics were felled by a 78-to-17 margin. Accusations surfaced that gambling interests fixed the outcome of the Rockford game by bribing some Washington Nationals' players to perform poorly. The allegations were fleeting and never proven. For purposes of this story, it didn't matter. Fame had been thrust upon young Spalding.

After spending most of the next three years with the Forest City club, opportunity appeared. In 1871, several major ball club owners from various cities formed the National Association of Professional Base Ball Players. The National Association was, among other things, formed to better organize and poise the professional side of America's National Pastime. For various reasons, including anticipating major changes in the gate receipts market, the Red Stockings moved from Cincinnati to Boston, and the twenty-year-old pitching sensation signed on with the Boston Red Stockings.

The National Association lasted through five baseball seasons. In the association's final year, Spalding tallied fifty-four victories, breaking his previously established record for most wins by a pitcher in a season. By the end of the final season, the Boston Red Stockings were reigning, four-time consecutive National Association champions. Spalding was the best pitcher in the game!

In February 1876, the respected pitcher joined forces with Chicago White Stockings Owner William Hulbert to establish the National League of Professional Baseball Clubs. The National League addressed many of the remaining issues in professional baseball and remains the same organizational framework that exists today.

The two National League organizers also worked out a blockbuster player arrangement. Spalding accepted Hulbert's offer to join the Chicago team's talented roster in a special capacity. Rather than remain in his present role as star pitcher for Boston, the Illinoisan accepted Hulbert's offer to become White Stockings' Player-Manager. The chicken had come home to roost.

The National League's inaugural season was a sensational year for Spalding and the Chicago faithful! In Spalding's first year as player-manager, the White Stockings won the National League Championship—and the euphoria flowed. As one of Chicago's two primary newspapers, *The Inter Ocean* offered the highest of praise in the issue published the day after the Sox locked up the championship.

> This game gives the pennant to Chicago beyond all doubt, and the Garden City may be congratulated on its possession of the finest nine that ever operated on the diamond field.

Despite the victorious glory of his first season on the job, Spalding abandoned his formula for success in the following year. The twenty-six-year-old remained player-manager; however, he would now play the first base position rather than pitch. At this point in his career, Spalding had hurled a baseball nearly four thousand innings—easily more than most professional pitchers throw in a lifetime. The sporting goods business he and his brother founded that very year demanded his attention—as did his role as club manager. For whatever reasons, Spalding would pitch eleven more innings in that next season after which he would abdicate his responsibilities as team starting pitcher.

The 1877 baseball season met with harsh criticism by White Stockings followers and the press. The magnificent Chicago team of 1876 narrowly escaped winding up in the league's cellar by closing out their schedule in second to last place. Spalding may well have escaped more embarrassment due to the team owner's humane handling of the situation possibly because Hulbert had intentions for the young man to contribute to the future of the organization. Regardless, Spalding was through as club manager, and his ball playing days, in any capacity, would also soon be over.

More than fame and the gateway to fortune, that July day in 1867 produced the beginning of an unlikely and complex friendship of the dearest kind that would last for more than forty years. Spalding first met Henry Chadwick on that summer's visit by the Nationals. The important relationship between these two future giants of baseball would persevere to the time of Chadwick's death, the same year that a prestigious commission would render a decision on what is arguably the most significant intellectual dispute to ever hit the American sports scene.

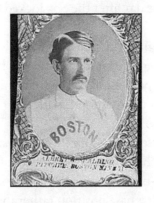

You can't judge a book by its binding.

—African journal American Speech,
1944

CHAPTER 2

An Invitation

*July 8, 1878—Fifth Avenue Hotel,
uptown Manhattan, New York*

The correspondent from the *Hartford Daily Times* looked out of place in the posh New York City hotel. His suit jacket and pants had visible wrinkles, and the fabric and tailoring left much to be desired. He entered the Fifth Avenue Hotel, the newest pearl of fashionable uptown Manhattan. The reporter walked across the luxurious lobby, opened the large door of brass and glass, and entered the spacious hotel bar within. The room was filled with the *after-work* business crowd. Threading his way past the clusters of finely attired business-people, he spotted a fellow reporter from the *Brooklyn Daily Eagle* seated next to a vacant stool along the lengthy bar. Standing behind the acquaintance, the Connecticut newsman said in a voice barely loud enough to be heard above the bar noise, "The *Daily Eagle* must be doing well these days. You're living high on the hog!"

The surprised man's face lit up. "Jenkins! It's been a while. Are you staying here?"

Jenkins shook his head. "Not hardly. The *Daily Times* spreads for decent hotels but not the nicest ones. Besides, I'd only take the stairs to my room, and most of the rooms are too high up for me."

Adams wondered, "The stairs? This hotel has an elevator! You're not afraid of that, I hope. They're fun. You don't have to pedal it, y' know—it's steam-powered."

"Doesn't matter," replied Jenkins. "I wouldn't take the thing, even if it meant getting an exclusive interview with President Hayes."

Adams responded, "I wouldn't walk across the room for an exclusive with him!"

"Oh, sure," Jenkins said sarcastically. "Tell you what, though. If you buy me a drink, I'll take the seat next to you so you don't look so friendless."

Adams responded, "What's your fancy?"

"I'll have the pretty drink you're having," Jenkins said as he sat down.

A bartender in silk vest with puffed sleeves immediately appeared.

Adams spoke, "Another Delmonico's Number One for my good friend."

"Very good, sir," responded the bartender.

Jenkins inquired, "Delmonico's Number One?"

"It's a simple drink," Adams replied. "Gin and vermouth, but what makes it spectacular is the touch of cognac they finish it with."

Jenkins then asked, "Tell me this, Adams, why would a reporter from the nation's fourth-largest city feel the need to wander over to my territory for a scoop?"

"The *Brooklyn Daily Eagle* isn't for want of news," Adams responded. "This is my day off! Besides, there's always a good crowd here on Mondays. In this place, I never know when I might overhear something worth writing about. And Jenkins, Brooklyn is not the fourth-largest city, it's third! Then, again, why do I suspect you knew that?"

The bartender delivered the drink, and Jenkins raised the glass and toasted, "Great place, great comradery!"

They both took a swig. Holding up the goblet and looking at it, Jenkins added, "This is fantastic!"

"It's a good'n," Adams agreed. "And the hotel is the best. If General Grant felt it good enough to kick off his campaign, it'll suit my needs. So, Jenkins, what brings a hotshot correspondent like you to the big city from the farmlands of Connecticut?"

Jenkins replied, "I came for a story that didn't pan out. Then, good fortune took me into her graces."

The *Brooklyn Eagle*'s Adams was listening.

Jenkins elaborated, "I walked into a fascinating drugstore hours later, and the face of 'Providence' smiled down upon me. I ran into someone I knew from years past when he sometimes wrote articles for the newspapers. He invited me to a most interesting party that's firing up about now."

"You mean to say you had me order a cocktail in this overpriced palace when you could be drinking for free somewhere else?"

Jenkins laughed. "Not hardly. There won't be any liquor at this affair."

"Sounds depressing," retorted Adams.

"Anything but," Jenkins of Hartford responded. "It will be 'uplifting,' and that, my friend, I say in the literal sense. When I tell you who the party is for, you'll be begging me to come along."

"First off," Adams began, "you said a reporter you knew. Might I also know him?"

"I don't think so," Jenkins replied. "Not a reporter, an occasional contributor. He's an attorney by the name of Henry Olcott. Henry Steele Olcott, Esquire! He goes by the designation of *colonel.*"

"Nope. Don't know him," Adams acknowledged. "So tell me about this fascinating group of people who practice abstinence?"

Jenkins asked, "Have you heard of Madame Helena Blavatsky?"

"No, no, no," Adams exclaimed. "Please don't tell me you're getting hooked up with *that* crowd of loons!"

Jenkins responded, "For with what judgment ye judge, ye shall be judged. That's Mathew 6 or 7."

"My comment is not of my opinion, friend," defended Adams. "It's what I've been told. I've heard many things about Madame Blavatsky and her cronies—mostly bad."

"I have a few seconds, Mr. Adams. Tell me what you think you know."

Adams inquired, "You really want to hear what I have to say?"

Jenkins patiently looked to the *Eagle*'s Adams without speaking.

"Russian born," Adams began. "Came over on the boat in rags. Hung around some local money and hooked up with an oddball attorney, and I assume the fellow you ran into is one and the same."

"They are, and I'm not sure why you think you know he's an oddball, but please, do go on," Jenkins insisted.

Adams recalled, "The woman is peddling some new form of Eastern religion, and she's assembled some followers, a few being up a ways on the social ladder. Shall I continue?"

Adams held Jenkin's attention, and again, Jenkins did not speak.

"I heard she's an upscale fortune-teller," exclaimed Adams. "The woman puts on séances for Christ's sake! I understand she's been kicked out of half the capitals of Europe for charlatanism."

Jenkins of the *Daily Times* chuckled. "No one's perfect! The woman is absolutely brilliant. She wrote a book—"

Adams blurted, "Perfect? That woman wrote a book that people say is blatant plagiarism. I expect she calls herself 'Madame' because it's good for business, but she'd likely rather call herself 'madam' because she screws everyone around her. And the summary of summaries, and these are not my words—'she weighs 300 pounds, smokes like a chimney, and swears like a sailor.'"

"I detect the slightest hint of disdain," Jenkins lightheartedly remarked.

"I try not to gossip—too much—but I see my description of her more as a biography of the Antichrist!"

"Madame Blavatsky," the reporter from Hartford began, "has occasion to be ill-tempered, and she does possess humanly traits. Nevertheless, you have it all wrong, sir. You really do. If you had printed what you said at the *Hartford Daily Times*, I'd call it shoddy journalism."

Adams laughed. "I won't respond to your crack on *shoddy journalism*, but suffice to say if I were looking to join a church, and Blavatsky were priest, I'd become an atheist—and this is a good Catholic talking!"

"I knew you were a *good Catholic*," Jenkins quipped, "the moment I walked into this place."

This time, Adams was stoic.

"Look," said Jenkins, "she wouldn't be my first choice for manning the pulpit either, but she'd never be a clergy person anyway. Madame Blavatsky has no interest in being any such thing. Fact is, you seem so judgmental that I fear you will not keep an open mind. If, on the other hand, you're willing to give what I have to say a listen, I think you'll be glad you did."

"Always game for a good story, Jenkins. I'm all ears."

"I know this woman," responded Jenkins. "Certainly not in the *biblical sense*, but I have had the pleasure of her company while in the presence of others. Everyone surrounding her are well-educated and of seemingly good character. Lend me those *ears* and an open mind, and I'll give you that 'story' you say you're willing to hear."

"I've said my piece," Adams replied.

Jenkins leaned toward Adams. "Helena is unlike anyone you or I have ever met. The woman speaks nine languages—fluently. She reads more languages than that—with proficiency. On almost any given night, she entertains groups of people in her apartment, and the preponderance of guests I sit with speak in a variety of languages that seldom includes the English tongue. These guests, men and women, are generally of uncommon intellect, and they seek *her* guidance and knowledge. Throughout the Madame's extensive worldly travels, she has studied with numerous thinkers of renown from all over the world. She's been to places like India, Tibet, Greece, Egypt, England, and other European nations, wherever learned people hang their hats or turbans as the case may be."

Adams's and the bartender's eyes met. Jenkins paused as Adams made a motion to the bartender who, in turn, acknowledged with a nod.

Jenkins slowly shook his head. "I dislike saying this against my own kind, but Americans are arrogant—or, at least, most of the white ones are that I know. They think we have the superior education and minds and philosophical bearing. Of all the cultures and nations in the world, we rank near last in terms of having an unbroken chain of philosophical development or knowledge. Yes, those countries have class systems and can cause some disparity, but overall, those places elsewhere have more than their share of superior thinkers, especially if you consider people of India and elsewhere with skin tones darker than ours."

"She's obviously smart and well-traveled," Adams noted, "but that doesn't give her a license to peddle some form of foreign religion!"

Jenkins retorted, "What she professes is not a religion! Her studies and the knowledge she possesses comes from the disciplines of philosophy, the sciences, and mathematics since the time of Pythagoras. She writes about these things and will be the first to admit that she was not the first human on earth to come up with many of the concepts to which she expounds. She does know of various religions though and gives her concepts a good dose of spirituality. The Madame freely mentions names of gurus and swamis and pundits who she's met, studied with, and corresponds. Madame Blavatsky has read more definitive works within her areas of interest than anyone I have ever known. The woman has an uncanny recall that if I had not personally witnessed the verification of what she recited while merely in passing, I would not otherwise believe such a warehouse of knowledge to be humanly achievable for any one person to absorb—with total accuracy. She is the most amazing, and, yes, charming person I know!"

"It's a good tale you tell," the Brooklynite Adams conceded. "I know little of the new religion or whatever it is she preaches, and you make a decent case that this phenom has one or two redeeming qualities. All the same, I can't forget what I understand to be the woman's many indiscretions from the past—and of the present."

"I was hesitant at first," Jenkins confessed. "*Theosophy* is the name of Blavatsky's movement. She may have come up with the term, *Theosophy*, I'm uncertain. Someone told me it was conceived by a religious leader in India. The words that make up the term come from the Greek language that, in combination, means *divine knowledge*. It isn't a religion though. The concept is more encompassing. I am not a member of the movement and am neither her most able defender nor the best person to describe the belief system they have. I can tell you though that Theosophy is more about understanding the forces of nature and the cosmos and how we fit within, rather than a basic belief system such as that of how most people define religion.

To imply that she *preaches* is also a misnomer. Theosophists don't recruit followers. Rather, they welcome men and women, of all races and creeds, when people desirous of becoming members indicate a sincere interest and are deemed to be worthy and of good intent."

Adams finished his drink, and his eyes were beginning to glaze over, but he continued looking at Jenkins.

Jenkins continued, "As for her indiscretions, one might consider that Madame Blavatsky has had to do many things over the years in order to survive as a woman in unfamiliar surroundings. I'm sure she regrets having done many things in her past. Anyway, that's the story."

"Come to the gathering with me," Jenkins urged. "It may provide you with some juicy—if not important things to write about. It could even prove interesting or, better still, life altering!"

"So then," asked Adams, "this Theosophy is a way of life?"

Jenkins replied, "It is but not without peculiarity! One final mention, out of curiosity, have you heard of the *brass teapot?*"

"I don't believe so," replied a puzzled Adams. "What is it?"

Jenkins thought for a moment. "My grandmother used to tell me a story when I was little. She said when Judas turned Jesus in to the Romans, he received a reward of silver shekels. Grandma showed me where the reference appears in the Bible. Judas supposedly became overwrought with grief and, prior to hanging himself, threw the silver away. The silver somehow wound up in a blacksmith's cauldron filled with molten brass. The blacksmith was making a teapot. Once forged, the pot wound up in the possession of an ancient king. The king discovered the teapot had magical powers and placed it in a well-guarded fortress. Where the famous *Chalice of Jesus* is thought of in a good way, the teapot is thought more to be of darkness and evil. My gram said it was owned by priests of the Spanish Inquisition, Genghis Khan, Marie Antoinette, Henry VIII, and as hard as this may be to believe, I recently read somewhere that the relic is, at this moment, in the hands of Jesse James, the bank and train robber."

"Why," Adams asked, "are you now telling me this ghost story?"

"Because," Jenkins acknowledged, "I understand from a highly reliable source that the Theosophists, both in India and locally, want it badly!"

Adams laughed. "Why don't they go to Missouri with guns a-blazing and get it? Preposterous! I will grant you one thing though. That yarn, in and of itself, was worth the price of your cocktails. I hope you don't believe all that balderdash."

"I won't be using it in one of my storylines any time soon," the Hartford reporter confessed. "My editor would throw the office tea-kettle at me—filled with boiling water! I love my grandmother, may she rest in peace, and yet I'd dismiss this as a tall tale if it were not for the many references to the ancient object from authoritative sources ranging from the Bible and other writings throughout the centuries."

"Let's get back on track," suggested Adams. "Where did you say you ran into that attorney fella?"

Jenkins inquired, "Have you ever been to Hudnut's?"

"The drugstore," Adams remarked. "Of course! I'm from here!"

Jenkins continued, "I was in the place an hour ago and spotted that attorney. He's hard to miss. A white crop of hair and an oversized scraggly beard to match. We hadn't crossed paths in some time. The Colonel is Madame Blavatsky's partner."

American Theosophical Society
Madame Helena Blavatsky, Henry Olcott, Esq.

Adam's seemed puzzled. "Partner? Do you mean 'a couple'?"

Jenkins seemed delighted with the question. "Aside from Henry and Helena, I don't believe anyone knows the answer to that question. They both live at the same residence, but they're both so peculiar that it's anyone's guess, and those two have not given out so much as a clue! I'm referring to their partnership in the Theosophical movement. Helena was the person who introduced the concept to the Colonel. She's an excellent writer and has the depth and breadth of knowledge to write about the doctrines and teachings of *the Word*. Although she almost died in a shipwreck or two, I will say that, when she lit in New York, she was penniless, friendless, and *dead in the water* when it came to promoting her concepts. Olcott is the antithesis of that. He has connections, money, and he's immediately likeable. With a long-standing interest in the spirit world and the occult, he soon became the ideal person to promote the Theosophical concepts. They cofounded the Theosophical Society. Henry is the society's president."

Adams remarked, "You say then the society *president* invited you?"

"That's right."

"What's the purpose of this evening's occasion?"

"It's a celebration for Helena," responded the out-of-towner Jenkins. "Madame Blavatsky was sworn in earlier today as a US citizen. It's a big deal all around. Henry told me that there'll be some prominent citizens in attendance. There may even be a few good stories for the *Daily Eagle*'s readership. Join me. Please. You won't regret it!"

"Tempting offer," replied Adams, "but I'll take a pass. I'll be ordering *meself* one more glass before hitting the road and heading back to Brooklyn." Adams thought briefly, "I wonder how your Theosophist friends are going to like it when they smell liquor on your breath."

Pulling a small tin container out of his vest pocket, Jenkins remarked, "Altoid mints. Picked them up over at Hudnut's. I'll take one or two of those spicy little devils, and no one will ever be the wiser. You may want one or two yourself, for when you see the missus later this evening?"

"I've had them once. Too strong for me," replied Adams. "Besides, my wife knows my indiscretions, and a little alcohol on my breath is the least of my worries."

"Well then, Mr. Adams, I'll be running along. Thank you for the drinks and the pleasure of your company."

"I enjoyed our conversation, Mr. Jenkins, amusing and informative. I'll be sure and pick up a Hartford newspaper at the newsstand tomorrow to read of your escapades."

"Keep in mind, Mr. Adams, that there are some reasons why they may not run the story at all, including whether I decide to write about it."

Both men stood and shook hands. Jenkins turned and abruptly departed. Adams hailed the barkeep and ordered one more Delmonico's Number One *for the road*.

If you see something that is not right,
not fair, not just, you have a moral
obligation to do something about it.

—US Representative John Robert Lewis

CHAPTER 3

General's Impressions

July 8, 1878—Manhattan, New York

During the late-afternoon hours of this summer afternoon, Colonel Henry Steel Olcott, cofounder of the American Theosophical Society, was hosting a celebration for the society's other cofounder, Madame Helena Petrovna Blavatsky. The event was taking place in the second-story Manhattan apartment they shared. The festivities were in honor of the Madame becoming an American citizen earlier in the day.

As the stream of guests entered the building and ascended the stairs, each step upward transformed the air. At street level, the odor of dung from the remnants of horse-drawn vehicles along the street was inescapable. At the top of the stairs, the odor was replaced with exotic aromas of curry, cumin, and turmeric. The savory scent emanated from the dining room where a bounty of culinary creations, largely of recipes from India and the Middle East, were laid out on the dining room table in anticipation of the many well-wishers expected to be on hand.

Although Colonel Olcott and Madame Blavatsky were not yet present, a few guests had already arrived. Every window was agape with curtains tied back in an attempt to mitigate the July heat within the suite. Cross ventilation within the room where all would assemble offered little relief from the outside temperature, other than an occasional puff of warm air from outdoors.

The second-story suite was comprised of a large sunny parlor, dining room, kitchen, three bedrooms, and Olcott's three-sided office. The parlor was furnished with an extensive and fascinating array of seemingly eclectic items with cultural and other worldly themes. Furniture and objects within the suite ranged from that of high intrinsic value to worthless and from ancient to modern. Walls were adorned with Japanese fans, pipes, woven rugs, and ritualistic primitive implements. A singing mechanical bird appeared on a wall at eye level, and a stuffed lioness head projecting a ferocious expression hung above the entry door. Cigarette holders, ash pots, and other objects of copper, brass, or inlaid woods were placed atop cabinets and tables that were largely of Middle Eastern origin. A gilded idol in the likeness of a primitive god of gold presided atop the center of the fireplace mantle. Divans and low couches were located throughout the main parlor for those willing to be seated not more than a foot off the floor. At the room's center was a large stuffed ape that stood on its hind legs with manuscript in paw, wearing a pair of spectacles balanced upon his nose, and sporting a necktie and white dicky around his neck, prompting the curious to wonder whether the well-dressed creature was mocking members of the Christian clergy. Olcott and Blavatsky also had a pair of canaries, Jenny and Pip, and a cat named Charles.

Retired General Abner Doubleday was one of the first guests to arrive. Doubleday spotted a small cluster of early entrants standing in the center of the room near the ape. The group was embroiled in conversation, and Doubleday decided to listen in to what was being said. Doubleday knew hardly anyone, but members of the Theosophical Society knew who he was.

True to the evening's theme, participants in the discussion were offering their views as to why they appreciated being American citizens. Upon concluding the topic, a man wearing a turban recognized Doubleday, introduced himself to the General, and stated, "General

Doubleday, most of us present would agree that President Abraham Lincoln was one of the great leaders of this nation. I understand you and President Lincoln were close friends."

Doubleday replied, "I visited the President's residence on occasion only, yet I take great pride in having known both the President and the First Lady. One of the most humbling moments of my military career was when President Lincoln invited me to ride on his train headed to Pennsylvania where he was to give the Gettysburg Address. I will forever consider President Lincoln to have been a good friend—not only to myself, but to the entire American people."

Another participant of the conversation inquired, "Did you, per chance, have the opportunity to attend one of the wayward First Lady's séances, or was your visit of a political or more personal nature?"

"My dear fellow," the General offered, "the First Lady was outspoken, however, 'wayward' incorrectly describes the woman. The First Lady had lost her second of four sons by the first year of the war, and as you know, she would soon lose her husband and another son. Mary dealt with a level of grief that was the equivalent to those families most adversely affected by the Civil War. Mrs. Lincoln was well-educated, didn't always follow the rules of cordiality, and prescribed to some unorthodox ideas. Aside from her occasional displays of anxiety, critics may well have considered many of the esteemed guests in attendance this evening, as well as our guest of honor, in a similar light. Mrs. Lincoln was a devout wife. She married a man in disfavor with her family, loved him dearly, and despite her Southern roots, heartily backed the President in…all political endeavors. Visiting with the First Lady and the President was enough of a rewarding experience, in and of itself, to last me during the remainder of my lifetime."

"General, sir," noted a man with a cockney accent. "I always thought your Civil War was about ending the practice of slavery in America. Lately, though, I've been reading about the perspectives of former Confederate officials that remain troubled with what most people seem to think were the precepts of the war. Those speaking out say that conditions for the enslaved had never been better and deny that slavery was the central issue. They cite the *more important reasons* for the war included the deprivation of freedoms guaranteed under the Bill of Rights. They argue that the South had little alternative but to arise and stave the Northern aggression resulting from Lincoln's *unreasonable* demands. Those speaking up submit that it was known that the acceptance of Lincoln's recommendations would have had the obvious consequence of ruining the region's economic order and devastating a comfortable and predictable way of life for millions of Southerners that had been blessed with these conditions for generations."

Doubleday, with hat in hand, stood before the *Brit* like a pillar, motionless and quiet, and held a stare upon the man.

The gentleman appended his commentary. "Do you agree with such accounts, sir?"

"May I assume, sir," Doubleday inquired, "that none of you are representatives of the press?"

Everyone looked at one another and shrugged their shoulders as if to say that they were not.

Doubleday began his reply. "The one fact with which I agree was that war would indeed impact *millions of lives*, but accepting the number in lieu of explanation leads to an incorrect impression. First, of the 600,000 war casualties, the largest number of losses came from the North. Severe injuries likely prove the same ratio. Further, although more marked in the South, economic hardship was experienced by families on both sides of the Mason-Dixon Line. It's true that the lifestyles for many of the nine million people living in the South were more dramatically impacted than people residing in the North. Keep in mind though that those lifestyles would not have been enjoyed to anything remotely close to what was the case had it not been for those of the south willing to enslave other human beings in order to receive such ill-gotten gains. More importantly, of the nine million Southern lives impacted, one out of every three Southerners were men, women, and children living in the cruel shackles of slavery. It is further noteworthy to point out that those three million slaves represent but one of many generations of slaves to have suffered such hardships."

"Quite frankly, sir," Doubleday continued, "I'm always surprised anyone does not quickly see through such a deception. Those arguments are not only wrong. They're wrongful! With all the complexities entering in, I'm confident a person representing either side of the argument could spend hours talking about why their thinking is justified. Rather, though, I choose to simply rely on a statement made by Abraham Lincoln: '*If slavery is not wrong, nothing is wrong!*'

A pleasantly fashioned lady offered, "I'm a geography professor. Just as you had visited Charleston, I too visited that city twice. The first time was as a young woman before the war. I again spent some time in that city years after the war had concluded. From the overall appearance of the place, in many ways, it was a model for cities to emulate—in part thanks to King Charles of England. The monarch wanted to make Charles's town a colonial capital. It was his seventeenth-century vision that led to the city's orderly layout, wide boulevards, and majestic buildings, which were still standing nicely at the time of my visit. Prior to the war, flowering gardens and magnolia trees with their colossal blooms and fragrances seemed to be everywhere. Finely appareled ladies and gentlemen strolled on the walkways, and elegant carriages filled the streets. Sitting on the edge of the great harbor, Charleston was the most beautiful city that American visitors might ever see."

"Prewar Charleston was indeed all that—and more," Doubleday recalled. "The streets were immaculate, and properties wonderfully maintained. Of course, there were the unforgettable scenes occurring every day in front of the Slave Mart at the center of town. Slave families were dragged through town in shackles and whipped when the traders or masters deemed appropriate. Charleston wasn't for everyone!"

"To be sure," the teacher admitted, "Charleston had a dark side. Everyone knew about the Slave Mart, plantations filled with slave labor appeared as soon as you left the downtown area, and a man named Rhett who published the *Charleston Mercury* made no bones about his position on allowing the South to keep the *tradition* of slavery."

Doubleday chuckled and shook his head. "Robert B. Rhett! I knew him, and he knew me. I was an active and unapologetic abolitionist, and he despised that. It was because of what he said about me in his editorials that confined me to my post at the fort in the harbor. His mouth and pen made it no longer safe for me to go ashore without facing serious and immediate danger. The man was a pip. He used to write and print news articles arguing that the Christians' God was proslavery!"

One of the listeners uttered, "That must have been some argument!"

Doubleday again shook his head in agreement. "You bet, but he'd come up with examples. One of his arguments was that, despite the prevalence of slavery and control of people in biblical times, both Jesus and the Bible never addressed the ethical question of slavery. Needless to say, however, I never bothered to verify any of that man's claims."

The professor offered, "When I returned years later, it was clear that the war had left its mark on the city, and yet, I could see some rays of light. I met a Negro man who was a long-standing member of the African Methodist Episcopal Church. Had you ever heard of it, General?"

"Yes, indeed," Doubleday responded. "Before the war, the fine white people of Charleston allowed the church to burn to the ground—more than once. The last burning happened after the South Carolina legislature made it illegal for Negroes to conduct church services! Of course, authorities never caught the criminals that set the blazes."

"That congregation's story," the lady commented, "is uplifting. While their church services were prohibited, congregants kept the church going. This had to place the members and their families at grave peril—death, the dire threat of being tarred and feathered, and separation from their families. Talk about bravery. Talk about an unwavering faith commitment to their God and religious beliefs! At the end of the war, the congregants rebuilt the church. It's an encouraging ending."

A man sounding and appearing as if from India spoke. "*Encouraging,* yes, but the *ending* remains to be seen. From what I read in the newspapers, your federal government's Reconstruction programs have not met with much success, and white Southern society seems to take their anger out on a regular basis by persecuting—and murdering—people of color, with little if any consequence. Speaking as a man with a skin tone darker than many of your countrymen, it scares me to imagine what sort of life I would have if I moved to that part of your country. To me, your war is far from over."

The professor extended her hand toward Doubleday and stated, "General, forgive me for not introducing myself earlier. Jen Brown."

They gently shook hands.

"Abner Doubleday."

Smiling, the professor said, "I see someone I must speak to. However, I have my class working on a project and would dearly love to speak with you again as I am sure you would have much to add. Are you local?"

"I live in New Jersey forty miles west of here," Doubleday replied, "but I'm here frequently. You can always reach me through Madame Blavatsky."

A nearby person blurted, "The deuce you say!"

The voice was that of Helena Petrovna Blavatsky. Her appearance was striking. Blavatsky was indeed a large woman. She had obviously found somewhere a red, white, and blue shawl for the occasion. She was wearing a necklace with a large medallion and wore as many rings on her hand as she had fingers.

As the group refocused their attentions on the guest of honor, a man barely of thirty years tapped Doubleday on the shoulder from behind. Doubleday turned to see who the person was. The General immediately recognized the man as the young inventor, Thomas Edison, whom Doubleday met soon after joining the society three days earlier.

Doubleday exclaimed, "Mr. Edison, how nice to see you again!"

Edison replied, "Please come with me, sir, if you have a moment. There's someone I'd like you to meet."

As Doubleday turned back around to say goodbye, he noticed that Madame Blavatsky had *gained command* of everyone around her, so he left with Edison unnoticed.

* * *

Edison escorted Doubleday over to where a tall athletic-looking man was standing next to a lady seated comfortably on a divan casually observing the people as they entered the suite.

Before Edison could make an introduction, Doubleday exclaimed to the lady seated, "Mrs. Churchill, nice to see you again."

Remaining seated, the young woman of not yet twenty-two years held upward her hand and replied with a flirtatious smile, "A pleasure to see you, General. You appear younger each time I see you."

Doubleday looked at the tall man while holding up three fingers, rolled his eyes, and referring to Churchill, said, "We met three days ago!"

Churchill stood up and continued, "Albert, as I told you, the General only recently joined the society. In military terms, he's our latest *enlistee*. Please allow me to introduce the illustrious General Abner Doubleday." Then speaking to Doubleday, Churchill added, "General, I'd like to introduce you to a dear family friend, Al Spalding."

Spalding, holding out his hand, responded, "Please, sir, call me AG."

Doubleday clasped Spalding's hand and inquired with astonishment, "*The* Albert Spalding? Of baseball fame?"

Spalding beamed. "One and the same, sir. You must be General Abner Doubleday of Civil War fame."

Doubleday jested, "Yes. Yes. They've been trying to hang that one on me for years!"

"Are you," Edison inquired of the General, "as much of a baseball enthusiast as I am?"

"I'm no aficionado of the game," Doubleday replied, "but anyone who reads the papers can't help but read of Mr. Spalding's exploits."

Churchill interjected, "Of course, it depends on which city's newspaper you read to determine whether he's an angel or the devil."

The three men smiled as Spalding forlornly nodded in agreement.

Doubleday asked Spalding, "Are you considering joining the Society?"

"Haven't thought much about it," Spalding answered. "I happened to be in town, heard of this event, and wisely invited myself." Glancing over at a table laden with food, he added, "I seem to have made the right choice for both dinner and conversation!"

Churchill spoke. "When Madame Blavatsky learned that Al would be in town, she insisted I rope him into coming to the commemoration. I thus convinced Albert to *want* to be here."

"Liz and I have known each other since childhood—her childhood," explained Spalding, "so now that Liz is all grown up, she'll believe as she will without my input. If the truth be told, I can't imagine having a greater honor than to meet you two gentlemen!"

Edison inquired of Spalding, "Have you met HPB yet?"

"Albert can't wait to meet her," Churchill stated and then quipped, "It's so rare to meet intelligent women such as us."

Spalding remarked, "If I were ever to make such a remark about the rarity of intelligent women during an interview with the press, the newspapers would have my hide, and at the first sign of gate receipts dropping, like the General, they'd *hang that one on me!*"

"That's nothing," Churchill pointed out, "compared to how you'd feel if HPB heard that! As for what the press would do to you, it's reassuring to know that the *battle* to eliminate the double standard in America between men and women can turn in the favor of the ladies on occasion. Who knows? Someday, we may be given the right to vote!"

"An impressionable youth," lamented Spalding.

"Speaking of *battles*, General," offered Edison, "and given the nature of tonight's celebration, this may be the only time I will ever have the opportunity to hear directly about the day the American Civil War began."

Doubleday paused and then replied, "It would be my pleasure. As I'm sure you all know, I participated in many battles over my military career, yet the Battle of Fort Sumter impacted my life more than all the other battles combined—and that includes Gettysburg. My experience at the fort became a defining characteristic as to the man I turned out to be. What would you like to know, Tom?"

Edison replied, "We're talking about a moment in time that changed the course of United States history. A description of that moment by you, General, would provide a unique perspective on this most important event. If you would, sir, kindly share with us your impressions as to what led up to that fight and the direct experience you had of the battle?"

At the insistence of the three curious guests, the former abolitionist began recounting his impressions from the Battle of Fort Sumter.

Doubleday began, "For perspective, I should first describe the overall circumstance leading up to the conflict."

"The Democrats' platform was silent on the issue of slavery, and thus, the Democratic Party was the party of choice for the South. The Democratic National Convention, coincidentally held in Charleston during April of 1860, failed to nominate one presidential candidate. The convention went into recess, and with the fear *the Dems* would split the vote with two candidates, alarm bells went off all over the South. When most Southerners' worst fears materialized, and Abraham Lincoln won the presidential election in November, the issue of slavery took center stage on the nation's political landscape. That same month, the South Carolina legislature convened and voted to become the first state to secede from the Union. Militias formed throughout the South only to converge on the city of Charleston. The everyday sight of fashionable ladies strolling with their parasols and fancy carriages was replaced with an inescapable military presence."

Most of the General's oration would represent a thin slice of his personal memoirs, later published by Harper & Brothers, Publishers of New York under the title, *Reminiscences of Forts Sumter and Moultrie in 1860–'61*.

"In January of 1861, Lincoln dispatched the *Star of the West*, a 1,200-ton, 220-foot merchant vessel bound for Fort Sumter to deliver desperately needed supplies and 200 Union soldiers to reinforce our garrison. General P. G. T. Beauregard of the South Carolina Militia ordered cannon batteries on the perimeter of Charleston Harbor to commence fire upon the ship prior to its sailing into range of the fort. *To the chagrin and disappointment of the men comprising the fort's Union garrison and tempered elation of the military and civilian bystanders in witness from the city, the ship reversed course for all to watch as the* Star of the West *slowly sailed off the horizon not to return.* Other such skirmishes were to follow that continued up to April of 1861.

"The fort housed sixty cannons within its five-foot walls, and to the untrained eye, Fort Sumter seemed impenetrable. The structure was comprised of millions of bricks and ten thousand tons of granite, sixty thousand tons of rock, and untold amounts of sand, mortar, wood, and metal. Despite the fort's enormous mass, Commanding Officer Major Richard Anderson and I knew a battle with secessionist forces would result in reducing the fort to rubble in a matter of days.

"That, my friends, is what led up to the Battle of Fort Sumter. As for the battle itself, you may wish to hear that story another time. There's so much for us to talk about tonight."

"Not on your tintype," exclaimed Edison.

Churchill chimed in. "General, you haven't seen any of us yawn yet."

Seeing that all were in agreement, Doubleday continued his story.

"*At the Alamo, Davy Crocket and his compadres were only outnumbered 15 to 1. Not making excuses, we were outmanned 100 to 1.* To make matters worse, Beauregard was aware of all of this.

"On April 11, 1861, Beauregard dispatched a large rowboat destined for Fort Sumter. The vessel, oared by slaves, carried three emissaries of the Confederate States. Upon the boat's arrival at the fort, Beauregard's representatives presented the text of a document outlining the terms and conditions for our surrender. The terms, stated in a cordial manner, guaranteed that my men could salute the flag upon departure and receive safe passage away from Charleston. My commanding officer, US Army Major Robert Anderson, born in the South and not adverse to slavery, remained true blue to the Union and kindly refused the offer. The Confederates said that Beauregard would have no alternative but to begin bombardment of the fort the next day.

"Beauregard's men commenced shelling Fort Sumter moments prior to 4:30 AM on Friday, April 12. Shells were incoming from a ring of artillery batteries surrounding three of the fort's five sides. The deafening thunder and explosions from the shelling throughout the early morning hours were loud and constant. On more than one occasion, I asked the major's permission to return fire.

"After the trauma from two constant hours of bone-rattling explosions without returning fire, a soldier sitting in a corner hailed me over to his post. He sat low to the ground to avoid the billowing cloud of smoke coming from the burning structures on all the higher levels.

Battle of Fort Sumter.

"'Captain Doubleday,' the soldier called out.

"I approached the soldier and asked, 'How's your strength holding out?'

"The soldier, a sergeant, replied, 'No less than yours, Captain. But I do have a question.'

"'I don't have many answers,' I replied.

"The sergeant thoughtfully responded, 'Sir. What are we waiting for?'

"'In what manner do you ask, sergeant?'

"The sergeant responded, 'Well, sir, why aren't we responding so we can knock out some of the Confederate batteries? We'll be in ruin soon. Are you and the major thinking about surrender?'

"Maintaining a sincere and composed demeanor, I looked at the sergeant through the morning darkness with only the light of the flickering fires within the fort through the smoke.

"The sergeant repeated his latter question, 'Are you and the major planning on having us surrender?'

"I recall kneeling down to where the sergeant sat. 'Surrender is a real option unless we can soon receive supplies and reinforcements, the prospect of which does not seem a pleasant one. I don't know about you, sergeant, but being associated with such failure from the onset of war could give the Confederates a serious boost of morale while not serving in the best interests of the Union or our reputations.'

"'No, sir,' replied the Sergeant.

"Upon arising, I stood tall, glanced down, and offered, 'Remain strong. I'll go and talk to the Major again.'

"In a bent-down position to avoid spraying powder from the incoming shells, I walked briskly toward the major's quarters. Upon consulting with Major Anderson, I returned moments later to the soldier.

"'Sergeant, I just talked to the Major. He said we are to wait until first light, at which time, we will have a clear view through the smoke and fountains of flame. Once we can see our intended targets, I will give you the word you are awaiting.'

"'Very good, Captain,' responded the sergeant. 'I'll look forward to the light of day, sir.'

"I replied, 'Carry on, soldier,' and left to tend to the other men.

"The time was 7:00 AM. While continuing to receive enemy fire at the rate of 100 shells per hour, I called out, 'Ready the cannons!'

"Within seconds, the Sergeant yelled, 'The cannons are ready, sir!'

"Pointing out the intended targets to the men, I shouted, 'Open fire. Fire at will, gentlemen.' Within seconds, the first shot was fired.

"The almost unbearable noise level from a continuing parade of one explosion following another over recent hours immediately doubled in frequency. From this moment, each explosion would be followed by but few seconds of quiet before the next explosion was heard and felt.

"*By 11:00 AM, the conflagration was terrible and disastrous. One-fifth of the fort was on fire, and the wind drove the smoke in dense masses into the structure's angle where we had all taken refuge. It seemed impossible to escape suffocation. Some of the men lay down close to the ground with handkerchiefs over their mouths. It was difficult to take solace that we had all but leveled our former encampment of Fort Moultrie because though now in safer climes, every one suffered severely...had a slightly change of wind not taken place as it had, the result might have been fatal to most of us.*

"*It was clear that the time to raise the white flag was near. The roaring and crackling of the flames, the dense masses of whirling smoke, the bursting of the enemy shells, and our own which were exploding in the burning rooms, the crashing of the shot, and the sound of masonry falling in every direction, made the fort a pandemonium.*

"*Through a variety of events and efforts, the terms of our surrender were soon agreed upon... These terms of departure were that which was embraced by the concept of honorable surrender. Personally, I always found the concept of surrender with honor a bit whimsical—in a dark sort of way. Regardless, something that I took away with me was a memory of the men and officers and how, to a man, they acted honorably and professionally.*

"*We had but one casualty during the entire battle, but regretfully, that one ill-fated soldier's death occurred upon 'departing the fort, during the one-hundred-cannon salute we insisted on having under our terms of surrender... This mishap was witnessed by a large population of foes in the waters surrounding us all about, for the bay was alive with floating craft of every description, filled with people from all parts of the South, in their holiday attire.*

"My brave and devoted wife, Mary, and I never had children of our own. The men I commanded who so proudly served their country and fought at my side were my children." The General ceased talking and those listening to his words were silent.

A man, though wise, should never be ashamed
of learning more, and must unbend his mind.

—Sophocles, Antigone

CHAPTER 4

Madame

The guest of honor drifted through the suite full of people at the end of the room farthest from where Churchill, Doubleday, Edison, and Spalding were standing. With each step she took, Madame Blavatsky *worked* the crowd, welcoming and thanking each friend she encountered, receiving salutations or warm jests and praises in return. Spalding's stature enabled him to spot different people in the crowd. He glanced toward the front door and noticed the arrival of a finely dressed man with an incongruous appearance. With flaring white hair and a long white beard, the gentleman wore a fashionable double-breasted jacket of textured white silk. Spalding and the man's eyes made contact. The fellow then began making his way toward the baseball player. Spalding thought the odd-looking fellow must be important because the man exchanged jovialities with each guest he passed while the crowd immediately in his path would continually spread slightly apart, allowing him to methodically move while leading with his drinking glass without breaking stride. It was akin to a Moses-Red Sea moment. The fellow arrived at Spalding's side and stood still, facing the others in the group.

Viewing the seated Mrs. Churchill, the odd fellow exclaimed, "Elizabeth, I might have known you'd be the one to be entertaining the Society's most notable new additions!" Rotating toward Spalding, the man's eyes lit up through the small lenses of his wire-rimmed glasses and exuberantly stated, "Albert Spalding, I presume."

"I am," enthused Spalding. "But you have me at a disadvantage, sir."

The man stated, "Colonel Henry Steel Olcott, Esquire—at your service."

The two men shook hands vigorously.

Spalding said, "Call me AG, please!"

Olcott responded, "I'll do that! And, you sir, may call me any of the names I just gave you. If you ask the Madame, she can even come up with a few additional descriptors." Olcott chuckled.

Spalding replied, "I'll just stay with the menu you handed me, Colonel."

Churchill stood and smiled. In a motherly tone, she inquired of Olcott, "Dare I ask, Colonel, where you have been to look so warm?"

"Pounding the hot pavement of Manhattan," Olcott exclaimed. "Stopped over at Hudnut's to see what new items they had on display. Ran into a chum I used to encounter during my more active days writing for the newspapers. When I was leaving, the store thermometer registered eighty-eight degrees. I can assure you, it's warmer than that treading on the sidewalk. That, my dear, is where I've been."

"Well," Churchill offered, "I can see right through your beard—and you look parched! Your glass is nearly empty. What can I get to cool you off? Water? Lemonade? Iced tea? One of the fruit juices, perhaps?"

"A refresher sounds delightful!" Olcott gulped the remainder of his drink and, gently handing the glass to Churchill, requested, "A glass of soda would be a special treat."

Churchill smiled at the Colonel. Prior to departing for the dining room, she stated, "I trust you will be at this station, at least until my return."

Looking at Churchill, Olcott replied, "Indeed, Mrs. Churchill." Next turning toward Spalding, Olcott said, "The Madame informed me you'd be in attendance but didn't say to what we owe the honor."

"I was to be in the area on usual baseball business," Spalding replied. "And Elizabeth invited me to what sounded like an intriguing evening. The guests have exceeded expectations, and your home is fascinating!"

"It's my sanctum sanctorum," Olcott replied.

With a delayed reaction to Olcott's earlier comment, Edison interjected, "Colonel, you mentioned Hudnut's. I love that place! Were you in search of a last-minute congratulatory gift for the Madame? Perfume, maybe?"

Olcott declared, "Perfume! Heavens, no! Why do you say that?"

Edison grinned. "It's my experience that women who wear jewelry as seriously as the Madame does find little fault with perfume."

"On occasion," Olcott acquiesced, "I do detect a pleasant scent on her, but I always thought it was aromatic oil to hide the evidence of her smoking. As I think of it, though, she does little to hide the nicotine stains on her fingers. Maybe she buys the stuff, and I don't know it."

Edison noted, "The owner's son received a degree in engineering. Junior makes his own line of perfumes on site. Hudnut's has as large a selection of fragrances as any place in the city that I know of."

"Maybe she does use perfume of sorts," Olcott conceded. "I may take a chance and get some mild perfume the next time I go there. When I need to buy her something, I never know what she'll like."

Having returned to the group and upon handing Spalding a plate of finger food, Churchill offered, "Men are generally happier not knowing everything about the women near them. Men have neither the capacity nor the comprehension to understand."

"Such wisdom from someone barely in her twenties," Olcott exclaimed.

"I knew Elizabeth when she was eleven," reminded Spalding. "And she was instructing everyone around her back then."

Churchill simply shook her head and addressed Olcott. "Incidentally, there's a small problem, Colonel. The soda machine needs the CO_2 cartridge replaced. Do any of you men know how to replace it?"

The men seemed to all step back at the same time—without a peep.

Olcott replied, "It must be too warm to use the CO_2. Those canisters are volatile in the heat, I've been told. Rather than risk explosion, and in lieu of a volunteer to fix the machine, I'd be most pleased with a cold glass of lemonade."

As Churchill was again departing on her mission, the men all acknowledged her departure with respectful nodding of their heads.

Edison asked Spalding, "I'm curious. Considering that New York no longer has a major league team, I'm surprised you have any *usual baseball business* in this town!"

Spalding inquired, "Do I detect disappointment in your voice, sir?"

Edison replied, "I was and am a devout Mets supporter, sir! Devout!"

"I see," Spalding noted. "It was too bad. I know what happened. The year before last, the New York nine was having a bad year. The owners of the Metropolitans felt they needed to save money by not traveling to some of the cities on the schedule, and that there would be nothing the National League or anyone could do to prevent them from doing so.

Grinning, Olcott nodded knowingly while observing. "When there's a ruling on anything, some New Yorker will open his mouth too wide." Olcott chuckled, adding, "It must be a cultural thing."

Edison frumpled his brow, Churchill gave but the hint of smile, and Olcott's eyes trolled the group for a reaction.

Spalding, nodding with raised eyebrows, continued, "League President Hulbert, who is also my boss, felt that the rights of the teams and fans for every franchise, without exception, must be protected. Hulbert similarly felt that, regardless of level of prestige, all teams must abide by what they agreed and not allow anarchy by rogue owners. So, inconceivable as it seemed, the league pulled the plug on the city of New York."

"Given the close relationship I know you to have with the league president," Edison acknowledged, "I believe what you say. I can even understand it, but it wasn't a popular decision with New Yorkers."

"Mr. Hulbert believes that if baseball aspires to achieve purity in competition with meaningful results, fairness must be maintained in all ways, without bias."

Noticing that Doubleday began smiling, a perplexed Spalding asked, "Was there something I said, General?"

"I found it ironic," Doubleday replied, "but I wish you no disrespect."

Madame Blavatsky, laden with jewelry and sporting her silk shawl with an uncharacteristic likeness of the American flag, appeared almost magically next to Olcott. Churchill arrived at the colonel's other side at the same time, handing him his lemonade.

Glancing briefly at Blavatsky and Churchill, Spalding nodded at Doubleday to continue the thought.

Doubleday began, "I thought about your comment that the National League president feels *strongly* that everyone must be treated fairly, *without bias*. He sounds like an abolitionist! It struck me as odd that his beliefs don't extend to the basic rights of others who have a different skin tone. It seems especially odd because such rights are not only *allowed* by the United States Constitution—they're *guaranteed* by it!"

Spalding retorted, "I absolutely see what you're saying, General, but it seems unfair to pin that fault solely on baseball rather than society. That sort of prejudice appears throughout society, and that is what prohibits baseball from overcoming the problem."

"Ending that attitude," Doubleday asserted, "is why so many made the ultimate sacrifice. It was what the Civil War was all about."

Blavatsky stepped forward toward the center of the discussion circle and offered, "Going to war allows the victor the ability to force and enforce compliance but seldom encourages understanding. It is only with understanding that future actions of the conquered will be willingly applied toward the prevailing philosophy. To achieve that objective, it is necessary to educate both the victor and the conquered."

"That, Madame, was beyond the scope of the war. That," Doubleday asserted, "was to be the next step."

"What was the objective," Blavatsky inquired, "of the war?"

Doubleday retorted, "To remove the shackles of slavery!"

"If you have dark skin," Blavatsky pointed out, "and you live in America, you still have shackles—they merely consist of a different substance."

Olcott, a war veteran, couldn't stand by any longer. "Now, at least, these people stand a fighting chance! Circumstances are not perfect, but things are improving. I do not wish for so many lives to seem as if they were lost in vain when I do not believe that the case!"

"Nor is it my intent to imply," Blavatsky replied. "I believe, however, that once a monumental event has concluded, that such opportunity should not be squandered. Rather, that is the time to revisit the entire approach toward the subject and determine how we can make best use of sacrifices from the past to the greatest benefit for the future of society."

Churchill asked, "Tell us, Madame, what is the role Theosophy would play in helping this country progress in the right direction?"

Blavatsky responded, "That, my dear, and fellows, is what I hope you will soon figure out, for the benefit of yourselves and for others."

A trio of people gently grabbed Helena and pulled her from the group.

Olcott offered, "I'm an older fellow, so I don't mind asking, What were we discussing before things turned painfully meaningful?"

Edison replied, "I had asked Mr. Spalding what *usual baseball business* he had in our fair city."

"Indeed, you did," Spalding cheerfully added, "but before we drop the last discussion, I have an uplifting note. It's a brief fun story."

There were now others listening to Spalding beyond Mrs. Churchill and the inventor, Colonel, and General.

"With respect to the topic of baseball excluding people of other races," Spalding began, "that only applies to major league baseball—and even that, General, may not continue too long into the future. Leagues do exist throughout the United States, elsewhere in America and the Caribbean that are almost exclusively populated with people of color."

Doubleday inquired, "And the benefit to major league baseball is...?"

"The benefit," Spalding enthused, "is that when it is time for major league baseball to open up to other races, there will be experienced talent, thus increasing the chances of longevity for the newcomers. Much more to the point, though, there's something else that happened—and it happened very recently!"

The listeners waited for Spalding to continue.

"Last week, I became aware of a Negro from Cooperstown, New York, by the name of Bud Fowler. Fowler is a paid baseball player—a professional—on an otherwise all-white team. His team competes in an organized league at a level of play that is but a half step down from the National League!"

Doubleday, with keen interest, asked, "How is he doing?"

"You like irony, sir," remarked Spalding. "As fate would have it, Fowler's team was scheduled the month before last, April, to play last year's champions of the National League, the Boston Red Caps. Fowler's team plays for Chelsea, Mass. I didn't catch whether the team playing the Red Caps was his team or an all-star team from his league. Regardless, the game was played, and Fowler played in the game. People say Fowler can play any of several positions. On this day, however, whether it was fate or some form of attempt at cruel torture to the minds of the Red Caps, his team assigned him the pitching duties."

Blavatsky was now somehow carrying on two conversations with her back turned. Spalding, however, now held the interest of ten listeners.

"The shortened version of the story," Spalding remarked, "is that Fowler's team won!" With some laughter in the group, Spalding continued, "They beat the reigning world champions! Fowler was the winning pitcher!"

Everyone thought the story humorous.

Blavatsky turned around and said, "Maybe there's some hope for the National League after all!"

Churchill recalled, "It seems to me, Albert, that when I was a little girl, I watched a seventeen-year-old pitcher from nowhere,

Illinois, beat the great baseball team which, at the time, hailed from the nation's capital! That was the day you instantly became a star!"

"Unfortunately, fairy-tale endings are harder for someone of color to secure," Spalding confessed. "Time will tell all, but so far, things haven't worked out well for Mr. Fowler. Even though I hear he is extremely well mannered, I understand that they already kicked him off the team."

Olcott asked, "For what reason?"

Spalding shrugged his shoulders. "Who knows? There's lots of possibilities. Pick one or pick them all."

Blavatsky turned around again and said, "I hereby rescind my comment that there's hope for the National League." Blavatsky then again turned her back, returning to her other discussion.

Churchill, wishing to get Spalding back on track, reminded, "Al, might you finally tell Mr. Edison what you were doing in New York?"

Spalding said to Edison, "I help Mr. Hulbert run the White Stockings. He's often in New York on league matters as he is now. I come here to seek guidance. I also started a sporting goods business with my brother the year before last, and I try to drum up business while I'm here."

Doubleday inquired, "How's business so far?"

"Business is booming," Spalding boasted. "We sell retail, and we also manufacture some items."

Edison addressed the group. "They make baseballs for the National League! I've read quite a bit about that in the papers."

Spalding shook his head. "Competitors can get pretty testy, especially when they think I had an inside advantage!"

"Yes," Edison remarked. "Some well buttoned-up people interviewed by the newspapers accused you or your company of bribing the National League by paying them a dollar for every baseball they use. Personally, I never understood what your adversaries were exactly saying."

Spalding laughed and shook his head. "Ya know, neither did I," Spalding began with a smile. "The truth is, that one person sees money spent to bribe while another sees it as budgeted corporate funds for advertising. There is no ill-gotten gain. No person or group is benefitting. There's no conflict of interest! The money goes to fund the continuation of the National League! Anyone could have struck a deal with the league before this if they wanted. The balls are more standardized than ever before and consistently align with league specifications. As for how I spend my advertising budget? So long as it's legal and anyone could have beaten me to the punch. I figure that is both figuratively, philosophically, and literally my business. Unfortunately, it's been in the newspapers, so our competitors got some of the damage they hoped for…just not enough to quench their palates."

Edison smiled understandingly and nodded. "In my business, competitors can be real sourpusses when they think they're at some sort of disadvantage. In my case, they get their nastiest when they think I may have stolen one of their ideas!"

Doubleday asked, "That's right, Tom. You must have a lot going on with your business interests. Whatever happened with the sound box your labs came up with last year? I believe it was a *phonograph*."

Edison groaned. "It's in patent hell at the moment. I understand you know something about that, General."

"Oh, my, yes," Doubleday responded. "After the war, I was in San Francisco for a time. Noticing all the steep hills, I came up with a patent for a cable car railway system. I had so much trouble with the patents that I wound up selling the patents off."

"I believe it," Edison noted. "It's probably the nicest thing you could do for yourself. My people may not get past all the patent issues on the phonograph for some time. We may not go into production for another ten years!"

"What a shame, Tom," Doubleday offered compassionately.

Edison cheerfully replied, "No reason to dwell on the phonograph though. That's old news! Have you heard about the incandescent light?"

Spalding asked, "You invented the incandescent light?"

"Invented, no," responded Edison. "Made practical, yes! Until the month before last, the globes would only stay lit for a minute or two. The filaments kept burning out. The folks in my labs recently came up with a filament that will soon enable an electric light globe to burn for a thousand hours continuous!"

Churchill exclaimed, "That's amazing! You made electric lights practical."

Edison said excitedly, "It will change the lives of everyone on the planet! My attorneys are progressing nicely on the patent for the filament."

Doubleday and Olcott shook their heads in near disbelief.

Edison boasted, "Businesses all over the world will soon be able to have their employees work into the night. It will lengthen family hours in the home and make the streets safer at night. Baseball games may even someday be played at night."

"Interesting proposition to play night games," Spalding observed. "I do, however, find it difficult to imagine that such an idea would ever meet with the approval of Chicago folks."

Olcott added, "I too take issue. I'm not excited about replacing gas streetlights with electrification. Gas lights are safe enough, and the prospect of walking on a sidewalk with electrified cables underfoot, especially walkways with cracks when it's raining, scares me terribly!"

Edison nodded in empathy. "Safety is everyone's concern. My people are paying particular attention to that issue. We feel confident that it won't be too difficult of a problem to solve. I'm the first to admit how catastrophic a calamity such as that would be to bounce back from."

Olcott inquired, "Tom, when will you be heading back to New Jersey?"

"In the morning, Colonel." Edison then asked of Spalding, "When will you be heading back to Chicago?"

"Not for a week or so," Spalding replied.

"How," Edison wondered, "can you stay away from your team for so long while in the middle of baseball season? You're not getting out of the game..."

"I sort of have already," confessed Spalding. "It makes sense in some important ways."

Olcott inquired, "Doesn't the prospect of retirement at your age scare you?"

Looking to Spalding, Edison added, "I must say that if I had talent such as yours, I would need to find a reason for retiring that is undeniably compelling and exceeds all doubt."

Churchill politely joined the jury and suggested, "Feel free to share your thoughts, Al. I wonder the same things."

Softening the serious tone of the conversation, Doubleday jested, "It should be illegal to retire at such a tender age! After all, that's even earlier than military retirement!"

Without pause, Olcott inquired, "Did your arm wear down?"

Spalding shook his head. "I've pitched nearly four thousand innings competitively, and my best days may be passed, but it's much more than my arm. There's a new type of pitch I have yet to master called the skewball that'll soon be an essential part of a pitcher's arsenal. The sporting goods business my brother and I began the year before last demands a fair piece of my attention. The best businessman in the game is willing to teach me the ropes of major league baseball from a business perspective with the team representing the land of my birth. Finally, the best reason of all, my wife, Josie, gave me a son this past October. Keith Spalding!"

The other members in the group expressed elation and congratulatory wishes. "Mazel tov!" "Congratulations!" "Bully!" "Wonderful!"

Spalding concluded, "An important consideration in all this is that I am not retiring from the game of baseball. I will no longer be a paid athlete, but I will get more involved with the forces and world of baseball."

Edison tactfully interrupted, "I'm glad you did what you did when you did it. As one who appreciates the sport, it was a treat to watch you play and read of your successes. As I recall, you led the league most every year that you pitched. Factually, how many times was that?"

"I was fortunate," admitted Spalding. "I led the league during the last five full seasons I pitched. It's been a good run."

Olcott pondered, "Never to be seen again?"

Spalding assured, "I can still hit a ball well. I can play if needed, but don't expect to see me standing on top of the pitchers' mound any time soon!"

Edison observed, "Baseball's faithful always appreciates greatness. You'll be missed, and I suspect you are constantly thinking how to spend time with your wife and little one in Illinois, as well."

"Thanks, Tom," Spalding replied. "Also, my wife and son are in New Jersey during the middle half of the year. I'll spend a day or two more in the city and then join my family while I'm out this way."

A surprised Edison asked, "Jersey? Not Illinois? Where in New Jersey?"

"On *the shore*," Spalding remarked. "Sea Bright, New Jersey. We still live in Chicago, but Josie loves summering by *the shore*. She wants to spend every summer for the rest of her life there!"

"I can understand that," Edison commented. "It's a beautiful place. A bit too rich for my blood, but I'm working on changing that," Edison said with a chuckle.

As Blavatsky turned to rejoin the discussion, Edison inquired, "Madame, I know the festivities are close at hand, but we have yet to hear a peep out of you expounding on anything remotely related to the cosmos or the ancients, nature, or anything Theosophy. You're not losing your enthusiasm already, are you?"

En-soph, the unrevealed forever, who is boundless and unconditioned, cannot create, and therefore it seems to us a great error to attribute to him a "creative thought," as is commonly done by the interpreters. In every cosmogony this supreme Essence is passive, if boundless, infinite, and unconditioned, it can have no thought nor idea. It acts not as the result of volition, but in obedience to its own nature, and according to the fatality of the law of which it is itself the embodiment.

Blavatsky added, "I think I got that right. There's more to the quote, but hopefully, you get the gist of it."

Olcott asked whimsically, "Did anyone other than the Madame understand what HPB said just now?"

Those in the conversation appreciated the humor within the question.

Spalding asked, "Isis Unveiled?"

"Why yes!" Blavatsky inquired excitedly, "Have you read my book?"

"No, ma'am," Spalding replied. "Lizzie showed me the book for the first time the other day. It's not the easiest of reading for a ballplayer."

"Please," Blavatsky begged. "I want you to read it! Elizabeth may be the youngest among us, but she grasps concepts as well as any of us. Mrs. Churchill can answer most of your questions, and for whatever questions you have that she can't answer, then call upon me—any time!"

"If I may add one thought for you and Mr. Hulbert to ponder," Blavatsky began, "my teachings would not be nearly so complete if they were to exclude the ideas offered by the great thinkers through history, many of which have darker skin than any of us. A preponderance of the Theosophical knowledge is the direct result of the intellectual workings by men and women from India, Africa, Egypt, and other lands of varying skin tone. It sounds like baseball has yet to appreciate the benefits of such inclusion. Lastly, it was a true pleasure for me to finally meet you, Albert! I hope to see you often in the coming days!"

A man tapped Olcott on the shoulder. Olcott spoke to the man, "William! I want you to meet some folks."

The man replied, "Later, Henry. For the moment, it's show-time. We need you center stage, along with HPB and the General."

Olcott gently took the guest of honor by the hand. As Blavatsky gave her attention to Olcott, he said, "My dear, the festivities are about to begin. You're wanted on center stage."

Looking across at Doubleday, Olcott stated, "General, you may wish to join us now. You'll be giving the first *pitch* of the evening, on the American ideal."

Upon the departures of Olcott, Blavatsky, and Doubleday to the middle of the room, Edison said to Churchill and Spalding, "I should likewise excuse myself. I'll be taking a position close to the action. We'll talk again before the night is out. I have more questions than your news reporter friends!" The inventor then followed in the path of Olcott.

Spalding was curious and asked of Churchill, "Who was that man?"

Churchill replied, "A cofounder of the society, William Quan Judge. I told a society member that I loved his name, and the member said, '*If you switch around his names, it sounds even better!*'" Churchill giggled. "You'll meet him later. I'll introduce you to him after all the hoopla."

"About meeting him later," Spalding began in a soft voice. "Elizabeth, would you mind terribly if I were to sneak out of here?"

"Albert! You didn't enjoy yourself?"

"Absolutely not! No! I mean quite the opposite! I enjoyed this evening immensely, but I suddenly feel the need for some quiet time and space, and I do have a meeting tomorrow."

Churchill looked at Spalding, and he continued. "The mere fact that I was unaware I would be meeting General Abner Doubleday or Inventor Thomas Edison threw me for quite a loop!"

Elizabeth looked puzzled. "But I hope you enjoyed meeting them!"

Spalding said, "Much more than *enjoyed!* This will be an event not soon forgotten—one that I expect to forever remember! Of course, throwing the Colonel and especially the Madame into the mix made it all the better, although HPB helped to make my brain yearn for a rest."

Churchill looked around the room. "Of course, Al. If it makes you happy, we can both sneak out. We'll hardly be missed, if at all."

"I'd like that, Liz. I'll find my suit coat, bid goodbye to Mr. Edison, and meet you outside."

"Five minutes, Albert. Five!"

Spalding walked over to Edison who was not involved in another conversation as he waited for the Colonel to kick things off. The two men had a brief exchange, albeit at a volume loud enough for the inventor to hear.

Once Olcott began speaking by introducing what he referred to as a special guest and the society's newest member, Spalding moved in the direction of the front door. A lady standing by the door asked Spalding, "You're leaving now? Things are about to begin!"

Spalding returned, "I only came for the free food!" He carefully snugged on his hat, gave it a tap on top, and departed.

Descending the flight of stairs, Spalding met Mrs. Churchill on the sidewalk immediately below. Churchill began slowly walking in the direction of Upper East Midtown, and Spalding walked alongside.

Churchill inquired, "Did you bid Mr. Edison a proper farewell?"

"I did," Spalding replied. "Upon him asking how I was heading back to my hotel, I said via Sixth. He told me to check out the streetlamps on Broadway. That's where he's first planning on phasing out the gas lights with electric replacements over the next two or three years."

"We're headed the opposite way from Broadway, Al. Do you think he was really serious about you checking it out?"

"He didn't strike me as otherwise," replied Spalding. "He suggested that if I'm not warm on the idea, to 'keep it to' myself."

Churchill shook her head.

Spalding then said, "I hope you don't mind me asking, but I'm confused about something."

"What's that, Al?"

"Mayer is your married name," Spalding observed. "I can see them calling you *Mrs. Mayer* or *Miss Churchill* when you use your maiden name, but why *Mrs. Churchill?*"

Churchill answered, "They address me both ways. Tell me something. Do you know anything about my husband?"

"I guess not," Spalding admitted. "No. Not too much at all."

"I married the man less than a year and a half ago," Churchill began. "I gave birth to his son, his only son as far as I know, and it all happened just this past winter while he and I were in Fort Wayne. I presently spend time in New York City, and my husband does not. What does that tell you?"

As they walked, Spalding listened.

"Do you know many German men?"

"Not really," Spalding admitted.

"They're not easy people to get along with," Churchill noted. "They're not easy to please."

Spalding consoled, "I'm sorry to hear that."

"Don't be," replied Churchill. Spalding appeared to be lost in wonderment. Churchill continued, "He wasn't my first love, Al. Out of curiosity, do you remember your first love?"

Spalding thought for a moment and responded, "I had a teacher in school who I often thought how wonderful it might be if she and I were more of the same age. Other than that though—not really."

"That's not exactly what I mean," Churchill observed. "I've been told that *first loves* are different for women than for men. I believe that, especially after what you just said."

Spalding listened intently.

Turning to Spalding as he looked at Churchill, she stated, "You were my first love, Al."

Churchill looked lovingly at Spalding. Spalding returned a look of surprise. "Are you serious? When I knew you back in Illinois, you were just a kid! You're talking adult love, right?"

Churchill sighed. "Al, girls mature earlier than boys. Yes, you were my first love, and as is often the case, I've never quite been able to release you from my heart or my thoughts. It wasn't just a googly-eyed little girl enamored with your abilities as a pitcher. Over the years, it became your manner—your pride, your humility, the sound of your voice, the enthusiasm I sometimes saw in you. You're brave, and you're scared, and," she said as she began to smile, "I very much like how you look. It was puppy love only briefly, if that's what you're getting at."

Churchill looked at Spalding in a way that, although her eyes had expressed that loving sentiment many times before, was recognized for what it was by Spalding for perhaps the first time. Spalding looked downward with humility, and glancing back at Churchill, his eyes returned the same caring expression toward her.

Spalding next began to talk. "I'm married to a good girl, but there's a bit of a problem with my feelings toward her, and I believe she toward me also. I suppose the problem began because I work in Chicago and have traveled a lot before now—the *life of a ballplayer* as they say."

Churchill patiently listened.

71

Spalding continued, "As I said earlier this evening, I'll soon be retiring as a ballplayer and will be spending most of my time at home in Chicago. Now, however, my wife wants to spend most of the pleasant summer months in New Jersey. Her interest in being with me isn't at the level it once was. What's worse is I feel the same way toward her." Spalding turned to look at Churchill and added, "With you and me, it seems like we simply wish to spend time together. I like being with you, Churchill! It makes me happy!"

They both looked at one another in the same special way as before, and Churchill nodded in agreement. She then reached over and gently clutched Spalding's hand as the couple continued to walk down street.

Upon walking quietly, arm in arm for a block, Churchill asked, "Did you leave your luggage in the bellman's closet at the hotel like I suggested?"

"I did," Spalding replied.

"We'll be coming up to your hotel shortly," noted Churchill.

Spalding cautiously began, "So then you're thinking that I should…"

"Albert," offered Churchill, "I'm thinking that we need to go to a wonderful saloon that I know of, not far from here!"

Spalding was perplexed. Before he could ask a question, however, the pleasantness of the walk was abruptly replaced with the thunderous rumblings of the elevated train that was rapidly passing overhead. As the train passed and Spalding was about to speak, the train's thunder was replaced by the loud, whooshing noise from the steam house that propelled the train. A moment later, the peace of the evening returned with only the gentle clip-clop of horses' hooves pulling a wagon.

"A saloon? Do you recall I don't drink? And unless you have changed as you say you haven't, you told me Theosophists don't drink anyway."

Spalding was walking between the roadway and Churchill as his mother had taught him to do when escorting a lady. Churchill gave Spalding a solid bump with her shoulder, making the tall, lanky pitcher wobble off the walkway and onto the road. Spalding looked at Churchill with a puzzled expression which, in turn, humored his lady friend.

"Not *that* kind of saloon," Churchill exclaimed. "An *ice cream* saloon, you silly but desirable man!"

"Oh," exclaimed Spalding. "That sounds like a great idea on a warm night. It must be eighty degrees at least!"

"That has nothing to do with it, Albert!"

They subtly unlocked arms. Spalding said, "I remain confused."

"Maybe men," Churchill began, "haven't learned to connect with ice cream the way women do—not unlike love." Churchill was humored by her own analogy and smiled at the athlete.

As they walked past Spalding's hotel, Churchill again intertwined her arm with his and responded, "Men are simply different. I'm in the mood to celebrate tonight, and I want some ice cream! The place is only a couple more blocks from here."

Spalding asked, "How do they serve it?"

"You'll see. First, you must decide whether you want ice cream, gelato, or a fruit ice. After that, then you'll have other decisions."

As the destination began to come into view, Churchill extended her arm forward and pointed.

"We're almost there, Albert. See the line of people?"

Spalding enthused, "This must be a popular place! Look at the line of people waiting to get in!"

Churchill chortled. "That's the tail of the line. The shop is around the corner, down the block, but you'll like standing in this line! Everyone is giddy because they know that they'll soon be eating ice cream."

"Although I'm not certain how this evening is going to come together," Spalding lamented, "I'm feeling really happy, though a bit nervous."

Churchill understood Spalding very well. As they joined the tail end of the line, Churchill caringly stated, "Fret not, Albert. Let this line we just joined make you feel secure, like when you wrap yourself up in a warm wool blanket. Just go with it. I will not allow anything, Al, to happen tonight that will make you feel the least bit uncomfortable! If it does, my woman's intuition isn't up to par." Pausing briefly, Churchill inquired, "Tell me this, dear. Have you ever heard of a writer named *Lyly*?"

Spalding repeated, "Lyly?"

"I didn't think so," Churchill responded. "Madame Blavatsky told me about him. John Lyly was a sixteenth-century writer and poet."

"I beg your pardon, Liz, but what does Lyly have to do with tonight—or ice cream?"

Churchill replied, "Lyly was the man that first said, '*The rules of fair play do not apply to love and war.*' Whatever may develop between the two of us, I think about what he said, and that's why I don't feel nervous. Look at it this way: once I've had my ice cream, there's nothing else you need do. It will be your turn for us to do whatever it is you want to do." Holding up her other hand, Churchill said, "You have my word on that."

As they reached the midpoint of the line, Churchill began looking to her left at the menus on the outside brick wall. The six-foot one-inch Spalding, on the other hand, was enjoying looking at the people over the heads of the ice cream lovers standing in front of them.

Churchill turned and faced Spalding. "I want the small 'Everything with Everything Sundae.' That's what you'll order for me."

"You do, ay? Everything with Everything?"

Churchill returned sarcastically, "If you're worried about the cost, Albert, I can always front you a loan."

Spalding laughed and continued to watch and listen to the line of happy throngs.

After a few steps more, Spalding turned to Churchill and affectionately observed, "Tonight was truly a special evening for me. I had the pleasure to meet three people of renown: Thomas Edison, General Doubleday, and Helena Blavatsky. It was great fun. Thank you for that! It just strikes me as so odd though."

Churchill interrogated, "Odd?"

Spalding lightheartedly began, "I know, for example, that I'm a famous athlete. I'm further respected as a sporting goods mogul.

You, however, are but a good ol' country girl from central Illinois. It merely seems odd to me that it would be you who would introduce that kind of person to me instead of the other way around."

Upon pondering the question, Churchill replied, "I will always be proud of my Illinois roots, Albert. That was my world at one of the times in my life. But that which you saw tonight, and that which you see, is now an important and permanent part of my present world, and I enjoy it immeasurably. Of course, with the Madame and all, there are some days I long to be back in Illinois."

Spalding began to laugh. "Don't think I don't have some rough days too," responded Spalding.

Churchill began to laugh. Spalding laughed harder. Churchill, still laughing, turned back to see how long the line had grown behind them. She noticed a few of the people standing behind them were straining to see who was doing the laughing.

Facing forward once more, Churchill said, "Well, Al, we've just earned our place in line."

Spalding was affixed on the fact that the line seemed to move much faster all of a sudden, and they were about to enter the doorway to the saloon. Spalding responded, "Pardon me, Elizabeth?"

Upon stepping inside the eatery, Churchill stated, "I'll tell you the plan in a moment, dear."

Spalding said, "Good. I've actually been wondering about the baby."

Churchill laughed. "My darling Durand! Fear not. Durand will be just fine! Things are well in hand," she said as she subtly goosed Spalding.

Spalding softly blurted out, "Good!" A few seated customers glanced over at Spalding but only briefly.

"I don't understand why you often seem so nervous," Churchill observed. "A tall good-looking athlete like you—a big-time star like you must have women throwing themselves at your feet constantly."

"It's not that simple," Spalding responded slightly defensively. "I never overcame my shyness until my early twenties, and then I got married."

Churchill commented, "To the victor goes the spoils."

"What's that supposed to mean?"

Churchill rolled her eyes. "Nothing, dear. Simply humoring myself."

The couple waited to be assigned a table. They were soon seated, and Spalding realized, "I need to look at the gas lights on Broadway that Tom was talking about!"

Churchill, looking at her menu, replied without looking up, "Next time I see him, I'll pass on that you 'think his idea is sensational.' For now, however, I have far more urgent business to attend to!"

Spalding reminded Churchill, "Strike me if I'm wrong, but I thought you already decided what you want to order."

"Tally one more for the women," Churchill boasted. "It is a woman's prerogative to change her mind, especially at a time like this!"

Spalding half-heartedly inquired, "You mean, even if it's about me?"

"No such luck on that one, dear boy," Churchill replied. "Over the years, I've tried but to no avail."

Spalding suggested, "Maybe you should stop trying to get rid of me."

Each looked at one another as they leaned toward each other.

Churchill inquired, "Are you thinking what I'm thinking?"

Spalding thought and replied, "It's about ice cream. Isn't it?"

Churchill looked sadly at Spalding and nodded in agreement. Then, they smiled at one another.

The two enjoyed their visit to the ice-cream saloon immeasurably—him in a way and her in multiple ways. Later, Churchill would have Spalding's luggage delivered to her place where they would retire for the evening.

* * *

With five months of citizenship under her belt, Madame Blavatsky departed the United States for England and India, accompanied by Olcott and two others. The Madame would never return.

Spalding never pitched another sanctioned game. He regretfully participated as a position player, however, in one more game. It was an important game near the end of the season that his team lost. The same Chicago newspaper that heralded the highest of praise for the White Stockings two years earlier capsulized the game and Spalding's final major league appearance thusly:

> The game was played and won on its merits. There was no luck, no falling to pieces and winning or losing in one inning, as often happens [to] Chicago's men. AG Spalding played second base and, as might have been anticipated, did not play the position as well as he might have done. In fact, he made five errors.

Spalding's life transformed over the next ten years. Upon Hulbert's death in 1882, the retired pitcher took over the reins of the White Stockings organization at a time when his sporting goods business was growing exponentially. During each year, he remained in Chicago during most of the six months of high baseball activity while his wife and son resided at the Spalding's ocean-side estate in Sea Bright. As is often the case in such circumstances, the lines blur as to whether the respective living arrangements of Josie and Albert were the cause or effect of the couple's drifting apart.

It takes two to tango.

—Songwriters Al Hoffman
and Dick Manning

CHAPTER 5

A Worldly Introduction

October 20, 1888—Chicago

A jolly affair! That's how the next day's edition of the *Inter Ocean* described the game. A lineup of White Stockings starters faced off against a team comprised of star players representing clubs from elsewhere around the league. It was an exhibition game filled with skilled performances, chants, antics, cheers, and banter. Despite the fun time, attendees were glad to see the game conclude. A northerly wind blew all afternoon, and as sunset approached, the day's high temperature of forty-three degrees had long since passed. Bundled-up adults within the crowd were thoroughly chilled while the children, free to run around along the sidelines, remained toasty as little furnaces. All said, there were no regrets.

The event, orchestrated by White Stockings President Albert Spalding, was the last chance Chicagoans had to watch professional-caliber baseball for some time to come. The game was a farewell appearance for members of the two teams. A privately chartered train would soon depart Chicago's Union Depot to begin a trek that would take the athletes to the opposite side of the world.

Spalding decided months earlier to organize an international goodwill baseball tour. He wanted to promote the sport in places where interest in the National Pastime might be cultivated. He also wanted to foster positive relations abroad. He did not want to duplicate the world tour of fourteen years earlier and with which he participated, where that effort focused on the British Isles. For the present trip, Spalding agreed to play exhibition matches in cities along the train route as the touring pros made their way west toward the Port of San Francisco. From there, baseball's ambassadors would set sail for the Hawaiian Islands and continue onward to the South Pacific Isles, New Zealand, and selected cities on the Australian continent.

Anticipating a last-minute mad dash to catch the train, Spalding's trip organizers reserved an ample number of carriages that were waiting for the freshly showered ballplayers to emerge from the ballpark's clubrooms. Players would then be whisked away and subsequently escorted to where their train awaited. By the time players were ready to leave the ballpark, close family members and friends invited to the final send-off at the station had already headed over to the departure point.

As people began to arrive at the assigned departure platform, a pleasantly dressed lady in her late sixties appeared. Walking aside the train, the woman became enamored with the scene. She looked up to discover she could not see the top of the locomotive that towered above her without stepping back a ways. Why bother now, she thought, when there'll be plenty of other opportunities for that! As the lady next walked past the fuel car, the remaining five cars came into view. Four distinctive train cars sat idly in front of the caboose at the rear of the train. Colorful banners were affixed to the sides of the four cars. Each banner, stretched from one end of its car to the other, read:

BASEBALL'S AUSTRALIAN EXPEDITION

The slogan-laden cars consisted of a long dining car, two Pullman sleepers, and a baggage car.

As the lady began to ascend the steps leading to the dining car, a station employee promptly arrived so as to offer assistance in boarding should such become necessary. Stepping up onto the staging of the car, unassisted, the woman proceeded to enter the dining car. A service attendant on board promptly appeared as the woman took off her hat, scarf, and overcoat. The train attendant asked for her name so that the outerwear could be placed in the woman's predesignated berth. As the porter was assisting with her gear, the silver-haired lady spotted the woman she was hoping to run into. The younger lady was seated comfortably at a table, sipping on a goblet of water. By chance, the seated lady casually turned, glanced in the direction of where the woman stood, sprung up like a Jack-in-the-Box and, with eyes agape and a big smile, called out, "Mrs. Spalding!"

With a facial expression of similar delight, Spalding approached the table. "Mrs. Williamson! We were worried sick about you earlier when you didn't show up for the parade!"

"I am so sorry," Mrs. Williamson pleaded. "Ned was supposed to tell you and your generous son, first thing, that I'd be going directly over to the train?"

Now seated in the chair at Williamson's side, Spalding remarked, "He sort of did. Once the parade dropped us off at the grounds, we observed a spectator in top hat giving your husband fielding practice by hitting balls over to him at the shortstop position. Given how the sportswriters say your husband is the most talented and popular third baseman of all time, I guessed the exercise on the field was secretly intended more for the benefit of the batter. At any rate, they stopped, and Mr. Williamson came over to us on the sidelines. He said you were having one of those very bad days."

Williamson groaned theatrically. "When I last saw him, Ed told me he was going directly to the parade. He was to tell you and AG, before the parade, that I would be heading directly over to the train. I didn't want anyone to fret!"

Spalding smiled, shaking her head. "Ballplayers. Through the years, I have often wondered why it is so difficult for them to follow the simplest of instructions."

Williamson laughed. "That, madam, may remain an eternal mystery!"

Spalding's expression transformed from a smile to intense curiosity. "Please. Tell me what happened, if it doesn't bring you discomfort. Is everything all right?"

The mild-mannered Williamson became melodramatic, replying, "First of all, Eddie, Ned has a birthday this coming Wednesday. I may try and look for a gift in the Twin Cities, but I already have a nice present. I didn't want him to know I have it. My bags are bursting at the seams, and I needed to smuggle it onto the train and have the porter stash it away until the big day. I used a tried and true technique to get the item on board without Ed's knowledge. I told him a little lie. I said I was running so late from all sorts of problems that I'd come directly here."

Spalding was perplexed. "And he never asked what any of your problems were?"

"No," Williamson said with delight. "He's really great that way. I get why the conniver avoids asking, but it's all for my benefit. I may not get as much help as some wives, but the inconvenience of having to do things on my own is a small price to pay for marrying a man who never cross-examines me. Besides, he's gone so much that I'm largely on my own, anyway."

Spalding laughed again. "So then, you didn't really have any problems at all!"

"No," exclaimed Williamson. "It turned out I had all sorts of problems. I had so many things go wrong after I sent Ed away that, once I tell you all that happened, you'll share my exasperation!"

Spalding laughed yet again. "In that case, hold the thought for later when we all need a laugh!"

Williamson giggled. "Deal! I'll tell you later about the gift too. Now you tell me what I missed! How was the parade? How was the farewell performance?"

Spalding stated hesitantly, "You knew the First Cavalry Band was supposed to lead all of us through the business district, right?"

Williamson nodded.

"Well, you missed nothing, dear! First, it was Captain Jack's Band who led the parade, but—"

Williamson excitedly interrupted, "I wonder if my husband will know of the change when I ask him about the parade later."

"If he doesn't immediately come clean," Spalding said in a whimsically evil tone, "why don't you wait until next Wednesday before you tell him about it."

Both ladies shared a good laugh.

"Anyway," Spalding began anew, "the change of bands was only the half of it, literally. Before we were halfway through downtown, Captain Jack and his merry band inexplicably separated from us. It was a potential disaster, and I'm not certain how Albert views the incident or how much he paid them, but it turned out fine. The parade watchers were wildly entertained as the scene unfolded. Besides, we did eventually wind up at the ballpark. My issue was with the cold! We sat in open carriages for a long while because my son said the sun would warm us up. I don't stay warm in the elements as I once did. Anyway, I won't be falling for another cockamamie scheme of Albert's any time soon!"

Williamson retorted, "Other than the voyage we are about to take?"

"Yes," agreed Spalding. "Other than that detail."

The two ladies both chuckled as they would, time and again, in the days ahead.

Williamson followed up, "Did many people show along the parade route?"

Spalding replied, "Not nearly as many as some would have liked. I overheard a few players saying how disappointed they were in the showing."

Williamson's eyes lit up as she gasped. "I think I know what happened! It's the talk of the town!"

Spalding's eyes encouraged Williamson to continue.

"Blaine from Maine is in Chicago," Williamson enthused. "Folks were saying that if all the people who showed up for the Blaine parade of earlier this morning had voted in the last presidential election, Blaine would be in the White House instead of Cleveland. I'm thinking that by the time our parade came along, Chicagoans had seen their fill of parading for one day."

"You could be right," admitted Spalding. "As for our little parade, regardless of the number of people who came out to watch, there was still a lot of enthusiasm. We had a good time and, at the game, Albert pitched remarkably well."

Williamson inquired in astonishment, "Your son pitched? Seriously?"

Spalding replied, "Seriously! Last week, the boys at the Board of Trade and some club men requested that President Spalding put on a uniform one more time and pitch today. Those caffeinated grain traders put together a petition containing four hundred signatures! Albert said he felt forced to accept the challenge, so he pitched the first four innings."

Williamson inquired, "And...?"

Spalding laughed. "The newspapers figured the young bats would knock my Albert's pitches all over the park, but it never happened. I was going to stick around until things turned sour, but they never did. He pitched four innings and only yielded a thrifty-five hits! Once he finished pitching, I ducked out. That's why I arrived here before the hoards descended."

Williamson observed what was going on around them—both inside and outside of the train. Noticing the high level of activity, the distracted Williamson mustered up enough tempered enthusiasm to reply, "That's nice."

During their conversation, Williamson and Spalding continued to glance through the windows at the crowd outside on the departure platform below. At first glance, it seemed sad to see the hapless families simply standing and looking at the train as they prepared to be left behind. Every one of those wives and children would certainly face new challenges and experience inconveniences in the coming months. Many of those standing in the cold remained forlorn—but only for a time. As members of families standing on the platform began to intermingle, smiles and laughter soon replaced expressions of fear and sadness. It was as if many of those remaining on the departure platform took solace in the comradery resulting from sharing a commonality of rare-but-like circumstance. The resilience of these *orphans* might have also been due to a realization that the authority for many family decisions would now be available for one of the other household inhabitants to pick up the slack. Having new rights and freedoms up for grabs, at least temporarily, might prove illuminating—and fun.

As departure time drew near, the dining car appeared to be at or near capacity. Several large men stood in the aisles clearly engaged in upbeat conversation. The Australian tour participants were in high spirits. It was one big loud party.

Through the crowd of men, Williamson spotted Mrs. Anson stepping into the car. The generally reserved Williamson stood and began waving her hands in a wide, sweeping motion. Williamson next gave a two-fingered whistle with a shrill loudness that transcended the noise level. Voices throughout the car hushed for a moment long enough for Williamson to shout and be heard.

"Mrs. Anson, over here!"

The wife of the White Stockings team captain acknowledged Williamson and began walking toward the table. As Mrs. Anson moved, the men in her path cleared out of the way. Upon arriving at the table, Spalding and Williamson could see tears in Mrs. Anson's reddish eyes. Assisted by two of her husband's teammates, Anson removed her scarf, overcoat, and hat. Mrs. Williamson sat back down. Mrs. Spalding motioned to an empty chair and commanded, "You sit right here, dear!"

Anson looked at the two ladies and, plopping down in the empty chair, gasped. "Am I glad to see the two of you!"

Expressing concern, Williamson inquired, "Are you all right? You look as if you've been crying."

Anson looked at Williamson with astonishment and exclaimed, "Me? Are you all right? Your husband made it sound like the sky was falling in on you!"

"Sorry, darling," Williamson began with a grin, "but I've been requested to give my official response to that question at a later time."

"Goodie," responded Anson. Turning to Spalding, Anson asked, "And where did you disappear to, Mrs. Spalding? I searched for you in the latter innings but couldn't find you…anywhere!"

Spalding groaned. "Once Albert finished pitching, I sneaked into a clubroom."

Anson teased, "Were any of the men showering?"

Chuckling, Spalding confessed, "Afraid not. I was merely warming up my tootsies." Spalding then asked Anson sympathetically, "Dearie, why the tears? Are you not excited?"

Anson giggled sheepishly and shook her head as if she were almost in disbelief. "It was so difficult saying goodbye to my children. My oldest daughter is heartbroken that both Adrian and I are leaving at the same time."

"Children are so resilient, though," Spalding remarked. "The next time you'll feel sad is when you receive a telegram in a week from now telling you they're having the times of their little lives!"

Anson nodded and sighed. "Probably so, Irene. Probably so." Addressing Williamson, Anson remarked, "I see Mr. Williamson is in high spirits having you along!"

Williamson nodded contentedly in concurrence.

Spalding then asked Anson, "Is Cap looking forward to the trip?"

Anson stated, "He's wild happy." Pointing to where her husband was standing, she continued, "Look at him! Happier than a clam! For him, this is more than a mere trip of a lifetime!" Anson paused. "After we finish up the next couple of days in the Twin Cities, the train heads over to where his kin all live, in tall corn country not far from Cedar Rapids. Of course, for some reason, my lovable lug gets nervous whenever he goes home to Iowa." Pausing into thoughtfulness, she continued, "I know he thinks Iowans are highly critical. Fortunately, he doesn't get too wound up over it. I reassured him, anyway, and now Cap couldn't be more excited."

The train whistle bellowed out a long blast that momentarily silenced the conversations. Once the ear-piercing sound ceased, train depot personnel in front of the dining and Pullman cars began shouting, "All aboard! All aboard for Base Ball's Australian Expedition!" As the station employees were making their final boarding call, Mrs. Anson stood while her eyes scanned the dining car. At that very moment, a lady approached Anson.

Anson exclaimed, "Mrs. Lynch! I was getting ready to send out the cavalry for you!"

Lynch, removing her outside wear with the assistance of two passengers and a porter, retorted, "No one in the First Cavalry, I pray." With increasing sincerity, Lynch added, "No power on earth was going to prevent me from getting here to this train! Not today!"

In synchronized movement, the three ladies motioned Lynch to sit in the fourth and only vacant seat at the table.

As Lynch took her seat, Anson began speaking to Williamson and Spalding, "Mrs. Lynch will be coming along with the three of us to the Antipodes where she will bail her husband out of whatever trouble he may have gotten himself into with the Aborigines."

Spalding looked at Williamson and said enthusiastically, "Leigh Lynch is our front man. He's the person who put together the foreign parts of our trip! He traveled ahead of us." Spalding added, "I only hope I feel strong enough to take advantage of Mr. Lynch's planning expertise. I'd really like to make the voyage beyond California, at the very least to the Sandwich Islands!"

"Please don't leave in the middle of the trip, Irene," Anson deplored. "With all these men, our opinions are terribly outnumbered! Besides, you're so enjoyable, and we may need your political clout!"

"Fear not, ladies," Spalding retorted. "Reinforcements are coming. The wife of the All-Americas team captain will be accompanying her husband. They'll catch up with us before we set sail."

"That's right," acknowledged Anson. "Mr. and Mrs. Ward."

Lynch asked, "Where are they now?"

"John Ward," Anson began, "is playing with the Giants for the Hall Cup. From the way things look so far, it appears the New Yorkers will wrap up the world championship soon." Looking at Williamson, Anson stated, "Ward plays at the same position as your Ned."

"Thank you," Williamson stated sincerely, "but if there's one thing I know about this sport, it's the left side of the infield. Shortstops and third basemen! Ed mentions Ward's name often."

Anson, upon reflecting how Cap talks incessantly about the world of baseball, became humored by Williamson's comment while, at the same time, was compelled to acknowledge her understanding.

Changing the topic, Lynch inquired, "I'm counting twenty-six travelers thus far: two rosters of ten, we four, Mr. Spalding and Mrs. Ward. Who am I missing?"

"Only a few more," responded Anson. "There are three sports reporters, a mascot, and two other gents, one of whom is none other than the all-time great, Mr. George Wright!"

Lynch wondered, "That's exciting! But did you say, Mascot?"

Anson replied, "Yes. He's a nice, well-mannered boy who will be making himself scarce."

Spalding noted, "When you mentioned the great George Wright, that reminded me, if anyone is interested, King Kelly who, after leaving the White Stockings…"

Lynch again asked, "King?"

Anson offered, "You may have heard him called by any of his many nicknames. People also call him the One and Only, or simply Only." Pausing, Anson continued, "My Adrian says that Kelly would probably attempt to use the alias, The One, if it were not for Kelly's fear of being excommunicated by Pope Leo XIII for blasphemy."

"Don't forget $10,000 Kelly," Spalding noted.

"Today's *Tribune*," Williamson pointed out, "called him Kelly the Great, but enough of that! Are you saying that Kelly is leaving the Beaneaters to come back to the White Stockings?"

"No," responded Spalding. "We can't afford to pay all the other salaries and pay him too! But he's playing for the All-Americas and will hook up with us in Denver."

Anson exclaimed, "Denver! He's already here! He played in today's game!"

Spalding commented, "He left for New York immediately after the game to dedicate his hotel."

Anson quipped, "That's vintage Only for ya'!"

* * *

5:55 p.m.

A series of lengthy blasts from the train's whistle set off a flurry of activity. The train's engineer was signaling for pedestrians on the platform to stand back—and for passengers on the train to be seated. Several ballplayers filed into the Pullman cars to find their assigned berths to begin settling in to what will be home for the next few weeks. Those few who were still standing in the aisles quickly found seats at welcoming tables. Conversation throughout the dining car continued to be as intense and jovial as before, but the noise level was more palatable.

As the whistle continued to sound, the dining car jolted and the train cars rumbled. This pattern would repeat as the train slowly began to pull away from the platform and head out of the station. As the train slowly gained momentum, the initial rumblings were soon replaced with a more subdued rhythm of wheels clacking on the rails along with the occasional blowing of the whistle warning those wagon drivers at the crossings who might otherwise be tempted to cross the tracks prior to the trains passing.

Throughout the beginning of the journey's first leg, only Albert Spalding remained standing. Gripping on to safety straps, the executive worked his way down the aisle to the table where the ladies were seated.

Dressed in a dapper suit, the host held a smile as he peered at each of the ladies. The four women looked up at him.

Anson broke the silence. "How's your arm, AG? Cap is giving fifty-fifty odds your pitching arm is going to fall off by the time they serve you your fruit cup."

AG nonchalantly replied, "Sorry to disappoint my loyal team captain, but I'm feeling on top of the world! Please convey to Adrian Constantine that I would have gone the entire game, but I'm not one to show off." Allowing the ladies to take in the sarcasm, AG inhaled and genuinely stated, "I only interrupt to give salutations to each of you, ladies, and inquire in earnest whether any of you might have outstanding problems or issues with which I may be able to help resolve, address, or otherwise assist. I'm anticipating all of you will have a wonderful time."

The women all shrugged their shoulders and looked at one another.

AG addressed each lady seated. "Mrs. Lynch? Mrs. Williamson? Mrs. Anson with the arm questions? Mother?"

Williamson said, "I'm the last person you need worry about. Ed and I are so happy…"

"That goes double for me," Mrs. Lynch volunteered.

"Oh, c'mon AG," Anson began, "my husband and I are both so very appreciative for everything you've done, and I mean that with all my heart! Now I'm only worried about when Adrian asks me, and he will, about your response to our little arm question that he insisted I ask. He's a big man, and when he gets real happy, it's kind of scary to be around him."

Pausing, Spalding retorted, "And without all my heart, Mrs. Anson, I thank you." Turning his attention to his mother, Spalding inquired gingerly, "Irene? Any comments?"

Mrs. Spalding raised her eyebrows and observed, "It looks so far like, between you and Mr. Lynch, you boys have thought about nearly everything. Nevertheless, dear, thank you for asking!"

Concluding, AG stated, "Please all remember to not hesitate to let me know if there is anything I can do to make your trip a better one!"

As the ladies and AG exchanged pleasant looks and nods, AG grabbed another overhead safety strap with his right hand and turned to face the table he next intended to visit. With the women now seated behind him, AG subtly massaged his right shoulder with his left hand, briefly grimacing in pain.

Spalding began walking from table to table, holding on to the handrails and leather straps as the train continued to accelerate on its 400-mile jaunt to St. Paul for the first of many stops westward.

Everyone on board, except for Spalding, was looking forward to the first two stops. St. Paul and Minneapolis were innocent-enough places for a person to enjoy themselves for a couple of days, but Spalding had a different take on it. First, these were two good-size cities and serious baseball towns in every sense of the word. Any slip-ups or losses by his teams would be criticized, something Spalding didn't want starting out on this kind of publicity tour.

There was a second reason that greatly concerned Spalding. He had a valid fear that, in the minds of Minnesotans, the Australian Tour already had *one foot in the ditch* before the teams arrived in the capital city. Nearly everyone in St. Paul enthusiastically supported the St. Paul Apostles baseball club. This club was an outstanding team. The talented local club was *rock solid* with quality position players and the brilliant pitcher-catcher combination of Duryea and Earle. Two Eastern ball clubs were presently trying to steal the Apostles' prized pitching combination—and the sports followers of St. Paul knew it. The most well-known of the would-be thieves were the Red Stockings of Cincinnati, a.k.a. *Porkopolis*, and the Chicago baseball team, a.k.a. Spalding's club. Spalding knew, before arrival, that the Twin City newspapers wouldn't send one sports reporter to cover the story. Rather, each newspaper would send a team of report-ers to cover the event. He knew that if he made so much as one brief move to talk to Duryea or Earle, the press would *eat him up alive* for attempting such a theft under the guise of a so-called goodwill tour. If Spalding were to attempt such a negotiation, he knew he would need to act in a highly presidential manner, by requiring intermedi-aries to perform his *bidding*. The citizens of St. Paul were excited to see such talent come to town, even if it were a "circus." Nevertheless, some level of skepticism held by the hosts should not have been a big surprise to Spalding.

October 21, 1888—St. Paul, Minnesota

The travelers arrived and were disembarking at Union Station in St. Paul, Minnesota. The four women were huddled together, try-ing to get off the train into the dense crowd on the train platform. Mrs. Williamson exclaimed, "There's a lot of people here, but I'm surprised. It doesn't look like there's many people to see us like in Chicago."

Mrs. Anson said, "I had a conversation with the conductor last evening. He said that Union Depot will handle eight million passengers this year. He told me that one hundred and fifty trains depart from here daily."

"They have a good local team," added Mrs. Spalding. "And talk is they support them to the hilt. I expect we'll see a good crowd of people to greet us once we get to West Seventh Street Park."

Mrs. Williamson observed, "St. Paul isn't so small. This may be a fun time like your son said, Irene."

"While the boys are playing," Mrs. Spalding offered, "they'd never know we were gone if we choose to do some sightseeing instead."

Mrs. Anson added, "I wonder where the biggest shopping district is."

The women all laughed and continued to follow the people within their group assigned to lead the way, at least for the time being.

On opening day of the tour, October 21, two games were played with two thousand St. Paulites on hand. The first match was between the two touring teams. The next game pitted the Chicagos against the St. Paul Apostles. The Apostles won! They beat Spalding's club. Prior to the train leaving for Minneapolis, Spalding awaited Harry Clay Palmer's arrival with the newspapers' early editions. The New York Herald's Palmer arrived and sat with Spalding.

Spalding said, "Yes, Harry."

"All right. You were concerned whether they might refer to you as a wolf in sheep's clothing and how they would interpret our visit overall."

"Something like that," Spalding responded.

Palmer returned, "Then, you're batting .500! I only bought a *St. Paul Globe*. It says it all." Pointing to the newspaper, Palmer said, "Take a look."

Anson Annihilated
The Chicago National Team Beaten by the Ruralists of St. Paul
Contests Between the Chicagos and All-
Americas Very One Sided

"I guess," Spalding began, "it was to be expected that the papers were going to tell their side of the story in a harsh way, especially given how protective they are of their darling Apostles. Have you read the article?"

"Of course, AG. This newspaper is for you."

"Thanks, Harry. I get the message from the headlines and don't feel like eating this *meal* in one sitting. I have enough of a taste in my mouth to last me until my curiosity gets the best of me."

"Very good, Big Al," Palmer replied. "Have a good evening. It will all get better from here on out!" Palmer then headed for his berth.

October 22, 1888—Minneapolis, Minnesota

In Minneapolis, the identical two contests held in Minnesota's capital city were replicated. The level of play seemed nearly the same as in the St. Paul contests, but the results were different due to what the city's newspapers felt were some nasty moves and biased calls by umpire Long:

**Laid Low By Long
Anson's Australian Contingent Outplayed
at All Points by the Apostles
The Umpire Couldn't See It, and the
Ruralists Were Whitewashed**

As a goodwill visit to the Twin Cities, the visit was not a success. It was thought by most to be more of a circus than quality sport. The Chicago team was referred to as "Anson's crybabies." The umpire, Long of Chicago, was accused of *extreme bias*, and it was reported that the attendees were gravely disappointed with the visitors' level of play. Spalding was glad to leave.

By the next morning, the group had been riding their train toward Cedar Rapids, Iowa. As the train began to near its destination, Spalding and Palmer entered the dining car for breakfast. They spotted the ladies on board sitting at the same table as the other days, tending to their breakfasts. Unlike the other mornings, the women were not talking to one another. Spalding walked up to the ladies' table. The women looked up to him with stoic expressions.

In a chipper fashion, Spalding said, "Good morning, ladies. How are our four chaperones doing today?"

The women continued looking up without speaking.

Spalding continued, "What's the matter? Nothing I've done I hope!"

Mrs. Anson inquired of Spalding, "Did you get much sleep last night?"

Spalding replied, "Except for the brief interlude, I slept like a baby!"

"None of us slept well, Albert," Spalding's mother said. "That *brief interlude* was quite upsetting to us all."

The episode to which the ladies alluded is best described on page 4 of the October 24, 1888, edition of *The Gazette* of Cedar Rapids, Iowa.

Mr. McNeillen [Macmillan], one of the press reporters, gives his idea of the trip to Cedar Rapids as follows:

> The Australian tourists woke up in a very dejected mood this morning. They left Minneapolis last night with every prospect for a good night's rest. This promise was fulfilled up to midnight. At that hour the devil broke loose in the heart of Tom Daly, the impish Chicago Colt. His satanic majesty began operations by impelling Daly to throw a tumbler of ice water upon the sleeping form of Van Haltren. He next secured a piece of ice and slipped it under the collar of Mark Baldwin's night shirt. Boston B. B. Brown peeked out of his [berth] to see what was up, and was greeted on the end of his nose with a bag hurled by the hand of the devil, alias Daly. Mr. Brown withdrew, and the devil having the field to himself proceeded to make things lively. He

carefully removed the shoe from each berth and placed them under the other fellows' bunks in order to [ensure] the proper degree of confusion in the morning. Then he pelted Fogarty, Carroll and Hanlon with pillows. Mr. Long, recently of Kansas City, interrupted the proceedings long enough to call the devil an opprobrious epithet. He was rapped on the head with a valise, but his shoelets' crowning achievement encompassed the ruin of "Old Hoss" Flint. That rosy veteran was sleeping the sleep of the pious in lower G. To him came the devil with a red lantern stolen from the rear platform of the train. Satan thrust the glaring luminary through the curtains of the berth and held it close to *old Silver's* face. The latter opened his sleepy eyes and saw the awful glare. He set up a cry of "Lord, Lord. I repeat," jumped up and bumped his head against the roof of the berth, and then went into a fit.

Spalding laughed. "You ladies let a little occurrence like that bother you? We're talking about a few ice cubes and a pillow or two!"

Mrs. Anson added, "Don't forget about the shoes, the valise, several other objects, and a few not-so-well-chosen words!"

Mrs. Williamson offered, "Your accommodations must be soundproof! I don't know about the conductor or the engineers, but there wasn't a soul on board this train that could sleep once the ruckus broke out."

Spalding's mother interrupted, "Albert, it took these ladies quite some time to settle things down. And don't think we didn't see you peeking out to see what was going on, only to return to your quarters! You said the trip would be relaxing and fun. Last night was quite the opposite!"

"If you look around you, Mr. Spalding," Mrs. Williamson commented, "most of your ballplayers aren't looking too bushy-tailed either. You may have been hoping that they'd play better than they did in Minnesota. I should think, however, that you will be doing good if they play *nearly* as well!"

Palmer, patiently listening up to now, pointed out, "It has always been my observation, ladies, that when AG terms something as *ideal*, one might translate that to mean *good with an occasional hiccup*."

"Precisely, Mr. Palmer," Spalding jovially agreed.

Speaking to the ladies, Spalding added, "You ladies said yourselves you felt responsible for keeping the men in proper order. And you performed splendidly last night! You should feel good about that! Feel free to grab the *bull by the horns* any time you see the need."

Palmer, knowing the routine, said to Spalding, "AG, we better grab that open table over there if we're going to get anything in our stomachs this morning. This may be another challenging day."

Spalding addressed the ladies, "Mother, ladies, we'll be going now. It's a new day! You'll like Cedar Rapids. The people are friendly, and I expect you will all have a relaxing time."

Spalding and Palmer left the ladies to be seated at the open table.

Hutchison entered the dining car. The lanky Chicago pitcher walked up to Spalding's table and sat down next to Palmer, wrestling his way into the small space at the table.

Spalding observed Hutchison's downtrodden face and said, "Why are *you* looking so down? You should be excited! You're going back to your hometown as a big shot! This is a moment of triumph!"

"You just described the problem," Hutchison replied. "We're talking about pressure here."

Spalding responded, "Excuse me? If I'm not mistaken, this train has been heading away from the pressure cooker and westward to the heartlands."

"I can see you need some educating," Hutchison retorted. "When you're from Iowa, performing any formidable task before an Iowan crowd would strike fear into the most courageous of souls. People of Iowa expect a lot from their neighbors. That's pressure! If you're not from Iowa, you'll never understand."

Spalding laughed. "You don't feel pressure in front of our usual audiences? Discriminating crowds that often hold us in contempt before we even arrive? Crowds that are many times the size of what we expect in Iowa? There's no pressure when you pitch for a world championship? Dear sir, there is something wrong with this picture."

Hutchison stood and sarcastically offered, "I'm so glad I came to you for your advice, *boss*. I feel so much better now! And if I may be excused…"

Hutchison left and sat down with a few ballplayers at another table.

Spalding said to Palmer, "I think that went rather well. Don't you?"

Palmer remarked, "If you believe that, AG, then at least you salvaged *something* from *the wreckage!*"

Spalding commented, "You know, Anson grew up in these parts too!"

"I might suggest then," Palmer replied, "that, for the time being, you avoid him."

Spalding sighed. "I'm just glad Minnesota is in the direction of the caboose! What time do you have, Harry?"

"I just looked. It's 9:00 AM, Big Al, and the train is beginning to slow."

October 23, 1888—Cedar Rapids, Iowa

For everything that happened or didn't happen in the Twin Cities, it all went smoothly in Cedar Rapids. Cedar Rapids was a young, economically healthy city of twenty-thousand and growing. The homes, buildings, and streets were all clean and new. The city had industry, jobs and opportunity, a river that emptied into the Mississippi River, and the occasional Victorian homes of unbridled opulence. Attendance was described as *3,500 of the city's best people.* The weather was clear. The game was close and exciting. The two favorite sons of the area coming on the tour both did well, and the spectators appreciated their efforts. The authorities were hospitable, and the crowd was pleasantly animated.

The next morning, Spalding entered the dining car, saw the ladies in a chipper conversation, and decided not to *rock the boat* before arriving in Des Moines. It was probably just as well.

Mrs. Spalding said to the other ladies, "I read an early edition of the *St. Paul Globe* that one of our reporters somehow found. I have the paper on loan. The reporter was looking to see the local news coverage to see what else was said about our visit to the cities. Turns out my son, PT Barnum Spalding, and the rest of us were upstaged."

Mrs. Anson inquired, "By what, Irene?

"Not what! By whom," Mrs. Spalding declared. "Sitting Bull!"

Mrs. Anson observed, "Sitting Bull is always big news in the Midwest!"

Mrs. Williamson commented, "Chief Sitting Bull was big news once, but one might think interest in the man would have waned. It's been years."

Mrs. Lynch responded, "He's the chief of the entire Sioux nation! That keeps him in the news!"

Mrs. Spalding appended the statement. "He's remained chief for more than twenty years! His people have faced one challenge after another. From all that I've read, there have been but few leaders in history who had the political savvy to maintain their reign for as long as he has!"

Mrs. Anson wondered, "What was Sitting Bull doing in St. Paul?"

"He was headed for the St. Paul Union Depot to catch the train to Washington. He's re-renegotiating a treaty," Mrs. Spalding noted.

Mrs. Williamson asked, "Were there many people on hand?"

"The article," Mrs. Spalding responded, "says he had a very large number of people with him to begin with. Remember that wide boulevard that went downhill for several blocks leading from the state capital down to the train station?"

"Of course," Mrs. Anson said.

Mrs. Spalding continued, "Apparently, Chief Sitting Bull and a large entourage walked down the middle of the street from the Capitol steps all the way down to Union Depot, and the boulevard was lined with onlookers. Of course, it's always difficult for us to compete with the publicity to someone like that. Sitting Bull simply did better than us!"

Mrs. Williamson observed, "Once a politician, always a politician."

With expressions of whimsical acknowledgment on their faces, the other ladies nodded in agreement.

With each future stop, there would be both challenges and memorable highlights, but the trip continued to go smoothly. It was clear that the ballplayers were enjoying the people at the places they visited, and the appreciation was continually reciprocated.

Des Moines, Iowa—Omaha, Nebraska—Hastings, Nebraska
Denver, Colorado—Colorado Springs,
Colorado—Salt Lake City, Utah
Next, onward to California—Los Angeles followed by San Francisco

Every stop while heading west to California had a good story, not unlike the first stops in Minnesota and Iowa. Of all the stops prior to arriving in California, the highest attendance occurred on October 26 in Denver. On that day, a total of six thousand interested spectators showed up.

On November 18, 1888, the group boarded the steamship *Alameda* bound for Australia by way of Oahu in the Sandwich Islands. Everyone was excited. The Hawaiian Islands were a paradise! It was also a panacea for baseball. Alexander Cartwright, famous for being the driving force behind drafting the first known set of rules for modern-day baseball, had relocated to the kingdom of Hawaii some years back. Since his arrival, Cartwright's successful promotion made the national game wildly popular on the islands, and everyone on the tour was aware of this. Oahu was baseball's paradise. Spirits were high!

Arrival at Honolulu was scheduled for the Saturday morning preceding Thanksgiving. A game was to be played later that same day. Sunday would be a day of sightseeing, socializing, and leisure because it was against Hawaiian law to, among many other things, play a game of baseball on Sunday. Spalding later commented on these *blue laws* in *America's National Game* by stating, "*Sunday ball was as 'taboo' in Honolulu as had been a whole lot of things when the heathens had been in full control of their island.*"

By unfortunate circumstance, Spalding was informed on Saturday that the *Alameda* would not arrive in Hawaii until Sunday. The new estimated time of arrival was early Sunday morning. The change in schedule was catastrophic unless he could find a way where baseball could still be played without going against law and tradition. By late that day, it became clear to Spalding that they would not be able to play without going against local law! He would not consider that, so he called a meeting for the early hours of Sunday morning with his team captains. They met on the main deck under lantern light.

The lighthouse on the watery outskirts of Oahu appeared off in the distance. Many of the passengers were waking up for the early morning arrival. The weather was calm and balmy. Team captains Cap Anson and John Ward arrived a few minutes early and were settling in to a pair of canvas lounging chairs on deck. A subtle hue from the day's sun was beginning to show. Spalding walked over to where the two men were lounging, grabbed an empty chair, and turned it to face the captains.

With a gentle smile, Spalding commented, "Good morning, gentlemen. I'm glad to see the two of you so bright-eyed and bushy-tailed." Addressing Anson, Spalding inquired, "Did you wake the missus?"

"Only accidentally," replied Anson. "She asked where I was going, and I told her I had a meeting."

Spalding retorted, "What did she say to that?"

"Nothing," replied Anson. "She covered her head with my pillow."

Spalding laughed. "Good for her! Meanwhile, I have some thoughts you may wish to pass on to your teams. If you can figure out how to appease the women folk, I would similarly appreciate the gesture."

Ward inquired, "Anything to be concerned about, AG?"

"I want you," responded Spalding, "to gently prepare the guys about what will likely transpire." Spalding took a deep breath. "I want you to let your team members know that, short of a miracle, we will not be able to play ball. It is illegal to play on Sunday here, and I will not breach public law. Monday is not an option to play a match as our next voyage begins on Monday morning. Although I am certain that we will be met with a cordial official welcome, not everyone will be pleased with our visit when we inform them that a game will not be played as planned. I don't want your baseball ambassadors to be too disappointed."

Anson asked, "Do you expect us to receive harsh criticism?"

"I don't expect so," replied Spalding. "I do think, however, that everyone should be made aware so that they might properly respond in dignified fashion, regardless of what may be said by any of our hosts."

Glancing over at the signalers waving their flags on deck at the shore, Spalding stopped a crew member briskly walking by and asked, "What are they saying to the people on shore?"

"No one on the islands knows that Henry Harrison won the presidential election," the deckhand responded. "With treaties and all, we were informed that emissaries to King Kalakaua recently stated that His Majesty wants to know—immediately—how the election went."

Ward exclaimed, "So that's the king's name."

Spalding pulled up his hand and began slowly reading something written. "His proper name is David La'amea Kamananakapu Mahinulani Naloiaehoukalani Lumialani Kalakaua. Did you get that?"

Anson glanced at Ward. "I don't know about you, John, but I'll be sticking close to AG's side!"

The three men laughed.

Ward inquired, "You know that for sure?"

Spalding showed writing on his palm. "Like the back of my hand!"

Spalding commented, "If all else fails, gentlemen, *Your Majesty* will do just fine. Oh, yes. You may also wish to lower your head should you address him, lest it be lowered for you."

Ward gazed at Spalding and exclaimed, "I'll flank your vacant side, sir."

After a few more minutes of conversation, the deck began filling up with passengers looking at the shoreline. People on shore were becoming visible, and large crowds had assembled on the various wharfs. Spalding would soon learn that his fears would be the farthest thing from reality.

November 25, 1888—Honolulu, Oahu, Kingdom of Hawaii

Upon docking, the ship was boarded by a delegation led by prominent citizen George W. Smith, who so happened to be Spalding's cousin. Greetings were enthusiastic and exchanged in earnest. As Spalding's party disembarked, leis were placed around the necks of everyone. Amidst a thick crowd with the Hawaiian band playing songs, the tourists were led to a long line of flag-laden carriages. Everyone was then whisked away to the Hawaiian hotel for a bountiful Hawaiian breakfast.

Following breakfast, a procession was formed to meet with the king. Led by His Excellency, US Minister resident George Merrill, the teams and guests marched by twos while accompanied by the band. After all appropriate ceremony and pomp, the goodwill tourists were escorted to the queen's residence so that they might meet and exchange all proper respects. Throughout the day, the pageantry was almost never-ending, except for a few occasional moments to play tourist and take in some sights. The boulevards, lined with palm trees and floral gardens, were clean, in perfect repair, and well-manicured. The palaces and government buildings were majestic with open air walkways. As the day progressed to sunset, the grid of electrified streetlights began to glow.

It was time for the grand luau. The host was His Majesty, King Kalakaua. Entertainment appeared off and on during the feast. All diners had colorful leis about their necks. Numerous toasts were given by the hosts to the baseball teams. Spalding stood and raised his pineapple. "I propose a toast to the finest host anywhere, a dear and important friend to the United States—and leader of this beautiful and most special kingdom—His Majesty, King Kalakaua. Long live the king, and may he enjoy a long and prosperous rule."

By day's end, the lei-laden passengers boarded the ship bound for New Zealand. On the verge of a lengthy voyage at sea, Spalding's group was on edge. They were thankful for the unsurpassed hospitality received yet felt badly for not having played a game of ball in this—of all places! Our sincerest apologies, Mr. Cartwright! Nevertheless, they departed Honolulu in the early morning hours of November 26th as planned.

A week at sea had passed when Spalding called a meeting with the entire party in the main hall of the steamer. Everyone assembled. Some were seated, and others stood motionless. Spalding began to speak.

"What's everyone so glum about?"

Cap Anson blurted, "We're all talked out, and we're curious as to why this meeting."

"You talked out? That'll be one of the memorable moments of the tour," quipped Spalding. The group continued their silence. "As for all of your curiosity, I'll alleviate that right now. In between the hoopla beneath the palm trees, I pursued a thought. I gathered international steamer schedules and talked with some higher-ups at two of the shipping lines. I may have figuratively *missed the boat* on planning our return trip home. I figured out a route home from Australia that is completely different from that which is planned. What I am about to propose will embellish our trip and enable all of us to do more good for baseball and America. At the same time, it will make a scheduling change that will turn this tour into an experience of a lifetime."

One of the reporters in the party asked, "Are you suggesting a delay in when we expect to return home?"

"No," Spalding enthused. "Rather than retracing our steps to return home by way of Hawaii to California and Chicago, we could go to Ceylon, Egypt, Italy, France, Scotland, Ireland, and England, and return by way of New York."

The group had blank expressions, and Spalding stood still in front of the group.

AG's mother volunteered, "Albert, my dear, I've heard that being at sea for extended periods of time can make even the most brilliant of people conjure strange thoughts, and some of us may be near exhaustion even when completing the trip as planned."

Several private conversations immediately burst out, and the noise level rose to that of a crowd of five times their size, with occasional belly laughs erupting. Spalding began speaking loudly.

"I figured out how to change our route home without delaying our arrival back to the United States. I might add, however, that I would need the assistance of several of you to make this pipe dream a reality. If we can pull this one off, we will return home on schedule. Moreover, this new route will also break up the long periods at sea. In the meantime, we will double our promotional efforts on behalf of baseball and the United States while greatly enhancing our overall experience."

Newton Macmillan of the New York Sun was intrigued with the prospect of returning by way of his hometown. "You're saying, then, that if we were to agree with your idea, it would be an easier trip, and we would hit the Middle East and Europe?"

"That is what I'm saying," Spalding responded.

A flurry of questions ensued near simultaneously.

"Are you committing to the additional funding?"

"Can we reschedule at this late date?"

"How can we schedule games on such short notice while on the move?"

"For those of us with commitments upon returning home, how is it possible to return home on or near our originally scheduled return?"

Spalding appeared to bask in the excitement of the moment.

"Please, allow me to address all your concerns," Spalding said. "I have several transport schedules, and some may change. There may be new and better possibilities also. Now then, I believe you all know that Mr. Leigh Lynch was the primary orchestrator of this trip. You probably also know that Mr. Lynch is presently in Australia. He and his wife, with whom I know you all know, will be returning to the United States with us. A part of this plan that I really like is, although Mr. Lynch does not yet know, he will be in charge of making this pipe dream a reality! If anything should go wrong, you can't blame me!" Spalding's eyes scanned the group. "And here's the other part I really like. Mrs. Lynch, would you kindly make your presence known."

Lynch was standing and slowly raised her hand. Containing more skepticism than enthusiasm in her voice, Lynch offered, "Yes, sir."

Spalding asked, "Might you know, Mrs. Lynch, who will be the one to inform Leigh of this small rush job we'd like for him to handle?"

Lynch said nothing. Spalding said nothing. The group became amused, especially the sisterhood.

Closing his conversation with Lynch, Spalding added, "Of course, that is entirely predicated on the assumption that I can later convince you to extend such a kindness." He smiled reassuringly. She acknowledged with a few comfortable nods.

George Wright asked, "When will we know if it's a go?"

"I'll try to solidify enough plans with the passenger lines to know we can do it. I can do this in New Zealand or by the first day in Australia," replied Spalding. "What other questions?"

The group was quiet again. "All right then," Spalding continued. "I'd like to see a show of hands as to those in favor of trying to go to New York by way of the Middle East and Europe."

Everyone raised their hands in favor. "Good. Then, I'll start preparations today. Don't let anyone leave the ship or take a swim. I may need your services." The group became mildly rowdy and a bit giddy.

Sunday, December 9, 1888—
Auckland, New Zealand

After two weeks of chasing the Southern Cross and having passed Fiji days ago, morning twilight offered the Alameda's crew first sight of the islands and peninsulas along the northern tip of New Zealand. The steamer would continue in a southerly direction for another one hundred and fifty miles. The ship's destination, Auckland, is New Zealand's largest city and known for being surrounded by a dramatic coastline of cliffs and black-sanded beaches. For members of the baseball tour, however, this mostly translated into meaning they would know within ten hours whether Spalding succeeded or failed to satisfactorily resolve a matter of potential embarrassment to everyone traveling in their group.

The expedition was in danger of repeating the disheartening situation that occurred in the Hawaiian Islands. Similar to the arrival at Honolulu, the steamer was again behind schedule by one day. Also, like Honolulu, the itinerary originally called for an early Saturday arrival, exhibition games to be played later in the day, and a departure time scheduled for Sunday afternoon. Consistent with Hawaiian custom, activities similar to playing ball on Sundays in Auckland were seriously frowned upon. Having already missed the opportunity to play ball in the Hawaiian Islands, a repeat of that event or nonevent would mean that Spalding would fail at meeting his primary objective at each of the first two international ports of call. To make matters worse, he no longer had control over what or how news was fed to the public. The number of correspondents on the tour had increased from an initial number of three to where, according to Auckland's *The Press, thirty-four journals* were now represented.

Everyone onboard knew there was but one good solution to the problem—*play ball!* No one wished to be caught up in what would surely be swarms of jokes the American sportswriters so reliably offer on such occasions to their hungry American readers. Faced with the obvious consequences upon first learning the ship would arrive at Auckland one day late, Spalding initiated action. He made a powerful *plea* to the Alameda's owners, the Oceanic Steamship Company, to allow for a full day's delay in departure. By the time of the baseball teams' arrival on Sunday, *The Press* learned of Spalding's request and the reply of the shipping line's ownership.

The Alameda was rescheduled to depart Auckland on Monday evening. The ballplayers were now free to introduce their beloved American sport while, at the same time, having some fun with the crowd by *hamming things up* and displaying their honed athletic skills to an inquisitive, appreciative, virgin audience. The extension of time also meant New Zealanders would avoid insult by not being brushed off in favor of nearby Australia. Then, too, the group of accompanying newspaper correspondents could write of their adventures while on tour rather than memorializing that Spalding was *zero for two* in traveling great distances to international ports for the stated purpose of spreading goodwill from the United States.

In *America's National Game*, Spalding wrote a solitary sentence describing the entirety of the New Zealand visit, "*Here a game was played to the great delectation of the New Zealanders, very few of whom had ever seen it, though many were proficient at cricket.*"

Auckland's newspaper, on the other hand, dedicated multiple columns to the touring teams' visit. The newspaper offered articles describing the aspects of the match, cameos on some of the athletes, and the rules of play. In its coverage of the event, the publication noted that attendance was only a thousand spectators but had the civility to not make much of the matter. Concurrently, a group of talented Maori athletes, indigenous New Zealanders, was in Manchester, England, playing rugby during a very successful world tour of their own. Again, it was kind not to make any comparison to Spalding's somewhat challenged expedition. *The Press* accurately described details and the essence of the match yet chose, rather than provide a final score, to note that...*both teams were loudly cheered on returning to the pavilion.*

In the shipping section of the next day's issue, Auckland's *Press* reported that the steamship Alameda, bound *for Sydney, sailed* on Monday at 5:10 p.m. From this point in the trip, the tourists would encounter two more issues, though of lesser consequence. One such event would occur in sight of the Nile while in the presence of

Cheops and the Great Sphinx; the other incident occurring while in the company of His Royal Highness, the crown prince of England.

December 14—Sydney, Australia

After a three-day sail, the ship arrived at the port of Sydney, Australia. All passengers were on deck as the ship pulled into port. While docking, amidst the hurried activity of the crew, Spalding announced that the changes in itinerary were already underway, and that their plans were in accord with what the group had agreed to.

Upon arriving on the continent amidst the summer heat of December, matches were played in four cities located in southeastern Australia. Over the twenty-five days while in Australia, Spalding's tour covered 1,500 miles by land. The teams appeared in Victoria at the cities of Melbourne and Ballarat, Sydney in New South Wales, and Adelaide in the state of South Australia. Crowds were consistently large, and it became clear that most people knew cricket, yet few had ever seen a game of baseball. Nevertheless, Spalding believed all were impressed with the sport and level of play. Importantly, Spalding believed bonds had formed between the touring party and the residents. He thus deemed the visit a success.

It was an unusual experience for all those on tour. It was Christmastime and the weather balmy. Christmas dinner consisted of that which was typical of the region—salads, cold meats, an array of seafood, and plum pudding. Locals filled the beaches on Christmas Day, and snowmen comprised of sand sculptures stood near the water's edge. Colorful decorations appeared along the streets and adorned the most modest of homes and business buildings. The differences in celebrating the holiday fascinated everyone on tour, and most people in the group seemed to miss sharing the experience with their loved ones back in the United States. It was obvious to the Australians the tour group appreciated their local traditions and the special comradery that resulted, both within the tour and among the citizens of this distant place.

January 6, 1889—Melbourne

One of Melbourne's newspapers, *The Age*, described the events of the tour's final day on the continent and the last impression left by the group:

> About 11,000 people assembled on the Melbourne cricket ground on Saturday to witness a mixed athletic exhibition given on the occasion of the American baseball players making their last appearance in Australia. Some disappointment was felt when it became known that Professor Bartholomew had not sufficiently recovered from his recent accident to undertake his balloon and parachute performance, but with baseball, football, and throwing the cricket ball the afternoon was pleasantly filled up. The Chicago team having scored 12 runs to 0 in a three innings game with the Melbourne baseball club, a football match was played between Carlton and Port Melbourne in which each side kicked 3 goals. Chicago then beat All America at baseball in a very pronounced fashion, scoring 5 runs to 0 in a five innings game. A competition at throwing the cricket ball concluded the afternoon's amusement, Crane, the New York pitcher, throwing 128 yards 10 1/2 inches, and Baldwin, of Chicago, 125 yards 8 inches. The Americans depart to-day for Colombo by the German mail steamer Salier, and will leave behind a most favorable impression of the marvelous skill at the national game of America, whilst socially Mr. Spalding and his associates have experienced and well deserved a very happy time in Australia.

After celebrating New Year's 2,500 miles south of the equator, the group departed Melbourne on board the steamer *Salier*. The ship passed through the Bass Strait, Tasmanian Sea, Indian Ocean, and the Suez Canal to arrive at Ceylon. Two days after reaching the island, a match was played in front of a large crowd.

Giza, Egypt, was the next destination. The two teams played games on the sizzling desert sands in sight of the Nile, under the shadow of Cheops and within feet of the Great Sphinx. All on the tour were taken aback by what Spalding observed as an overwhelming sense of history. Spalding failed to mention that some Egyptians were troubled after observing ballplayers freely bouncing baseballs off the Great Sphinx, with one tosser hitting the right eye as the intended target.

Next, the teams' ship entered the Bay of Naples to arrive in Italy. The tour went ashore to teach the Italians how to play the American game. The first game in Italy was played at the base of magnificent Vesuvius. In what was among the most favored of experiences on the trip, the ballplayers partook in a match in Rome on the grounds of the Villa Borghese, considered one of the world's most fabulous estates. His Royal Highness, King Humbert of Italy, students enrolled at the Roman College of the Catholic Church, and many others were in attendance. The Americans soon departed Italy but not until a visit to the *city of Michelangelo*—majestic Florence.

Upon leaving behind the generosity of the Italian hosts, the Americans headed for Paris, France. Here, the teams played a game before a large group of knowledgeable Americans and a gathering of newcomers to the sport. The contest was played on the grounds along the Champ de Mars by the foot of the nearly completed Eiffel Tower. After playing a couple of games, several of the athletes and their tiny entourage of journalists decided to get a bite of French cuisine. They spotted some cafés on the street where they were walking. One place, a bistro, had a menu painted on a wooden likeness of a chef, although they did not know what most of the offerings were. The American contingent courageously walked into the café and looked around. There were some empty tables. A host came up to the party and asked a question in French that no one understood.

Noting the confused expressions during their nonresponse, the host spoke in English, asking with a smile, "How may I help you?"

Harry Clay Palmer exclaimed, "You speak English!"

"You are surprised, monsieur? People of France speak many languages. It is only the Americans who do not."

"You're right," conceded Palmer. He continued, "My associates and I are looking for a café where we can get some good food before departing for England."

"Monsieur, there is no such thing as a bad restaurant in Paris, and there is no better food than right here—and if you are off to England shortly, you need to eat here. The food is not good in England."

Anson inquired, "Not good?"

"They can't understand the concept of a great sauce. The only decent food England ever invented are crumpets and Boeuf Wellington, and neither is anything you can write your mother back home about. Please," the waiter said as he motioned to an open table, "be seated and we will soon make your palates cry with pleasure."

Palmer was in suit and tie, although the others were still in uniforms.

A man sitting alone at the next table said with a French accent, "I saw the contest. It was very entertaining. You are all well skilled."

"Merci, monsieur," replied Cap Anson in an outrageous accent, proudly showing off what little French he knew.

"What do you think of le tour Eiffel?"

"Impressive," responded Anson. "When will the tower be complete?"

"Soon," the Frenchman responded. "It must be finished for the opening of the Exposition Universelle in a few months from now."

Making conversation, Anson inquired, "The Universal Exposition sounds like a big event, n'est-ce pas?"

The Parisian replied, "Our exposition will have displays and visitors from many nations. This fair of the world will be here but once." The man continued, "You are going to England to play another game?"

"Yes," exclaimed Williamson. "We were told we may meet the Prince of Wales at a game near London."

The Frenchman laughed. "The Prince of Wales!" He uttered something indiscernible in French.

Williamson inquired, "Does that seem funny to you?"

The patron replied, "The Prince is known to be quite a character!"

"How so?"

Conversation was interrupted as the waiter, with a white towel draped over his shoulder, silently laid down empty goblets and place settings, and presented a menu to each of the hungry diners. From large carafes, the waiter partially filled the goblets and glasses with wine and water. The waiter stood still as the Americans tried to decipher the menu, leaning forward to answer each question, and take the group's orders.

As the waiter departed, the patron continued, "The hommes in France are considered to be romantic, but the Crown Prince should be a professor on the subject!"

"We were told he very much loves his wife," Anson replied.

The patron laughed again. "The Prince loves many things. He loves his food and drink. He loves his cigars and friends. The Prince loves his wife—and many women. Do you know Lillie Langtry?"

"Sounds familiar," replied Anson.

"The Prince knows Lillie Langtry, and the Prince knows many others like her," said the Frenchman.

Williamson offered, "I expect we will hear much about the Prince soon."

"Not if you are going to England. They will not talk about this. The French have the guillotine when you berate royalty, but the English have shackles and irons. The guillotine is fast. In England, death is slow."

Palmer interrupted, "You seem to know a great deal about the monarchy of the Commonwealth."

"My countrymen," replied the patron, "enjoy acting like they know the English so that they can talk about them. It is not often we have a person with such sinful ways. A Frenchman dines on good food, good wine, and sinful conversation. The royals are the pièces de résistance."

There was no response from the Americans. The patron added, "Why do you think the Queen, who will soon celebrate her seventieth birthday, does not give up her throne? The Prince is not yet ready to be king."

"I have not seen a picture of him," Williamson commented. "Is he tall and thin as I'm told most British kings have been?"

The patron, finishing up his meal, dabbed his mouth with a napkin, stood up, and said, "You will soon see for yourself. They say the Prince can smell the manure on the ground better than all other Englishman." The man then laughed. "You will soon understand! Adieu, monsieurs."

It was as fine a meal as any of the travelers had ever experienced. Their plates cleaned off and the wineglasses emptied, the Americans departed the café and returned to their ship to depart for England.

* * *

England! The ball clubs were welcomed in grandiose fashion at the Surrey County Cricket Club with many dignitaries on hand. The guest list included the American consul; Dukes of Beaufort and Buccleuch; Earls of Coventry, Chessborough, Sandsborough, and

Sheffield; Lords Hawke, Littleton, and Oxenbridge; Sir R. Hanson; Attorney General Sir W. C. Webster; London's Lord Mayor; and other notable figures. It was the first of what would be many generous, humbling receptions throughout this hosting land. English hospitality would be second to none!

The first and most memorable matches in America's sister country was held in London at Kennington Oval grounds. It was thrilling for the teams to see such a large crowd as was on hand, though the players expected to see the Prince of Wales and were clearly disappointed in the Crown Prince's absence. Spalding also felt disappointment at the absence of the man that would one day be king, especially after hearing what his ballplayers said about the Prince's reputation. The local club team was designated "home" club and were first to take the field.

The game had just begun when the appearance of two dignitaries silenced the crowd, and timeout was called. The two finely dressed men were escorted onto the field by an entourage consisting of, in part, tall guards dressed in formal military uniform. One of the two men was quite tall, and the other was short in stature. Spalding was standing by one of the team benches when a British official came up to him. The official explained that the two men in question were the Prince of Wales and his brother-in-law, Prince Christian. The two royals proceeded to step onto the ball field while play was halted.

The seated players, eager to see the Prince and having been briefed on proper protocol, arose from their benches and, along with those at play a moment earlier, watched the Prince of Wales approach. He was clothed in a dapper, stylish outfit; however, he did not appear as the playboy they had imagined. The Prince's clothes were impeccably tailored; however, he didn't look like a stereotypically thin Englishman. Prince Edward was maybe five foot five inches and stout.

One of the ballplayers said to another in Spalding's presence, "I think I understand why the Prince can smell the manure so well."

Spalding softly barked, "Boys, there are times to cut up and make jokes. This is not one of them. Straighten up your act—now!"

After the players and Spalding watched the Prince make his way to the visitors, the teams initiated a "three cheers and a tiger." One of the team members shouted, "For His Majesty, the Prince." The standing players shouted in unison, "Hoorah!" The Prince nodded his head politely. A second cheer was given. "Hoorah!" This was followed by a third cheer. "Hoorah!" The Prince nodded regally with each cheer.

The crowd became excited and began to randomly make numerous and enthusiastic cheers in a variety of forms with the Prince continually nodding his head in appreciation. The two princes and the handful of people accompanying them were escorted to the royal box at the foot of the grandstand. Play was then resumed.

Spalding was standing on the sideline when a "gentleman in waiting" walked up to him. The man said, "Sir, the Prince requests the pleasure of your company and wishes for you to be seated alongside His Highness and Prince Christian in the royal box."

As the man awaited an answer, Spalding glanced over at the royal box. "My privilege," Spalding replied.

Again, the game was momentarily halted as the players watched Spalding's departure. Spalding was escorted to stand between the two princes. The royals stood motionless as they formally received Spalding. Facing the Prince of Wales, Spalding bowed his head and said, "Your Highness, this is an unexpected and welcome honor!"

Both princes made kindly nods with their heads. The Prince of Wales leaned toward Spalding with a stiff neck and said, "You did very well, Mr. Spalding. The last American we invited to a royal box called me 'Your Majesty.' Her Majesty Queen Victoria was in attendance that day. The Queen has an uncanny pair of ears and can hear the softest of utterances. When I was previously addressed as *Your Majesty*, I was obligated to instruct the fellow on when to use the word, *majesty*, and when it was appropriate to say what you now said."

Spalding noted what appeared to be a large and painful swelling in the form of a boil on the crown prince's neck. Being the tall man that Spalding was, AG leaned downward in front of the Prince of Wales so the prince needn't turn his neck while, at the same time, minimizing the upward angle of the Prince's eyeballs. "Your Highness, I'm glad I asked the American consul about rules of etiquette. What you spoke of was the first rule he mentioned."

The Prince laughed and responded, "Jolly good!" Turning to Prince Christian, the crown prince noted, "Remind me to make a treaty for increased trade with our cousins in America."

Spalding chuckled. "If you are in need of sporting goods, I will be most pleased to hear from you." The Prince nodded.

Play resumed, and being early in the game, there was no score. The home team was now at bat with no outs and runners on first and second base. The batter held the bat with both hands and struck at the ball, sending the white leather orb about twenty feet down the third baseline. The batter was thrown out at first base, but the other runners advanced to second and third base.

Prince Christian seemed pleasingly interested in the game and began asking a series of questions. "What was that?"

Spalding responded, "The batter made a sacrifice bunt. It's a new strategy some batters started to use in the last couple of years."

"Sacrifice?"

"Yes," said Spalding. "The bunt advances the runner to scoring position, but the batter is thrown out at first base. The batter sacrificed himself."

"Scoring position?"

"Yes. When a runner gets to second base, it increases their chances of scoring when the batter hits a single to the outfield."

"A single?"

Spalding was most pleased to be hearing such questions; however, due to the boil on his neck, the Prince of Wales would not turn his head, but he wanted to hear the discussion. He would partially lean sideways in front of Spalding to overcome the crowd noise and hear the explanation to each of Prince Christian's questions. Each time the Prince of Wales leaned in front of Spalding, Spalding would talk to Prince Christian over the top of the future king's head. Prince Christian resumed watching the game, and the Prince of Wales returned to his proper seated position.

Prince Christian would continue to ask one question after another.

"Why do they allow the catcher to get between home plate and the runner trying to score from third base?"

"Why did the runners freely advance after the umpire said, 'balk'?"

"Why are the batters allowed to constantly argue with the umpire?"

"Why did the batter hit the ball and dive headfirst into first base?"

Spalding kept quite busy answering Prince Christian's questions while talking above the ear of the Prince of Wales. Everyone in the royal box remained for the entirety of the game and would respond with applause when a good fielding play was made or when a sound crack of the bat caused the ball to sail far or enabled base runners to advance.

At one point during the game, the Chicago's Captain Anson hit a long fly ball that couldn't be caught by the outfielder. Anson lumbered past first and second base, reaching third.

Out of the excitement, the Prince of Wales slapped Spalding on the leg and exclaimed exuberantly, "That was a hard clip!"

Williamson came to bat after Anson and hit a hard ground ball that shot by Woods covering first base, and Williamson made a dive into first.

Spalding slapped the Prince of Wales on the back and said, "What do you think of that?" Spalding was merely attempting to return the favor of familiarity with the crown prince; however, the crowd gasped and had expressions of horror on their faces on such a breach in protocol.

At the end of the game, a reporter from the London edition of *The New York Herald* approached the stout prince. With pencil and blank note card in hand, the reporter said, "Your Highness, would you care to tell my newspaper's readers what you think of this American game of ball?"

The Prince reached out and gently grabbed the note card and pencil. He then wrote something down on the card and handed the card to Spalding, gently ordering, "Please hand the card to our distinguished newsman once you have read my comment."

The card contained the following handwritten words: "I consider baseball an excellent game, but cricket a better one."

Upon the game ending with a good time had by all, the Americans and British exchanged cheerful goodbyes. In the days that followed, and prior to departing on a ship bound for New York City, nine more sets of matches would be played at eight additional cities in England, Scotland, and Ireland. Each visit was as highly rewarding as the one before.

Members of Baseball's Australian Expedition departed the island nation, and their ship steamed across the Atlantic scheduled to arrive at New York City in early April 1889. Prior to the end of their voyage, Spalding asked of Palmer, "Do you think the tour was a success?"

Palmer exclaimed, "Unquestionably, sir!"

Spalding came back, "Excellent! It was a wonderful visit for all of us, I think. The people of all the lands we visited now have an appreciation for Americans and their game."

Palmer replied, "Our travel companions all enjoyed themselves."

"I so hoped that would be the case," conceded Spalding.

Palmer inquired, "Not our primary purpose?"

"I wanted to show off the goodness of our fellow Americans and introduce the world to our national game," responded Spalding. "Do you question whether those objectives were met?"

"Not in the least," exclaimed Palmer. "I should think though, that the experience your ballplayers had was an important learning experience. We watched them intercourse with peoples of many cultures while enjoying themselves in the process."

Spalding returned, "And you find that an important part of the tour?"

The sportswriter retorted, "In order to enjoy any dance, you must have two willing partners rather than one. Our dancing was merely of a different form."

Spalding placed his hand on the shoulder of Palmer. "It was a remarkable tour, Harry. A remarkable tour!"

A sensational event was changing from
the brown suit to the gray the contents of
his pockets. He was earnest about these
objects. They were of eternal importance,
like baseball or the Republican Party.

—Sinclair Lewis, Ib.

CHAPTER 6

Americans

With all the experiences savored by the touring Americans, one of
the most memorable events was not a landmark. It wasn't like the
Great Sphinx, Colosseum, or Eiffel Tower. The memory wasn't about
attending an extravagant gala or lavish luau, gazing at a snowman
made of sand on a beach at Christmas time, or basking in the presence of kings and other royalty. It occurred at a time that would
have otherwise been just another lengthy day at sea. It was Spalding's
announcement that instead of returning home from Australia by
way of Hawaii to San Francisco, the group could now reenter the
United States at the Port of New York *via* Southern Europe, Egypt,
and Ceylon.

The touring party was jubilant when they first heard the news,
and for good reason! This was a huge travel bonus to everyone: exciting destinations that were the cultural roots of nearly every ballplayer
on tour. Additionally, the Americans would no longer wind up the
tour by facing the stress and unenviable monotony of having to spend
twenty-six days at sea with but one day's break on land. Additionally,
group members could take pride to know the reach of goodwill they

were spreading in the names of baseball and *apple pie* would soon extend beyond Hawaii and two distant nations to now include the Middle East and America's most strategic European allies. So much good news at once, and without returning home a moment later than as originally planned!

Despite the euphoria, something didn't *feel* quite right, especially to the half of the group representing the Chicago contingent. Spalding wrote specifically about this topic two decades later in his landmark book entitled *America's National Game*. In the book, he stated that the idea to reroute did not come to his attention until "before leaving the Pacific Coast." That delay in Spalding's epiphany, rather than having his realization at an earlier date when the trip was being planned, resulted in avoiding a public relations headache.

On the day the tour began, Spalding could still get all the attention he relished from his adopted hometown of Chicago. If Spalding was one to be *up front* with everyone, he wouldn't have any bad news in which to disappoint his team's *friends* with the fact that New York would now be host to the primary *returning home* celebration, rather than Chicago. There would still be a reception at Chicago's luxurious Palmer House Hotel, but that event would no longer enjoy the same prestige or serve the same level of purpose as initially anticipated.

On this evening, none of those irregularities mattered. Tonight, members of the tour were celebrating their safe return home to the United States. The tour group was ready to come home, and they were being welcomed back at nowhere less than the grand hall of the nationally renowned Delmonico's Restaurant of New York City. What better place to host the most extraordinary banquet of its kind ever held in the United States? It was an affair that members of the tour and others fortunate enough to be in attendance looked forward to with grand anticipation.

April 8, 1889—New York City

Earlier that day, and prior to the banquet, the Chicagos and All Americans put on an exhibition game for a local crowd.

The banquet would be the next activity for the ballplayers, and the event had been well-publicized. Deemed to be newsworthy by editors of the nation's major publications within this highly competitive news business of the 1880s, a multitude of reporters were in attendance. Writers for sports publications, newspapers of major cities from coast to coast, and members of the Associated Press were on hand to *spread the word*. Lengthy articles covering the many proceedings of the evening would be written—and transmitted—through the night so that the stories would make press time deadlines for getting onto the front pages of the newspapers' morning editions. The lengthy stories generally varied from one to two full columns of the big city papers that spread from the *Boston Globe* and *Philadelphia Inquirer* outward across the nation.

Other than reporters and participants of the occasion, there were also sports figures, politicians, and bureaucrats at all levels of government, and other influential citizens in attendance. Democrats and Republicans were well represented, and there was even one person who would one day become the only US president to be elected as a member of the Bull Moose Party. Elected officials and those aspiring to future public posts always work the crowds at these happenings—and there were more than enough of them to go around.

The list of invited guests was an impressive one. The head table was configured in the facsimile of a baseball diamond. Mills sat at the head of the speakers' group with Spalding seated at his right. At the pitcher and catcher positions were Chauncey Depew, Esq. and Judge Henry Howland. Depew was Cornelius Vanderbilt's attorney, a national politician and president of the Grand Central Railroad while serving as a director on numerous other railroad companies; Howland was a well-known personality and longtime friend of Mark Twain. The symbolic infield positions were taken by Pennsylvania politician and orator Daniel Dougherty, Esq.; Orestes Cleveland, mayor of Jersey City and former US congressman; Erastus Wilman, Philadelphia financier and builder of such projects as the rail tunnel under the Verrazano Narrows connecting Long Island to the city; and Mark Twain at shortstop. The symbolic outfielder positions were filled by W. H. McElroy, US consul; G. W. Griffin; and Mayor Chapin of Brooklyn.

Delmonico's was a most impressive location for the dinner, and the extensive decorations arranged especially for the evening's affair made the place even more so. Signs and posters with baseball and nationalistic themes and other posters depicting the foreign lands visited appeared in every direction. Several American flags were posted in different spots within the great hall and displayed in trophy position. A truckload of flowering plants was brought in with the larger plants on the floor and the smaller ones atop the tables.

Prior to dinner, guests standing throughout the great hall were greeted with an abundance of hot hors d'oeuvres served on silver trays and an overabundance of champagne. Prior to dinner, the guests were taking advantage of the selection of invitees to socialize freely with any of several politically important or well-connected guests.

The event was the *brain child* of Spalding's longtime ally and dear friend, former president of the National League and New York area attorney, Abraham Gilbert Mills, Esquire. As it was getting near time to begin serving dinner, Mills was working his way back toward Spalding, who was standing in conversation near the front of the hall where the head tables were located. Not far from where Spalding stood were two of the guest speakers engaged in conversation—Daniel Dougherty, Esq. and Chauncey Depew, Esq. Prior to approaching Spalding, Mills decided to join in the conversation with Dougherty and Depew.

Placing one hand on each of the attorney's shoulders, Mills said, "You see the power of baseball, gentlemen? It brings people together who might not otherwise ever speak to one another—you, Mr. Dougherty as a Democrat on the national level, and you, Mr. Depew, a devout high-level Republican!"

"I'll say this, Abraham," Dougherty began, "I mentioned to Mr. Depew that I need to lie low these next four years now that Benjamin Harrison won the election, considering it was I who gave the nominating address for Grover Cleveland's reelection bid at last year's Democratic National Convention."

"And I, Abraham," added Depew, "reminded my esteemed-though-naive Democrat friend that, although I am a Republican, Mr. Dougherty is in a better position than I to receive favors from our newly elected Republican president. I needed only remind Attorney Dougherty that, at last year's Republican National Convention, I didn't release my hundred delegates to nominate then-presidential *wannabe* Harrison until after the third ballot. That move put me in the presidential *dog house* for Harrison's entire first term!"

Mills laughed. "Regardless of our many differences, gentlemen, I can confidently say that all three of us will agree on two things this evening. First, despite all else, baseball is good for the national spirit. Second, the tour was good for Americans and people of other countries to get to know one another, and that both baseball and diplomacy perform important roles in our great nation's future."

Dougherty and Depew both nodded in affirmation. As Mills began to make his final steps toward Spalding, Depew declared, "Councilor Dougherty and I were wondering why you hit the two of us up for some of the fifty thousand dollars you were raising and spared Vanderbilt and the Roosevelts."

Mills laughed, replying, "Those are my *go-to's* for the big deals!"

As Mills stepped away from the two politicians, he was stopped by a dashing, poised twenty-eight-year-old named Elliott Bulloch Roosevelt. Mills casually knew Elliott through Elliott's older brother. They cheerfully greeted one another as Mills led the two of them to where Spalding was concluding a conversation with a prominent local attorney.

"It was good talking to you, AG," the attorney said as the two men shook hands.

"We'll talk again," Spalding replied, "when we discuss possible business arrangements on our next exchange."

Mills spoke as the lawyer turned to walk off to another conversation.

"AG, I have an enjoyable introduction to make. This is Elliott Roosevelt, socialite, always welcome at any affair, and like you, a world traveler."

"None of the attributes Mr. Mills mentioned," Roosevelt responded, "are redemptive qualities, Mr. Spalding, but contrary to public belief, I do have some redeeming characteristics."

"In this town," Spalding began, "when your surname is Roosevelt, you are prequalified for having traits of a noble nature."

Roosevelt chuckled as Mills bowed out of the conversation. "This is truly a pleasure to meet you, sir."

"The pleasure is mine, Mr. Roosevelt." Spalding briefly paused. "Do I take it correctly that, as a well-traveled man, you have been to some of the same destinations we visited on our tour?"

"I have," Roosevelt admitted. "I adore every culture and land I have seen. I can ill imagine tiring of returning to those places, but there's so much more to see and experience, and so little time—even for those most fortunate—to fulfill my thirst."

Spalding was reflecting on his recent travels, and Elliott continued.

"When traveling with my family, it is grandly rewarding to watch their eyes light up at new and intriguing experiences."

Spalding inquired, "You have children then."

"Three and one wife—all intelligent and beautiful."

Spalding smiled. "*One* wife, you say! Sounds like you've been to the Sandwich Islands observing their matrimonial nuances."

"Beautiful place, the islands," remarked Roosevelt. "but some of their traditions are not something my family would appreciate bringing back from my travels. More to the point, I am eager to hear of your travels."

A familiar figure joined the twosome. "Mr. Spalding," offered Elliott, "allow me to introduce someone I did not mention, yet also love—my big brother, Theodore."

Spalding turned to Theodore and quipped, "One who is loved as a 'big brother' has achieved a high station."

The older Roosevelt said to Spalding, "I could never hope for a better brother than Elliott. He is intelligent, persuasive, and his potential is great. I concede that my love for such a talented man as Elliott, much less being of my own flesh and blood, drives me all too often to play the role of big brother—a pest in the hopes that he may pursue accomplishment worthy of his formidable and untapped potential."

The mildly embarrassed younger Roosevelt brother with an increasing level of impatience interrupted his older brother's critique to address Spalding. "Again, my heartiest congratulations on your important achievement, Mr. Spalding! It was an honor to meet you. I now depart knowing you to be in the capable hands of the more able side of the Roosevelt family."

Elliott stepped back and gracefully exited the conversation.

Changing the topic, Spalding said to Theodore, "I've heard great things of you and your noteworthy and beneficial efforts in the political workings of New York and the safety of its residents."

"Your kind words should be shared by me with many others," Theodore Roosevelt noted, "though my last campaign manager would publicly disagree, and one who understands the compliment should know well enough that there is so much more work that needs to be done at the city and state levels, and more especially on the national horizon. You, sir, have helped this nation of ours at the highest of those levels."

Spalding silently assimilated what Theodore Roosevelt had uttered.

Roosevelt continued, "Americans have long accepted our isolation as a nation by the mere presence of two great oceans lying on either side of the continent. Most would rather read a newspaper in their favorite armchair than address America's isolationist policies. You, sir, took an entirely different route. You and your baseball companions could have basked in the opulence the game has provided, yet this did not occur. Together, with your leadership and initiative, you helped to spread the word of who Americans are, what they stand for, and what our nation can offer the world. Making such friendships will one day pay dividends beyond what most people imagine and in ways you or I cannot yet know. I wanted to meet you, in part, because I am an admirer of what baseball and its finest athletes represent, but of far greater importance to pay tribute for your accomplishment in achieving a greater good. I thank you for that. You have my admiration, sir!"

Spalding replied with a rare sense of humility that was more than he knew how to contain. "I feel like replying with a speech, but I think we're all about to hear enough of those this evening. I can only say that you have bestowed upon me a compliment of the first magnitude, and I will keep your words in my songbook."

The two men shook hands, and Roosevelt said, "I hope and expect to frequently cross paths in the years ahead and will look forward to those days. In the meantime, my constituents are being neglected."

Mills, who had subtly departed the conversation minutes earlier, was now at his place at the head table and wanted to get things underway. He used the likeness of a miniature baseball bat to rap on the table in an effort to call the dinner and proceedings to order. It was the end of the cocktail hour, and the 250 people present began to hurriedly take their places. Mills, Spalding, and the other guests standing by the guest tables only moments earlier promptly disappeared from sight. The dinner was about to commence.

As the *Boston Globe* reported,

> At 7 o'clock Chairman Mills with AG Spalding and the guests entered the room. Then came old man Anso[n] and John M. Ward, followed by the Chicago and All-America players. Cheer after cheer greeted them.
>
> At 7.30 o'clock, when pitcher Depew made his appearance, there was tremendous cheering, and catcher Howland and First Baseman Dougherty were received with manifestations of high popular favor.

Hungry patrons were each provided with a nine-page menu for the "testimonial banquet," bound with lace and filled with color artwork depicting landmarks and images of locations visited. The menu also contained lists of tour participants, speakers, and leaders of the several toasts, sponsors and organizers, guests, and "The Dinner in 9 Innings." The nine courses in the styles of several countries visited, each with multiple offerings of food and beverages, included oysters, broths and soups such as red snapper, numerous vegetable dishes and condiments, beef, champagne, capon, sweet breads, Roman punch, Plover salad, burgundy, pudding Schiller with fancy ice cream pyramids, fruits, coffee, cakes, cheeses, and multiple liqueurs.

Meanwhile, a few ladies associated with some of the banquet guests and numbering approximately a dozen were enjoying themselves in a small banquet room on the restaurant's second floor. If the servers within the room did not outnumber the ladies, it was a difference of narrow margin. Within the room, a bartender attended a fully-stocked bar of wines, liquors, and the finest champagne. Hors d'oeuvres and artistically prepared staples in wondrous variety from around the world were being served from a table near the center of the room. The conversation among the women was so loud, cheerful, brisk, and filled with such constant laughter that the muffled noise from the banquet crowd below was hardly noticeable.

Dignitaries at the head table had been served first, and to the delight of host Mills, everything was going like clockwork. As Mills and the others at the head table began to finish eating their main courses, Chairman Mills thought it would be prudent to begin the speeches on what would surely be a long evening while the other guests were *over the hump* with the delicacies they were continuing to conquer. With the assistance of some of the other guests at the head table, Mills and some fellow dignitaries began clinking their respective goblets with their spoons. The call to attention was heard throughout the main dining hall, and the banquet floor became remarkably quiet. One of the women in the small banquet room above the main floor similarly heard the customary call to attention and said in a loud voice, "Ladies! It's showtime!"

As Mills stood to commence the proceedings, he was upstaged in a manner best described by a reporter from the *Philadelphia Inquirer*.

> Before the speeches began a number of ladies, including Mrs. AG Spalding, Mrs. Anson and Mrs. John W. Ward, appeared on the balcony beside the band, and were greeted with shouts of

welcome by the guests below. When they waved
their handkerchiefs in reply to the tumultuous
chivalry displayed by the men, it was so overpow-
ering that the band, in desperation, began to play
"Yankee Doodle" which the audience joined in.

Once the music finally paused, Mills took swift action to stymie
the civil unrest caused by, what everyone in the hall knew to be, the
actions of the baseball players' charming and not-so-innocent ladies.
The chairman again attempted to commence giving the audience a
hearty welcome. On this occasion, his efforts met with success.

Chairman Mills, in a happy little speech, welcomed the double teams home, and described
in fitting language the glories of baseball and the
paralyzing effect on the degenerate sons of old
dynasties. It was a game of essentially American
origin. (A voice, "No rounders," and cheers)

Mayors Cleveland of Jersey City and Chapin of Brooklyn
would be the first to officially offer words of welcome. The *Globe* and
Inquirer reported that Mayor Cleveland began his punchline-laden
talk by admitting that he had never attended a game of ball, and
thusly, his speech would be brief because he was not qualified for it to
be otherwise. Upon saying that, a member of the audience shouted,
"No flies on him!"

The speech of Mayor Chapin was also entertaining. He claimed
Brooklyn to be the birthplace of baseball, which was believed by
many at the time. Upon stating that the "citizens of Brooklyn try
nevertheless not to be unduly proud," another voice from the audience with a Brooklyn accent exclaimed, "He's a dandy!"

Upon conclusion of the first two speakers' remarks, both of
which received a hearty applause at the end of their talks, eight toasts
were given to "our guests, AG Spalding, and his party of representative American ballplayers." Although the remainder of speeches and
presentations that followed contained frequent elements of humor

with lighthearted reminiscences and other stories and despite other continual interruption caused by impromptu *toasts* tendered throughout the orations, it soon became evident to everyone in the hall that the line dividing intellectual and athlete was nonexistent. Each of the many successive speeches met with similar levels of cheering, laughter, and irreverence. Anson, as but one example, had a bit of a challenge speaking amidst loud chants and shouts of "baby Anson" and "three cheers for the double team." Overall, however, Anson's speech was exceptionally well received.

Every speech was laced with comments regarding the prideful characteristics and benefits of being a citizen of their great country, and the cheers that resulted were often excessively loud and, in some instances, continued for a minute or more. Once the amateur speakers and the speeches given by the several skilled politicians concluded, it was time for the most highly anticipated articulation. The guest speaker was author and lecturer Mark Twain.

Twain had previously spent time in the Sandwich Islands and knew that Oahu and the tiny independent nation was the Australian Tour's first international port of call. As a result, Twain decided to discuss his humoresque theories on the residents of the island nation and how the author believed those people's ways were similar and different from the attitudes and approach of Americans. His words were constantly received with exuberant laughter. A small excerpt of the speech, making assumptions of differences in accounts between the *Boston Globe* and *Philadelphia Inquirer*, follows:

> That peaceful land, that beautiful land, that fair home of profound repose and solitude where life is one long, long Sabbath celebration! A land where it is one long summer day and where the good, who die, experience no change, but merely fall asleep in one heaven and awaken in another. (*Laughter.*)
> And these boys have played base ball there! Base ball, which is the very symbol of the outward and visible expression of the drive and push and

rush and struggle of the raging, tearing, booming nineteenth century! One cannot realize it, the
place and fact is so utterly incongruous; it's like
interrupting a funeral with a circus. Why, there's
no possible point of contact, no possible kinships
between base ball and the Sandwich Islands; base
ball is all fact and business, while the islands are
all poetry and sentiment. (Loud laughter.) In
base ball you've got to do everything just right or
you don't get there; in the islands you've got to do
everything just wrong or you can't stay there. You
do it wrong to get it right, for if you do it right,
you get it wrong. There isn't a way to get it right,
but to do it wrong and the wronger you do it, the
righter it is. (*Laughter.*) The natives illustrate this
every day. They never mount a horse from the larboard side, they always mount him from the starboard. On the other hand, they never milk a cow
on the starboard side, they always milk her on
the larboard side; it's why you see so many short
people there—they've got their heads kicked off.
When they meet on the road they don't turn out
to the right, they turn out to the left.

...When a child is born the mother goes
right along with her ordinary work without losing a half day. It's the father that knocks off and
goes to bed 'til he gets over the circumstances.
And these natives don't trace descent through the
male line, but through the female. They say they
always know who the child's mother was. Well,
that odd system is well enough there, because
there a woman often has six or seven husbands,
all at the same time—and all properly married to
her and no blemish about the matter anywhere.
Yet there is no fussing, no trouble. When a child
is born the husbands all meet together in con-

vention, in a perfectly orderly way, and elect the father, and the whole thing is perfectly fair; at least as fair as it would be anywhere.

Of course, you can't keep politics out; you can't do that in any country, and so if three of the husbands are Republicans and four are Democrats it don't make any difference how strong a Republican aspect the baby has got, that election is going Democratic every time…

Twain migrated his discussion to politics and other contemporary subjects and themes. The man with the name Samuel Langhorne Clemens continued to carry on for some time. He ended his speech on a complimentary note, not without more humor, regarding the importance of the tour to display Americans in their best light while establishing a vital channel of fellowship with our foreign neighbors.

The banquet ended within moments of midnight. Newspaper reporters were generally among the first to race out the door so they might meet their respective newspapers' press deadlines for making one of the next day's editions. It was an exciting evening containing ingredients their readers would be entertained in reading about—tales of high society, decadence, world travels, famous people, and anecdotes. These were the ingredients that enticed the public to read the articles.

That which was important to convey, however, was the primary theme of the evening under the guise of welcome back—a spirit of nationalism. Be proud to be an American. Support your country. Every message conveyed to the attendees of the banquet by the speakers included the importance of maintaining and building the American spirit and ideals, the strength Americans can get out of the physical and intellectual benefits of baseball and other sports, and the wisdom and benefits of ensuring that America's geographic separation from other world powers the result of two oceans does not emulate the close relationships we must have with nations possessing strengths and ideologies that complement those of the United

States. These were the true messages those contributing to the evening wanted the public to take away.

A theme of comradery and the American spirit was effectively and directly reinforced among influential US citizens in the most powerful of ways—through an evening of cheer and merriment. And thanks to the members of the press, the general public would be availed the same message. It wasn't all the public, but it was a majority of the public. It was the relevant public. It was what mattered to those who *mattered*. It was white society.

The banquet at the Palmer House in Chicago would go off as scheduled and would also be a memorable affair where a long line of niceties flowed throughout the evening, beginning with providing guests with menus enveloped in jackets of silk. Aside from important games or victories or actions that baseball or some players took or may take in the future, the dinner at Delmonico's would be an event that wouldn't be surpassed for fifty years until the dedication ceremonies of the National Baseball Hall of Fame in Cooperstown, New York.

The priorities of white male America were clear—promote self-interest and pleasures to be shared with family while helping America to have a more secure place within an increasingly uncertain and symbolically shrinking world. It was as if the losses from the Civil War were deemed more than adequate sacrifice to help a portion of America whose suffering was now less than the seemingly incomprehensible levels it once was.

Baseball would remain segregated within America, but America would attempt to assimilate within the world. Baseball had been used as a tool to that latter end. Baseball had not even begun to emulate those Americans with a conscience and empathy to brothers and sisters continuing to suffer injustices within our nation's borders.

If you do not know where you are
going, you'll end up someplace else.

—Yogi Berra

CHAPTER 7

The Commission

Beginning of March 1905—Otis Elevator
Co. satellite office, Manhattan

At the southernmost tip of Manhattan island, Abraham G. Mills, Esq.,
was sitting in his large office at the satellite offices of Otis Elevator
Company. The stocky-figured executive, with handlebar mustache
and balding pate, had aged fairly well since the Delmonico's banquet
of fifteen years earlier. Mills was waiting for a meeting to commence;
however, he did not know why Albert Spalding requested the get-together. Spalding mentioned that he wished to discuss the subject
matter with Mills and one other attendee on a face-to-face basis in a
place most convenient to Mills.

The meeting's third participant, James E. Sullivan, had just
arrived at Mills's office. Sullivan was presently secretary and cofounder
of the national Amateur Athletic Union. Within the office, Mills
had a set of plush chairs and a sofa placed opposite the desk for
such occasions. The two men were comfortably seated, engrossed in
conversation.

Mills inquired, "Any idea why we three are assembling here
today?"

Sullivan responded, "Possibly," Sullivan responded. "But AG said it may be a surprise for you. I don't want to be the spoiler."

"He'll be here soon enough," Mills exclaimed. "No snow on the ground left over to cause any delay today!"

Sullivan observed, "This has certainly been an odd winter, weather-wise. Snowiest December on record and we're only getting into March, and it's been two weeks since the last good storm."

Mills chuckled. "Let's not rock the boat on that, knock on wood. We've surely had our share of the white stuff, and March is often full of little surprises too!"

"Yes, sir," Sullivan replied. "I must say, Colonel, this is a very nice facility. I had expected your office to be across the river."

"Yonkers is the larger facility most assuredly," Mills responded. "But this is a great spot for me!"

"Do you live nearby?"

"I wish," Mills enthused. "I live in Summit City."

Sullivan inquired, "I believe AG mentioned you have a missus at home."

"And two spinster daughters," Mills added. "Mary and Francis, twenty-six and thirty-one. They're both nice, smart, and pretty. They spend more time worrying about me than I do about them though, so if you want to do me a favor…"

Sullivan laughed. "Find them a pair of amateur athletes?"

Mills furled his bushy eyebrows. "Please, make them employed ones—with decent jobs."

"There's the rub," Sullivan conceded playfully. "How's the commute?"

"Not bad," Mills conceded. "The trains are quick, and they come often. What I like best about this location is the setting. Rather than being in more of a factory area in Yonkers, we're in a serene part of Manhattan."

"That's for certain," Sullivan observed. "You're right by the harbor and the Hudson [River]. Quite scenic."

"And the park," Mills sweetly boasted.

"So tell me, Colonel, how did a famous sports figure like you wind up as an executive—doing whatever it is you do for Otis Elevator?"

Mills was tickled by the question. "How did I wind up at an elevator company? After receiving my law degree from Columbian Law School, I moved from DC to Chicago. During my years in Chicago, I had worked for Hale & Co., the large elevator manufacturing outfit. I subsequently moved back to the New York City area where I grew up. A few years ago, Otis was building new facilities out here. I guess they couldn't let a *prize* like me get away, so they hired me." Mills laughed again. "They gave me a vice president title and this office. Closing sales deals and lots of legal matters to keep me busy, and Manhattan is close to where I need to conduct most of my business."

Mills paused briefly. "Now, Mr. Sullivan, since we're getting the introductions out of the way, I must ask, how did such a young fellow like you get anointed over all of us old geezers desirous of being responsible for the prestigious job you so recently concluded?"

"You refer to the Olympics, I trust," replied Sullivan. "I was fortunate. I wanted the role and made certain the right people knew it. Then again, Mr. Spalding reminded me when I was on the *stick* [phone] with him the other day that I was *walking in* his *footsteps.*"

Mills thought over Sullivan's last statement and burst into laughter. "Of course!" Mills laughed again. "He was in charge of the United States delegation to the last Olympics before yours." Pausing to change manner from *humored* to *serious*, Mills continued, "He has his faults, but he has some wonderful qualities that are hard to ignore. You'll never meet another one like him!"

"I'm glad he said what he did," Sullivan began. "It didn't bother me in the least, and I always like to get to know the person with whom I'm dealing."

Mills commented, "I closely followed the Summer Games. From all reports I've read, your efforts warrant hearty congratulations! With the games concluding only weeks ago, I suspect you have yet to shed the sense of relief you must be feeling from successfully pulling off America's first hosting of the event!"

Sullivan responded, "Participating in producing the games of the third Olympiad, although arduous at times, was the highlight of my career. Just the same, four and a half months of games made all of us, including the people of St. Louis, anxious to see the affair come to a conclusion."

"With the US having walked away with the *lion's share* of the medals," Mills noted, "your AAU buddies must be thrilled with the outcome!"

Lightheartedly, Sullivan returned, "It wasn't so difficult for us to do as well as we did. Of the ninety events staged, half of the competitions were manned solely by the red, white, and blue. Some people are referring to the 1904 games as *Uncle Sam and the Eleven Dwarfs*."

"That's the fine print," bellowed Mills sarcastically. "It's still an impressive feat. I read there were 650 athletes from around the world."

Sullivan returned the sarcasm. "It's wonderful when the newspapers take press releases, as stated, in order to tell the truth, but not necessarily all of it. If such other truths be told, for every one athlete provided by the rest of the world, America sent nine. The 'deck' was stacked in our favor! I do take an enormous sense of national pride in seeing so many American athletes dedicate themselves as they have—both young men and ladies. There were only six American women competing, but they came through particularly well."

"Frankly," Mills began, "I thought six a surprisingly small number, but any blame for such a light turnout most assuredly can't be pinned on you! After all, it's mostly the country's fairer sex who discourages athletic competition by the ladies!"

"Oh, I've been catching some of the blame," remarked Sullivan, "and I'll catch more in the future. Between you and me, I know I could have supported the women more, but I had several so-called *top* priorities. Regardless, I'm committed to encouraging better participation in the years ahead."

"Hopefully, you'll achieve success," Mills lamented. "Men win points in most sports with their strength, and that gives them the upper hand. It is my observation, however, that women seem to have a few tricks up their skirts. They're more graceful—maybe more coordinated, and they seem to have some sort of superior athletic intelligence to that of their male counterparts. Don't quote me on this, but from a purist's perspective, women seem to be the superior athletes when one considers grace, form, strategy, and quickness of reaction."

"There's some validity to what you say," began Sullivan. "For society to change its position on women in sports, both men and women, it will take some time. Nevertheless, I'm confident the time will come."

The tall clock outside Mills's office chimed twice, and there was a knock on the office door. The door opened, and the secretary ushered Spalding into the office. As Spalding entered the room, the secretary subtly closed the door behind him while the two seated gents struggled to quickly stand from their deeply seated positions.

Spalding walked over to Mills, and standing toe to toe, the two men shook hands vigorously. With an uncharacteristically high level of enthusiasm, Mills said, "Great to see you again, AG! You obviously know James here."

Spalding blurted, "Of course, I do!" Spalding walked over to Sullivan, and the two men shook hands in warm fashion. "Nice to see you, Mr. Sullivan. Thank you kindly for coming on such short notice!"

"My pleasure," Sullivan replied exuberantly. "It's not every day I get to converse with such baseball notables."

Mills interjected, "I suspect you know, James, but AG retired to the good life some seven years ago."

"Semiretired," Spalding corrected. Turning to Sullivan, he continued, "I now am a Californian residing on the southwestern edge of San Diego."

Mills again interrupted, addressing Sullivan. "The property Mr. Spalding purchased is so picturesque, you'd think he's rich. The Spaldings' abode overlooks the Pacific. They have a most unique home with a lovely yard and flowering gardens."

Looking at Sullivan, Spalding subtly blushed. "We're in a little community called Point Loma. It was initially more my wife's idea than mine, so I have much to be thankful for with Elizabeth, of course, being my greatest blessing."

"Is Elizabeth from California?"

"Not hardly," Spalding replied. "Elizabeth grew up in Illinois as did I. We were childhood friends. I never realized how much I loved her until my later years. After my first wife, Josie, passed away, I made up for lost time by convincing Elizabeth, then a widower with the name Elizabeth Mayer Churchill, that I was worthy enough to marry."

Sullivan inquired, "How did Elizabeth know of Point Lomas?"

"Point Loma," Spalding corrected. "Our home is located in a community organized by members of the American Theosophical Society. Through the years, Elizabeth has remained quite active with that group, and I have since become the same. When the colonel said my house is 'unique,' he alluded to the dome centered within the structure. It resembles an Arabic mosque. I think the design is supposed to prompt me to think on a higher plane."

"It all sounds lovely," concluded Sullivan. "You said you and Mr. Mills are friends of many years."

Mills responded, "Mr. Spalding and I had the same boss during our professional formative years. William Hulbert." Turning to Sullivan, Mills inquired, "Have you heard of him?"

"I've heard a great deal about him," exclaimed Sullivan. "He was one of the early organizers of the sport when baseball began turning professional. I believe he also owned the Chicago Cubs."

"Precisely," Mills replied. "A great man who taught me the fundamentals of the philosophy and tactics relating to the business side of baseball! Regrettably, Mr. Hulbert passed away far too young."

"Nearly thirty years ago," Spalding began, "Mr. Hulbert was my greatest mentor. You are correct that Mr. Hulbert owned 'the Cubs,' but it was called—"

Sullivan interrupted, "The White Stockings! Next, they were Colts, and many people call them the Cubs now."

"Correct," Spalding replied. "When I was playing for the club, Mr. Hulbert became league president and was frequently off to New York. He needed someone to handle the day-to-day operations of the team, and he gave me the Chicagos' front-office duties. He was acutely aware of how some teams, the St. Paul Apostles immediately coming to mind, were continually being raided by other teams. As league president, he didn't think highly of the practice."

> *It so happened at that time that, …then living at Chicago, [a solution to the problem] appeared on the field of reform. In a published article, the author, of which was no less than Mr. Mills… severely criticized the reprehensible practice…of League clubs visiting cities, accepting their hospitality, and then stealing their players…he outlined a plan showing how this abuse could be done away with and called upon…the League to put a stop to the pernicious custom. Mr. Hulbert was very much impressed, and…immediately sent an invitation to the writer, asking to call upon him at his office… to consult with him on [such] matters. Mr. Mills accepted the invitation, and from thence forward, [we] were close personal friends.[1]*

"So, then, the two of you," said Sullivan as he glanced at Mills and Spalding, "are old compadres."
Spalding responded,

> *After their first meeting, Mr. Hulbert told me [he] had…found just the man we are looking for; and when he said Abraham's name it sounded familiar. I later realized that, shortly after the end of the war, I was offered the role of pitcher on the Washington Olympics club along with employment at the US Treasury by the club's president. I did not accept the generous offer, however, I subsequently recalled the*

---

[1] *America's National Game* by AG Spalding.

man [running the Olympics club at the time] to be
Mr. A.G. Mills being, of course, one in the same.[2]

"And obviously," observed Sullivan, "you two gents hit it off well."

"No question," Spalding responded. "Over the years, Mr. Mills has done many a thoughtful thing for me, not the least of which was a heck of a feed he put on for me and 250 of my closest friends at Delmonico's."

Sullivan recalled, "I vaguely recollect reading that Hulbert led a crusade against the evils that alcohol and gambling wrought upon baseball."

"Yup," replied Spalding. "Mr. Hulbert was quite the crusader!"

Sullivan, in a rare showing of heart on sleeve, conceded, "I know we must begin, but may I say that hearing the stories and perspectives of such accomplished contributors to baseball, and listening to your particular impressions of some of the past influencers of the nation's great sport, is fascinating. Thank you."

Mills reacted. "I thank you, James, but please keep in mind that Mr. Hulbert is far more than a 'past influencer' of the game. He wove the best of outside influences into baseball while purging the bad. He had the fortitude to do this and the vision to find and mold people that would carry on in the finest of tradition. I believe I speak for AG when I say that, as author Frank Baum might say, we and other accomplished men of this sport are *munchkins* compared to a giant like Bill Hulbert. He paved the way for league success that is felt to this day."

"Well said, my friend," Spalding admitted.

The three men respectfully paused for a silent moment.

Spalding offered, "It is now time to get on with the business at hand."

"And James and I," quipped Mills, "would be thrilled to know what that *business* may be!"

---

[2] Ibid.

"You shall soon both know," Spalding noted. Looking at Mills, Spalding asked, "However, I first have one last question of you, Abe."

"Fire away, AG," Mills said.

"I can't help but notice that little man on your desk carrying those buckets of water on his shoulders," Spalding observed. "The little guy's pin-sized feet appear impossibly balanced on the pedestal beneath him. How does he do that without falling over?"

"A birthday gift from my three daughters," boasted Mills. "They're all full grown, but they thought the little contraption a good way to keep my mind entertained while I sit in my office doing nothing all day. I think of it as an experiment in gravity with buckets of water." Turning toward Sullivan, Mills chuckled. "Who better than you, James, would appreciate an experiment—like when you mixed heat and water with athletes?"

Sullivan gave a sigh and responded, "I suppose you're referring to the drinking water controversy during the marathon."

Mills said to Spalding, "The newspapers said James limited the number of water stops in the marathon to one while the runners chugged along on dusty roads for twenty-five miles with a temperature in the nineties! The newspapers had, excuse the pun, a 'field day.'" Mills chuckled.

Sullivan groaned. "I didn't make the decision lightly nor to be an experiment. I nurture amateur athletes, but I won't baby them. They're a tough bunch and not so pampered as the professional athletes are today!" Sullivan then stated, "Let's begin, gentlemen."

The meeting participants plunked their bodies onto the overstuffed chairs and sofa.

"May I assume," inquired Spalding, "the two of you have read the recent articles written by Henry Chadwick?"

Both listeners nodded in acknowledgment.

Spalding exclaimed, "First, be it known that, over the years, he's become my oldest and one of my most dearest friends. In recent years, the old man has served dutifully as the editor of my *Spalding Sporting Guide*. Unfortunately, as they say, *once an Englishman, always an Englishman*. The man can't shut up about how baseball is merely an offshoot of British games. After all that I have preached to the contrary, he became something of *a thorn in my side*. Recently, he's put pen to paper on the matter, and that was the *last straw*. His writings struck a nerve—a big one! I recently approached Henry and suggested that we settle this argument once and for all."

Mills said to Sullivan, "This must be where we come in!"

Spalding answered, "Eureka! To resolve our dispute, I suggested we form an independent commission to decide the matter."

Mills questioned, "An *independent* commission? Does Henry know that yours truly might be a part of this commission?"

"He does," exclaimed Spalding. "I mentioned both of your names!"

Mills prompted, "And?"

"He thought it *a capital* idea," Spalding noted.

Mills laughed, and Sullivan sat forward in his chair.

Sullivan observed, "Now, we're getting somewhere, I think."

Spalding responded, "I propose the formation of the Mills Commission."

Mills noted, "This idea has suddenly taken an ominous turn. Do I sense that this *Mills Commission* will publicly determine what is, in your mind, a foregone conclusion—that baseball is of American origin?"

"That would be," Spalding retorted, "the ideal outcome!"

Sullivan asked, "Might there not be an easier way than forming a full-blown commission to resolve your differences?"

Mills added, "It does seem, AG, that you want us to do your bidding."

"It is not as if I am forcing the two of you to publicly make a statement on my behalf," Spalding replied. "Even I will not cross that line. What I ask for is of more noble purpose than settling a dispute between Henry and myself. This is about America!"

"As a clarification," Sullivan pondered, "you mean the United States."

Spalding nodded, acknowledging agreement.

Sullivan recalled, "Though not particularly familiar with either Mr. Chadwick's arguments or those of yours, AG, I have always assumed baseball emanated from English games. It seems intuitively obvious. Our nation is laced with British customs and culture. Cricket was popular on our shores for many years. It seems only logical, regardless of what Mr. Chadwick says, that baseball has English roots."

Mills smiled and sighed. "Oh, boy!"

Spalding declared, "The English games and baseball are so dissimilar! *Cricket is a gentle pastime. Baseball is a war! Cricket is an athletic sociable, played and applauded in a conventional, decorous, and English manner. Baseball is an athletic turmoil, played and applauded in an unconventional, enthusiastic, and American manner.* Those of English descent travelled the perilous ocean to become Americans because they took serious grave exception to the ways, customs, and outlook of those that remain in that land. The two games, that of cricket and of baseball, have such serious departures from one another in approach and spirit as to be as similar as golf is to tennis."[3]

"Granted," Sullivan admitted. "There are marked differences between the English and American variations, but doesn't it strike you that we originally played the British games, and that the modern game of baseball might merely have evolved over time to that which it is today?"

Spalding returned, "In our *melting pot*, we have people whose ancestors were Dutch, Greek, French, and so on. All of them brought stick and ball games to this nation from what they learned growing up in their original homelands, and their descendants often carried on the traditions. Explorers have found pictures of this general type of game on the inside walls of the pyramids. Even the original tribal Americans played stick and ball sports long before your granddaddy or mine ever hit these shores! Canadians play lacrosse big-time. In Mexico, they play jai alai. Both of those countries' games originated with tribal peoples. The Cherokee had large gatherings and played stickball in organized tournaments, and they were serious about it! Ironically, had they recorded evidence in pictorial form that we might know about anywhere, this entire project might take on an entirely different tact."

---

3   Ibid.

Spalding paused to catch his breath. "The English don't have a corner on this market. I've studied the game from mounds of documents uncovered over the years. I know a great deal about the games of yesteryear that were once played in America. They bear little resemblance to cricket. Stick and ball sports like the Massachusetts game, townball, and all the variations of old cat were played on this continent long ago by a majority of people descended from many lands other than England. In frankness, the modern game of baseball has little resemblance to any of the primitive stick and ball games of our past."

"I agree that the game as we now know it is markedly different from cricket," admitted Sullivan. "There's no question that baseball today is purely American. I should think, regardless of origin, that is enough to be able to wrap the Stars and Stripes around the sport! Moreover, there are more than enough sports authorities and historians to go around in this country, and none have yet been able to determine the origins of baseball one way or the other. Your thesis may be unprovable. Certainly, it would be a daunting task to show otherwise. Why do you feel it imperative to nail the lid on the proverbial coffin long after the body has already been buried?"

Spalding blurted, "To begin with, there was once a time when, in the words of Alexander Dumas, it was *all for one and one for all.* That message among our countrymen has become lost. America has fallen into the doldrums, and this is the wrong time to have that happen. At this moment in history, there are conflicts of enormous consequence occurring outside our country's borders. The Kaiser is dissatisfied with his neighboring countries. The Russians are at war with China and Japan. The King of Serbia was recently murdered. South of us, there's a new dictator in Colombia. Even our civilized friends in England recently completed the Nigerian conquest. These are examples of the increasing unrest and militarization around the globe. And what of America?"

Mills and Sullivan remained patient and silent.

Spalding continued, "The United States has become weak and isolated. The American populace has become apathetic and lethargic. Despite the general strength of our economy, there are serious signs of weakening. This country is both weak and vulnerable. Now that he's in for a second term, our old friend, President Roosevelt, wants to again focus on rallying around the flag. To that end, baseball can help! It can help to reinstill that waning American spirit.

Spalding spoke once more. "Don't quote me on this, but that son of a bitch John McGraw's big mouth caused the feud that led to the cancellation of this past year's World Series. Baseball has a black eye. Proving the origins of the sport as American would kill two birds with one stone: promote baseball and help the American spirit to get balanced and back on her feet—not unlike the little man on your desk with the buckets."

Sullivan stated, "If this is primarily about professional baseball, I wonder why I'm here. You two gentlemen are intimately involved with your sport. I, on the other hand, am more of a general practitioner of sports."

Spalding responded, "Your perspective, James, is particularly important for what I propose. Professional baseball receives most of the news coverage, but the vast majority of interest in baseball rests with other than the professional. The multitudes that observe or play the game don't do so for money. The overwhelming preponderance of interest in baseball resides in the hearts of amateur athletes and people from all walks of life. I have an idea that requires the perspective of the professionally minded and, more importantly, that of the amateur. If nothing else, your proven love for athleticism, the competitive spirit, and America's position within the sports world, in and of themselves, qualifies you for what I hope you will consider the complement of my request for your presence here."

Spalding next looked to Mills. "I'm talking about embracing the course of history, something that you can be a part of. I refer to proving, once and for all, that the history of baseball attests to the great American game and is indeed that—a purely American invention and tradition. In almost all ways, it seems this country has its roots from every nation but the United States. Our Constitution is based on the Magna Carta, and the republic is based on ideals resulting from the French Revolution and the apex of Greek civilization. Our citizens come from England, the rest of Europe, Africa, and every other continent. We have little to claim as our own. And what's worse, even baseball is said to be nothing more than an offshoot of that childish English game. In brief, I am merely looking for a commission to determine the origin of baseball."

As if in a school setting, Mills raised his hand. "I may know where this is going but will nevertheless ask, where are you going with this?"

"Americans need to be more supportive of and proactive with their country," Spalding insisted. "President Roosevelt thinks we need it, and I believe you two agree. Diverse political views within the halls of government are stagnating progress to resolve our nation's problems. If we see our ideals threatened abroad, will there be an adequate number of citizens who would volunteer to go out there and help? And what if we are called to war? We need to recapture the national pride! This country needs to get back the enthusiasm it once had!"

Mills furled his bushy eyebrows. "Since when we last met, AG, I am wondering whether you have gained a preponderance of thought that may be emanating from some illusions of grandeur to make you believe that we three and a bat and ball sport can make such a contribution toward influencing the thought processes of our fellow citizens."

Spalding retorted, "There is clearly no one solution to rebuild the spirit of '76. Getting back the enthusiasm of our country's people requires a multitude of activities experienced throughout the US, but I am certain that we three can get the proverbial ball 'rolling'—in a big way."

"I have yet another issue," Sullivan added. "It seems as if we are trying to prove an argument rather than discover the answer to a lingering question. Are you expecting that our effort would be to prove one and only one thing—that baseball was invented in America?"

"I want to clarify something," Spalding declared. "I fervently desire to prove the origin of the game to be American, but not at the cost of ignoring the obvious, should you discover evidence to the contrary. I clearly recognize that proceeding to hide such evidence would...

be an act of disloyalty to the commission that was appointed at my suggestion…, with instructions to consider all available evidence and decide the case upon its merits, were I ever again to enter upon the details of that vexed controversy— except in order to prove the righteousness of the verdict…rendered.[4]

Sullivan asked, "How do you expect the commission to find proof which has thus far eluded knowledgeable people on this topic?"

Mills added, "In sales, we teach our people to follow the prospective client into the water closet and don't leave without a signed order. Are you suggesting that James and I banish ourselves to the library and not return until we have uncovered the evidential proof of support?"

"Hardly that, gentlemen," retorted Spalding. "It's quite simple, really. We'll go to the people. We will ask all Americans if they have evidence to prove the origins of baseball. We will solicit evidence from the old and young, in cities and hamlets, and from East to West. We'll accept any relevant stories they have been told, events they have witnessed, and letters or other documents they hold in their possession."

Mills sarcastically offered, "Seventy-six million conversations may take some time to complete. If you require us to take notes, add some—"

Spalding interrupted, "Nothing of the kind. We will have a thousand newspapers throughout the forty-five states and territories publicize what we are attempting to do, what evidence we seek, and how to contact us if they might have something of relevance to share."

Sullivan inquired, "Have you thought about how much money it will cost to get one or more notices in each of a thousand newspapers?"

---

[4] Ibid.

Mills added, "I was wondering how you will get people interested in what we're doing? For that matter, do you have a plan on how to get people interested enough to even read the notices we provide?"

Spalding was pleased with the questions. "Do you want the short answer or the longer one?"

"I know you well, AG," Mills replied. "Let's start with the short answer before we decide where next to go."

Spalding laughed. "My response then is nothing, yes and yes."

Sullivan responded, "No cost to us?"

Spalding reminded, "Throwing all modesty aside…"

"Modesty has never been your strong point, AG," Mills jested. "By all means, throw modesty out!"

Spalding replied, "My name is still a drawing card. We don't need to pay for notices. I'll write a letter to the editors explaining what we are attempting to do. I'll write a related article containing little-known historical facts and anecdotes of interest to followers of sport, as well as a description of the Mills Commission's intentions. At the end of—"

"Hold on one moment, Mr. Spalding," Mills ordered. "Please don't use the term *Mills Commission* when I have not consented to be a part of this scheme of yours. It serves you little benefit to play to my ego."

Spalding continued, "Correction, as well as a description of the commission's intent. At the end of the piece, we will encourage a response by knowledgeable people and inform them where to send a brief of what information they have."

Sullivan wondered, "Am I the secretary of the commission?"

"That you are," replied Spalding, "if you are gracious enough to accept."

"Suppose that we receive a million replies," Sullivan said.

Spalding remarked, "That would be a dream come true!"

Mills exclaimed, "Either a dream or a nightmare!"

"Okay," Spalding admitted. "I could specify what we want and also tell people what would not be of interest to us. In fact, I will suggest that we already know that Alexander Cartwright and his teammates' first codified modern baseball rules in 1845, that we are looking for evidence of the game prior to that time. These sort of considerations should mitigate the issue of receiving an overabundance of correspondence."

Spalding received no response and then continued, "If we are inundated, I'll spring for the cost of support staff, if necessary."

"You'll need to have credibility," Mills declared. "Otherwise, this may wind up like the person who is having a party, hires the caterers and brass band, and then no one shows up."

"Credibility will be the least of our worries," Spalding proudly asserted.

> [The]…commission rendering this important decision [will be] composed of such able men and well-known friends of the game…[as those names I am about to provide to you.][5]

Mills asked, "Do you not think the men of such high repute will have some of the same questions James and I had for you today?"

Spalding reached into his leather bag and pulled out three pieces of paper. "You're right, Abe! They did have those questions! The list of proposed committee members I hold in my hand have reputations beyond question and are well-suited for this task. I should add that whatever inquiries they have made or will make have either been answered or will soon be addressed to their satisfactions."

"May I presume," Mills asked, "that these men of greatness have already been directly approached by you, Al?"

"Yes," Spalding proclaimed. "I have discussed this, in person, with most of the potential members already. Additionally, the individuals on this list have been approached in writing, and I have responses from each of them. I now present you with a copy of the list."

---

[5] Ibid.

Spalding handed Mills and Sullivan carbon copies of the original list that Spalding retained in his hand. Mills and Sullivan began reading the lists with noticeable anticipation.

Spalding prompted, "Shall I begin, gentlemen?"

Both of Spalding's recruits continued reading.

Spalding began to read the names while providing remarks on each committee candidate.

"First at bat is the Honorable Arthur P. Gorman, former United States senator from Maryland. Shortly after being able to grow facial hair, Senator Gorman became a founding member of the Washington Nationals Baseball Club, America's first official baseball team. He became quite the star pitcher. When the Nationals went on tour back in '78, I was the only opposing pitcher to beat their squad. Arthur didn't pitch against me that day because he didn't join up with the Nationals until the tour hit Chicago. On the rare occasions I see Arthur, I like to remind him how fortunate he was for not pitching against me that day and avoiding falling prey to the arm of AG Spalding, a teenage boy from Smallville, USA."

Mills commented as he shook his head. "Please, AG, you really do need to learn to let go of your modesty!"

Spalding continued without breaking stride. "The senator was also the fourth president of the National Association of Baseball and, anecdotally, was unanimously and officially voted in as the first chairman of the Senate Democratic Conference held last year. That last remark, however," stated Spalding with tongue in cheek, "is more for your ears only, given the number of Republican voters crawling around these parts."

Mills, with a chuckle, said, "Go on, Al. Go on."

"Next is the Honorable Morgan G. Bulkeley, former governor and United States senator for and from the state of Connecticut. I might add that he has business executive experience as president of AETNA Insurance for the past twenty years or so. Of significance, Bulkeley was also the first president of the National League and was, in fact, replaced by Abraham's and my esteemed mentor, Mr. Hulbert."

"You forgot to tell James the best part," asserted Mills as he faced Sullivan. "At the league's first annual board meeting, Bulkeley never showed his face. Needless to say, that is how Bulkeley ended his brief term in office as league president!"

"In the senator's defense," Spalding replied, "Bulkeley didn't show up because he only agreed to a one-year term, and his term was over. He never really had any ties to baseball prior to that anyway. The only reason he was roped into the position, to begin with, was because he was from out east, and everyone thought that was better than having someone from the Midwest become the first head of the league. From my point of view, his résumé thereafter, along with his brief stint in baseball, such as it was, well-qualifies the gentleman in my mind."

After a moment of silence, Spalding continued. "Next at the plate is Mr. Nicholas E. 'NE' Young of Washington, DC."

Mills exclaimed, "Good choice, Al! NE was a major help to me in my post as National League president, and I liked him!"

Spalding looked over at Sullivan. "Mr. Young was the first secretary of the National League and later served as league president. He was quite involved with league affairs, knows a lot of people, and is a true aficionado of the game."

"Our sixth recruit is Mr. Alfred Reach of Philadelphia," boasted Spalding.

Sullivan inquired, "Sixth choice?"

Spalding responded, "The two of you were my first two choices—if you're wondering why *six* and not four."

"I wondered whether you would rope Reach into this," remarked Mills. "This choice should surely please Chadwick!"

Again, turning to Sullivan, Spalding added, "A cricket player originally from London, England. In that respect, he has a similar background to Mr. Chadwick. Reach has me by ten years in age and began playing baseball after I did. He claims he's 5'6", and although that's a stretch, he was one heck of a complete ballplayer whom I admired—infield or outfield, it didn't matter. He was good enough to become professionally paid as a player with the Philadelphia Athletics. He was older than all his teammates yet was one of the best batters in the National Association, having batted better than .350 as I recall. At one time or another and even up to a few years ago, Reach was manager, president, and a part owner of the Phillies."

"We should add, James," said Mills to Sullivan, "that Reach built a prominent sporting goods company that competes with Al's company."

"I believe the A. J. Reach Company," admitted Spalding, "is a bigger outfit than mine, certainly, a formidable competitor. And if all this does not make him qualified as a commission member, he's a student of the game as well. Just as Chadwick has been the editor for my company's baseball guide, Reach is intimately involved with his company's production of a comparable sports guide which," boasted Spalding, "is almost as good as the *Spalding Baseball Guide*."

Sullivan commenting, "That's solid. Not originally American erases the perception of commission bias as to the national origin of the game, and the man is obviously well-rounded."

"Very true," remarked Spalding. "Did I say he even umpired some?"

Looking at the list of names handed him by Spalding, Mills offered, "AG, we'll need to move this meeting along as I have some business matters that I will soon need to tend to. Thus, and finally...?"

"Finally," continued Spalding. "Also, a businessman who happened to have been one of the finest ballplayers of his day, Mr. George Wright."

"I know well of his level of play," Sullivan proudly interjected. "As a shortstop, there were none finer!"

"So true," concurred Spalding. "My familiarity with George goes way back. At one time, for my money, he was the best player in the game! He played with baseball's first professional club in Cincinnati. Also, so as to appease Mr. Chadwick, George came from England. After moving to New York City, he began his career as a cricket player. As Abraham knows, George accompanied me on my World Baseball Tour. Anecdotally, when I was first discovered as the teen pitcher of the Forest City nine, George was the opposing player I feared the most! His brother, Harry, is well-known in baseball circles too."

Spalding began gathering up his papers and concluded, "So there you have it, gentlemen. I hope you're both pleased."

Mills bellowed, "I'm impressed! And you say these men are on board."

"After but a few more formalities, the answer will be yes."

"Formalities," Mills repeated.

"Mere formalities," Spalding replied.

Mills furled his brow once again and briefly glared at Spalding. Spalding did not notice, or at least, he didn't appear to notice.

"I have a question, AG," Sullivan added. "Do you think that Mr. Chadwick will accept the verdict of the commission if our conclusion disagrees with his beliefs?"

"It doesn't matter," Spalding replied. "He'll have to—or raise the ire of every member on our panel. We will outpublicize him. I guarantee you, we will see little or nothing from him on his greatest platform—the *Spalding Baseball Guide*. Besides, I know Henry. For all that Henry is or is not, he's a gentleman and man of his word. If he says anything, it will be but a peep, and even our 'Father of Baseball,' as President Roosevelt labelled him, will not carry the weight of the commission in this matter."

"Suppose," pondered Sullivan, "that we find evidence and the proof we discover points in the direction of baseball being a direct descendant of cricket or rounders?"

"I'm not worried about that," Spalding exclaimed. "We can handle whatever issues may come along. In other sporting words, we'll la*crosse that bridge when we come to it*."

Sullivan and Mills rolled their eyes at one another.

"Fair enough," Sullivan replied. "I'll *throw my hat in the ring*. My only issue is whether the workload becomes a conflict with our deadlines."

As the lobby clock chimed four o'clock, Mills said, "Quickly, Al, what are their time constraints?"

"It's wide open," Spalding declared. "*All in good time* as they say."

"I have no more questions," Mills said as he doodled a few words onto a notepad he had in his lap.

Spalding coyly tried to see what Mills had written, but Mills casually prevented anyone from reading the words, *No thank you to the assignment. Will participate only as the other commission members will.*

Mills walked over to his desk to collect papers for his next meeting. There was a knock on the office door. The door opened, and two ladies working in the front office appeared. They were holding Spalding's and Sullivan's overcoats and hats.

Spalding inquired of Mills, "When might you let James and me know whether you will kindly accept the role of commission chair?"

Mills replied, "Soon, my friend." As Mills was exiting his office, he said, "Good meeting, gentlemen. I'll be in touch. Nice meeting you, James. Always a pleasure, AG."

With those words, Mills disappeared down the hall, and the two men put on their spring weight overcoats and hats.

Spalding offered to Sullivan, "I'll buy you an ice cream."

Sullivan inquired, "An ice cream?"

"Why certainly," exclaimed Spalding. "Cool spring days are the best days for ice cream! I know a place that has pistachio nut flavor. You'll love it!"

Sullivan replied, "It's nearly dinnertime."

Spalding laughed. "If there's one thing I've learned from Lizzie, it's the importance of ice cream. Dinners come and go. You amateurs need to show more backbone! I'm telling you, you'll be glad you tried it!"

Sullivan did not reply. The men said their *goodbyes* to the staff and left.

Sullivan asked, "So what do you think, AG? Do you think we got him?"

"Hook, line, and sinker, James! Hook, line, and sinker!"

* * *

Three weeks later, Spalding received a typed letter from Mills on Otis Elevator Company letterhead, stating,

> *I am not inclined to take up the baseball question again in any of its aspects, [although] I will not be the one to break the chain, in other words, if all the others will serve I will.*

Upon returning to California, Spalding replied to that letter with a handwritten letter, dated April 13, 1905, stating, among other things:

> *I was gratified to receive yours of the 27th...expressing a willingness to serve on the proposed Base Ball Committee.*
> *...I am pleased to say that all have accepted...*
> *...It is now up to our friend Sullivan to collect the necessary evidence and formulate into shape so it will take little of your time to consider it.*

Within a matter of weeks, evidence would be submitted to the committee that would ultimately determine the course of the commission and the conclusion it would one day publish as its findings.

Exitus acta probat...the outcome
justifies the deed.

—Publius "Ovid" Ovidius Naso,
Roman Poet (year 0)

CHAPTER 8

Birth of a Legend

Early December 1905—Midtown Manhattan

Waiting for Spalding to do a late checkout of his room and arrive, Mills and Sullivan had just ordered three lunch specials while seated at a table within the intimate main floor bar at the Algonquin Hotel. The Algonquin was one of New York City's newest and finest hotels, having opened its doors for the first time two years earlier. The bar, with its rich wooden-paneled walls, was sparsely lit. Although the noon-hour customer rush had subsided, leaving the bar nearly devoid of customers, the two men requested a table in the innermost corner of the room to ensure privacy.

Sullivan commented, "Great idea you had, Mr. Mills, having the three of us stay here."

"Once I committed to this in my calendar," Mills began, "I didn't want anything to go wrong. When the weather doesn't cooperate during this time of the year, with the Christmas rush and all, I wanted to make certain the scheduled meeting would go off as planned."

Sullivan offered, "All the same, it's nice not having to deal with our winter gear during the meeting—and this is one beautiful hotel.

I slept like a log. And speaking of which, maybe I should check and ensure AG is on his way."

"No need," Mills said. "I instructed the front desk to check on him, and I left him a note also."

Sullivan was mildly puzzled. "A note?"

"The note," boasted Mills, "informed AG that we're waiting in the lounge. It also instructs him to pay our bills when he checks out."

Sullivan laughed. "Hopefully, he won't complain too loudly about that!"

"Trust me," Mills consoled, "he won't utter a peep."

Sullivan chuckled. "I see the battle lines are being drawn."

With exasperation, Mills stated, "He knows I didn't want to be a part of this effort to any extent beyond how the others are also involved, and when he wanted the three of us to meet, I knew what this was about!"

"I'm partially to blame for that, Abe. We came across some important evidence, and AG asked me if I thought you'd be willing to meet with us. I said time has passed since last March, and that your heart seemed to be in the same place as ours when we last met."

"I don't blame you in the least," Mills admitted, "because as important as you may be in the world of athletics, you're merely the soldier here. He's Rasputin."

Sullivan laughed again. "Rasputin?"

"Self-proclaimed holy man," Mills responded. "Our friend Spalding just never learned to take *no* for an answer!"

"I don't know about that, Abe," Sullivan stated. "But as I said when you called me the other day, we may be near a solution."

"Don't hold your breath," Mills replied. "There could be bad news."

Sullivan wondered, "Hopefully not based on our two-minute call."

"Once you mentioned the names *Graves* and *Doubleday*," Mills responded, "I had a bad feeling."

Sullivan asked, "You know these men?"

"I believe so," Mills admitted. As Spalding came bounding through the door from the lobby, Mills continued, "But allow me to bring that up. I know you don't like to ruin a good surprise."

Spalding weaved his way between the empty tables and chairs to where the two earlier arrivals were seated. Picking up his napkin, Spalding sat down, laid the napkin on his lap, and addressed the two men. "Abe, James, good afternoon."

Mills said, "I hope you rested well after your arrival from California, and I trust things go well for you and the missus."

The bartender made his way to the table as Spalding replied, "I slept extremely well, and we're just fine! Thank you for asking!"

"Good afternoon, Mr. Spalding," propounded the bartender. "I'll be taking your order and understand you don't partake in the *spirit world*."

Suddenly devoid of anonymity, Spalding pondered the words of the bartender while observing the smirks on his fellow diners' faces.

The barkeep continued. "I mean to say I assume you are not interested in an alcoholic libation—spirits, which is no problem, sir. The Algonquin has a wide selection of nonalcoholic beverages. What may I bring you?"

"An effervescent water with a twist. Also, I'd like to see a menu."

"Sir," replied the bartender. "Your friends took the liberty of ordering for you. I hope that is to your satisfaction."

"Friends," quipped Spalding. "Then, that will be all. Thank you."

The server bowed graciously and said, "Your drink and the food will be out shortly." The bartender walked off, disappearing through the set of swinging doors behind the bar.

Mills joshed, "You must frequent this bar often."

Spalding exclaimed, "I've never been here before!" The response made Mills and Sullivan laugh.

Spalding then inquired, "If I may ask, what did I order for lunch?"

"The daily special," remarked Sullivan. "Salad. A large Russian salad. We're all having the same thing!"

Mills added, "It's in honor of your spiritual leader, the Madame. The salad comes with a scoop of caviar on top. We took the liberty of having your optional anchovy strips on the side!"

Spalding exclaimed, "Just so that I understand, the current price of caviar leads me to wonder who is springing for lunch?"

Mills retorted, "Why, I assumed it was Spalding Brothers!"

Spalding looked up and politely smiled as he watched a waitress gently set his beverage down by his place setting.

Spalding asked of Sullivan, "Did you bring the correspondence?"

"The more important pieces. Shall I take them out?"

Spalding instructed, "Everything except the Graves documents. Just don't spill your caviar on what little evidence we've accumulated."

Rising from his chair and walking over to a nearby table, Sullivan pulled the table up to where the three were seated. He then retrieved a small group of letters and envelopes out of a portfolio and laid the items atop the empty table.

Turning to Sullivan, Spalding said, "James, why don't you show the committee head what you have."

Mills interjected, "Does this meeting need to be called to order?"

Spalding asked, "Any volunteers?"

The three men looked at each other in expressionless fashion.

"I'm not volunteering for anything, AG," Mills said, "but merely wondering why I'm here after the last discourse we had on the subject was a letter sent by me making my position quite clear on this matter."

"My dear friend Mills," Spalding began, "I can think of no better friend I have than you. You know my situation. An important turn of events has occurred, and we wish to run something by you. You'll understand when we bring it up. Will you kindly humor me this once?"

Mills responded with great sincerity, "For you, I will do it, dear friend. Is this another of your surprises?"

Spalding replied, "It is!"

Mills smiled gently and responded, "Nothing like a good surprise I always say."

Spalding looked at Mills with mild wonderment.

"Very well," Mills offered. "Just to refresh, would either of you gentlemen state each committee member's name and whether or not anything has changed as to their certainty of remaining committed?"

With an air of humble frustration, Spalding began reciting. "The Honorable Arthur Pue Gorman, the Honorable Morgan G. Bulkeley, Mr. NE Young, Mr. Alfred J. Reach, Mr. George Wright, and you two comprise the remainder of the seven. I do not have any updates on status at this time. To the best of my knowledge, all remain committed."

The salads were served almost unnoticed.

Mills exclaimed, "Look at this presentation! I move to take a brief recess whilst I dive into this wonderful daily special!"

Sullivan declared, "Second!"

After a brief intermission for eating and light conversation, Sullivan ate faster than the others and finished eating first. He then scooted his chair toward his papers and began to speak.

"We've had our solicitation for information covered in a thousand newspapers, as agreed, from sea to shining sea. It seems like we've had almost as many responses. The bulk of what I received was eliminated from further consideration, but we have a few good ones."

Mills inquired, "Might you enlighten me as to your process of elimination for the letters you deemed as unworthy of consideration?"

"Most assuredly," replied Sullivan. "It is a far simpler explanation than describing how we had to distribute those newspaper articles all over the continent!"

Spalding offered, "Mr. Sullivan was a real *trooper*, Abe."

"As was Mr. Spalding," Sullivan conceded. "The press services helped big-time too."

Mills inquired, "Press services?"

"Mostly the AP," Spalding responded. "The Associated Press."

Sullivan continued. "The vast majority of correspondence was easily concluded as irrelevant, unverifiable, or not credible. Quite frankly, most items we received were not close to the specifications of what we requested in the solicitation. Of the letters that were not immediately eliminated, it was clear that many of the remaining replies were simply describing variations of prior American ball bat games, such as the old cats, town ball, barn ball, and so on. These games bear little similarity to the national game of today, and we thus weeded them out."

Mills inquired, "When you say *we*..."

Sullivan replied, "Me and my unofficial consultant, Mr. Spalding."

Addressing Spalding, Mills observed, "You recruited the committee members. Your name is associated with the commission's search for information by way of your byline. The public knows of your involvement. Given you make no bones about the fact that you have your own personal ax to grind with Henry, I must ask, Other than playing instigator of this crusade, how much involvement have you had in the review process?"

Sullivan offered, "Other than coordinating the distribution of articles to the news concerns, not all that much, Mr. Chairman."

Mills sharply turned his head toward Sullivan. Sullivan continued, "Sorry, Abe. I misspoke. It just seemed so natural, I felt compelled to say it. I'll continue. Most of the work, if I may say so, has been on my own, with assistance from my administrative people and the occasional athlete unfortunate enough to wander by my office at the wrong time. Beyond that, AG's involvement was limited to reviewing letters I deemed as candidates for further consideration. Over the past year, our conversations were limited."

Mills looked at Sullivan and cautiously nodded in approval.

Sullivan declared, "I'll get back to my summary of items I removed from consideration. In addition to the letters I already described as irrelevant, other replies to our call for information described gatherings of cricket players, without any evolution mentioned, thus they were eliminated. A majority of other recollections were from experiences around or after the time of the Civil War, which is after the game had become popularized which was, in turn, after 1845 and the days of Alexander Cartwright. Then too, some respondents seemed set on proving that baseball was derived from English games, the Egyptians, Dutch, Germans, and several other countries, referring, once again, to sports far removed from what we know to be our national pastime. Incidentally, by 'far removed,' I'm not speaking geographically, but rather in terms of the rules and layout of the modern game. There was a reference by one historian to the writings of Lewis and Clark that bear witness to observations of related types of games played by our indigenous friends in areas where the white man had never previously been. There was no detail or corroborating evidence, however, and the likelihood of reasonably close similarity seemed remote. Thus, that reference was eliminated."

Placing his hand on the stack of folders, Sullivan added, "Once all the correspondence was received and refined and upon adding a couple of letters out of AG's files to what was left, you wind up with this small pile of potentially valid responses sitting on the table before you."

Neither Spalding nor Mills offered any comment, and Sullivan began pulling correspondence from the top of the pile, reading the highlights from one letter after another. As each letter was introduced, Sullivan would hand the papers to Mills. Mills would then glance at the item and subsequently place the document facedown on the growing pile of papers adjacent to the place where the colonel sat.

"Here's a letter from a Phillip Hudson of Houston," stated Sullivan. "In this instance, however, I require more information and will soon reply to Mr. Hudson with that request."

Sullivan continued, "This next letter is from a business owner, H. H. Waldo, who lives in AG's childhood *neck of the woods*. This response references the year 1835, four years prior to our earliest credible account. I take some issue of the letter from Waldo, however, as he describes more of a childhood-type game than what we know as baseball today."

Sullivan grabbed the next letter. "Here's an interesting letter from a Mr. Henry Sargeant who references several places in or around Massachusetts, Brown University in Rhode Island, and down to Richmond and elsewhere. In the letter, Mr. Sargeant confesses a weakness of memory for detail, and he jumped around in his topic frequently. This response, taken without subsequent inquiries, may not hold up well under scrutiny. It's still a possible, though. Thus, it remains subject to further investigation."

"Then, there's a letter from a judge hailing from Mount Vernon, New York," Sullivan continued. "The judge wrote an intriguing one-pager describing a game of ball that occurred near where Alexander Cartwright's team played in the Newark area. Unfortunately, the event the judge described was after the magical year of 1845 when Cartwright codified the infamous twenty rules of baseball. The judge's letter does, however, have historical merit with much of what he included."

Not slowing down, Sullivan held up the next letter. "Here's a piece of correspondence from AG's files from last November. It was written by a Mr. John Lowell of Massachusetts. Although we are awaiting a reply from our request for more detail, my expectations are beginning to wane. It certainly would not further the cause to show the game as he described it. His description infers baseball is rooted in British tradition. Of course, we will have but little choice to include this as evidence if the story proves out."

Grabbing the next document, Sullivan observed, "This letter I next hold is actually from AG asking a reverend in Brooklyn to provide insight on what he had previously commented on in a discussion with AG. In my personal opinion, it holds little promise. Several months have passed since my follow-up inquiry, and as of this date, the minister has yet to reply to our request for further detail."

Pausing briefly, Sullivan stated, "There are other responses here, but on second thought, these have similar issues to what we have with the reverend's account, and I won't waste your time, at least not now."

"Finally, we have one prospect that shows promise."

Mills inquired, "And this is the letter you and I briefly discussed?"

"It's one person who wrote the initial letter," Sullivan replied. "And he submitted a second letter in response to our request for clarification and additional detail." Holding up a file folder, Sullivan pulled out the papers. "These are letters AG and I have conferenced on previously."

Mills repeated, "Conferenced?"

"Talked," Sullivan returned.

During the entirety of Sullivan's review of the letters thus far mentioned, Spalding was uncharacteristically quiet. He was presently using his fork to gently toy with the tiny black specks of caviar that remained in his salad bowl.

Mills responded, "I see. Frankly, James, the letters we've discussed thus far are somewhat disheartening."

Mills returned the stack of letters previously handed to him, and Sullivan placed all of them into one of the empty folders within his briefcase.

Next, Sullivan commenced a methodical explanation.

"I have before me a set of three letters and a couple of newspaper clippings that address a testimonial by one Abner Graves. Mr. Graves is a mining company executive who has resided in Denver, Colorado, for many years. The three letters will—"

Mills interrupted, "I thought you said two letters."

"My reference to 'three' includes the letter we wrote to Mr. Graves for more information. As I began to say, with the written explanations of Mr. Graves's recollection, we feel it can presently be argued that the game of baseball, as we know it, was invented in a way that seems likely and in a manner consistent with how the game may well have been created. Although the gentleman is unable, with certainty, to pinpoint whether what he witnessed occurred in 1839, '40, or '41, Mr. Graves gives an extraordinary account of what he personally witnessed unfold. Mr. Graves points out that he was one of the younger boys then assembled to play a game of ball."

"Marbles," Spalding pointed out. "The younger boys were playing marbles but knew the older fellows were about to play a game of town ball, I seem to recall."

Sullivan did not break stride. "By this eyewitness account, the moment of inception took place on a school playground located within the village of Cooperstown, New York. Have you heard of the place, Abraham?"

Mills replied, "On rare occasion. Never been there."

"It's a tiny scenic town upstate. Have you perhaps heard of James Fennimore Cooper?"

"*Last of the Mohicans*," Mills replied. "One of the great American novelists. Very prolific. Wrote several novels of similar circumstance. Is he the person the town named itself after?"

"His father, but the author grew up there."

Mills appeared mildly impressed.

"Abner Doubleday grew up there also," Sullivan added.

"I believe you to be in error, sir," Mills recalled. "I happen to know General Doubleday grew up in Ballston Spa."

"He was born in Ballston Spa, one county over," Sullivan corrected. "But the General went to school as a child in nearby Cooperstown."

Mills inquired, "How do you know this?"

"The town office verified it for me," Sullivan retorted.

With no response from Mills, Sullivan continued, "In front of several boys of varying ages then assembled…"

Mills inquired, "If I may ask, do you know the range of ages?"

"School ages," Sullivan replied.

Mills held to his question. "What grade range?"

Sullivan hesitantly stated, "A wide range from beginning of school to graduate."

"Where did Graves fall into this range?"

"He was amongst the younger boys," Sullivan conceded.

"Age six?"

"Probably," Sullivan admitted.

Mills thought for a moment. "I've seen Doubleday's birth year a hundred times. In 1839, he would have graduated."

"I expect," replied the exasperated commission secretary.

"And you said the event may have occurred as late as 1841," Mills recalled. "AG, when was the General a cadet at West Point?"

"I don't know, Abe," Spalding said, shaking his head. "Where are you going with all this?"

"I don't know," Mills replied despondently. "Please continue, James."

"Mr. Graves recalls that he and the other lads witnessed Doubleday using a stick to scratch out a diagram in the dirt. Mr. Graves provided his recollection of the diagram in one of the letters.

The drawn image of a base path was in the shape of a four-sided diamond. The base path included four bases—complete with a pitcher's circle in the middle of what would be considered as the infield. He then placed marks in the dirt where ten fielding players plus a pitcher were to be positioned. As I stated, we've had one back and forth with Mr. Graves, and he admits to not being certain of some of the specifics due to his age and the length of time since he was a boy. Nevertheless, Mr. Graves provides us with a sufficient level of detail. You must admit, Abe, it is a likely scenario of the way in which baseball might very well have been invented. The Graves story appears to be a highly plausible explanation."

Mills asked, "Has Graves provided the names of any of the other boys so that we might seek corroboration of this story from other eyewitnesses at the time?"

"I asked for some names," Sullivan responded. "In his reply, Graves provided several names of those present. Unfortunately, this all took place sixty-six years ago, and most, if not all, of the young fellows then present are either deceased, in declining health, or their whereabouts are unknown to Mr. Graves."

"I don't care to give any *official* advice, but it would be good," Mills recommended, "if you investigate this matter more thoroughly. Might you reapproach Mr. Graves and press him to locate or identify any of those present with whom we might verify the details of the event?"

"We can certainly try," Sullivan chimed.

"If we could hear from just one other person," Mills pleaded, "it would go a long way toward establishing the credibility we all desire. In lieu of his providing such understanding that this took place long ago, I would hold the Graves recollection suspect of not being true."

"It's a good suggestion, Abe," Spalding stated. "If neither of you mind, I have talked with the gentleman and may have better luck. Please allow me to take a crack at it."

"I certainly have no objection," replied Sullivan.

"Nor would I," Mills added. "Any headway you make would be important to what could be finding the holy grail of our quest. May I see the group of correspondence and review it for a moment?"

"Of course, you can," replied Sullivan as he handed over the papers to Mills. "I only ask that you keep the articles, letters, and envelopes in the order in which I have them."

Accordingly, Sullivan handed over the papers. On the top of the documents were two clipped articles from the *Beacon Journal* of Akron, Ohio. Mills unfolded the first document, a complete newspaper page.

"The first article," offered Sullivan, "came out of the weekend edition published on Saturday, April 1, 1905. This is the piece written by our very own Albert G., where at the end, AG requests any information relating to the origins of baseball to be sent to me at my work address."

The Spalding article, located on page 6 of the newspaper, was entitled, "The Origin of the Game of Baseball" by AG Spalding.

"The large half-page story," Sullivan summarized, "began by telling of the debate between the article's author and Henry Chadwick, all the while giving Chadwick high praise for his contributions to the game. In the article, Spalding presented both Henry Chadwick and AG's respective arguments as to whether the game was of English versus American origin. To be frank, the article spent most of the time debunking Mr. Chadwick's arguments while bolstering those held to be true by AG."

Mills glanced at the article, refolded the piece of paper, and set it down. "I've seen some of the solicitations for information already."

"Pretty much the standard request for information we submitted to the various newspapers," Spalding reiterated. "I grant that the solicitation for information is a little slanted in our favor. However, I didn't think Chadwick would mind when considering how highly he was praised in the writing. Besides, ol' Henry knows me so well that he could hardly expect anything less. He won't complain."

Sullivan added, "Nor does it hurt that Mr. Chadwick's primary vehicle for espousing his thoughts is the *Annual Spalding Baseball Guide!*"

"That too," commented Spalding.

Mills observed, "I've seen some of the articles you've sent on to the newspapers. Although I may question why you would want to expend so much effort describing your disagreement with Henry, as opposed to emphasizing that you're making inquiries for the sake of 'Old Glory,' I'm not certain. But it's good stuff! Besides, most people know your position on the flag and motherhood, and as you said before, your name draws a crowd of readers who follow and appreciate the sport. I only suggest, as we go forward, that you try to remain distant from the next process of determination—in the unlikely event that you can muster up the strength to do so."

Mills began looking at the second news article. It was a quarter-page extract from page 5 of the *Beacon Journal's* April 4 edition entitled, "Abner Doubleday Invented Baseball, Abner Graves of Denver, Colorado, Tells How the Present National Game Had Its Origins."

Sullivan elaborated, "The article you see appeared on the newspaper's sports page. Within the article you're now viewing, a brief introduction by the editor is followed by what was alleged to be the complete text of the Graves letter of April 3, from first paragraph to last. Due to the potential importance of the Graves account, however, we felt it imperative to see the actual letter itself to verify that no details were inadvertently omitted. I requested that Mr. Graves provide us with a carbon copy of the actual letter. Graves stated that he had only created one carbon of the letter, however, and upon our request, he sent the carbon copy under agreement that we return it to him."

With eyes scanning the article, Mills nodded while he continued to read.

As Mills looked over the letter, Sullivan noted, "The letter notes that the number of players was limited to eleven position players, rather than having unlimited players as town ball rules had always allowed. This important modification met with resistance from the younger crowd as they knew it lessened the likelihood that they would be allowed to play. Nevertheless, it was a significant improvement in terms of equalizing both sides in the competition while lessoning the frequency of injuries from collisions that so often occurred when an indefinite number of players were allowed to take the field at the same time."

Mills laid the news clipping on top of the first newspaper article.

Sullivan commented, "Of the letters you hold, the first one repeats what you just read in the second news article. The second letter, however, is a carbon copy of what we sent to Mr. Graves. In that letter, aside from asking for a copy of Mr. Graves's letter to the Akron paper, we asked for additional detail, inclusive of the names of witnesses, to verify the facts and get some additional information. Mr. Graves's response, dated November 17 to my request of November 10 for additional information, is the third and last letter."

Mills hastily scanned the first two letters, set them on the newsprint he previously looked at, and picked up the second Graves letter that replied to the commission's inquiry. Mills then began reading the two-page reply of Abner Graves in earnest. Sullivan and Spalding were silent while Mills perused the letter.

Upon completing his review of the last document, Mills looked up and asked Sullivan, "These three letters represent the sum total of all correspondence between the commission and Mr. Graves?"

"Pretty much," Sullivan replied.

Mills eyed Sullivan skeptically and continued his interrogation. "Pretty much? What does that mean?"

"Everything of consequence," Sullivan said.

Mills stated, "I'm not understanding."

"The only thing you don't have," Sullivan retorted, "is the standard very brief *thank-you* letter I often send to respondents."

Mills asked, "Did you happen to bring it with you?"

"I did," Sullivan returned. "Do you wish to see that also?"

"Why the hell not," Mills replied. "Let's make it a complete set."

Sullivan went into his briefcase, pulled out the one-page letter, and handed it to Mills.

As Mills looked the document over, Sullivan noted, "It's dated April 6."

"I see that," Mills said as he continued to look at the brief letter.

Mills put the thank-you letter down. "What strikes me," Mills observed, "is that Graves claims this was the first time that anyone, anywhere, drew a diagram—in dirt or otherwise. He cannot make such a claim. He can't possibly know whether someone else did the same or a similar thing prior to the event he alleges occurred. Further, Graves isn't even certain of the year!"

"Not knowing the precise year vexes you," Spalding observed. "If you don't like that, we can pick one of those years. They're close to one another so that should not present a problem."

"That's not my issue," Mills returned as he wrote what appeared to be a list on the top sheet of a pad of yellow paper.

Spalding inquired, "What is the issue then? And what are you writing?"

"Making a list," Mills conceded. Remaining on his train of thought, Mills recalled, "Abner [Doubleday] had a huge class ring from West Point. You couldn't miss the thing. He was proud of it. He would say that no other college graduates of his age had class rings. He used to boast the academy was the first school in the country to have them. The graduation year on the ring, as I recall, would have put him into the academy by then—especially if the year Graves identified was 1841!"

"We'll just pick a date," Spalding concluded. "Make it 1839. If someone points out that it may not have been that year, I'd respond *close enough*. They'd be *splitting hairs* over a year."

Mills did not respond.

Spalding chimed in, "Your point for Graves's statement of being the first time anyone drew a baseball diagram is valid, however, in attorney speak, the issue is 'irrelevant.' From all the correspondence we have thus far received, Mr. Graves describes a field of play prior to the year 1845, and if true, the diagram and description of play predate all other such similar claims we know of. If we might come to agreement that the Graves account is valid, I expect our commission's official findings can emphasize *the event* and how it seems to fall together."

"Do I understand," inquired Mills of Sullivan, "that I now have all the Graves evidence before me?"

"At this time, yes," Sullivan stated. "Four letters and the news articles."

Mills continued, "I have some questions. First, have either of you briefed Mr. Chadwick as to what evidence you have collected thus far? And if not, do you intend on doing so?"

Spalding responded, "Being the type of analyst that the old man is, I'm certain Henry is curious. Even his curiosity though is not enough to compel him to make such a request, and I have no desire to offer anything to him—at least not at this time.

"As for you, AG," Mills continued, "I suggest that, except for recontacting Graves, you minimize further involvement as we go forward. Please allow James to perform the primary functions."

"Gladly," Spalding enthused. "I appreciate your position on the importance of minimizing the 'appearance' of bias on what is ultimately determined and voiced by the commission under your namesake."

Mills retorted, "Quite frankly, I hope that we minimize more than the *appearance* of bias. In a perfect scenario, I would hope to eliminate the reality of bias, period! No bias. None. I fear, however, that may not be achievable, but you can at least *try* to work in that direction."

Spalding spoke up. "Sure. There will be a perception of bias, but who cares? I know in my soul that baseball is, indeed, of American origin. Further, no matter what, there will always be skeptics prepared to debate the origins of baseball. There's always *someone* with an ax to grind. That especially goes for the news correspondents trying to make a name for themselves. If a person is so moved, he or she could make an argument for or against the commission's findings. The vast majority of Americans, however, will cherish the positive and reject any negative."

Mills let out with a soft moan of exasperation. "So then, you're saying that you don't expect there to be any definitive proof, one way or the other, to enable the commission to form a conclusion that can hold water under scrutiny?"

"Look, Abe," retorted Spalding, "our commission is membered by men of integrity and position, and all are well-versed on the business of baseball. Regardless of what journalists or stubborn old cricket players might say to the contrary, nothing will change. Americans want to believe in their country but need something to latch on to. We can give them that!"

Mills turned to Sullivan, saying, "Mr. Sullivan, you may recall that I said earlier there may be some bad news for the two of you. Well, sir, the bad news, if you haven't noticed, is unfolding. My next question is a simple one, and it is in the spirit of letting you know what you may be getting into the middle of rather than in a role as a litigator. Has Big Al informed you of either his relationship with Mr. Graves or with both Al's and my associations with Abner Doubleday?"

"More or less," replied Sullivan. "I'm aware that AG met Mr. Graves on the train a few times. They both happen to frequently take the same train. I've elected to call that *serendipity*."

Mills bellowed a short sharp laugh while Spalding and Sullivan retained their stoic expressions. "Serendipity! We best save *that* word for after I tell you how AG and I came to know the General."

"James," Mills volunteered, "I want to first make certain you understand the relationships that AG and I had with Abner Doubleday so as to get all the liars on the same sheet of music—in the unlikely event that you two go forward with the Graves pitch. What has AG told you about our familiarity with the General?"

Spalding interposed, "I didn't have an opportunity to explain that side of things, though I had planned on doing so."

Mills retorted, "Quoting Robert Burns, '*The best laid schemes o' mice an' men.*' No better time than the present to let Mr. Secretary learn the true meaning of the word *serendipity*."

"I'm all ears," Sullivan declared.

"Interestingly," Mills remarked, "it is coincidental that AG and I knew the General. Baseball is neither the common thread nor applicable to one iota. I was an officer during the Civil War. After the war ended, fraternal groups comprised of war veterans sprung up all over the country. It so happened that I became in charge of the same veterans' outfit that Doubleday was a member of. It was at those gatherings, over the years, where I came to know the General. As for AG—"

Spalding interrupted, "I'll handle this one, Abe, but thanks."

Mills motioned his hand in concurrence.

Spalding asked Sullivan, "Do I correctly surmise, based on the Russian salad jokes, that you are familiar with the Theosophical Society?"

"Not as much as I should," Sullivan replied. "Go ahead, AG."

Leaning forward toward Sullivan, Spalding began his explanation.

"The American Theosophical Society is an organization that promotes a concept outsiders often misconstrue as a religion. It's a movement of sorts—quite a brilliant concept, really. It follows the teachings of one Madame Helena Blavatsky when she briefly lived in New York City thirty years ago. The Madame settled in Manhattan for a time. Theosophy is largely based on many past and present cultures, philosophies, religions, and academic disciplines from around the world. The Society in America was centered in Manhattan. My wife was and is active in the movement, having been one of the Madame's first pupils. When the society was in its second year, the group had a special occasion that I and Elizabeth attended. General Doubleday had just joined the society. Elizabeth and I met the General at that function, and I would then after get together with him, occasionally, up to his death some dozen years ago."

Sullivan remarked, "So you've been wed to Elizabeth for some time?"

Spalding took a deep breath. "Elizabeth and I have known each other since our childhood. She married another fellow, and I took a bride of my own. I frequented New York where Elizabeth lived for a time. Later, Elizabeth moved back to Illinois where we would cross paths on occasion. We remained friends through the years, and after we both became widowers, we subsequently married each other in the year 1900. When I met Doubleday, Elizabeth was living in New York City where I met some society members through her relationship with some of the Theosophists. That, sir, is the whole kit and caboodle."

Mills turned to Sullivan. "Our relationships with General Doubleday were fairly close—so close that AG and I were pallbearers at the General's funeral when he was laid in state at New York City

Hall. As far as tagging this national hero, dear friend Sullivan, that is *serendipity*!"

Mills paused. "Let's now discuss how AG was so fortuitous as to meet Mr. Graves. Not only is that something that might interest James. It is something I would like to hear more about too."

Sullivan offered, "All that I know is AG and Graves somehow met on the train from Chicago."

"If you will allow me, gentlemen," Spalding pointed out. "Mr. Graves frequently travels from his home in Denver to attend board meetings held in New York for a client of his. The Denver train connects through Chicago. When I travel cross-country to New York, I usually check up on my business interests in Chicago en route to the city. We're both enamored with the 20th Century Limited that goes from Chicago to New York. When…"

Mills inquired, "Even after the big wreck a few years ago, you still like the Limited, ay?"

"As they say," Spalding returned, *"Greatest train in the world!"*

Mills interjected, "Better than the Orient Express?"

"For my money, absolutely," Spalding replied. "The Limited lays out a massive scarlet carpet on the platform for all their customers to walk upon. Once on board, the service and the Pullman sleeper cars are first rate all the way. The train takes a scenic route, and the trip takes but twenty hours from Chicago to New York—and they're always on schedule! There's a barbershop, secretarial services available, the food is extraordinary, and there's plenty of other amenities too."

Mills remained on the same line of thought. "So Graves connects through Chicago because he likes the Limited too?"

"He'd connect through Chicago anyway, but yes, Mr. Graves thinks the Limited is the best thing to ever happen to train travel," Spalding responded. "He can't stop talking about it, especially considering that the train from Denver to Chicago is a three-day noisy, bumpy, jerking ride—and that's if there's no problems, like snow in the Rockies!"

"Carry on, Al," Mills urged.

"Simply stated," Spalding remarked, "Graves and I travel first class, and we ran into one another twice—once departing Chicago and the other time departing New York."

Mills blurted, "Whoa! Whoa! I had vaguely recalled you mentioning him, but it suddenly hit me. Isn't Graves the same character you told me about previously that you think is crazy?"

"I did," Spalding submitted, "but when I told you—"

Mills interrupted, "A kid playing with marbles, ay? I seem to recall you telling me that this character had *lost his marbles* prior to you ever meeting the man! He's the guy with the outrageous claims, being at the forefront of history in the development of the old west!"

"One and the same," Spalding rebutted, "but I was wrong, Abe!"

Mills retorted, "Wrong?"

"It turns out his claims aren't so *outrageous* after all."

Mills retorted, "He claims to have been a Pony Express rider. You said that! I don't recall what years the Pony Express existed as I'm no expert on intellectual Americana, but I do know the Pony Express never got off the ground, symbolically speaking. After a year and a half, the operation folded before the Pony Express could expand delivery beyond a handful of western cities, none of which consist of any populations of note. Then, there was Graves's claim that he was one of the original 49ers seeking fortune during the California gold…"

Spalding returned the interruption. "Turns out his claims are true!"

Mills inquired, "For both? How can you possibly know this?"

"As for being a Pony Express rider, he would have been living in that part of the country and probably of the right age at the time. Nevertheless, I'll focus on his having been an original 49er. I admit he struck me as quite the character when I first ran into him, especially after having made such claims. I subsequently ran into him again, however, on board the Limited. The time when I saw him most recently, I lightheartedly asked him if he had any more tall tales to tell me, like the 'original 49ers' tale. Get this! Graves pulls a ruffled piece of paper out of his briefcase. It was an old passport he'd been carrying around for a half century—with the proof he was a 49er! He said he carries it because he likes to tell stories of the gold rush days, but no one seems to ever believe him."

Mills quipped sarcastically, "I can't understand why not! I now recall you also telling me he built and owned his very own railroad spur. As I think about what you just said though, a passport? What does a passport have to do with the gold rush or anything?"

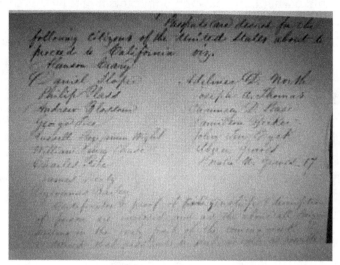

Courtesy: Ancestry.com

"I wondered the same thing," Spalding confided. "Graves refreshed my memory of what I've learned since becoming a California resident. He explained that, at the time of first discovering gold at Sutter's Mill, California was a republic—however briefly. California didn't enter the Union until the year 1850, so a passport was required of all US citizens wishing to gain entry to the Republic of California."

Mills projected a robust laugh. "You outdid yourself on this one, AG! This is rich! And you say you saw it? It was a US passport that was stamped showing entry?"

"You laugh, friend Mills," replied Spalding. "First, I wouldn't know that background. It happened before my time. I was born in that year! As for the passport, it wasn't a *passport* per se. The sheet was a passport *application.* The requisition was handwritten on one page."

Mills laughed once more. "Handwritten?"

Spalding forged ahead. "It contained a list of nine or ten names of which Abner Graves was on the list. Yes, I saw it! As for the document, it was smartly written, and the form of the document would not be unlike what other passport applicants might have used at that time—and the document was definitely old!"

Mills raised his hand, motioning to stop talking and hurriedly began looking through the Graves documents that Sullivan had provided.

"Here it is," Mills stated. "Graves's first letter is addressed to you, Al. Why? The instructions in the ad say to send information to James. When you saw him on the train the last time, did you put him up to this?"

Spalding was indignant. "No! I did not, sir! Absolutely not!"

"It sure seems fishy," Mills reacted.

"It's not," Spalding returned.

Interrogating further, Mills asked, "And he says he knew Doubleday?"

"Of course," Spalding replied. "The General was well-known in those parts. Graves says most people around Cooperstown crossed paths with the General at one time or another."

Mills wondered, "Then, why didn't he previously brag about that one?"

"Graves was just a kid when he met him," Spalding explained. "Then, they both moved away from the area. Who the Hell knows? Graves is contactable. Why don't you ask him yourself!"

"For now, I won't dwell on the gentleman's credibility—or sanity—so let's simply leave it at that," Mills told Spalding.

Spalding did not speak.

"Should we accept this tale as *the Gospel according to Graves,* then allow me to recap what we know thus far," Mills stated. Flipping to the top page of his yellow paper pad, Mills began to read. "That…

1. AG, purely as a matter of chance, ran into the man who, as a very young child, witnessed the birth of modern-day baseball;

2. That the witness claims to have been one of the original 49rs and rode for the Pony Express for its brief existence and now claims to have witnessed the birth of our national sport;

3. The witness happened to be passing through Akron, Ohio, the day the Spalding article was published in the *Akron Beacon Journal* shortly after running into AG and had never responded to any of the other thousand publications in the year prior to speaking up;

4. We can't seem to find any of the many other witnesses;

5. The man who invented modern-day baseball, to which you and I were completely oblivious, was a close mutual acquaintance of both yours and mine, Al;

6. The great American sport was invented by an American war hero of almost biblical proportion including having been the first in charge of Union forces at the infamous Battle of Gettysburg;

7. A mere child had brilliant recall and hung out with lads thrice his age;

8. No one knows with any certainty as to the day—much less the year—when this historical event occurred; and

9. Mr. Sullivan's thank-you letter was written *two* days after the original Graves letter was published when it takes a person five days to travel direct from Denver to New York on the fastest train in America, and it takes the mail even longer."

Have I made any errors or omissions, gentlemen?"

"I can explain that last one," Spalding offered.

Mills shook his head. "Unless Graves, in addition to all else, is also a close personal friend of Orville Wright and coerced him to pop up to Denver via the Rockies from Kitty Hawk, I'd rather simply relish this moment!" The litigator Mills continued, "Or maybe you just happened to run into the man on the same day he was hand-carrying the letter, hot off the press, for delivery to James. For the moment, AG, let's simply leave it at that—at least for the time being."

Spalding stiffened up without speaking as Sullivan tacitly observed the proceedings.

A somewhat exhausted Mills continued speaking. "Look, guys, I don't want to declare to the inhabitants of the cities and farmlands across America that this is our finding, and that it is based on the Graves letters, at least, not for the moment. I'm still wondering when Doubleday entered the Academy. You know Graves, AG, and he's still sketchy in my opinion—and the sketchiness doesn't end there, my friends. Look, the man likes to talk. Further, there are people around who know that both you and I knew Doubleday. Moreover, there is one person—in particular—who could shoot this entire story out of the air."

Spalding realized, "Mary!"

Sullivan asked, "Mary? Was that Doubleday's wife?"

Mills answered, "His surviving widow! I know she's still around, and though the ol' gal must be well into her eighties, I expect she's still sharp as a tack. She *could* validate what you two suggest. On the other hand, she could immediately shed a bad light on things if the General never once uttered a solitary word to her about baseball or this allegedly infamous day in the history of our great pastime. As much of a rubber stamp as our fellow committee members may be, some will expect verification of Graves's recollection and may well ask whether there is someone that was near to the General who could attest to all this—*prior to* publicly backing your recommendation. You and I, Al, were indeed close to the General, however, not once did he ever utter anything about baseball or that magical day. Have either of you, per chance, approached the widow Doubleday?"

Sullivan looked toward Spalding, and Mills did the same. No response from Spalding appeared forthcoming.

Mills added, "I didn't think so, nor do I expect you have intent to do so."

Again, there was no response by Sullivan nor Spalding.

Mills declared, "You wanted my opinion. I simply can't back you two up on this, not unless this story line changes dramatically. There are always skeptics who pursue the truth—especially when the nature of the findings hold such a high profile of interest to millions of Americans. I can assure you that both the English and American newspapers would dine on such a farce. I no more wish to be a part of embarrassing this nation of ours—either domestically or abroad— then seeing the three of us hanging next to one another from the flagpoles at the nation's capital in effigy. If Graves is lying, or heaven forbid, you two somehow manufactured some of this story, should someone else catch wind of it or find some other valid evidence of origin, God forbid, it will frame all our legacies in a very bad light. I suggest you shelve this option and move on to seek something—anything—that might be offered as an alternative solution."

Sullivan suggested, "We've shot our cannons already, and I am not optimistic that much more evidence exists or, at least, will be forthcoming in future months, however…"

Mills turned toward Sullivan. "However?"

"I'm thinking through what may be a suggestion," Sullivan offered. "There might be a way to resolve our dilemma."

Mills and Spalding glared at Sullivan with four eyebrows raised.

"Suppose," Sullivan proposed, "that we say we have reviewed volumes of testimonials and literature, and based upon all evidence reasonably and practically obtainable, the commission concludes that the sport of baseball was not invented, but rather, it simply evolved. We would…"

Spalding remarked, "Score one for the English Commonwealth and Henry."

"Hear me out," retorted Sullivan. "I'm certainly less of an expert on baseball than either of you, but common sense tells me that the American game of baseball doesn't have to be purely or even mostly of British descent. There is evidence to suggest that, as you intimated, Al, the Dutch, Germans, French, Egyptians, Ethiopians, Celts, and even the indigenous people of this country potentially had hands in developing the sport. In that instance, even dear Chadwick would be hard-pressed to declare 'victory,' while at the same time, our efforts would not appear to be in vain."

Mills remarked, "Your suggestion is intriguing, Mr. Sullivan. The idea may have merit! It's almost too simple. People would wonder why we needed a commission to come up with that explanation."

The table was quiet.

Mills went on. "We could suggest that our game is unique, not unlike the *melting pot* analogy that people use to describe this very country of ours. That would make baseball purely of American origin. It would not be an invention of one American, but due to the ingenuity of several—and Alexander Cartwright and his fellow Knickerbocker club teammates would simply be the *icing on the cake*."

"There's a lot of new information with which I was not previously aware," Sullivan remonstrated. "You must have nerves of steel, AG. The case of weaknesses in the argument made by Abe should be enough to scare anyone! Not trying to *blow my own horn*, it would solve our dilemma. With my suggestion, you'd get your wish, AG. We would make the sport of baseball an American tradition. It's the sure money."

Spalding stated, "Your idea, James, has its merits. It sounds mildly promising. I also appreciate your naming me in what could become a conclusion of longstanding note. Nevertheless, I am not yet willing to give up on our quest."

"Nor do I choose to do so," replied Mills. "We still have time, though it is beginning to wane. Although this is not what either of you were hoping to hear, I suggest you two continue on for a while and reconvene at a later date, informing the committee members that we are still wading through volumes of evidence that continues to come to our mail stop. What do you think, James?"

Sullivan raised his eyebrows, but did not speak, opting to avoid debating the matter further.

Spalding asked, "Although I said earlier that I could communicate this to the board members, in view of what you earlier stated, I'll ask, How would you like for us to pass along to our partners the status of where the process is at?"

"It matters not to me," replied Mills. "It's your skins in the game."

Mills pushed back his chair and stood up. "Gentlemen, I work for a living and must be off. James, you and your semiretired boss here may wish to caucus further."

As Spalding and Sullivan arose from their chairs, Mills exchanged expressions of goodbye. "Tallyho, gents and Big Al, thanks for a tasty and most entertaining lunch!"

Spalding retorted, "Let's not forget a good night's sleep."

"You'll get there, fellas," Mills assured. "I know you will!"

The remaining twosome sat down at the table, now next to one another, while Mills promptly departed the bar, heading back to his room to collect his coat and hat, and get home to see his family.

Sullivan asked Spalding, "Do you wish to talk further before we go our separate ways?"

"Let's do this another time. I've suddenly grown weary of attorneys. That lawyer put me through the thrasher today, and I need to sleep on all of this. I'll be back in town in a couple of months. We'll surely talk then—or sooner if my telephone company out west can figure out how to connect with whichever company you use."

"That being the case, I'm headed back to my room to get my wraps," Sullivan said. "Thanks for one doozy of a lunch, AG."

As Sullivan began walking toward the door to the hotel lobby, Spalding called out from behind, "I'll be in touch. Until next time, my friend."

Sullivan waved as he left the bar. Spalding would remain seated at the table for a while longer. He would soon depart for Chicago and would not return to New York City for some time. The proceedings would be left in the capable hands of Sullivan who understood the objectives. Besides, Spalding thought, he was not on the commission—not technically anyway. Returning to the sun and serenity of Point Loma, Lizzie and, yes, even Madame Tingley, sounded pretty good to him.

Sometimes it's more noble to tell a small
lie than to deliver a painful truth.

—Theodore Roosevelt

CHAPTER 9

All In

*April 11, 1907—the Fourth Polo Grounds,
Fifth Avenue at 110th Street, New York City*

Spalding and Sullivan were outside Polo Grounds ballpark at Coogan's
Hollow in Washington Heights, Manhattan. They were surrounded
by snowdrifts that remained from the mid-April snowstorm of the
previous day. Lines of people, men and women all dressed in fine
overcoats and hats, were streaming by on shoveled paths to enter the
stadium.

Sullivan asked, "Why are we standing out here in the cold, AG?"

Spalding responded, "Mills has our tickets. It's no warmer where
we'll be seated anyway."

"If it weren't for the crowd," Sullivan remarked, "you'd never
guess it was Opening Day."

"I always know when it's Opening Day," Spalding declared.
"After being in baseball for forty years like I've been, you grow an
internal clock that tells you it's time to play ball—training, preseason, and opening day."

Sullivan inquired, "Is it just the three of us?"

"There'll be four," Spalding replied. "Abraham is bringing a
member of the commission, Alfred Reach."

"Alfred Reach," exclaimed Sullivan. "I've been looking forward to meeting him."

"You may not be able to get rid of him when you do," Spalding warned. "Try not to sit next to him at the game. He'll spend half the time trying to talk you into buying his products for your AAU activities."

Sullivan laughed. "We buy from several sporting goods concerns. On a more timely vein, what do you think about today's teams?"

"It's a good matchup, James. Giants versus Phillies. That's the team Reach used to own. He sold the Phillies the year after I sold the Colts. *Monkey see monkey do!*"

Mills and Reach walked up to the two men.

"A fine day for a ball game, gentlemen," bellowed Mills. "Greetings, James, AG. Good to see the two of you looking so rosy cheeked! May I assume you both know Mr. Reach."

"Nice to see you, Al," Spalding said graciously.

Reach smiled at Spalding, and his eyes lit up when he looked at Sullivan. "You must be Mr. Sullivan!"

"Mr. Mills obviously warned you I was coming," Sullivan said.

Sullivan and Reach took off their right gloves and shook hands while Reach handed off a business card. Reach said, "Are you kidding? It is I who have been looking forward to meeting you, sir!"

Spalding chuckled, saying to Sullivan, "I warned ya."

Reach looked at Spalding, observing, "Nice tan you have, AG. I hear interesting things about your castle with its view of the Pacific."

Spalding replied, "It's comfy, warm—and it came with a loving wife and lots of groundskeepers too!"

Reach inquired, "I should think, AG, that if you dare out of San Diego this time of year, you might rather catch one of the openers in Chicago. After all, with last year's cross-town series, wouldn't you rather be there? You can't lose with either team."

"In some ways, it's difficult to go," Spalding replied. "It was more fun when I was at the center of it all. You, on the other hand, seem to have maintained your enthusiasm with the Phillies. I trust you brought us tickets for seating in the owner's box?"

"Afraid not, Al. Mr. Mills informed me he already had seats for the game, and I should shut my mouth and like them, regardless of where the seats may be. That's dandy with me. I just need to satisfy the Phillies by attending the game. They're customers of mine as are Connie Mack and the Athletics."

Spalding replied, "Both teams—customers, ay? It's nice that you pulled that one off. Sounds like business is good though. Maybe I should consider opening a large office in Philadelphia, unless you're in the state of mind to allow me to buy your company at a fair price."

"Y'know, I don't recall even the Bible having a *Jonah eating the whale* story," Reach bragged. "Maybe I should consider buying *your* company, if I could ever figure out how you made that coup by selling all those balls to the major leagues."

"Friends," Mills began.

Reach retorted, "You said it, Abe. I didn't!"

"No, Alfred," Mills gently corrected. "I was beginning to say something. Friends, let's save the *big dick* contest for another time! There will be plenty of time for that. I'd like to get inside and find our seats. Game time is 1:00 PM. The show is about to begin."

Mills led the other three into the stadium, up the inside ramp, and entered the ballpark. An usher approached the four men. Mills held up the tickets in fanned position for the usher to see. After glancing at the passes, the usher led the group down the aisle closest to home plate and stood in the aisle by the entry to their seats in the first row. They filed in—first Reach, then Sullivan and Spalding. Mills sat by the aisle.

While settling in to their seats, Spalding whispered in Sullivan's ear. "I warned you not to sit there."

Sullivan softly replied, "I can handle it, AG. After all, look how I've been able to handle you."

Spalding laughed, slapped Sullivan on the knee, and said, "That you have, James. That you have, my boy!"

Albert G. Spalding

It took no time for Reach, Mills, and Spalding to become drawn into soaking up the electricity within the park. Banners representing National League Championships for 1904 and 1905 waved atop two large flagpoles placed on the far side of the outfield boundary ropes and fences. In view of the weather, the modest showing of 17,000 spectators was most acceptable. Those standing outside the outfield barriers were soon cramped, and the seats in the grandstands were rapidly filling. The bands' marchers were tuning their instruments, the teams were assembling to take their customary Opening Day walk across the field, the color guard was in formation, and dignitaries were lining up to give their presentations.

Sullivan reached behind Spalding and tapped Mills on the shoulder. The two men leaned forward to look at one another.

Sullivan exclaimed, "Abraham, these are fantastic seats! These are the best seats in the house! The very best!"

Mills replied, "I try and go to Opening Day every year if I can. It's not easy getting decent seats on Opening Day, y' know."

"I know. I know!" Sullivan added, "How did you get these seats?"

"The Giants president," Mills replied. "John T. Brush gave them to me."

Sullivan inquired, "Will Mr. Brush be joining us?"

"No," said Mills. "That's why he gave them to me. Curious, isn't it? He must be watching from some other spot."

Sullivan shook his head and then did a 360-degree scan of the ballpark. Mills leaned back in his seat, again intently watching the crowd. Sullivan again reached behind Spalding, tapping Mills on the shoulder. Both men leaned forward.

Sullivan softly exclaimed, "Abe, I am impressed!"

Neither Spalding nor Reach were paying attention to the conversation.

Mills pondered the statement and replied, "My dear James, you're younger than the rest of us here, so I will take the liberty of saying this to you. As important and accomplished as you are within the sports world, even old guys like us still have some connections you'll never have."

With a large smile, Mills continued, "When I lecture you on the superiority of your elders, keep in mind that I like and respect no man more than you. For now, I just want you to enjoy the moment."

Mills and Sullivan both sat back. Spalding flicked Sullivan on the leg. The two men looked at one another.

Spalding said, "Great idea Abraham had, allowing us an audience with him provided it be to keep him company on opening day. I'm certain this meeting will end more pleasantly than the last one we three had."

Ceremonies on the field soon began. A tribute to the flag, marchers, the band playing, introductions, speeches, and the opening pitch were soon concluded. Following the pomp, the Giants took the field amidst applause and enthusiastic cheers. The Phillies would be first to bat.

After the first inning, Spalding noticed that Reach was affixed in a stare toward center field. "Mr. Reach, what are you looking at?"

"That hill in center field that rises up to the fence. It's amazingly steep!"

Spalding laughed. "Steepest grade in baseball. I have a good *Cap Anson* story about that!"

"Cap Anson," exclaimed Reach. "There's a reprehensible character for you! He's a drinker. Not something, as you well know, that was ever good for the game. Worse yet was the way he halted games whenever he saw a colored man in the opposing team dugout. I never understood why you recruited him, befriended him—and then made him captain!"

"I counseled Anson many a time on his misgivings," Spalding defended, "but he was one of the best ballplayers I'd ever seen! He was my star. He batted cleanup, had one of the highest batting averages in the league…

Reach interrupted, "Oh come on, Al! You weren't counseling Anson. You were aiding and abetting him. At the time the American Association was fixing to admit Toledo to the major league, you knew what was going on. And you must know that a decade ago when the major leagues officially banned people of color from club rosters, the verbiage came from a document Anson previously had a literate person create for him. Do you remember the name Moses Walker?"

Spalding remembered, "Middle name Fleetwood. That's who Cap had a run in with."

"Twice," exclaimed Reach. "My clipping service was sure to give me the newspaper articles. The *Daily Blade* went so far as to say he was *a scholar and a gentleman*, and the writer added *literally*."

"That was all twenty years ago," defended Spalding. "Clearly a sign of the times."

"Nonsense," argued Reach. "It seemed evident that the team's management, the local newspaper, and even most people in the good city of Toledo were behind Walker! And I'll never forget what your star player and team captain was quoted as saying after he gave up his argument that first time, '*We'll play this here game, but won't play never no more with the nigger in.*'"

Sullivan, looking a bit uncomfortable, interrupted, "Big Al, I'd like to hear your story."

Mills added, "Me too, AG!"

Spalding was still quiet when Reach pleaded, "Come on, Al, let's hear your funny story, please."

Spalding began, "*Cap* was a big man—taller than me and had a lot more meat on his bones. Great hitter but slower than molasses on the basepaths. He had some stolen bases, but that's only because he was on base nearly half of the times he batted."

As Spalding gained the attention of Mills and Sullivan, he continued his story. "Our White Stockings were playing the Giants back here in '89. The field was wet. Anson was at bat. The big fella whaled a shot over the Giants' center fielder's head. The ball rolled all the way up to the outfield fence. The center fielder tried in earnest to scratch and claw his way up that hill, but he couldn't do it. He kept sliding down. All the while, *Cap* lumbered his way around the bases and eventually crossed home plate, winding up with an inside-the-park home run. The crowd didn't think it was funny, but my guys thought it was hysterical!"

Mills and Sullivan were amused, though Reach remained expressionless.

"You had to be there, I guess," Spalding concluded.

As the game progressed, each of the men would occasionally talk among one another, providing facts and anecdotes.

At one point, Spalding wished to have some fun with Mills, stating, "It's too bad, Abe, that those two National League pennants flying high only have one World Series banner to complement them."

Mills rolled his eyes and shook his head. "You know fully well, Albert, John Brush said the reason for his refusal to play his team in the 1904 World Series was due to his opinion that the American League was inferior, and the National League pennant was all that he had hoped for. I should add that, when Brush was taking the heat from the newspapers with other theories, Brush called them outrageous lies. Besides, Coach McGraw said he felt the exact same way."

"That was a major event," Spalding asserted, "and I read several newspaper articles on it. Sources said Brush was in a tizzy for the American League placing another New York team–the Yankees–minutes away at Highlander Field in an effort to drive him out of business. And McGraw had his own ax to grind with the other league too."

Mills looked Spalding square in the eye and said, "I'm missing watching the pitcher warm up for this next inning." Mills then turned his attention back to the game. Spalding did likewise.

With the City of New York's recent passage of an ordinance to no longer support large-scale private events, the usual force of policemen for crowd control was not on hand. It would now be the responsibility of private security people—with but a handful of security guards on site.

By the latter innings, the Giants were trailing the Phillies by a score of 3-to-nil and spectators in the grandstands had grown discouraged with the score. Everyone, especially those standing beyond the outfield ropes, were cold, wet, and restless. Many people wanted to leave the park before the game's end to avoid the tumult. A small number of attendees sporadically began to take the shortcut to the best exits by jumping the grandstand railings and running across the field of play. The security force was too small to have much impact on stopping the phenomena.

The officiating umpire halted play each time a rogue spectator made a dash across the field, and each time, the crowd *booed* with an enthusiasm that was greater than the time before. There must have been a lot of single tickets sold because there was a constant flow of one or two people at a time continuing to run across the field. Some of the runners undoubtedly had a warped sense of humor and ran onto the field to further agitate the crowd. As this continued, the noise level from the boos reached a deafening pitch.

Suddenly, with undetermined motive, a swarm of people standing outside the outfield ropes raced onto the field. Soon thereafter, a thousand people had taken their places in all areas of the grounds of play. Seat cushions and other personal objects were flying onto the infield en masse. So voluminous were the items finding their way onto the field that, soon after, cushions were flying from the infield back into the grandstands. Thinking that things were beginning to get out of hand, the umpire declared the game a forfeit. The Phillies were deemed the victors. Giants President John Brush was nowhere to be found.

Reach snidely spoke. "That's some show you New Yorkers put on for Opening Day! Y'all must think we're pretty dull in Philly!"

"This has never happened here before as far as I know," Mills shouted to have his voice heard above the noise of the crowd.

Spalding noted in a loud voice, "Absolutely correct, Mr. Mills. Trust me, I know. There has never been an Opening Day forfeit in the history of the major leagues—anywhere!"

Sullivan half-heartedly inquired, "Do you think we should stay here?"

Mills chimed in, "Remaining close to the backstop is the safest place we can be. Trust me. I too know this for a fact. Watch out for bottles!"

Spalding leaned toward Sullivan and asked, "Do you know where we'll all be meeting after the game?"

"I was hoping you'd know," Sullivan stated.

Mills reached into his pocket and pulled out a key. "As if treating us to his seats for a most memorable afternoon wasn't enough, Mr. Brush has also made a conference room available for the four of us to use."

"Better make that three," Reach called out. "I know a few veteran players on the Phillies, and after today's turn of events, I'd love to hear their take on today's reception. I'll trust you three to conclude."

As Reach shuffled by the three men, he said, "A pleasure, James. Love your tan, Al." Handing Mills his business card, Reach said, "Always a good time, Abe. Please express my compliments to Mr. Brush, and do let him know that if there's anything his team might need in the way of quality equipment or throwable objects not to hesitate to contact me. Ciao, gentlemen."

Reach joined the moving hordes headed up the aisle toward the exits.

A moment later, Mills led the other two men up the aisle as they made their way in the direction of the clubhouse. As they passed the clubhouse entrance, John McGraw, team manager for the Giants, came shooting out the door. Spotting Mills and Spalding, McGraw walked up to the three sports figures and said, "None of you saw me. There'll be more reporters than flies on shit, so I'm taking my leave. I need some time to come up with a few witticisms. You have the conference room for as long as you need, but should you prefer, feel free to use my office as an alternative."

As McGraw began quickly threading his way down the hall toward the teams' exit, Mills shouted, "Thanks all the same, John."

With back turned, McGraw waved as he walked away.

Mills walked up to a door and placed his key into the lock, turned to Sullivan, and said, "Like I said before, I still have pull in your world!"

Upon opening the door, the three sports executives entered the room. The room was tiny, more resembling a walk-in closet than a conference room. Except for a few coat hooks and coat hangers, the freshly painted walls were devoid of all else. A small table in the corner had a linen cloth with a Giants emblem and colors draped over it. The table was crammed with a small vase holding four red carnations, bowls containing sauerkraut and other condiments, a pitcher of ice water, two domed platters, an ice bucket containing three bottles of beer, and a set of four glasses, paper plates, silverware, and brown paper napkins. A monogrammed note card with a New York Giants emblem was wedged between the flowers. On the card was a preprinted message that read, "Compliments of President John T. Brush."

Sullivan was first to shed his outer wear and went to the food table. Upon removing the domes on the platters, he discovered a stack of sausage sandwiches on one of the trays, with the other containing four cupcakes along with a selection of fresh handily cut vegetables. Sullivan loaded his plate, poured a drink of water, and placed his supper at the miniature conference table where he took his place. The other two followed suit and were soon seated also.

Mills said, "I'd rather be in here than McGraw's office with the sports reporters swarming around like hornets. We three are all known, and I'm not in the mood to answer their questions."

Spalding added, "I have no need to see McGraw's desk memorabilia."

"I'm good too," Sullivan responded between bites.

Spalding pulled a small news clipping out of his inner suit coat pocket and said, "Mary's obituary from the March 13 issue of the *Brooklyn Daily Eagle*." He recited, "Here's the entire article. It gives her name, when she died in Washington, DC, that she was born to a Baltimore attorney, and lists the accomplishments of the General. That's it."

"Disgraceful," commented Mills as he pulled a slightly larger clipping from the same day's issue of the *New York Times*.

Spalding observed, "With all due respect to Mary, I see that great minds think alike."

"Such a shame," commented Mills. "James, were you aware that Mrs. Doubleday passed away last month?"

As Sullivan continued eating, he briefly looked up and said, "I was aware. AG told me."

Mills opened, "Other than the very sad note on Mary's passing, what's new on the committee's efforts?"

Spalding and Sullivan briefly looked up. Neither man responded.

Mills inquired, "Nothing?"

"Nothing of consequence," Sullivan offered. "We went to Cooperstown. It would have almost been quicker to take the train to Denver. Quite isolated but a pretty little place."

Mills wondered, "Did you learn anything while there?"

"Nope," Sullivan replied. "They didn't know much at the village office other than seeing some of the witnesses Mr. Graves had mentioned and informing me that they had either died or were no longer in the area. The staff at the *Freeman's Journal* didn't have much more to say. They were all quite busy at the time."

Mills pleaded, "What then do we have, James?"

"Nothing except to pick an option or come up with a new explanation. There's the solution I offered over a year ago—the baseball-evolved theory—versus the story that Graves witnessed the invention of baseball by Abner Doubleday at Cooperstown in what would best be in the year 1839."

Mills looked over at Spalding. "AG?"

"You know my thoughts, Abe," Spalding said. "If I had a vote, it would be for Cooperstown. It's an ideal American setting."

Mills addressed Sullivan. "How strongly do you feel about your solution?"

Sullivan asserted, "It's the option I prefer. It's the safe way out of this matter, and it meets everyone's objectives."

The trio briefly focused on their food and drink.

Mills stated, "If we opt for backing Graves's story, it could be our undoing, friends."

"I have no issue with this," Spalding remarked. "If the story does not somehow *hold water*, no one would likely ever be the wiser. I know the people of Cooperstown won't take exception with any of this. It gives them something to take pride in—more than having an author born there or a General that briefly lived in that place. They might even make a few bucks from selling souvenirs."

"I'm not sold on it," Mills asserted. "It isn't the villagers I take exception with—it's everyone else!"

"The biggest uncertainty was Mary Doubleday," Spalding pointed out. "May her lovely soul rest in peace. She might have backed us on this anyway. Unfortunately, it's too late to know now."

"I only hope the dear woman won't be turning over in her grave at high speeds," Mills lamented. "She may be revving up at this moment."

"For you *believers*," Spalding predicted, "she'll be smiling down upon all of us. Besides, if the Graves story is not true, it would begin to even the score for all that credit the General deserved yet never received."

The room was anything but soundproof, and the three could hear the ruckus in the locker room on the other side of the inner wall. A body slammed against the wall. The loud *thud* was subsequently followed with a groan of pain.

"Jocks," Mills boasted.

"Professionals," Sullivan jested.

"Right," Mills commented sarcastically. "Men, we have little need to defer any longer. It's decision time. James, there's one issue I have with your evolution theory. I am not suggesting anything by this, but frankly, it feels like an admittance of failure. That, after two and a half years, we didn't find a thing despite our best efforts and all this time."

"That's the down side," Sullivan conceded.

There was a lengthy pause that seemed like several minutes.

Sullivan proposed, "I wish to make one request. Hopefully, neither of you will think me the worse for this, but I see no need for me to officially sign and approve the final report. After all, I see my function as having been the compiler of information and the coordinator of what we received—not so much as a baseball historian."

Mills listened and changed the subject. "Not in the same vein as James, I hesitate to use the name of Mills Commission as you originally suggested, AG. There are others involved with more prominence than yours truly. We need another name that sounds more official. More important. Catchier."

"I had thought on that but didn't want to take away your glory," Spalding admitted, adding, "Let's not forget we still need someone designated to head the committee."

"There's still time for that," Mills replied. "Any ideas on the committee's name?"

Spalding replied, "Let's continue along the lines of where James has been leading us, maybe the Special Baseball Commission."

"I have no problem with that," Mills responded, "if you don't, James."

This time, Sullivan pulled two pieces of another news article out of the inner pocket of his suit coat. The first of the two pieces was a full double-column clipping from the front page of the June 5, 1906, issue of the *Baltimore Sun*. "May I assume you two know that Senator Gorman passed away nearly a year ago?"

"I'm aware," Mills acknowledged. "I previously mentioned it to James. You might recall, AG, that you mentioned it to me some months back. I haven't seen the article that you're holding though."

Handing Mills the article, Spalding stated, "It's yours."

"In view of what Mr. Sullivan said earlier and with which I have appreciation for, we have a total of four other members whose signatures will be required. As you previously stated, Abe, I won't be signing the news release as a member."

"I suddenly feel all alone," Mills lamented.

"We'll be behind you every step of the way," Spalding joked. "Throw an acknowledgment for me into the final report. I'd like that, and you won't feel so alone any longer."

Mills inquired, "Be there anything else we need to discuss at this time?"

"Not from me," Spalding replied.

"Good," Mills said. "And you can sell the Graves story to the committee?"

Spalding exclaimed, "They'll each lecture me on the importance of truth and then sign the attestation."

Mills kiddingly posed the question of Spalding. "No fear of a curse being placed on your beloved Cubs?"

"With the preseason trades the Cubs made, they're a *shoo-in* to win it all this year," Spalding boasted. "Mark my words."

Mills continued the jab. "And the seasons thereafter?"

Spalding retorted, "Dynasties may fall apart in China, but not in baseball. We're doing this the American way. Barring any dismantling of the team which the newly named Cubs supporters would never stand for, the Cubs will win more than their share of championships long after the year's 1908 season has come and gone."

Mills preached, "May the good Lord have mercy on our souls, for we may not know what we have wrought."

The three men stood, faced one another, placed their hands in the center of their huddle in unity, and as one offered the words, "For America", they all exuberantly declared, "For America!"

* * *

On October 12 of that year, Sullivan issued a letter on Amateur Athletic Union letterhead to Mills and the other committee members. The letter was accompanied by what Sullivan stated as being relevant evidence that he was "practically finished...collecting all the information possible," solicited additional member input, recommended acceptance of the Doubleday/Cooperstown theory, requested each member to expediently perform a review of the evidence with a prompt reply, and mentioned that it would then be determined whether or not a final meeting would be necessary.

* * *

The 1907 baseball season came and went. Detroit won the American League pennant but lost to the Cubs in the World Series by a tally of four wins to none. The Special Baseball Commission's findings, dated December 30, 1907, was issued in early 1908. That would be the last time the Cubs would win a World Series for more than a century.

In December of 1907, the same month the commission report was dated, eighty-three-year-old Henry Chadwick would be hit by a car. From there, Chadwick would enter a period of declining health. Once the commission's findings became known in 1908, Chadwick authored an article in the March issue of *Spalding's Baseball Guide*. Spalding followed suit and published the commission's report at the beginning of April when the same monthly publication was produced in the following month. The report is reproduced on the pages that follow. The article included the esteemed names that membered the commission. Later that month, on April 20, Henry Chadwick passed away at the age of eighty-three.

Spalding had the last say between the two men. Some years later, he would make an unsuccessful bid to become US senator representing the state of California. Albert Goodwill Spalding, the man anointed by the National Baseball Hall of Fame as the *Father of Baseball*, passed away in San Diego, California, on September 9, 1915, one week after his sixty-fifth birthday. For such a short life, he had quite a positive impact on the sport of baseball—truly a *giant* of the game.

Abner Graves lived for several years thereafter. His later years were spent with his second wife, Minnie, in a nice-looking brick home located in Denver. Minnie was forty-two years his junior. When Graves turned ninety years old on February 27, 1924, Minnie was forty-eight years old. Four months after his birthday, Graves and Minnie were engaged in a heated argument over a deed of property. As the *Denver Post* reported it, Graves, who was wheelchair-bound, shot Minnie with his shotgun and mortally wounded her. The authorities arrived in time to hear some of Minnie's final words. Minnie stated that she forgave her husband for what he had done. Graves was tried for murder in the first degree. He was found to be innocent by reason of insanity. Graves was thereafter confined to an insane asylum for the six remaining years of his life.

Mills lived for more than a score of years after rendering his final decision. Mills died less than two months before the stock market crash of 1929 and just short of a decade prior to the publication of a definitive article that appeared in a New York City Public Library Bulletin, written by a librarian that would greatly challenge the commission's decision. Abraham G. Mills died in Falmouth, Massachusetts, on August 26, 1929.

The story surrounding the tactics, deceptions, importance, and outcome of the debate over the Doubleday myth was far from over.

* * *

FINAL DECISION OF THE SPECIAL BASE BALL COMMISSION

New York, December 30, 1907

MR. JAMES E. SULLIVAN, Secretary, Special Base Ball Commission
21 Warren St., New York City

DEAR SULLIVAN:

On my earliest opportunity, after my recent return from Europe, I read—and read with much interest—the considerable mass of testimony bearing on the origin of Base Ball which you sent to my office address during my absence. I cannot say that I find myself in accord with those who urge the American origin of the game as against its English origin as contended for by Mr. Chadwick, on "patriotic ground." In my opinion we owe much to our Anglo-Saxon kinsmen for their example which we have too tardily followed in fostering healthful field sports generally, and if the fact could be established by evidence that our national game, "Base Ball," was devised in England, I do not think that it would be any less admirable nor welcome on that account. As a matter of fact, the game of ball which I have always regarded as the distinctive English game, i.e., cricket, was brought to this country and had a respectable following here, which it has since maintained, long before any game of ball resembling our national game was played anywhere! Indeed, the earliest field sport that I remember was a game of cricket, played on an open field near Jamaica, L.I., where I was then attending school. Then, and ever since, I have heard cricket spoken of as the essentially English game, and, until my perusal of this testimony, my own belief had been that our game of Base Ball, substantially as played to-day, originated with the Knickerbocker club of New York, and it was frequently referred to as the "New York Ball Game."

As I have stated, my belief had been that our "National Game of Base Ball" originated with the Knickerbocker club, organized in New York in 1845, and which club published certain elementary rules in that year; but, in the interesting and pertinent testimony for which we are indebted to Mr. AG Spalding, appears a circumstantial statement by a reputable gentleman, according to which the first known diagram of the diamond, indicating positions for the players, was drawn by Abner Doubleday in Cooperstown, N.Y., in 1839. Abner Doubleday subsequently graduated from West Point and entered the regular army, where, as Captain of Artillery, he sighted the first gun fired on the Union side (at Fort Sumter) in the Civil War. Later, still, as Major General, he was in command of the Union army at the close of the first day's fight in the bat-

tle of Gettysburg, and he died full of honors at Mendham, N.J., in 1893. It happened that he and I were members of the same veteran military organization—the crack Grand Army Post (Lafayette), and the duty devolved upon me, as Commander of that organization, to have charge of his obsequies, and to command the veteran military escort which served as guard of honor when his body lay in state, January 30, 1893, in the New York City Hall, prior to his internment in Arlington.

In the days when Abner Doubleday attended school in Cooperstown, it was a common thing for two dozen or more of school boys to join in a game of ball. Doubtless, as in my later experience, collisions between players in attempting to catch the batted ball were frequent, and injury due to this cause, or to the practice of putting out the runner by hitting him with the ball, often occurred.

I can well understand how the orderly mind of the embryo West Pointer would devise a scheme for limiting the contestants on each side and allotting them to field positions, each with a certain amount of territory; also substituting the existing method of putting out the base runner for the old one of "plugging" him with the ball.

True, it appears from the statement that Doubleday provided for eleven men on a side instead of nine, stationing the two extra men between first and second, and second and third bases, but this is a minor detail, and, indeed, I have played, and doubtless other old players have, repeatedly with eleven on a side, placed almost identically indicated by Doubleday's diagram, although it is true we so played after the number on each side was fixed at nine, simply to admit to the game an additional number of those who wished to take part in it.

I am also much interested in the statement made by Mr. Curry, of the pioneer Knickerbocker club, and confirmed by Mr. Tassie, of the famous old Atlantic club of Brooklyn, that a diagram, showing the ball field laid out substantially as it is today, was brought to the field one afternoon by a Mr. Wadsworth. Mr. Curry says "the plan caused a great deal of talk, but, finally, we agreed to try it." While he is not quoted as adding that they did both try and adopt it, it is apparent that such was the fact; as, from that day to this, the scheme of the game as described by Mr. Curry has been continued with only slight variations in detail. It should be borne in mind that Mr. Curry was the first President of the old Knickerbocker club, and participated in drafting the first published rules of the game.

It is possible that a connection more or less direct can be traced between the diagram by Doubleday in 1839 and that presented to the Knickerbocker club by Wadsworth in 1845, or thereabouts, and I wrote several days ago for certain data bearing on this point, but as it has not yet come to hand I have decided to delay no longer sending in the kind of paper your letter calls for, promising to furnish you the indicated data when I obtain it, whatever it may be.

My deductions from the testimony submitted are:

First: That "Base Ball" had its origin in the United States.

Second: That the first scheme for playing it, according to the best evidence obtainable to date, was devised by Abner Doubleday at Cooperstown, N.Y., in 1839.

Very truly yours,
A.G. Mills

We, the undersigned members of the Special Base Ball Commission, unanimously agree with the decision expressed and outlined in Mr. AG Mills' letter of December 30.

(Signed)   *Morgan G. Bulkeley*
Nicholas E. Young
Al Reach
George Wright

* * *

So nigh is grandeur to our dust,
So near is God to man,
When duty whispers low, "Thou must,"
The youth whispers, "I can."

—Ralph Waldo Emerson

CHAPTER 10

The Librarian

Spring 1910—South Shields, United Kingdom

In the northeast corner of England, a stone's throw from Scotland
lies the medieval city of South Shields, Durham. London is 450 kilometers to the south; Edinburgh, Scotland, is less than half that distance to the north. Bordered by the great North Sea to the east, the
city's local economy is self-sustaining and diverse. Major industries
include coal and other mining activity, shipbuilding, the merchant
trade, glass manufacturing, the fishing industry, and services in support of its 75,000 residents. The local tramway system installed a
couple of years ago enables people of limited means to move freely
throughout the city. The main business district is heavily built up,
and its wide sidewalks are filled during the day with businessmen,
laborers, mothers with children or baby carriages, and a rainbow of
others from all stations. South Shields, a jaunt away from any large
cities, is a vibrant working-class place.

A popular spot for couples to pass the time is to sit on benches
placed where the mouth of the River Tyne opens up onto the expansive beaches and white cliffs along the waters' edge of the North Sea.

Robert Henderson and Lucy Lawson are of the same age, twenty-one years, and had grown up together in South Shields. Like many other young couples, they frequently share moments at this spot. Presently, they are sitting on a bench watching a pair of tugboats pull a large ocean vessel from the sea—up the center of the River Tyne channel destined for repairs at the boatyards complex one kilometer away.

Henderson exclaimed, "I'll never tire of this, Lucy!" Lawson remained quiet, and Henderson continued, "And what a day! It all seems so perfect! Doesn't it?"

Lawson replied, "Robert, something's on your mind. What is it?"

Henderson asked, "Why do you continually ask that question?"

"I don't," Lawson responded. "I ask the question sometimes, and every time I do, I'm glad I did."

Henderson insisted, "Nothing is the matter. Should there be?"

Lawson replied, "You should know by now that you can't hide anything from me without eventually being found out. You've been making small talk. That's unlike you. Yesterday, you needed to go to King Street. Your mum told me you were gone for some time and said it was because you went to Mac Black's."

Henderson wondered, "What's wrong with that?"

KING STREET SOUTH SHIELDS LOOKING EAST.

"You spent a long time in that place," Lawson answered. "You don't need any clothes, and you don't have the money to buy nice clothes even if you needed them."

Henderson didn't have a comeback. Lawson continued, "What's on your brilliant mind, Robert? I deserve to know—now!"

Henderson took Lawson's hand. "I've been meaning to tell you. I've decided to go to America."

Lawson was silent.

He added, "It's something I must do."

After more silence, he continued, "I'm leaving soon." With a deep breath, Robert stated, "As soon as I'm settled, I'll come back for you. I promise! That is—if you'll have me."

Lawson was stunned. "When did you come up with this idea?"

"I've been thinking about it for years. You and everyone who understands me know I have an unbridled adoration for books. You've heard my mother call my reading 'an obsession'—and admittedly, it is! I want my life to revolve around two things: a home with you and working with books, journals—items written of knowledge and fact."

Lawson rhetorically asked, "I have known in my heart that your future would involve an occupation with books. Although that is *fait accompli*, what does that have to do with the need to go to America? If you want to work near or with books, the surrounding kingdom has more bookstores, libraries, publishers, and archives than you can count." Pointing southerly towards London, Lawson added, "And the largest city in the world is in that direction. There are more opportunities there than you could ever hope to have anywhere else."

Lawson shook her head in frustration and continued to express her annoyance. "I understand why your future may not be here in South Shields, though I love it so. But America? There's so much for you in England and Scotland. Why do you feel so drawn to America? The English ways are already established and of greater sophistication."

"That's the problem," Henderson retorted. "All the institutions in England that work with books were organized long ago. They're stagnant. They're outdated. Most every library in this country is inadequate, and nothing is being done about any of it. People stay in jobs for a lifetime. I will never have any opportunities to do something of consequence if I stay here. I wouldn't even know where to begin if I stayed here."

"You know the ways of the Americans even less," Lawson noted. "Do you think you know where you will go once you get there?"

"New York City," Henderson responded.

"When do you plan on leaving?"

"Soon."

"How soon?"

"Next week."

Lawson declared, "Next week! Why the rush? Why next week?"

"I have an immediate opportunity," Henderson boasted.

Lawson slowly shook her head. "We can get to that later—if there is a later. First, what is your grand plan for us?"

"I will come back for you. We'll have a church wedding here."

Lawson retorted, "When will that be?"

"In a year," Henderson replied. "No more than two?"

"So then, you are saying," Lawson remarked, "you expect for me to wait for you for some long, indefinite amount of time. Am I correct?"

Henderson stated, "I love you. I love you! I'll miss you every day. Please know I will want to get back with you as soon as possible."

"Have you asked," Lawson wondered, "whether I want to leave my family and friends and everything I know and enjoy to go thousands of kilometers away from here to a foreign land?"

Henderson remained silent. Lawson continued, "Does your mother know what you're thinking?"

"Heavens, no!" Henderson went on, "I wanted to tell you first. I felt she would make a bigger thing about this than you would. I was hoping that you might back me up on the plan."

"Plan? Robert! This thing is so messed up that *the messed up* is messed up! You're barely making it here in South Shields on your own! How do you intend on making ends meet in America? You're from a little place in England that no one over there has ever heard of. You will be in a giant city—friendless, jobless, with no contacts, no money, and very little experience of working! Further, I still don't see why you feel the need to travel so far to find what you wish to do in life!"

"You should see what I plan," Henderson said excitedly. "We need to go to my mother's house. Please come with me right now!"

"Your mother's house," Lawson exclaimed. "Do you rather mean back to your place?"

"The place where I'm living is a shoebox," Henderson responded. "I had to keep what I want to show you at my mother's place. She allows me to keep things in my old room there. Please let me show you! Please!"

Lawson replied, "I need some quiet time alone now! Without any money, I still don't know how you think you can get there—much less survive if you make it to America!"

Henderson pointed to the dark-blue waters of the sea. "It's that way, and I've already made arrangements."

"That way," Lawson commented. "Right. The only ocean steamers we ever see around here are the ones being towed by tugboats up the river to the boatyards. Besides, what arrangements? With what money?"

Henderson said, "I'll work my way across on a freighter."

Lawson commented, "Robert William! You don't know the first thing about sailing! Even if you did, those crusty sailors will have your skinny bones rattling the moment you step on board!"

"I've already been assigned to a ship. The *Arabic*! It's bound for New York Harbor. It's almost 200 meters in length! She's an eight-year-old beauty! I've seen pictures of her."

Lawson stood up abruptly, and Henderson followed suit.

"What? How did you get the job," Lawson interrogated, "if I may dare to inquire?"

"I've recently read a great deal about ocean ships," Henderson boasted, "and I had an interview with the shipping line the other day. The man in charge asked me several how-to questions, and I knew the answers to even the most complicated ones. I did exaggerate a bit by saying I've worked on a ship in the past. At the end of the interview, they told me that my level of experience is perfect for the voyage! The man in charge reserves the company's right to assign me to any task he deems appropriate. That's fine by me. And, yes, I've heard at least as many sailor stories as you. I assure you—I can take whatever they dish out."

Lawson again shook her head to clear the cobwebs. "How are you going to get a job—any job—in that metropolis?"

"I have that problem solved," Henderson boasted while pulling an envelope out of his pants pocket. "I've been carrying this letter around for weeks, waiting for the right time to tell you the good news. It is the answer to both of your questions."

Lawson inquired, "And the solution to all this is contained in that envelope? It must be some letter! What is it?"

"It's a job offer," Henderson responded.

"You're telling me," Lawson began, "that a twenty-one-year-old who has little job experience and has never set foot outside of Great Britain has an offer for a job in New York City?"

Lawson extended her arm toward the letter with palm upright. "The time to show me this was a while ago," she said as she took the letter Henderson just handed her. Lawson began reading the document.

Henderson remained silent.

Lawson inquired, "Is the Astor Library a medical library?"

"No," replied Henderson. A respectful smile quickly came over his face when he realized why Lawson had asked the question. "The man who signed the letter is a surgeon who happens to be a brilliant librarian! Doctor John Shaw Billings. He has extensive experience with building libraries, having worked with the wealthy American financier Carnegie who built numerous libraries in North America as well as some over here."

"I know about him," Lawson stated. "There's a Carnegie library I've been to a hundred and fifty kilometers due south of here in Leeds."

"Dr. Billings is also an architect!" Henderson chuckled as Lawson patiently gazed at him, and thus the young man continued, "The Astor is like a regular library, except it isn't a lending library. It's for reference only. It's a wonderful library, though, and people can use the library's services at no charge."

"I don't see it," Lawson began. "I don't understand why you think this Astor Library is such a special place to begin your career."

"The Astor," Henderson enthused, "is great, but it's merely a stepping stone. It will soon be merged into an entirely new library destined to be one of the great libraries of the world. That library will be the New York Public Library." Lawson listened patiently, and Henderson continued, "There's a wealthy foundation called the Tilden Trust that is holding a vast sum of money earmarked for library-type expenditures in New York City. The Trust is joining with the Astor Library and another one, the Lenox, to create one world-class library in Manhattan." Henderson continued his momentum, "What a way to get in on the ground floor of a once-in-a-lifetime opportunity! What better place to learn my craft? And besides, if—"

Lawson finished reading and interrupted, "Robert, the letter doesn't say he's making an offer to hire you. It merely says *as a matter of policy, the library does not make offers of employment without first conducting an in-person interview.*'"

As Lawson handed the letter back to Henderson, she added, "He's not telling you that you have a job or even an interview. The man at the top—at the top, mind you—is telling you why he elected *not* to hire you."

"Please, Lucy! We have to go to my mum's house," Henderson insisted. "You won't be so crazy after I show you what I have for you to see."

Lawson asked sarcastically, "I'm the crazy one?"

Henderson took Lawson by the hand and, initially meeting with some resistance, began leading her back toward town at a quickening pace.

"Robert, slow down," Lawson ordered. "I don't compete in speed walking like you do."

"You set the pace, my love," Henderson agreed.

After the brief walk, the couple arrived at the place where Henderson's parents lived. Being the afternoon, only Henderson's mother was home.

As they entered the house, Henderson called out, "Mum, it's only me and Lucy."

Henderson's mother replied with a voice that could be heard from another part of the house, "Hello, Lucy. Lucy, be a dear and make sure Robert doesn't leave things around the house."

"Don't worry, Mum," Henderson remarked. "We'll be in my room."

Henderson escorted Lawson to his room and closed the door. His bedroom was furnished with a twin-size bed with hardly a wrinkle on the sheets, a small desk loaded with books and magazines on its surface, two overstuffed bookshelves, and a dresser bureau. He began furiously pulling magazines and old newspapers off his desk and out of the bookshelves and began laying one publication after another, most having been published in the United States, methodically on to his bed. He then pulled out two files of periodicals clipped from various newspapers and magazines and laid them on the bed also.

Henderson's mother entered the hallway leading toward the bedroom. Noticing the bedroom door was closed, she walked up to the room and, without knocking, opened the door. His mother observed that the bed had piles of magazines spread across the sheets.

Henderson asked, "What is it, Mother?"

"Nothing, dear," his mother replied as she rolled her eyes and closed the door and left.

Every magazine had pieces of paper serving as bookmarks placed within. He would grab one publication after the other to have Lawson look at. The articles within the files were all labelled as to source and date. He first grabbed the news clippings.

"Look at this," Henderson requested. "It's from page 18 of the *Hartford Courant*'s January 21, 1908, issue. It says,

> *'It may astonish some readers to learn that there are books and pamphlets in the Astor Library which can be found nowhere else...'"*

"It lists all these departments," he said as he pointed to the article, "categorized by language or national source. In this one department, it says, '*In the Print Department there are upward of 60,000 different subjects...*'

"That's just one department in one of the libraries that are being consolidated into the future city library!"

Henderson took out two more articles. "These are both from *The New York Times*. This one is a year old. It's from page 48 of the March 28, 1909, issue. This piece is titled 'Greatest of Public Libraries.' It discusses massive costs and effort. Look here where it talks about the marble quarried for construction. It says *120,000 tons were rejected before the selection of 30,000 tons was made.* The article discusses the process of awarding construction contracts back in 1897 when all this began! The construction of this incredible library has been going on for the majority of our lifetimes! I want...no! I need to be settled and in place before the doors open to the public. I want to be a part of this when it opens. I need to be a part of this as it all comes together!"

Lawson inquired, "How did you find this on page 48? Where did you find the time? Where was I?"

"You were most likely sleeping," Henderson replied. "I often read by lantern light."

"What a busy little bee you are," Lawson exclaimed.

Henderson continued, "This article is from the Sunday edition of the paper dated June 23, 1907. It says here," as he pointed to the applicable part of the clipping, "*When the new system is in complete working order, with thirty-nine more branches open to the public...*' Thirty-nine new branches! New! Do you have any idea of the transformation that is going on? It is huge!"

"It says *page 54* and was issued back in 1907," Lawson observed. "Have you been finding and collecting all these articles for all this time without making a peep?"

"Of course," Henderson admitted. "I'm not going to say anything if it seems doubtful that I could ever do it—but this is important to me!"

Lawson laughed. "Do tell!"

Picking up a magazine, the lad said, "Look at this artist's renderings once the building is complete. Isn't it beautiful? The building looks like a temple for the gods—dedicated to books! It's two blocks wide! That grandiose, beautiful building has been under construction for a decade! The main branch is on Fifth Avenue too! Fifth Avenue. New York City! America! Even your aunt's maid has heard of Fifth Avenue!"

Lawson began flipping through some of the publications. Beneath a *National Geographic* and a *Saturday Evening Post* was a copy of the *Ladies' Home Journal*. Lucy held the magazine up and inquired, "What do you need with this?"

"More related information," Henderson responded. Continuing in a sarcastic tone, "In America, even women like to read!"

"Funny little boy," Lawson retorted. "Look, Robert, I can see that you've done your research, and I've seen quite enough already! This is obviously what you want. I would never stand in the way of that. My next question is a simple one."

"I'm ready when you are," Henderson happily jested.

"Do you intend on asking me to marry you?"

"That's the general idea," Henderson replied, "if you'll have me."

Lawson stood directly facing Henderson, grabbed his hands with hers, and stared into his eyes. "At such time that you make your proposal, dear sir, you better do it properly—and it will need to be very, very soon if you expect me to wait for you! All that, of course, is based on the premise that I say *yes* to you."

Henderson grabbed Lawson and hugged and kissed her. "I will! I will!"

Lawson exclaimed, "An agreement to propose to me. My, that was so much easier than I could have imagined! Now, how do you intend on handling this American matter with your mom?"

"That one is not so easy! Allow me some time to think about it," Henderson requested.

"Oh no, you don't," demanded Lawson. "I wanted to know how you were to explain it—not when. When is today, once we're finished!"

Henderson thought for a moment. "I don't like it, but I'll do it if I must. I will, of course, need you to back me up."

"I'll be here to make certain you do what you say you will," Lucy said. "But, you and you, alone, shall find the words to fend for yourself."

"I wonder," Henderson quipped, "whether New Yorkers are tough enough to handle a girl like you."

"Don't you worry about those New Yorkers. You need only concern yourself with you and us," Lawson returned. "You, us, and our future family, Robert. That is where I suggest you focus what little attention you give to other than your livelihood, or one of the speed-walking competitions you enter so frequently to add to your already-large trophy collection."

"They don't have that sport in America," Henderson lamented.

"Then, you will bring the sport to the Americans," Lawson suggested, "just as others before you taught them cricket so they could modify it to their own peculiar liking."

Henderson's mother was at the outside of his bedroom door; however, this time, she knocked. Lawson said to Henderson, "Do it now, my love."

Henderson called out, "Yes, Mum. Come in."

Henderson's mother asked, "Would you children like to stay for the evening meal?"

"Mother," Henderson began, "I have something much more important to discuss with you."

Henderson's mother, looking mildly concerned, asked, "What is it, child?"

Henderson's mind went momentarily blank.

His mother continued, "Robert!"

Henderson next embarked on the journey to explain the situation to his mother as best he could while Lawson presided over the confession.

Though Henderson's mother was clearly worried and wondering what was in store for Lawson, his mom wished him the best. Upon Lawson leaving for her home, Henderson pleased his mother by informing her that he would soon propose to Lawson. On the next day, Henderson asked Lawson to marry him, and she accepted, conditionally. Henderson left port on the *Arabic* during the following week heading across the Atlantic, bound for the port and city of New York. While performing his duties as a deckhand, the many hours of mopping the deck and during his time off, Henderson had the opportunity to think and plan for what he must do next. The first big step was in progress. He was headed for America.

* * *

May 2, 1910—New York City, New York

On the first morning after his arrival in the United States, Henderson dressed up in his English tweed suit jacket and made his way through Midtown Manhattan to the Astor Library. Upon entering the building, he approached a security guard, or rather, the guard approached him.

Henderson pulled the letter out of his pocket so that the security officer could see that the letterhead of the document was officially from the library. "I arrived from England yesterday to fulfill the invitation of Dr. Billings. Would you mind directing me to his office?"

"Do you have an appointment scheduled, sir?" the guard asked skeptically of the twenty-year-old.

"Yes. I came here on his invitation," Henderson responded.

The guard drew a clipboard from within his podium. "What is your name?"

"Robert W. Henderson."

The watchman scanned the top page of his group of papers from top to bottom. "I don't see your name on today's list. Are you certain your appointment is for today?"

"It's an open invitation," Henderson replied. "He will see me. I can assure you of that!"

"Without having your name on the list," the security man began, "I am not allowed to permit you to go further."

Waving the letter in front of the guard, Henderson stated, "This letter signed by Dr. Billings specifically invites me to stop by. I have just sailed the Atlantic to meet with him."

The sentry was skeptical of such a young man being invited to have an audience with Dr. Billings. "May I see the letter, please?"

"This letter is of an extremely personal nature," Henderson asserted. Holding out the letter once again, Henderson covered the text with his hand and exposed the letterhead, Henderson's name, the introduction, and the signature of Dr. Billings. "I don't see any harm in showing you that the letter is addressed to me personally and signed by Dr. Billings. It will serve both of us well to promptly guide me to his office. I have identification if you wish to see it."

"This is out of the ordinary," the guard began. "Why don't I do this? I'll go to his office and inquire? It will take a few minutes though, so please be comfortable until my return."

Henderson responded, "My time is limited. I do have other appointments after this. May I come with you? It will save both of us some time."

The security officer looked at Henderson's extremely thin physique and tweed jacket. "I don't see a problem with that. Please follow me."

The two men walked through the lobby and a pair of hallways to arrive at a set of heavy double doors. The guard grabbed the brass handle, pulled one of the doors open, and waved Henderson in to an exquisite office suite. A fashionable lady of conservative dress was sitting behind a large desk in the common area outside four offices.

As the woman looked up, the guard said, "Ma'am, this man says he has a personal invitation from Dr. Billings. He just arrived from England. I saw enough of the invitation to know it appears to be Dr. Billings's signature on the letter. However, the correspondence is said by this gentleman to be very personal, Mr. …"

"Henderson. Robert W."

"That will be all, Sam," the lady said.

"Very good, ma'am." The guard humbly departed.

"Mr. Henderson, may I see the invitation, please."

Henderson said, "It's actually a letter, but it's quite personal, though I can show you parts."

"You needn't worry about the contents, Mr. Henderson." Reaching out and holding her hand outward, the lady continued, "I won't alert the media" was her sarcastic reply. "I am Dr. Billings's personal executive secretary, and Dr. Billings requires I review any such documents."

She pulled out a large silver nameplate with her name and title and placed it on her desk. "Do pardon me, Mr. Henderson. I normally have that big thing on my desk, but there were no meetings scheduled for today, and I appreciate the additional desk space when it isn't needed. Dr. Billings is preparing for a speaking engagement. The letter, please."

Henderson placed the letter in the assistant's hand. She read the letter rapidly yet thoroughly. While she read, the woman remarked, "So you just arrived from crossing the Atlantic?"

"That is correct," Henderson responded.

"Your voyage was a pleasant one, I hope," the lady said.

"You'll never know how much," Henderson stated. "Have you ever traveled to Britain?"

"I don't like the water," the assistant remarked. She then looked up at Henderson. "You say this is an invitation?"

"Well, ma'am, I took it that way," Henderson responded.

After glancing at the letter once more, the woman stood and continued to hold the letter. "Please wait. I won't be but a moment."

The woman opened the nearest office door and, without closing the door, took the letter inside the office and entered into a softly spoken conversation unintelligible to Henderson. She exited the office, closing the door behind her. As she walked toward Henderson, about to speak, the office door opened, and a very distinguished-looking man came out carrying the letter. He walked up to Henderson with a welcoming smile and handed the letter back to its owner.

The man said jovially, "John Billings, sir. I understand you arrived recently from jolly old England."

"I did," Henderson replied.

"Welcome to the Astor Library, Mr. Henderson." In a playful tone, Billings added, "On behalf of the denizens of the City of New York, I would like to welcome you to our island municipality!"

Billings and Henderson shook hands. "Please, Mr. Henderson. Follow me."

As Henderson followed Billings into the office, Henderson began to close the door behind him.

"Please, young man," Billings instructed, "that won't be necessary. Leave the door open."

After ten minutes, Henderson came out of the office, and the door closed behind him.

"No broken bones, I hope," the secretary said.

Henderson was again holding the letter.

Henderson offered, "No! It was a great meeting!"

"I take it, Dr. Billings hired you," the executive secretary said.

Smiling from ear to ear, Henderson replied, "It couldn't have been better! Fastest interview I've ever had—and I got the job!"

The executive secretary was visibly pleased. She laughed and retorted, "Few of Dr. Billings's meetings take long, and many don't have such a happy ending. My congratulations! May I surmise that Dr. Billings shared the details of what you will be doing and when you begin?"

Henderson responded, "He said I start Monday at the standard entry-level rate."

"Did he say where within the library you will be assigned?"

Henderson replied, "Dr. Billings said he reserves the right to assign me to whatever he or his staff *deems appropriate*. I am to report to you at 9:00 AM Monday morning."

The executive secretary again sat down. "I know all I need to, the people I need to speak with, and the questions I must ask. I make only two requests of you, young man."

Henderson was a bit taken aback as to how the woman addressed him just now. There was a brief pause.

"First," the executive secretary began, "ensure you arrive by my desk on Monday morning not a moment later than eight o'clock sharp. You will begin your first day an hour earlier than usual."

Henderson replied, "Yes, ma'am! You said you had *two* requests."

"My second request," the executive secretary responded, "is more of a favor to you. It will serve you well during your future time at the Astor Library. We function as a well-oiled machine here. Trust is something that is assumed—and required. Every employee offers this and expects the same respect in return. Candor with brevity. Do yourself a big favor in your future dealings at the Astor Library—no more embellishments or distortions. When you have some news for me or anyone else around here, tell us what it is—not what you wish it to be."

Henderson uncomfortably smiled and nodded.

"May I ask," Henderson wondered, "what my starting salary will be?"

"Why don't we save the minor details for when you return? Dr. Billings personally hired you. You won't be disappointed. Until Monday, Robert, have a good time enjoying the wonders of our city. There is a lot to do here, but if a place doesn't look inviting, stay out. Welcome to New York, Robert!"

The executive assistant's attention refocused on her work. She began to hurriedly shuffle papers on her desk while Billings called out something unintelligible to Henderson. The assistant then took some papers in her hands, entered Billings's office, and closed the door.

As Henderson was leaving the executive office area, the security guard met him and began to escort Henderson toward the exit.

The security guard inquired, "Will we see you again, sir?"

"Monday slightly before 8:00 AM," Henderson cheerfully replied.

"I see," the guard responded. "Welcome to New York and welcome aboard!"

Upon stepping outside the library onto the pavement, Henderson would reflect on what happened in those offices and thought about the executive assistant's words. *Welcome to New York, Robert!* He was going to have a delightful weekend. His plan was on target. Robert W. Henderson was to be assigned as a book page, but as far as he was concerned, he was a librarian now—and an employee of the prestigious Astor Library!

Never interrupt someone doing
something you said couldn't be done.

—Amelia Earhart

CHAPTER 11

Positioning

*May 24, 1911. Noon hour—Off Fifth
Avenue, Manhattan, New York*

Bryant Park is adjacent to the Fifth Avenue branch of the New York
Public Library. With its thousands of benches, moveable chairs and
tables, the shaded areas and open spaces within the park invite visitors to find a peaceful spot and take a moment to relax amidst the
chaos of Manhattan.

It was noon hour, and a librarian stepped outside the library's
rear exit to find a spot to eat his lunch. He recognized a friend seated
by a small table near the building and walked over. The seated man
spoke first.

"Mr. Lawrence," exclaimed Henderson. "Join me."

"I was hoping…," Lawrence responded.

Lawrence sat down and pulled a banana and a sandwich
wrapped in wax paper out of a brown lunch bag, asking, "How's
things, Robert?"

"No complaints, John," replied Henderson.

"You really like this spot," Lawrence noted as he began eating
his sandwich. "You don't eat lunch often, but I've seen you this time
of day often since we've been trying to get the building ready."

"It's more convenient now that we're no longer at the Astor Library. I've enjoyed observing the construction activity both from here and in the front of the building," Henderson said. "Making sure they didn't mess up the place where I'll be spending a third of the rest of my life. I only wish I'd been able to see the installation of the columns out front."

"I saw that," claimed Lawrence. "That was three years ago—before you joined us at the Astor. It was quite the project!"

"Oh well," Henderson said. "I was there yesterday. That has been my number one objective years before I came to America. How could the day possibly have gone any better!"

Lawrence returned, "Like a dream! Everything went off perfectly. I was three feet from the William Howard Taft! Four feet tops!"

Henderson observed, "President Taft is big—figuratively and literally!"

"You can say that again, friend," Lawrence exclaimed. "You know about the presidential bathtub, right?"

"No," Henderson replied. "Is it gold-plated or something?"

Lawrence laughed. "No! *Big Bill* weighs over 300 pounds. Word is he got stuck in the old White House tub shortly after moving into the residence. Either he or someone ordered him a larger one. Several of the newspapers printed a photo of the new tub with four men sitting in the thing!"

"I didn't know that. It's not the sort of thing that makes the main edition of the *London Times* and *that's* the newspaper where I first read about this place, years ago. Of course," Henderson confessed, "if it had been the president of France, the *Times* would have put the bathtub photo in a space on the front page!"

Lawrence laughed. "I'm sure. Ancient feuds!"

"This morning's paper," Henderson began, "said more than 50,000 people passed through the doors once the ceremonies ended, and I can assure you, by the end of the day, my brain felt like it!"

"My sister came for the dedication and was somewhat disappointed," Lawrence commented. "No one around her saw even a glimpse of the president slipping away from here. Nor did she like that the speeches were held indoors for but a fortunate few. From where I was perched, it looked like the seats were filled with a bunch of bald heads seated next to several *hats of brilliant plumage*. My sister's highlight was watching Governor Dix get into his gasoline carriage. She said it was easily spotted with New York state flags plastered all over the thing."

"I told her it was also difficult for me to tell much of what was going on," admitted Lawrence. "I was assigned to a side reading room. I took a few moments to listen to the president though. From all the campaigning he did, his voice is loud and was easily heard. Unfortunately, I couldn't hear the bishops, the governor, Mayor Gaynor, or anyone else, only that band which was loud enough for my ancestors to tap their feet!"

Henderson listened to Lawrence but did not speak.

"Out of curiosity, Robert," Lawrence asked, "where were you assigned?"

"The front desk," Henderson replied. "I couldn't hear things much better than you could."

"Front desk," Lawrence exclaimed. "You're definitely one of the chosen few, Roberto! Always working hard. Hired by Billings himself."

Henderson, shaking his head, replied, "Not hardly. I do work hard though. I enjoy everything they ask me to do—and I do what I'm told. As for being chosen, aside from yesterday for a moment, I haven't seen Dr. Billings in some time. I haven't broken into his social circle as yet!"

Lawrence gazed over at Henderson.

Holding up a newspaper, Henderson offered, "Here's today's *New York Tribune*, all sixteen pages. Worth every bit of the penny they charge for it!"

Lawrence laughed. "Thanks for the sales pitch, Robert. Just give me the highlights. I need to finish up here and get back to work. Anything in there about us laborer types?"

Henderson exclaimed, "It's a good recap! As for the *worker bees*, only what the president said." Pointing to a place in the article, Henderson stated, "It says how Taft gave credit to the generosity of the benefactors—and then mentioned by name the Astor, Tilden, and Lenox families, as well as to Andrew Carnegie and others. Taft then said 'the real credit should go to *the librarian and the trustees of these various foundations that I would convey my profound felicitations.*'

Lawrence exclaimed, "The librarian! Other than being a vote getter for sure, that should make Dr. Billings strut around for some time to come."

"Well deserved," Henderson commented. "I think we all should take pride in what has been accomplished here."

"It does feel good," Lawrence admitted, "and really strange! This morning, I could hardly believe I was working under the largest vaulted ceiling in the world! The main reading room blows me away. And something else—now we'll have time to date the ladies again."

Henderson chuckled. "You'll have to go looking stag! My lady is waiting for me back in South Shields, England."

"Being assigned to the front desk," commented Lawrence, "is a big deal. You'll be making good money to bring her back here soon enough."

"It'll take time," Henderson confessed. "The cost to set things up for her here is one matter—and the cost of travel for two of us is yet another…and that's assuming we return second-class at best!"

Lawrence balled up the lunch bag with the banana peel and wax paper within it. He hurled the bag dead center into a trash receptacle.

As the two young men stood up from the table and began walking toward the front of the building, Lawrence said, "Doesn't it all seem so strange? We've been working as long and hard and as fast as we could in getting ready for opening the library. All of a sudden, things have shifted to a normal, easy pace."

Henderson exclaimed, "*Easy?* I don't see that yet. Right now, this library has thousands of books and documents that are irretrievable due to being misfiled. It's a mess. The consolidation and move may have gone brilliantly, but the sheer volume…"

Lawrence responded, "How can you say *it's a mess*? The stacks and all look as good as they've ever been at the other libraries."

Henderson stated, "I've been one of the so-called *mushroom people* working beneath the main library. Forget about all the books the patrons can see. You know as well as I, there's eighty miles of subterranean shelving filled with books. Do you have any idea how many books that represents?"

Lawrence admitted, "I'm well aware of the vastness of the storage down below. We put a lot of publications down there!"

"True," said Henderson. "Counting books of all sizes, maps, rare documents, magazines, pamphlets, and all, we must be talking well into the eight digits! That's tens of millions of items! And remember, that's just overflow beyond what the customers see above ground! With everything we've moved, there are enough errors in need of correction that should keep us going for a long time."

As the two entered the front doors of the library, Lawrence noted, "You're going to go far, Robert! Catch ya later!"

* * *

It was nearly one and a half years since the library consolidation was complete—and nearly two and a half years since Henderson left his home in England, but he finally made it back to South Shields. Lucy had waited for him. Thereafter, Henderson would be forever grateful to Lucy for the patience she had exhibited.

The two were married in 1912 during an early October ceremony at the Ecclesiastical church in their hometown. Days later, the Hendersons boarded the RMS *Cedric* bound for America out of Liverpool, England. The famous ship was no longer the largest in the world as it was when originally launched a decade earlier. Nevertheless, the vast size of the ship with its five decks gave some security to its passengers who were sailing while the recent sinking of the *Titanic* was still on people's minds. Traveling with Lucy and as a paying passenger on this trip, the eight-day crossing of the Atlantic was a more pleasant experience for Henderson than the first time he had made the voyage. In fact, it was a most exciting time for the couple—both jointly and severally.

They arrived at Ellis Island on October 26, 1912, and within days found a place to live in the Bronx. Two months later, on Christmas Day in their new home, Lucy baked Robert his first homemade birthday cake in America. This would be their home for several years until they would one day find their dream house elsewhere in the New York City area. It would be slightly more than a year after the couple's arrival in New York before a pleasant turn of events in the couple's lives would motivate the hardworking Robert Henderson to find additional employment to supplement his present income from the New York Public Library.

* * *

The Racquet and Tennis Club was located within blocks of the library's main branch. One summer's morning in 1914, Henderson's superior instructed him to attend *a meeting* at the Racquet and Tennis Club. The meeting was scheduled to begin at 1:00 PM. Upon Henderson's timely arrival at the club, the librarian was greeted by a security guard.

As the guard began to speak, a man seated in a nearby leather chair spotted the slim librarian, stood up, and said, "It's all right, James. Mr. Henderson is here to see me."

"You are Mr. Henderson, I presume," the man said.

"I am," Henderson replied. "Are you Mr. Halsey?"

"I am, sir," Halsey responded. The two men shook hands. "It is a pleasure to meet you! Please follow me. I have a quiet little spot picked out so that we might chat."

Henderson was quite puzzled. He had never been inside such an elegant club. Would this be the *meeting*? Although men standing or seated within the lobby area were in conversation, the place had a sense of silence. You could not hear a sound. Halsey and Henderson entered a small but finely appointed conference room and sat down in two chairs facing one another.

"You look befuddled," Halsey observed. "Are you doing all right today?"

"I am indeed," Henderson replied, "except I don't know why I'm here."

Halsey laughed. "Management! Did they tell you anything other than time and place?"

"They told me a little about you," Henderson answered. "And I knew so little detail about the Racquet and Tennis Club that most of what I know is based on the research I did following the briefing."

Halsey asked, "What did you learn from your research?"

"I know," Henderson observed, "it helps if your last name begins with the letter *R*."

Halsey thought for a moment and then laughed at a marginally acceptable decibel level within the club. "That's rich! That is rich! Why the letter *R*?"

"Rockefeller, Roosevelt, Rothschild. Yes, sir! That *is* rich!"

"What else do you know about the club?"

"This is an exclusive club with a distinguished membership list," Henderson observed. "The club caters to traditional indoor sport and games, with all the proper amenities, including fine dining."

Halsey responded, "Well said, my boy! Are you aware of my role here at the club?"

"No," Henderson confessed. "However, I know something about you. You graduated Harvard law school. I was told that you're a trustee of the New York Public Library, and that you, personally, have a wonderful collection of fine and rare printings. I also understand you to be a member of the Grolier Club—something of particular interest to me."

"The Grolier Club is quite special," Halsey admitted. "Is that a club you wish to one day join?"

"Someday," Henderson stated. "Bibliophiles have so much in common yet are so different from one another. There is so much to share! Avid readers, printers, illustrators, collectors, editors, authors, publishers, and the worst of them all—librarians."

Halsey returned, "First, I thank you for the kind words you said about my collection. It's a great source of pride for me. As for bibliophiles, we are an odd lot, yet I continue to be fascinated by the various perspectives as to what enables a book to be considered *of greatness*."

Halsey continued. "As for my capacity here at the club, I am the chair of the Library and Art Committee."

"May I inquire, Mr. Halsey, as to whether I am here regarding your collection or in an official capacity on behalf of the club?"

"May I beg your pardon," Halsey requested, "by asking you one question before I answer yours. May I?"

"Of course," Henderson blurted. "By all means, do!"

"It's really a philosophical question," Halsey began. "My question is, If you wanted to build up from scratch a world-class sports books library, and you wanted to focus to whatever extent necessary in the club's best interest, what would that library look like if you were its creator?"

Henderson thought. "I hope, sir, that you will beg *my* pardon by allowing me to first ask you one question before I answer yours."

Halsey announced, "Of course! Please do ask!"

Henderson began, "You know the club and its members. You know what members want or need and how much in the way of resources they're willing to commit. If it were you answering your question, what are your thoughts?"

"*Touché,*" Halsey remarked. "Now, then, I will offer my answer to the question we asked each other. Here is what I believe to be the ideal scenario. My committee members and I would hope to obtain volumes that address traditional outdoor sports, such as angling, hunting, and the associated necessity of horsemanship. Also, this club has a tennis court where we follow many of the same rules used by athletes during the reign of King Louis XVI of France. With that in mind, I would also be interested in stick and ball games that includes tennis, squash, golf, baseball, cricket, and other games of similar attributes from around the world. It would also be good if we could cover topics, such as fast-walk racing—like you do—and other sports here and there that could answer questions club members may have from time to time. No complete voids on any well-known sports. Those are my thoughts."

"I was born and raised in England," Henderson began. "After hearing your answer, it would not have surprised me had you been British, so it is a treat to hear such words from an American. I can ill imagine a more welcome answer than the one you provided!"

Halsey said, "Some of the committee members and I have a common vision. We wish to build—for this club—a world-class library with books relating to traditional sport. Accordingly, I have been informed by people I hold in high regard at the New York Public Library that, although you are young, you are most capable and already seasoned enough so as to be able to help us in achieving our goal. We are particularly interested in procuring descriptions of the sport at its time of inception, written at or near that time, whether of the 15th century or what have you."

Henderson subtly laughed and shook his head. "For someone like me, pursuing such an endeavor would be a dream come true, if you were in a position to overcome the primary obstacles."

"What primary obstacles?"

"Obtaining substantial financing," Henderson noted. "Having the time to accomplish the feat. To whatever extent collections similar and of the level like what you aspire to exist, their creation was due to the diligence of years of effort by talented individuals with a substantial budget of the type rarely found by other than wealthy individuals or with the greatest of institutions the size of libraries like the one in New York or located in other world capitals."

"Time is a commodity we have," assured Halsey. "As for financing, you let me worry about that. I will get what you need out of the skin flints running around here. Of that, sir, I can assure you. I know they're good for it."

"I do have another issue," Henderson offered. "It is one of a more personal nature."

"That is of importance to me," Halsey empathized. "To whatever extent you feel comfortable in talking to the issue, I am ready to listen."

"Although I aspire to accomplish that which you describe and am driven to enjoy greater achievements than I am presently in a position to do," Henderson said, "my job at the library is what I have always dreamed of having. The stability of my job and my potential career path is of vital importance to me and my family."

"I believe I can put your mind at ease, Mr. Henderson. However, if I may ask, how large is your family?"

"At present, there are two of us," Henderson conceded. "But there is a third on the way."

Halsey appeared elated. "My wife and I were never so blessed, but I'm thrilled for you! How exciting!"

"Very exciting," Henderson admitted, "but I worry about the future. I don't have the personal funding of the type you see around the club."

"I have been told that you are interested in earning more money," Halsey confessed. "What I am proposing will help to achieve that goal."

"It's more than a paycheck that has me concerned," Henderson said. "I love the library and what I do there. I work hard and am convinced that, so long as I continue to do so, I will have a fulfilling future. Of greater importance, I am secure in those halls and would fear for the long-term financial security of my family if I were ever to leave."

"Oh, I see," Halsey declared. "You think I'm trying to hire you away. Is that what you are thinking?"

"I don't know. I pray that I am wrong."

"Your prayers have been answered, Mr. Henderson," Halsey exclaimed exuberantly. "I am not trying to hire you away from your employer. In fact, it is of vital importance that you remain in their employ!"

Henderson was again perplexed. "I wonder how I could make a significant contribution toward your vision if I continue to work for the library. I expect that I would need to spend many hours if we were to put together a collection the likes of what you describe."

"I can dispel your wonderment quickly," Halsey began. "First of all, you are in the catbird's seat for this quest. Your placement within the public library—and where I believe you will be in the future— places you in a position where you will be able to locate the rarest and best books for the club's future collection. The vastness of the New York Public Library commands the attention of almost every collector of books or institution anywhere in the world."

"What of..."

"Allow me to finish, please," Halsey continued. "The club's committee is looking for you to function as a club employee in the capacity of a consultant. You will be in charge of the project. However, you will soon learn that we do not see your value as you might see it. We are not interested in utilizing your services for your ability to catalogue or file or resolve logistical problems. That's between you and your present employer. We are interested in your knowledge at a higher level of task. You have been recommended as a man that can find out where to locate any book and then acquire it. I have been told, in no uncertain terms, that you have the energy, dedication, knowledge, and natural abilities to guide you toward helping us in our quest. I am fully aware that you work five days per week, and I am asking for one additional day per week. I will gladly work with the library's trustees to ensure you never work Sundays, if that is of importance to you. Working for the Racquet and Tennis Club will only serve as another feather in your cap when you toil at the library. People there—important people toward your long-term success— will know what you are trying to accomplish on behalf of the club. When you are present within this club's walls, you will be given the autonomy, guidance as you may require, authority, and my personal assurance that you will have the type and level of resources you need."

A butler of sorts entered the room and asked if Halsey or Henderson might like to have a beverage.

Halsey asked, "What can we get for you, Mr. Henderson?"

"I don't drink alcohol," Henderson stated, "but thank you for asking."

"If there's any type of drink served in New York," Halsey boasted, "we have it. Are you thirsty at all?"

"A cold glass of milk would be fine," Henderson said.

Halsey's eyes lit up. "Have you ever tasted a chocolate egg cream?"

Henderson inquired, "An egg cream? No, I've never heard of it!"

Halsey beamed. Addressing the man, he said, "Two chocolate egg creams, please."

"Very good, sir. Right away," the server replied as he dismissed himself with dispatch.

Turning to Henderson, Halsey continued. "This beverage has milk in it. It is far better than any alcoholic beverage I know. It was recently invented by an owner of a candy store in Brooklyn. It's guaranteed to bring tears of pleasure to your eyes! Once we resolve any issues you have—and I have no doubt that can be done—we will have an egg cream toast to it all!"

The librarian sat patiently.

"Let's get back to your issues," Halsey said. "What have I not yet addressed?"

"I don't believe you missed much of anything," Henderson responded. "I am certain, however, that I will soon have more questions to fill in the blanks. Based on what you've said thus far, I'm thinking that this may not be such a bad day after all," Henderson jested.

"Quite the opposite," Halsey declared. "This is a great day for you, me, the club, the world of sport-book collecting, and above all, your family—both present and future!"

"Before I fail to mention it," Halsey added, "I should tell you that we're not long for these digs. The club will be moving to Park Avenue over the next two years, but it won't be much farther for you from either the library or Grand Central Station. I hope you won't take issue with the extra half-mile walk from the library or Grand Central Station, especially given how fast I believe you can walk a half mile," Halsey concluded with a big smile.

Henderson beamed with pride. "That presents no problem, sir. I'll think of the additional walking distance as part of a conditioning program."

Halsey stated, "Outstanding! And, incidentally, I know you went through quite a move when the Astor was consolidated into the New York Public Library. Although I am certain that was quite a chore for you, our move will be a slightly different experience. This time, you will merely point your finger, and thy will be done."

The egg creams were placed next to each man. Henderson had more questions, and Halsey elaborated more about the project and Henderson's future role. They reached a most satisfactory accord, and Henderson began his employ at the Racquet and Tennis Club.

Henderson was on his way toward building a world-class collection of sports books while, at the same time, retaining the great job where he would continue to flourish.

* * *

Over the course of the next five years, Henderson's wife would give birth to a daughter and, later, to a son. At the New York Public Library, Henderson would be placed in charge of stacks—a powerful position of responsibility within the library with many people working under his demanding guidance. The librarian had achieved such influence with the library system that he could have an audience with the most exclusive book collectors and cultural institutions throughout the world. This became highly beneficial when seeking out the rarest and most valuable of sport books. Soon thereafter, the Henderson family would move out of their Bronx apartment and into an apartment five miles from the club where he would often speed walk to work for conditioning. Later, the Hendersons would move again; this time into a nice brick home in White Plains, New York. Henderson would somehow find the time to coach his son's *midget* baseball team when the time came. During this period, Henderson succeeded in building what was arguably the greatest collection of rare and important sports books of its kind in the world. Henderson would also become an active participating member in good standing at the prestigious Grolier Club.

The librarian was well-connected, brilliant, and loved what he did. Where some would sit back and take stock, Henderson became increasingly more motivated to perform extensive research. He became what many believed to be the world's most knowledgeable authority on the history of sports, not the least of which was stick and ball games. As a result, none of the aforementioned beneficial changes to his life could prepare Henderson for the immense controversy in which he would soon become embroiled.

Controversy equalizes fools and wise men
in the same way—and the fools know it.

—Oliver Wendell Holmes Sr.

CHAPTER 12

Controversy

At the peak of the Great Depression in 1933, one-third of the country's workforce was unemployed. Whether employed or not, few American families could insulate themselves from the tension of the nation's reality. By late 1935, economic signs had improved slightly; however, prosperity had not returned by any stretch, and the national psyche was wearing thin. Throughout these trying times, baseball had become increasingly popular. The game was a welcome diversion from the reality of life's hardships. Followers of the game could root for teams and players and enter enthusiastic conversations with family and friends. As the severity of economic hardship began to soften, the American public began replacing their tensions of financial insecurity with a preoccupation of Hitler, Mussolini, Stalin, and other international leaders having potential future consequence.

Through all the trials of American life, the topic of baseball remained wildly popular. Little wonder, as unheralded as advance notice of the news was, that the first-ever public announcement of the National Baseball Hall of Fame seized the national interest. In the slumber of an early February in 1936, a press release came out of Chicago before a handful of sportswriters.

The communication listed the names of five former ballplayers who would become the first inductees to enter baseball's national

Hall of Fame. At the time of the announcement, few Americans knew there was a Hall of Fame. The Hall lacked official sanction and took up little more than one room in a small building within a tiny village. Few people in America had heard of this town located *out east* in the mountain forests of central New York state. Nevertheless, numerous newspapers with a wide range of circulation decided to print articles written by Paul Mickelson of the Associated Press. Mickelson's and other reporters' articles covering the announcement appeared in newspapers whose locations crossed the continental United States. Whether someone wanted to read about the Hall of Fame in the *Spokane Daily Chronicle, Miami Herald, Boston Globe, Los Angeles Times*, or points in between, the news item was well-covered.

Three years later...
Village of Cooperstown, New York—Spring 1939

Three years of planning and effort to celebrate the centennial of baseball were drawing to a conclusion. On this spring day in 1939, the Village Club of Cooperstown, New York, was the site for a regularly scheduled planning and status meeting of the Program Committee of the Baseball Centennial Celebration. Typically, attendees at these meetings included Cooperstown Centennial Celebration Chairman Theodore Lettis, not present, Program committee chairman Lester G. Bursey, Harris Cooke, Village Mayor Sprakel, other committee chairs and members, and those representing local commerce, community organizations, schools, celebration participants, occasional other interested parties, and reporters representing the Cooperstown *Freeman's Journal* and other area newspapers. Well before the scheduled time of the meeting, a large crowd was already assembled. Many of the moods of those present ranged from concerned to irate. Bursey had yet to arrive.

A man standing in the center of the crowd and wearing a straw hat with a leather band held a copy of *The New York Library Bulletin* in his hand.

"The man is trying to make a mockery of baseball's upcoming centennial celebration! He says that Abner Doubleday did not, repeat, did not invent baseball in Cooperstown in 1839—or in any other year. His eight-page article consists of five pages of written text with the other pages containing illustrations from books of long ago."

A lady with a floral hat asked, "What does he say to dispute the Doubleday event?"

The man replied, "He's cited various rare books with diagrams or descriptions of similar games dating back as far as 1744. That's almost a century before Albert Spalding claimed that Doubleday invented the game. This so-called expert speaks to a variety of books published prior to when Doubleday drew his baseball diagram on the school grounds. The 1744 book is the oldest one. That book was published in London, England, and this bulletin, here, says it was entitled, *A Little Pretty Pocket-Book, Intended for the Instruction and Amusement of Little Master TOMMY, and Pretty Miss POLLY.*"

"The book uses the term *base-ball* and gives instruction on how to play the game. This librarian says the rules and layout have striking similarities to our national game. He makes a convincing argument."

As Bursey entered the room, another person inquired, "What does Mr. Librarian say about Doubleday? That he was a fraud?"

"No," replied the man with the bulletin. "The author said that Doubleday did not invent the sport but was given credit for *being…a strong link, to be sure—but merely a link in a long chain in the evolution of the game.*"

Another person asked, "That's a pretty weak effort to appease us. Who is this man who wrote the piece?"

"Robert W. Henderson. Our local librarian gave me this bulletin and said that Henderson is a high-ranking librarian employed by the New York Public Library. She also told me that Henderson was born and raised in England. Doesn't that just fit!"

Rather than acknowledging, Bursey was intending on calling the meeting to order, when a committee member stated, "Lester, you may wish to allow a conclusion to the present discussion before you begin the more formal proceedings of our meeting."

Bursey addressed the man in the straw hat. "I heard the last of what you said. Where did the article appear?"

"In the *New York Public Library Bulletin.*"

Bursey gave a sigh of relief and stated, "At least you didn't say *The New York Times*! When was the article published?"

"In the April 1937 bulletin."

Bursey exclaimed, "*Nineteen thirty-seven*! That's two years old! This is like quoting a text from a book on ancient civilization. Several of us knew of that article, but nothing of consequence ever came of it."

"You don't understand," the man in the straw hat responded as he waved a similar looking publication in his other hand. "He just came up with a considerably stronger article in the latest library bulletin published just the other day in the April 1939 issue!"

"How is this latter piece *stronger* than before?" Bursey inquired.

"Henderson cites more examples than he did in 1937, except this time, the librarian says that baseball appears to be tied directly to the English game of rounders."

Bursey asked, "Was any credit given to Doubleday?"

"Maybe a backhanded compliment, but that's all," the man responded. "I'll read what he says to that topic: *Abner Doubleday seems to have had fame posthumously thrust upon him—at least as far as baseball is concerned. There is no record that he made personal claim to be its inventor. No contemporary records exist connecting him with the game. His obituary in the New York Times of January 28, 1893, makes no mention of baseball, nor does the memorial volume published by the New York State Monuments Commission in 1918.*"

Bursey inquired, "Is the circulation of the bulletin primarily within the New York Public Library system?"

"No. They print over a thousand copies. These bulletins go to libraries, educational institutions, newspapers, and other interested parties throughout North America. Some copies are mailed to England and elsewhere around the world!"

"Has it even appeared in the press? After all, they did miss, for the most part, the first time around," Bursey observed.

"Personally, I'm aware of a few specific papers, but I've been told by someone I talked to at the New York Public Library that news articles have been showing up literally everywhere. Our librarian handed me this article issued the other day in Rochester's *Democrat and Chronicle.*"

Bursey said, "That's the closest in-state big city newspaper to us. Please don't tell me they are taking Henderson under their wing."

"Quite the contrary," the man responded as he stepped onto the small stage where Bursey was standing. "Here's what is said early in the article.

"It seems a little bit late in the game to challenge the [baseball origin] *decision—in this year set apart for the hundredth anniversary of the birth of baseball—yet Robert W. Henderson in the Bulletin of the New York Public Library is putting up an argument.*

"The end of the news article shows a further understanding of our position on the matter.

"Doubleday probably got his ideas from prior sources. He should not properly be called the 'inventor' of the game. Yet there seems to be no doubt that he started it on a new course, that it was owing to him that baseball became the national game. At any rate, baseball as it is now known, grew from this time, whatever the names and rules may have been before that, nobody was building million-dollar stadiums in which to play it."

The group began applauding.

Bursey wondered, "Is that how all the newspapers are receiving Henderson's journalistic dagger?"

The man in the hat replied, "I was told the articles are all over the map—both figuratively and geographically. Of course, I haven't personally seen that."

Someone shouted out, "Why don't we form a little delegation and go to New York City and show him our appreciation for trying to give us a black eye. Maybe we can return the favor."

Another person shouted, "I'll get a picture of the man and pass it around so that we can give him a real Cooperstown welcome."

Yet another man said, "I'll help you on that one."

Mayor Sprakel took control of the discussion. "There won't be any of that! We're not like that around here! Besides, I need to inform all of you that US Congressman Schwert stopped by to see me earlier. A couple of assemblymen from Albany came along with him. The congressman wanted to check up on his constituency and how our plans for the celebration were progressing. He did tell me generally of this article but said it would be of no further problem. First, he said that Congress has passed some Acts of Congress. June 12 will be a national holiday, and the post office is in the process of printing special centennial postage stamps for the occasion. Further, as many of you know, our congressman played professional ball with the New York Yankees, and he reassured me that he feels to have a personal stake in the matter. I can tell you he knows the right people to talk with, and he knows where this librarian is employed."

The village mayor then added, "You might wish to point out that we have all of major league baseball solidly behind us. That includes Baseball Commissioner Landis, National League President Frick, and the other illustrious members of the major league's Executive Committee for the Baseball Centennial. Let us further not forget that baseball legends the likes of Babe Ruth, Cyrus Young, and a host of their other cronies will be at the podium giving speeches. Besmirch us and you besmirch them."

One committee member offered, "What the politicians or ballplayers don't get done, we can do peacefully right here. There are several events of importance unfolding on the celebration's first day. Near the beginning of the day, we have our parade. To begin the parade, we've secured the assistance of two of our state's military academies. They alone will be bringing thirteen busloads filled with two sizeable bands and an additional 400 marching cadets. To paraphrase 'The Battle Hymn of the Republic,' with the use of the cadets as but one example, our Lord will be *trampling out the vintage where the grapes of wrath are stored.* No one will even remember that the little man in the big shoes exists by the time the day is out."

"People," Bursey said, "we will let this matter take its course. I have only allotted so much time here at the club for our regular meeting, so I'm going to get started."

As Bursey pulled out his gavel to begin the meeting, a disgruntled citizen standing by the door shouted, "You can't make all of us follow your commands, Bursey! If this Henderson character is half the genuine baseball historian he implies, he will either be present to witness the ceremonies, or he's a fraud! Some of the local schoolkids will make great spotters. Taking care of Henderson will be as easy as pie." The man then left the club.

Bursey spoke to those that remained. "Friends, let's not allow one hothead to project an image on behalf of our community that ignores the good intentions I know all of us have."

Striking the gavel, Bursey declared, "I hereby call today's meeting of the Program Committee of the Baseball Centennial Celebration to order."

The acting chairman announced, "In view of the delay in beginning the meeting, this will be an abbreviated meeting, and we may have a special session later in the week prior to our next scheduled committee meeting. In the meantime, for the sake of time, I will not follow the usual procedure of calling upon each committee member to speak. Rather, I will give all of you a brief on where we're at.

"First, all rights are in order for the sacred ground where General Doubleday first drew his baseball diamond, the baseball field has been certified as ready, and the grandstands will be able to handle a capacity of 10,000 spectators. In short, Doubleday Field will be dedicated as planned and on schedule."

Bursey continued to rapidly provide other details.

"Lastly, I want to give all of you an update on the progress of readying the main building for its June debut."

By this time, the group only consisted of the committee members and a few onlookers. Bursey unrolled the blueprints of the C-shaped two-story building's interior onto a large conference-like table. He then proceeded to quickly go over the progress of the different rooms, halls, and exhibits within the building.

"The completion of the outside is also at hand. The landscaping of the courtyard had to wait until planting season which is now, and the completion of the yard is imminent. Also, everyone present should have observed that the pillar columns by the entryway are finally in place. We are additionally in receipt of the four marble slabs that will serve as the outside steps, the white granite keystone with the baseball carving, and the wrought-iron fencing to complete the external entryway. All in all, the target date for completion of the facility to house the collections of the National Baseball Hall of Fame is expected to be absolutely ready for the big day."

Bursey began to roll up the building blueprint, and a committee member asked, "Mr. Bursey, have you or Chairman Lettis heard anything of late from the Baseball Centennial Executive Committee?"

"Oh yes. We do have some deliverables to them," Bursey recalled as he pulled some notes out of his briefcase. "Here it is. Yes. I have the proposed agenda items for their next meeting. It is, of course, not final. The committee will be providing us with a list of baseball officials and players that will be staying overnight, whether arriving by train or driving up, so that the Otsega Hotel and other lodging hosts can release any remainder of the blocks of rooms we've reserved for others. We will also need to coordinate with the Cooperstown train depot about the special train from Albany where the New York City train makes its connection. You will want to ensure that the facilities we're providing for the photo sessions are immaculate and ready to go." Bursey continued to scan his notes for any other items. "It looks like the other items are the responsibility of the executive committee—raising of the centennial flag at the All-Star Game, bringing the umpires, balls, uniforms, equipment, league coordination between team owners for the players that will be participating, etcetera. For whoever wants, I can be available today at the café down street at 3:00 PM. I can bring you the details of what some of you need then. I'd hope you know who you are by now."

The lady committee member gave the thumbs-up. Bursey then called an adjournment to the meeting.

The attendees of that day's session had listened intently to the proceedings. The excitement, robust enthusiasm, and sense of pride felt by all in attendance seemed to remain intact once the rocky start of the morning had concluded. If Cooperstown was not previously *on the map*, the dedication of the National Baseball Hall of Fame would soon put it there! A good number of citizens, both adults and schoolchildren, would continue to remain heavily involved in the preparations. If all went well in the coming days and weeks, the people of Cooperstown and the participants from professional baseball were ready to strut their stuff on the 12th day of June in front of the American public, relying on newsreels, newspapers, sports magazines, and live radio broadcasts to spread the word from the Hudson River Valley to the farther reaches of American audiences.

* * *

A synopsis of the bulletin issued for April 1939 appears below. The article began as follows:

> RECENTLY Miss Beatrice H. Gunn, of Boston, presented to the New York Public Library an edition of the *Boys and Girls Book of Sports*, published in Providence, R.I., in the year 1836. In so doing she unwittingly reopened a long dormant controversy: Is baseball an offshoot of rounders?—for this innocent little juvenile work, printed three years before the date when Abner Doubleday was supposed to have "devised" the game of baseball at Cooperstown, N.Y., contained a set of rules for "the great American game." The acquisition of this book naturally inspired a checking up for other editions, earlier if possible, and this search led to the surprising results which are herewith recorded. We do not hold Miss Gunn responsible for the findings of this article, but we do wish to record appreciation for her initial interest and generosity, and for her continued helpfulness.

Words within Henderson's introduction to the article are defensive. He must have known the article would stir up controversy. Selective phrases appear to be an attempt at misdirecting blame for the motive to write this article a mere nine weeks prior to the ceremonious culmination of a multiyear effort to open a new building to house the National Baseball Hall of Fame and Museum. Capsulized, this might be boiled down to read, "RECENTLY Miss Beatrice H. Gunn...reopened a long dormant controversy: Is baseball an offshoot of rounders… We do not hold Miss Gunn responsible for the findings of this article…" It was not typical for Henderson, a man generally of few words, to make an otherwise meaningless statement that we "do not hold Miss Gunn responsible…"

Other than this paragraph, the balance of the article presented factual evidence to back up Henderson's claims. Preceding the text appears a page displaying two diagrams. Both illustrations depict a picture of six or seven boys standing on a field having the attributes of a baseball diamond. Both illustrations had two infielders, a pitcher, batsman, catcher, and an umpire of sorts. Both pictures also were published prior to when the alleged 1839 event was said to have taken place. The first pictorial was reproduced from *Children's Amusements*, New York, 1820. The second image reillustrated from *The Boy's Book of Sports*, Providence, 1839, has one extra player than the first illustration, and the lad is standing near a likeness of second base and appears to be a base runner.

The text that follows the introduction consists of example after example appearing to disprove the published conclusion by the *Mills Commission*, often with Henderson's offering a discussion of the examples' perspectives or backgrounds. The article ended with a "Summary: How Baseball Developed" and was finalized with no less than a "List of References to the Game of Baseball Before the Year 1840."

The list, each item detailed with a short paragraph, then followed. The first four items on the list appear below:

> 1744   *A LITTLE pretty pocket-book, intended for the instruction and amusement of Little Master Tommy and Pretty Miss Polly*, London, 1744. Contained a rhymed description and cut of baseball.
>
> 1748   *Letters of Mary Lepell*, Lady Hervey. London. 1721 "Baseball, a play all who are, or have been school boys, are acquainted with." …November the 14th, 1748

1762 A reprint of *A LITTLE Pretty Pocket Book*...New York, 1762

1778 *The Military Journal of George Ewing* (1754–1824), a soldier of Valley Forge. Yonkers, N.Y., 1928. "In the intervals play[e]d at base." P. 35. Perhaps the earliest record of a game of baseball played in America.

The above was followed by ten more examples from the years 1787, 1815, 1820, 1823, 1829, 1830, 1845, 1835, 1836, 1839. Each example appeared with citation and comment of relevance as to why the reference disproves the *Mills Commission's* conclusion that baseball was primarily of American invention. The evidence relating to the origins of baseball had been entered in the public record for posterity. The debate regarding the relationship between baseball and rounders was reignited.

* * *

Since opening its doors in 1884, the Grolier Club has been membered by those accepting the club's invitation to join. The club's charter encourages book collecting and an appreciation for the highest standards of book production in all facets of the publication process. Each member is deemed an accomplished bibliophile in these pursuits. A variety of ever-changing exhibits produced throughout the year feature exceedingly rare book collections of extraordinary quality. Although reservations are generally required, many exhibits are available to the viewing public at no charge.

The club's facilities are located on East Sixth Street where Midtown Manhattan meets the fashionable Upper East Side. Upon stepping onto marble steps outside the Neo-Georgian structure, visitors enter a lobby that radiates an old-world charm. Within the first-floor main room, a grand staircase ascends from the highly polished wood floors. The flooring and Persian rugs give way to Doric columns that appear to hold up the pleasantly designed ceiling.

Furnishings are both useful and of fine craftsmanship. The modern display showcases blend in nicely. Floors above the main level offer spacious hallways and decorative rooms used for receptions, private showings, and meetings.

The Grolier Club, Manhattan, New York—Early May 1939

David Wagstaff, a collector of rare publications relating to hunting and fishing, was standing in the club's lobby next to the assistant librarian's desk that was typically vacant during the noon hour. Wagstaff had an appointment with Robert Henderson and was awaiting his arrival. Moments later, Henderson appeared in his usual tweed sport jacket.

"David, thank you for agreeing to meet with me today on short notice."

"I was glad you contacted me," Wagstaff exclaimed. "After receiving the honor to give the keynote on your exhibit last year, I can ill refuse to honor any request of yours."

"Outdoor sporting literature in America is a fun topic," Henderson noted. "And you, sir, were the perfect man for the task."

"You're a man after my own heart," Wagstaff replied. "You are a man that adores books, and you apparently find my favorite hobby of outdoor sport interesting. I never did ask you this before. Are you a hunter, angler, or both?"

"None of the above," Henderson responded. "I have no time for that. Maybe someday."

Wagstaff watched Henderson begin to pull note papers out of a valise and observed, "I wonder why we are both so fascinated with such diverse topics as sports on the one hand and of books on the other."

Henderson had his own take. *There is a natural affinity between sport and book collecting. The objects of pursuit differ, it is true, but the joys of the chase and the exultation in achievement after an arduous hunt, whether of fox, pheasant, or folio have much in common.*[6]

"You nailed that one as you usually do," Wagstaff concluded. "So, my friend, what's new?"

"Other than the fact that I just became a grandpa, I was wondering whether you—"

Wagstaff interrupted, "A grandfather? Heartiest congratulations! Was it a boy or girl?"

"Frank Chapman van Cleef," Henderson boasted. "And this next part is extremely important—the third!" Henderson chuckled at his sarcasm.

Wagstaff was humored by the latter remark too. "Yes, there's a lot of thirds, fourths, and fifths running around here! Please, I didn't mean to interrupt. You were saying…"

Henderson continued, "I am thinking about putting together a second exhibit, and as with my first one, I may require some of your tutelage."

"Hard to imagine," Wagstaff began, "that you might rival your exhibit of last year. Many great books on sports were published over the course of American history. Whereas the last exhibit was entitled, *The Growth and Development of Sporting Literature in America*, I can't imagine how you could top that!"

"Try this one for size, David, *Manuscripts and Printed Books Relating to Sport Produced During the Last Six Centuries.*"

Wagstaff looked at Henderson in astonishment. Before he would say a word, the two were politely interrupted by a member of the Racquet and Tennis Club.

"Mr. Henderson," the man said, "Mr. Cromwell knew I was coming over here and asked that I convey a message. Cromwell said that he needs to see you at the racquet club at one o'clock."

Henderson inquired, "Thank you. Did he say why?"

---

[6] Robt W. Henderson, The Grolier Club Exhibition Catalogue: Six Hundred Years of Sport, "Forward", D.B. Updike, The Merrymount Press, New York, December, 1940, p. vii

"He did not" was the reply. "He sounded serious. So serious that it could be regarding your recent article in the library bulletin that everyone seems to be talking about. He had young Charles Scribner with him."

"Was it Junior?"

"No. He'll have to wait on the *Junior* designation until his father steps aside," the man joked. "I think he's Scribner IV, but I have difficulty keeping count."

"Interesting," Henderson responded. "Young Scribner is not yet even a member of the club—unless he was there to somehow pass on information. I'll be there. Thank you for passing along the word."

The man winked and departed in the direction of the Grolier Club manager's office.

"Cromwell, ay," Wagstaff stated. "I know the name. I'm fairly certain he owned a finance company and sold it to First City of New York at the same time you and I worked on your last exhibit. Is he a literary type of the kind to provide you with guidance?"

"Mr. Cromwell," Henderson began, "is in charge of the Library and Art Committee. He is my mentor at the club. He has a private collection of printed materials not unlike yours. Phi Beta Kappa student newspaper at Princeton. He can surely keep up with me—if that's what you are asking. He's a good man and does well at his position on the committee."

Wagstaff wondered, "Let's get back to what you propose."

"I was wondering what you think," Henderson reminded.

Wagstaff shook his head. "I've never heard of anything close to a 600-year exhibit. I'm having difficulty merely wrapping my head around the concept! You obviously think you can somehow pull off a *six-hundred-year* exhibit—with the actual books. Is that what you are saying?"

"I can," Henderson declared. "I already control some of the items at the club, and the public library has some extraordinary collections also. On many of the other manuscripts, I have letters of commitment, or I expect them soon. For any other works, I know who has them. Whether the owners be museums, other institutions, or individuals or caretakers, we will be required to give assurances of proper security arrangements."

"I won't question your veracity," Wagstaff conceded. "And you have obviously done your homework as always. Can you cite any of the older or exceedingly rare publications you plan on bringing to the exhibit?"

The lobby clock in the Grolier Club chimed that it was 12:45 PM.

"The older manuscripts are varied between treatises, manuscripts, folios with remarkable hand coloring, books, pamphlets, and so on. I have more than 150 items that will go on display. The earlier manuscripts are on vellum or parchment—animal membranes—and as you might guess, falconry was quite popular. I have a heavy concentration of sixteenth-century works that will total more than forty in number. The oldest document, dated 1340, has treatises on falconry and veterinary medicine by J. Ruffus. It is accompanied by delicately executed colored drawings as illustrations that were created by an Italian artist."

"My word," exclaimed Wagstaff. "Security arrangements, you said. Sounds like half of the entire New York City Police Department will need to be on call for this one!" Wagstaff continued, "Quite frankly, Robert, I don't know what to say! To the best of my recollection, I am unaware of any exhibit of this magnitude for what you are attempting to have been produced anywhere in the world!"

"So then you like the idea?"

Wagstaff blurted, "Like it! This is so astonishing, what's not to like? Who are some of these people you're in communication with, if I dare ask?"

"Some are members or caretakers on behalf of the various royal houses of Europe. There are other individuals that are part of families of great wealth. Still others are go-betweens with religious orders that range from the most disparate monasteries to the Vatican. And, of course, then there are the commonly known institutions such as those in education, in libraries and museums, and so on," Henderson offered. "I became an American citizen a quarter century ago. I'm a citizen through and through, yet I can play upon my European birthright when that is appropriate. Anything that works!"

"Have you run your idea past anyone here at the Grolier Club?"

"From the top," Henderson replied. "I've been working on this since the last exhibit we had closed. Numero uno wanted me to get your opinion on the feasibility of the matter. I assure you, however, that I would have asked for that anyway."

"I'm no expert on the security that will be necessary," Wagstaff responded, "but I'm all in on this. Talk about exciting! If it's only half as good as what you say, it's still a good deal!"

"My two objectives have been met," Henderson said. "First, you have been brought up to speed for us to soon begin collaboration. Second, I believe to have received your concurrence and approval."

"In spades, sir," responded Wagstaff.

"With that I must be off to see Mr. Cromwell."

"You better walk fast," Wagstaff encouraged. "Hope he doesn't want to see you about your recent library article."

As Henderson finished packing up his papers, he said, "I trust Mr. Cromwell's opinion fervently. I never worry about such things at the club, so long as I have all my *i*'s dotted."

Upon shaking hands, Henderson began heading toward the Grolier Club's exit. "Tallyho!"

A well-dressed man who had been patiently sitting elsewhere in the room sprung to his feet and quickly approached Henderson. He began, "Mr. Henderson?"

Henderson acknowledged.

"I have been a New York Yankees fan since my father first brought me to a game as a child. I wish to discuss your recently published article on the evolution of baseball. I take grave exception to what you have done."

Henderson replied, "I'd be delighted to discuss this with you, sir. However, I have a pressing engagement elsewhere. Please do discuss the matter with my partner, Mr. Wagstaff."

As Henderson approached his exit door, Wagstaff called out, "I'm sure we will be in touch again soon."

As Henderson opened the door, he turned, laughed, and left.

The man followed Henderson out the door, but the legs of Henderson moved so swiftly that he was already a half block away, and the man did not follow in pursuit. Henderson would think about the possibilities of his next meeting and what his responses might be if the *baseball origins* article were to come up as a topic of discussion. He would think of those thoughts for the entirety of the six-minute brisk walk to the Racquet and Tennis Club.

* * *

The Racquet and Tennis Club had been located at its Park Avenue address for more than twenty years. The building is far from what might be considered a tiny structure, and yet it seems dwarfed by the surrounding tall buildings of glass and steel. The club is housed in a good portion of a four- to five-story structure that displays a powerful facade of limestone and brick. There are also large Romanesque archways along the front side of the edifice that resemble that which might represent a Federal Reserve Bank building. The structure's footprint covers a city block.

There are no signs signifying the club's presence, other than a long green awning that stretches over the sidewalk with the sole inscription a number that represents the Park Avenue street address upon it. Henderson entered the front door leading to the luxurious lobby of marble flooring and dark wood-paneled walls with vaulted ceiling, and hurriedly passed through the room and past the elevator en route to his office at the rear of the lobby. No one had yet arrived. As he stepped into his office, the lobby clock chimed to signify the one o'clock hour.

As Henderson sat down to neaten up his desktop, the twenty-year-old Scribner stepped into the office door threshold. Henderson immediately recognized the finely tailored gent as the youngest Charles Scribner whose father and grandfather, all of the same name, used to occasionally bring young Scribner to the club.

Henderson enthused, "Why, come in, Mr. Scribner! Please come in!"

Scribner offered, "My apologies, Mr. Henderson. We started lunch late. I've been sent as Mr. Cromwell's messenger to inform you that he'll be right along."

Henderson responded, "Quite all right, Mr. Scribner! How have you been, and how is your father?"

Scribner remarked, "For all the years you addressed me as 'Master Scribner,' 'mister' will take some time to get used to. I feel more comfortable being called *Junior*."

"So then, they've passed the baton to you already," commented Henderson.

"That's right," Scribner replied with a hint of sheepish smile. "We're both doing well. Father is working harder than he ever has, and I'm now enrolled at Princeton so that I can soon go to work in the family business. I hope I will be able to call upon you from time to time, if for no other reason than to receive council on matters of the book world."

Henderson replied, "I'm not certain if I would be the best person to answer your questions. I know about books that exist and how to acquire them, but the world of publishing is on the opposite end of the continuum. You produce copy and then try to sell it. Of course, I'd be glad to provide assistance any time. What brings you here today?"

"It's a treat for doing well at St. Paul's," Scribner replied. Then, noticing a short pile of neatly placed magazines on the credenza behind Henderson, he added, "I see those magazines behind you."

"Yes," said Henderson. "I replace the older magazines in the library for newer ones each Thursday morning."

Scribner returned, "I see you have the March issue of *Scribner's Magazine* on top! The portrait of the cowhand's rugged face on this month's cover is hard to miss."

"It's an excellent magazine," responded Henderson. "It's quite well-read within the club."

Scribner interjected, "My grandpa began that magazine more than a half century ago. Through the years, he and father improved upon it. Dad is proud of what the magazine has become."

"As he should," responded Henderson. "I heard talk from some people in the business though that the magazine's days may be numbered."

"I was at dinner the other night," Scribner offered, "and the magazine was the lead topic of conversation. Although the family seldom brings work or reading material to the dining table, Father brought the March issue to dinner. It's a great magazine. Do you ever look at it?"

Henderson replied, "I look over every issue. I always read that which catches my eye—and usually the featured short novel. It would be a shame if—"

Without allowing Henderson to continue, Scribner interjected, "I understand the staff has attempted to expand the magazine's circulation over the years by making changes to the format in an attempt to add subscribers. Unfortunately, their efforts were not good enough to save the old magazine."

Henderson inquired, "So the sad news I heard is true?"

Scribner returned softly, "That's why Father was allowed to bring the magazine to dinner. He has a great deal of remorse from it all. The way he described it, the family and magazine staff's refusal to compromise journalistic integrity keeps the costs of producing the magazine at a higher level than what we bring in for subscription and advertising revenue. The month of May will be the magazine's final issue. If I may ask, where did you hear it was closing down?"

"When several people from a fine company, such as Scribner Sons, begin looking around for jobs at the same time, people in the business suspect there's a problem. Several people at the Grolier Club continually have their ears to the ground."

"We found positions," Scribner volunteered, "for several of the staffers elsewhere in the company beginning next month. For those we couldn't find positions for, writers and the like, we'll have to let them go over the coming weeks. It's quite sad, really. Everyone at the magazine had become like a family long ago. The news of the magazine's finality has yet to be publicly announced."

"Such a tough business," commented Henderson. "That's one reason I like burying myself in the books themselves. I never need to deal with those kinds of ups and downs."

An uncharacteristically disheveled Jarvis Cromwell hastily entered the office. "I must apologize for my tardiness. I've been running behind all morning. Good afternoon, Mr. Henderson. I see you're engaged in conversation with Junior."

"I believe we're finished," responded Scribner. "I don't want to hold you two up. Shall I wait in the lobby, Mr. Cromwell, while the two of you have your meeting?"

"By all means, stay," replied Cromwell.

Scribner acknowledged the invite.

Henderson mocked, "By the sound of this, you're not giving me my walking papers as yet."

Cromwell laughed. "What? Nothing of the sort! Nothing of the kind, my dear Mr. Henderson. You're a feather in the club's hat. Why would you think such a thing?"

"I didn't know," responded Henderson, "whether you might be troubled by the *baseball origins* article I recently wrote."

The usually serious Cromwell laughed. "I am aware of your latest entry into the kingdom of journalism," replied Cromwell as he lightheartedly added, "Painfully aware."

Henderson queried, "Painfully?"

Cromwell chuckled. "Some have decided I'm guilty by association. I don't really feel any real heartache over it. First, what you wrote simply lays out the evidence. Second, I'm thick-skinned. Importantly, I respond by informing your critics that you wrote the column as an employee of the New York Library rather than as one of the Racquet and Tennis Club. That seems to defray any lingering conversation on the matter."

In a humble tone, Henderson asked, "All the same, do you, in any way, regret my writing?"

"Again, no, I don't," responded Cromwell. "People wonder why you chose to write the article now—weeks prior to one of the biggest events in New York state this year. I tell people they would need to ask you and then add that I am highly confident it is for none other than the reasons you stated. I have added that, in the years I have had the pleasure of your acquaintance, I have seen nothing to dissuade my confidence that your motives are honorable and not of an antagonistic nature." Cromwell continued, "I even had a little fun with it. One not-so-polite banker I know with bank stock holdings in the Oneonta region thought the article was most inappropriate. With the way he said his piece, I had to respond by suggesting he might wish to be more concerned about financial bonds representing holdings in countries having borders with Germany where Hitler is amassing large numbers of soldiers and tanks. It didn't go over that well, though I somewhat enjoyed the exchange."

Henderson looked pleased at Cromwell's response and then turned to Scribner and asked, "Did you see the article?"

Scribner responded, "I read about it in the newspaper but haven't discussed it with anyone before now. What I have learned at the dinner table, however, is that publishers are the last people to want to censure any valid writing. My understanding is that anything including fact and truth can and should be printed without disclaimer or regret."

"So then, Mr. Scribner," Henderson asked rhetorically, "you would have published what I wrote?"

Scribner smiled and gently offered, "In my family's business, *censorship* is an unfriendly term. Sometimes, however, we might consider the timing of when we allow some things to be said. In my mind, based upon the nearness of the upcoming events, I would only question why you did what you did at this particular time."

At the moment Scribner paused, the club doorman leaned into the office from the hallway and said, "Excuse me, Mr. Cromwell, but your ride is waiting for you out front. May I pass on a message to the driver?"

"That won't be necessary, Charles," returned Cromwell. "Both Mr. Scribner and I will join them in the next two minutes."

"Very good, sir," the doorman replied as he then turned away and left.

Cromwell next turned to Henderson and sarcastically suggested, "You may wish to wear body armor when you visit Cooperstown."

"I'm not certain that I will be attending," Henderson admitted. "I want to. I feel it a significant sporting event that I should attend, but I've had second thoughts as of late. I have no need to rain on anyone's parade."

"Based on my sense of responses to your bulletin article," Cromwell surmised, "I think you wise for thinking the matter over. Do let me know though should you decide to make the trek to attend."

Cromwell added, "I understand why you might feel it important for you to witness the dedication ceremonies, and the club would have no problem with your absence if you opted to go. You would not be there representing this club, however, in any capacity. I also think it unwise if you think there may be trouble by your attending."

Henderson did not respond, and Cromwell concluded, "Please keep me advised on whatever you ultimately decide to do. I must now be off."

Cromwell and Scribner departed Henderson's office.

Henderson thought about the discussion that had just transpired throughout the remainder of the day and weeks that followed. During this period, Henderson would be confronted in one way or another every day he spent at the New York Public Library. Each such incident was unsettling. It all seemed unfair. Henderson felt that his article had only addressed the truth in a factual manner. Nevertheless, it was the human element that was so troublesome. Especially now that he was a family man, he had an important decision to make. Should he attend the centennial celebration? He would be asked that question more than a hundred times during the month that followed. There is no evidence to imply that Henderson ever gave anyone an advance indication as to whether he was going to attend the celebration.

Paradise is surrounded by hardships, and
the Fire is surrounded by desires.

—Muhammad

CHAPTER 13

Final Preparations

Early June 1939

By this, the self-proclaimed centennial year, baseball had changed immeasurably in the ninety-four years since Alexander Cartwright and his teammates codified rules of the game. The change was not so much about the rules, the parameters of field, nor tactics of play. The size of the crowds and ballparks changed considerably; however, that is similarly not the type of change heretofore referred to. Back in the days of Cartwright, there were two types of leadership essential to playing the game: a team manager and an umpire.

Over the years, the sport's following grew exponentially, and the athletes transitioned from amateur or near-amateur status to that of being professional ballplayers. The sport became a business—a big business. Gate receipts were the favorite tallies of club owners. Contracts, business ethics, and negotiations were ever-present and covered all aspects of the sport. Baseball became organized in the strictest legal sense. Expansion of telegraph services on a nationwide basis, followed by the invention of the telephone, teletype, and radio enabled people on one side of North America to learn the results from thousands of miles away on the same or next day. Many times the amount of information became available to the American public, and the game's colorful aspects and players added to the fun and spectacle for white society. Sports programs were now beginning to appear over the radio airwaves regularly on a coast-to-coast basis. The quality of play had improved to where the athletes regularly made plays previously considered impossible.

Of course, the increase in information along with the improvement in the quality, depth, and speed of the communications made life more complicated for people living in the bubble of the game. Among other things, enhanced media services paved the way for an entirely new level of public scrutiny. The three factions of the game—owners, players, and *fans*—although this latter term had not yet come into being—were often at odds. Further, the issues were not merely between these groups but within each of the three groupings as well. Things were no longer handled within the confines of the clubhouse. Secrets and private grievances were now in the open.

As the third decade of the twentieth century progressed, the drawn-out trauma of the Great Depression began to give way to the threat of war by national powers on the other side of increasingly navigated oceans. As some of life's problems and fears went away, there was always a treasure trove of new ones to take their places. Baseball was a splendid diversion from these problems for millions of men, women, and children. Virtually everyone in America, die-hard sports follower or not, knew of the great players and significant events relating to the national pastime.

Having to deal with the ballplayers was not an easy task. Dealing with the owners could be even more challenging. More daunting than working with the owners and players combined was dealing with the American public. The game had gained so much prominence and influence, it was now part of the national trust. Although the spectators did not participate nor make financial investment in the game, no longer were owners and players the only ones with rights—and the investigative news reporters and sports journalists made certain such rights were claimed by their readership. To make matters more difficult, one might easily accuse the press of being biased toward one faction or another or one team or another, but you still couldn't shake them off very easily. It didn't matter whether there was bias. If there was an issue, you had to address it, or it didn't go away. To society's most evil, that's democracy at its worst.

Effective guidance from the pinnacle of major league baseball's power structure requires highly talented leaders. Success dictates the need for someone with vision and all that is necessary to gain the attention and respect of owners, players, and the various interests of the public alike. The league's *top dogs* may not be endearing souls, but the ideal leaders must have qualities beyond merely having the confidence to be decisive. The qualities of honesty, forthrightness, and candor are the building blocks of the required character traits. An effective leader commands respect with an aura of honor and possesses all the important qualities our hearts hold dear while maintaining the highest standards in order to keep the *wheels* of the giant sport machine turning. Resolving issues in the immediate is more of a tactical exercise not unlike warfare. Issues of the present must quickly become matters of the past.

At the highest level, leadership's every move has an eye on the future. Baseball's heads of state must protect and nurture the best of what the sport has to offer for posterity—consistent with the American psyche, norms, and best-held values. At the same time, it is desirable to know that there will be a strong sense of continuity for generations to come.

From the analogy of steering a great ship from one port to the next, baseball's leadership generally got it right. As far as the long-term, high-level influence was concerned, it won some and lost some. Encouraging players and owners to get involved in community matters was good. Encouraging all associated with the game to try and set good examples for children and the rest of the American public, such as promoting good sportsmanship and honesty and punishing that which was not was generally good. In promoting human rights, the executives and the owners, players, and sadly, the fans too fell far short.

Next week's centennial celebration would showcase the best of what baseball has to offer while securing the sport's heritage for future generations. In short, next week would be—both figuratively and literally—a monumental moment for baseball.

Three years ago, the two *heads of state* not owning a league franchise decided to become and remain personally involved in the centennial celebration and Hall dedication. One of these two men was Kenesaw Mountain Landis, Commissioner for the American and National Leagues of Baseball Clubs and for the National Association of Professional Baseball. Now in his seventies, the slight of build Landis, with a full head of wavy white hair, was completing his eighteenth year since being elected to the lifetime term of becoming the first commissioner. Over that time, the former federal judge had become known and referred to more often than not as the *Czar of Baseball*. For the most recent five years, Judge Landis had worked closely with youthful National League president, Ford C. Frick. Frick was the person who first approached Landis with the centennial celebration idea a couple of years ago and had been anointed in charge of the project. The two men were having a previously scheduled telephone conversation.

Telephone Conversation—Thursday, June 8, 1939

Landis: Good morning, Ford. I can only imagine how busy you must be with days to go, so I'll be quick.

Frick: Good morning, Mr. Commissioner. Don't worry about my time. Given the characters involved in this affair, things are as in control as I could have hoped for—knock on wood. Besides, I can always use another set of capable eyes to scrutinize an important moment for all of us.

Landis: Thanks for that, Ford. Before beginning, I must say that, vivid as my recollection is from the meeting we all had last week at the Commodore Hotel, I recall with equal clarity the day you first approached me with this idea of yours.

Frick: That's pretty good, Judge, considering all we've been through over the past four years. Please remember, though, that this celebration wasn't my idea to begin with.

Landis: I'll rephrase my statement. You liked the idea when you heard it, you sold me on it, you stuck with it, and due to your invaluable efforts, it all becomes a reality on Monday.

Frick: Thank you. How do you wish to begin, Mr. Commissioner?

Landis: I have the minutes from last week's get-together. Being unaware of any new issues, why don't we go over open or fluid items remaining from our June 1 meeting?

Frick: This is how I had hoped we would proceed. I too have the meeting minutes in front of me. First, though, I'm pleased to report that the Cooperstown contingent is alive and well and doing fantastic. The grounds of Doubleday Field are immaculate by any standard. The new grandstands are ready to seat 10,000 spectators, and the infield diamond is as green as the Emerald Isle.

Landis: (*Laughter*) Good!

Frick: The museum—all displays, space, and surrounding grounds are ready to go and looking good. Everything the Cooperstown folks are supposed to be doing they're doing—the staging platform for the speakers, the *Cavalcade of Baseball* parade, coordination of the special trains, contests, coordination of law enforcement and security, events and performances by local groups—for all that, I'm sitting back enjoying the show.

Landis: Good! Very good! Speaking of the trains, what time does Farley arrive?

Frick: Postmaster General Farley arrives from New York at the Delaware and Hudson station nine-ish Monday morning. The Chicago follows within the hour. Incidentally, I've been instructed to get you over to the post office immediately following your arrival. The postmaster general has a little surprise for you.

Landis: President Roosevelt perhaps?

Frick: (*Laugh*) Nothing so dramatic.

Landis: Just wondering. FDR's a New Yorker. Did you ever hear why the president elected not to attend?

Frick: He's giving the commencement address at West Point.

Landis: That's a good reason! We'll worry about the national game. He can worry about the national defense.

Frick: No complaints here, Judge. I think we'll have more fun.

Landis: I'm banking on that, Ford. And you say the locals are doing their part?

Frick: They are! Over the past three-plus years, I've grown to know several people in the village, and quite frankly, I'll miss working with them. Returning to our agenda, to finish up on discussing outstanding items the responsibility of the Baseball Centennial Executive Committee...Hotel and travel reservations—over the past week, our travel coordinators made all effort to identify everyone in need of accommodations. I've already been informed that arrangements for those in need have been secured, and the guests have either been instructed as to what they need to know or understand when they will be notified. All round-trip tickets have been distributed, and those driving have been sent reimbursements for the cost incurred by those taking the train. Also, the Georgia Peach is driving here with his wife and son. Knowing that, we took care of Cobb's family's accommodations.

Landis: Who are the coordinators doing all this?

Frick: It's a network of people, and I'm confident everyone knows their responsibilities. If you want specifics...

Landis: No. I was merely thinking how important it is to properly handle all the many details for all those concerned.

Frick: I'll remain on task. The equipment is also taken care of. That includes the four dozen balls for the game.

Landis: Did we get the umpires we wanted?

Frick: We did. We even have places for them in the parade!

Landis: (*Laughter*) Don't tell me they're leading the parade...

Frick: Quite the opposite. The tail that wags the dog, sir.

Landis: Hmm.

Frick: It'll be good for a laugh, sir. One of the townspeople assured me that the boo birds will be out in force.

Landis: (*Laughter*)

Frick: I believe our choreographers have everything and everyone in proper order for the cavalcade. They'll be at their stations where the parade assembles to ensure that all those making any sort of appearance are at the right place at the proper time. Finally, the scripts on the cavalcade have now been distributed within the league offices as necessary.

Landis: Everything else on the old agenda was already taken care of. I don't have anything else unless you do.

Frick: I do. One item. It's really more in the form of a question.

Landis: Yes, Ford.

Frick: I'm thinking about the New York librarian—our naysayer.

Landis: Robert Henderson! We briefly discussed him last week at the Commodore Hotel. Is he still *beating his* drum?

Frick: I don't know. Nothing I'm aware of. Every day though, some newspaper with decent circulation has a prominent article discussing somewhere Henderson's findings—where the words *Doubleday* and *Cooperstown* continually find their way into the conversation.

Landis: If you're thinking about cancelling everything (*laugh*), you better get on the horn, Ford!

Frick: C'mon, Kennie. We both have the same high hopes for next week.

Landis: Surely you don't think Henderson jeopardizes next week!

Frick: Based on Henderson's credentials, his sources, and where he published his findings, his arguments seem highly credible. Baseball was not invented in Cooperstown, nor was it invented a hundred years ago.

Landis: So what's your point, Mr. Frick?

Frick: I fear all of us could soon be the butt of jokes as early as next week. If not, one can certainly expect for this matter to appear and remain well beyond your lifetime and mine.

Landis: Baseball is on the precipice of a monumental, shining moment. There will be nothing but jubilation for the sport.

Frick: Dedicating the National Baseball Hall of Fame in the tiny village where this great sport was supposedly invented matters. The fact that we're doing all this on baseball's supposed one hundredth anniversary matters. It's the whole point why we're doing it at this time in that locale.

Landis: Regardless of where baseball was or wasn't invented, did you say the people of the village were a deserving lot? Is this not a community of good, honest, hardworking Americans who have endured over generations? A place where anyone could envision this to be the place where it all once began? Is it not a place of such natural majesty that, as Americans, we are proud to show off what our lands offer?

Frick: You and I know that, but people of future generations will reflect and speak on the fallacy of it all. It'll be a big joke, and quite frankly, so will we!

Landis: Nonsense! In time, this will become nothing other than another interesting anecdotal facet of the sport.

Frick: You have tougher skin than I, Kennie, probably all along.

Landis: That's not what it is. Why do you say that?

Frick: From the beginning of your reign, not that anyone can blame you, you kicked some of the game's most popular and talented athletes out of the game—and that was *after* a jury had acquitted them!

Landis: They were guilty as sin. Their gambling buddies stole and burned the real evidence. *That's* why they were acquitted.

Frick: The players were wrong, but they had a legitimate beef. Commiskey was paying them a fraction of their worth.

Landis: They signed contracts. They agreed to their earnings.

Frick: They had no choice. Back then, they had to take the offer or get nothing and don't play.

Landis: Those were the league rules back then.

Frick: Innocent unless proven guilty.

Landis: You were quite young back then, Ford. I was a federal judge. I remember the matter well. From a timing perspective, what they did could not have been more injurious. The year before the *Black Sox* scandal, we were coming off an extremely tough year for baseball—and as a nation. Due to the *Great War*, the 1918 Series was played in early September at Fenway Park at the beginning of the Spanish flu epidemic. Within days thereafter, hospitals hit capacity with Boston's death rate topping a hundred souls daily. Shops, the public-school system, amusements in Boston—all closed—but it was too late. It was an awful year for the world and America, and Boston was devastated. Major league baseball was criticized for allowing a ballpark of people to help spread the deadly disease. The next year, *Shoeless*

Joe and the other boneheads pulled their stunt. It wasn't that I had tough skin. Those eight desecrated the honor of baseball on the coattails of national tragedy and criticism of our sport. Throwing the 1919 World Series was a shameful act that shook the confidence our clients—the paying customer—had in our sport! Those players deserved what I gave them and more!

Frick: You're right, Kennie. *Tough skin* wasn't the best term to use.

Landis: Not even twenty years later, what does the public memory retain about the Series of '19? Promoting an epidemic? The gambling scandal?

Frick: The *Curse of the Bambino*!

Landis: Precisely. The Red Sox haven't won a championship since. People of today think old man Commiskey was a great and wonderful man. You needn't worry about the librarian!

Frick: So then, in the unlikely event we receive any inquiries from the reporters in the coming days and weeks, we will simply down-play the matter?

Landis: I wouldn't suggest that you inform a reporter you'll cut off his sources of information, although it would not be a surprise if he were to fall in disfavor with sporting news sources. Most sports writers have no desire to dishonor baseball, insult an entire vil-lage, nor raise our ire or that of the game's past greats or present stars involved in this wonderful event.

Frick: No further questions, Your Honor. The prosecution rests. That is all I had—and you, sir?

Landis: Nothing else on my end. Sounds like you have everything well under control. I'll finish with a cinematic tidbit, Mr. Frick. Might you happen to know the name of the full-length movie that was the first all-talking, all-color film to ever be made?

Frick: Of course! *On with the Show*!

Landis: Until Monday then. On with the show! (*disconnect*)

Upon hanging up the stick phone, Frick's eyes scanned the sur-face of the table where he was seated. He stared at the piles of mes-sages and telegrams requesting prompt replies. Clasping his hands behind his head, he leaned back in his chair to take a momentary break from all the thoughts spinning in his mind.

Years of plans and countless ideas would soon converge. Why didn't that *pain-in-the-ass* librarian bring the Doubleday fallacy into the open earlier, and then for Henderson to come up with a weak reason why the blame for the timing of his conclusion should be placed on the generosity of some hapless book collector. It may have changed the timing of the celebration—and whether the celebration and dedication would ultimately take place in Cooperstown or else-where. Even if things would not have resulted in a change as to what, where, and when the events were to take place, the explanations as to why might have been expressed in cleaner fashion. Regardless of it all, what a special and well-done event was planned! How could there possibly be a better choice for the location of baseball's cen-tennial celebration and the repository for baseball's heritage than Cooperstown village!

Frick reflected back to his first visit to the village. On the side of the main road at the village's outskirts was an historical marker he stopped to investigate. A mound not larger than two grave sites appeared within a plot of land the size of a modest home site. The parcel was guarded by a wrought iron fence. A small bronze sign sits atop a metal post by the entry gate: "Indian remains excavated in this field were reburied in 1874 at the base of this mysterious mound."

A tablet placed over the mound in 1899 by a local reverend offered his perspective:

> White man, greeting!
> We, near whose bones you stand,
> were Iroquois. The wide land
> which now is yours was ours.
> Friendly hands have given back
> to us enough for a tomb.

Generations earlier, a son of the man from whom the village took its namesake became a literary giant of early America. James Fenimore Cooper became a prolific novelist who wrote extensively about his perception of the lives and times of the region's indigenous peoples. Those people, the true earliest pioneers of the area, once represented more than ten nations with populations numbering in the tens of thousands. Given Cooper's notoriety, it is no wonder that every generation of children within this community grew up with a familiarity of the author's writings and an associated awareness of a rich history of the area long before white man arrived—taking the land for his own.

Cooperstown rests at a place where the Catskill and Adirondack mountains meet while offering a bird's-eye view of the lake that is the source to the Susquehanna River. The road leading to the 150-year-old village offers frequent vistas of majestic mountain panoramas along the Hudson River Valley, a favored subject of artists that once comprised the esteemed Hudson River school. To this, consider a Main Street of well-maintained buildings that stem from the earliest days of the village.

What better place to find a community of good-hearted, courageous guardians for the national heritage? Could there possibly be a better choice for the location of baseball's shrine? Frick thought things were indeed shaping up nicely!

Give the people what they want...

—The O' Jays

CHAPTER 14

The Hall

June 12, 1939—Cooperstown, Central New York

A way of life as it has existed since colonial times will change today. The change will be dramatic and permanent. Until now, out-of-state visitors to this village were rare. Greetings with the people one passes while walking have always been exchanged because you either knew them, or you knew someone else who did. Main Street was wider than it needed to be. Sidewalks were spacious. In the heart of downtown, a person could park their vehicle in front of the store where they shopped. Aside from stopping for a visit, errands were quick and effortless, though the pace seemed slow. Storefronts rarely changed and often advertised sales on useful products for daily life. In the future, except for the winter months, all this will be a memory of how village life once was.

Feelings of melancholy anticipated by Cooperstown residents for times soon gone by are easily overcome with an immense sense of euphoria. Like elsewhere throughout the nation, ten years of bad economic times hit families hard, and many continue to suffer. For most people who lost businesses, jobs, or savings, their dreams are farther away now than they were a decade ago. Whether by direct experience or through inescapable empathy, memories will remain brutally vivid for years to come. To Cooperstown residents, the significant positive economic impact to the community resulting from establishing a world-class shrine to the nation's most popular sport is obvious. To do so at this particular time is precisely *what the doctor ordered*. Today, that dream becomes a reality.

5:25 AM, Sunrise

It was sixty-nine degrees and clear at dawn. Village streets were awake. Townspeople and visitors were milling around. Downtown building facades had been readied. Store windows appeared colorful and welcoming. Banners, flowering pots, and buntings in the nation's colors were hanging from the fronts of buildings, and American flags were waving in the morning breeze. What few parking spaces allowed for today's use are taken. A temporary stage is set up on the sidewalk in front of the Hall.

The buildings serve as echo chambers that magnify the sounds of hammers and wood saws presently being employed by workmen in a frantic effort to complete construction on a variety of concessions that will be in use. It is as if the colors and movement and sounds are singing harmoniously. In less than seven hours from now, three years of planning and a dream that began years before that will usher a village's hope into reality. The only sports museum in America was coming to Cooperstown, Otsego County, New York.

Over the next four hours, cars and trucks will line the sides of neighborhood streets and the two roads leading into town. Clusters of parked cars and trucks will fill designated lots, front lawns, and nearby fields—for a price. The sounds of workmen will have been replaced with the constant hum of a large crowd the likes of what gathers in a ballpark prior to the beginning of an important game. Eateries were overflowing with diners and other hungry patrons awaiting their turn at breakfast. Retail establishments were deluged the moment their doors opened for business. The streets and sidewalks would be filled with vendors selling souvenirs and people standing together in tight quarters. Some of the area's youths were finding vantage points high atop buildings that overlooked the center of activity. State police and Otsego County deputies were visibly present to assist directing arriving traffic, crowd control, and in the provision of security to dignitaries, downtown merchants, and residential neighborhoods.

9:30 AM

It seemed difficult to believe that the train station was no longer used for its originally intended purpose. A crowd standing shoulder-to-shoulder packed the arrival platform from front to back and side to side. Newsreel people and photographers huddled together at the center of the platform awaiting the arrival of the first of three trains.

A delegation of local Democrats grouped together near the tracks. Local postmaster Melvin Bundy stood in formal uniform at the front of the group. Deputy State Attorney General Joseph P. Leary, chairman of Otsego County's Democratic Committee, stood at Bundy's side.

"I'll tell you what," Leary told Bundy, "that's big stuff, Melvin, having Postmaster General Farley tell your chain of command and the biggest Democrats in the state that he wanted you as his escort! He must have really taken a shine to you!"

"Never met the man," Bundy confessed. "I figured it was Mr. Frick who came up with the idea."

Leary declared, "Frick! He's peanuts! To James Farley, he's a puppet on a string! Mr. Farley does whatever he wants! Since you never met, I must ask what you know about him."

"I know what I need to," remarked Bundy.

"Is that so," Leary retorted. The deputy attorney general interrogated, "Tell me what you *think* you know about your boss of bosses."

"I know Mr. Farley was given his cabinet post at the beginning of President Roosevelt's first term," boasted Bundy. "I know that the Post Office Department always lost money until he came along, and now, it's profitable. I know his relationship with the president goes way back."

Leary interrupted, "Goes way back with FDR? Forget *way back*! He *made* FDR, and everyone knows it—including Eleanor! What else?"

"How did he supposedly *make* the president?"

Leary gave a short burst of laughter. "Mr. Farley was FDR's campaign manager when he ran for the governor's office of New York. He beat the political machine—in part by revolutionizing how we interpret polling statistics! Mr. Farley was the president's campaign manager for both terms as president. Why do you think he's postmaster general? It's considered a cush job—but do not quote me on this—normally reserved for campaign managers. What else do you know?"

Hesitantly, Bundy replied, "I know he's Irish American Roman Catholic. I know I'm really nervous!"

Leary laughed. "Nervous! *I'm* nervous around *you*. You're the chosen one. He picked you for whatever reason."

Bundy smiled. "I have no idea why! Oh. Also, I know he used to be head of the New York State Democratic Party."

"Just for your edification, Melvin, I'll make—"

Leary was interrupted by a series of loud blasts from the whistle of the approaching train. The shrillness at such a volume rattled the nerves of everyone on the station platform. The New York Special was arriving. The train station became noticeably noisier with the excitement of the impending arrival. Thirteen Pullman cars were carrying several ball clubs with the New York Yankees being one of them. Onboard there were also retired legends like Babe Ruth, a variety of dignitaries in and outside of baseball—there was a little something for most everyone.

Leary continued by raising his voice over the increased noise level. He shouted, "Melvin, just so you know, the man with Mr. Farley is the *acting* state Democratic party chairman because when Mr. Farley became chairman of the Democratic *National* Committee, he didn't step down from his state position. Mr. Farley remains state chairman. Also, as you are probably aware, there's a consensus out there that it would be wrongful for FDR to break tradition by running for a third term for president, and if FDR doesn't go for a third term, Mr. Farley is possibly the odds-on contender to run as the Democratic nominee for president. Incidentally, you never heard that from me!"

"On my mother's eyes," Bundy replied.

The train was quite a sight. The sixteen cars behind the engine made this train the longest one to ever have been destined for this station. The length of the train dwarfed the size of the platform; and the ground shook noticeably.

As the hissing from the engine pistons slowed, the squeaking and clacking noise from the wheels softened as did the crowd noise. Within the station, the cars inched their way and rumbled to a halt. A brief loud hissing from each set of wheels sounded as the brakes and pistons released steam and air. Station personnel would occasionally shout instructions at one another. State police continued to hold everyone back from the train except for people designated to facilitate those about to disembark. Small steps were placed at the points where passengers were to get off the train.

As the first person came out of one of the train car exits, the crowd erupted. The crowd on the platform had come alive as passengers began appearing at several of the exits. Out of the exit door of the Pullman at the front of the train and nearest the delegation appeared a large man donning a suit and Yankees baseball cap. It was US Postmaster General James Aloysius Farley. Acting state Democratic Party chair Vince Dailey appeared behind the dignitary.

Farley and Dailey descended on to the station platform, and as if by magic, reporters appeared near the train car—storming past the police.

One reporter shouted, "Mr. Postmaster General, how about a scoop?"

Farley replied, "You tell me! At the Postal Service, we're always the last ones to know anything!"

Another reporter called out, "Where's your boss today?"

Farley responded, "She's at home watching the kids."

(Subdued laughter.) The reporter retorted, "President Roosevelt!"

"He'll be handing out sheepskins at West Point commencement."

Another voice chimed in, "Surely you and the president have synchronized messages!"

"The president and I," Farley began, "consistently have synchronized messages because I support the administration's policies absolutely, but I'll let the president beat his own drum. I am here at the president's will and pleasure to support the spirit of the centennial celebration of an important American tradition"—as Farley raised an envelope with stamp in a small frame for all to see—"and sell this stamp commemorating the one hundredth anniversary since Abner Doubleday invented baseball."

Elsewhere on the station platform, cheers would frequently erupt as popular baseball well-knowns would appear.

"Do you intend on selling enough copies to pay for your train ticket?"

Farley smiled and looked at the framed stamp. "We're hoping this'll be the most popular commemorative of all time. I expect to sell a million of these beauties."

"Any intentions to announce your plans to run for high office?"

"You must do Christmas shopping in July," Farley theorized. He then turned his head toward Dailey. "You see, Vince, someone had to go and spoil it all by bringing politics into this—and starting such a rumor!"

Dailey gently took Farley by the arm and turned to the reporters. "Boys and girls, we'd like to chat more, but we have people to see. See you at one of the clambakes! Thank you!"

Ignoring further questions from the press, the state police opened a short path into the crowd to facilitate Farley and Dailey's escape. The two men headed directly toward the awaiting delegation of Democrats.

Easily recognizing the uniformed local postmaster, Farley made a beeline toward Bundy. Farley and Bundy introduced themselves, and at the same time, the acting Democrat State Committee Chairman Dailey and Otsego Democrat County Committee Chairman Leary greeted one another. A lengthy flurry of greetings and introductions ensued between the other Democrat hosts and the two arriving passengers.

Following the exchanges, Farley said, "Folks, I am in dire need of a shave, and with my associate, Postmaster Bundy, we must take our leave for the barbershop. I'll see all of you again immediately after the dedication ceremony at one of the clambake seatings."

Bundy and Farley headed toward the station exit. Once outside, the two men began the short walk toward town. Farley glanced back at the depot and said, "For this size of town, that's a fine stone building you have for a train station. How often does the train come?"

"It doesn't. Not anymore," Bundy replied. "The building is a beauty. It's only eight years old. The train company owning the spur constructed the building. They apparently had plans for our village, but a change in management decided to put their time into more profitable routes and left us high and dry with only this empty station to show for it."

"Such a fine station to go unused," Farley offered. "It served its purpose today though. It was quite the convenience getting here!"

"I'm sure, sir," Bundy responded.

"Call me Jim," Farley requested.

Bundy grinned. "I go by Mel or Melvin—either-or."

"Fair enough," Farley replied gently. "Also, I have a question about the supervisors I sent up here from Washington. They were supposed to assist you in getting ready for today's stamp sale and to prepare to send the hundreds of thousands of First Day issue mailings. I heard from them that things have worked out well over these past weeks. I wanted to hear your perspective. What's your take?"

Bundy enthused, "Everything has worked out well! They've helped with managing the fifty people we hired. We're also getting help from the Leather Stocking Club, a local group, and your folks have helped to coordinate with the members of that club also."

Bundy paused briefly and added, "I must admit, I needed all the help I could get. We've been working around the clock with no complaints from anyone. Your people knew how to plan things out. That was especially helpful to me because frankly, I've never done anything like this before. The people you sent to help are all likeable too. We're getting done all that we needed to."

Farley bellowed, "Outstanding! I wanted to believe what my people told me, and now, I do! I especially like the last part you mentioned about getting done what was needed."

"I have another question on a different topic, Melvin, but I don't know whether you will be able to answer it."

"Fire away, sir."

"Might you happen to know the present whereabouts of Judge Landis or your friend, Mr. Frick?"

"Not certain," Bundy replied, "but I suspect they're presently together."

Farley inquired, "Why do you *suspect* that?"

Bundy replied, "When Mr. Frick called the other day, he informed me that it would be my *duty to hold* your *hand*. He said he was going to do the same for the commissioner."

Farley responded pensively, "I see!"

Bundy laughed. "May I inquire why you ask?"

Farley responded matter-of-factly. "When League President Frick informed me that you would be available *to hold* my hand, I asked if he *might similarly be willing to hold the hand of the commissioner*."

Bundy wondered, "The commissioner?"

"Yes," commented Farley. "I want to personally sell the first stamp to Judge Landis. We've never done that sort of thing before, and the sooner we get the commissioner over here, the sooner we can get the ball rolling on the day's stamp sales."

As the two men moved ever more slowly due to the intensifying crowd, Farley asked, "Are we getting near our first destination?"

"We're very close," Bundy offered. "That's the Hall of Fame up ahead on the left." Pointing to the right, Bundy added, "The post office is across the street. Gage's Barbershop is a block up. Best shave in town!"

As the denseness of the crowd intensified, Bundy took the lead as the two began walking in single-file order as Farley followed close behind.

Bundy turned around and looked back every ten steps to make certain the postmaster general remained right behind him. Farley patted Bundy on the shoulder and said, "You're not going to lose me, Melvin. I've decided to take *you by your hand!*"

They crossed the street to arrive at Gage's Barbershop. All customer chairs were taken, and those standing were in tight quarters, but the barbers' chairs were empty. Bundy walked ahead and said something to one of the barbers. The barber waved to Farley, summoning him over to the chair the barber was standing next to.

Bundy said to the barber while gesturing toward Farley, "The Postmaster General of the United States needs a shave. Do you think you might accommodate him?"

The barber slapped at the chair with the sheet he was holding. "Sit yours down right here. The name is Harry Yule. Pleased to be making your acquaintance!"

Farley and Yule shook hands. "Hello, Harry. Jim Farley."

"A real honor, sir," said Yule. "Make yourself comfortable. You're among friends. We're mostly Democrats in here."

Farley sat down. Conversation in the shop ceased while everyone watched the dignitary. Yule pulled a fresh linen out of a cabinet and placed it on top of Farley's clothing.

Farley continued, "I understand from Postmaster Bundy that you give a good shave."

Yule asked rhetorically, "Do I give a good shave? No, sir! I'm not good. I am the best! When you step out of this chair, you'll feel and look twenty years younger."

Farley responded, "That's good to know. I suspect my wife, Elizabeth, would like being with a younger man."

Yule laughed. "Excellent, but I suggest you don't make me laugh once I strop the blade."

The postmaster general smiled and didn't say another word until after the process was complete—the slow and methodical stropping of the razor's blade, hot towel, lathering, shaving, application of the Barbasol aftershave lotion, and Yule's fanning of Farley's face and back of neck to soothe the burn. Yule removed the barber's linen covering Farley's suit and turned the Postmaster General toward the wall mirror.

"Great shave! I feel twenty years younger! What do I owe you?"

"Not a wooden nickel, sir," Yule responded. "This one's on the house!"

Farley said, "No, sir. I insist!"

Yule responded, "If you run for president and win, I'll take a set of free tours at the White House."

Farley laughed and then said in a suspicious and serious voice, "Why on earth did you say that?"

Yule paused. "Well, sir, if your horse needs shoes, go to a blacksmith. If you want to know politics, go to a barber."

Farley smiled, nodded, shook Yule's hand, and departed with Postmaster Bundy. The two post office gents walked down the street toward the Hall and post office. As they began crossing the street in front of the Hall of Fame building, Farley spotted the delegation of Democrats that greeted him at the station earlier. The Dems stood near the newsreel cameras set up alongside the stage in front of the Hall of Fame.

While the Democrats stood and chatted with Farley, one of the local Democrats commented in a lowered voice that a man with one leg was seated by one of the newsreel cameras near the stage.

"I wonder if one of us should help the poor man," the woman said.

Farley turned to the lady and replied, "Excuse me for one moment. There's someone I need to see."

Farley walked over to the man with one leg and began talking to him. The two men could be observed shaking hands and quickly entering into a serious conversation. As Farley talked with the man, they couldn't help but pause as a loud series of blasts of a train whistle from the direction of the train station echoed between the buildings along Main Street. After the train whistle blasts subsided, Farley and the man by the camera concluded their conversation, and Farley rejoined the group.

Acting state Democratic chairman Dailey asked, "Do you know that man?"

"We never met until now," Farley replied. "But I knew who he was—and so will you when you hear the name!"

Dailey asked, "Who is he?"

"That," Farley responded, "is the biggest sportscaster of them all. That, my friend, is Bill Stern of NBC."

Bundy exclaimed, "That's Bill Stern? The one-legged man? What did you say to him, if I may ask?"

"I introduced myself and asked him if he lost his wooden leg."

Dailey asked, "And?"

Farley continued, "Stern said he didn't feel like bothering to put it on. He said he can get around faster when it's not getting in his way…that if someone doesn't know who he is without the prosthesis, the person isn't important enough in the sports world for him to bother with!"

Dailey further inquired, "That's all you said to him?"

"Heavens, no," Farley replied. "Meeting him was too big an opportunity. I told him that, should he see Commissioner Landis, to send him right over to the post office so that we can begin selling our first day commemorative stamps before the waiting customers get unruly."

"He must have liked that," Dailey said.

Farley laughed. "He did. Stern said the train whistle we all heard just now was announcing the arrival of the Chicago Special. Stern said he'd be sure to pass along the message. He's a newsman. Those guys like passing along that kind of message when the commissioner of baseball is involved. It's a good war story for him. It's also a fun story for me to pass along to FDR at the next cabinet meeting. When you're in public office, it's good to befriend someone with a national audience and a microphone. Maybe he'll mention me when he's broadcasting his coast-to-coast show this week."

"That would be something." Dailey chuckled. "I take it then that President Roosevelt knows you're here."

"He does," Farley replied. "He might have been here if he wasn't giving a speech today at the West Point commencement ceremonies."

"Will the president be sending a message to the Army or maybe to the world?"

"I guess it won't be a secret much longer," Farley said. "I haven't heard the speech, but I know he'll be passing along that he's going to Congress for more military funding. As I recall, his message will be along the lines of cautioning people not to *mistake America's desire for peace to be a sign of weakness*. If I know the president, he'll probably be handing out the diplomas too."

Turning to Bundy, Farley continued, "We better get over to the post office. I want to meet the people and get ready for the start of the first day issue sale."

Farley informed the group that he and Mr. Bundy had to depart and that they would all meet up for seafood at lunch after the dedication ceremonies. Farley and Bundy crossed the street toward the postal building and walked up the steps. The custodian was waiting for them by the main entrance to the post office.

Someone from the street shouted to the custodian, "Hey, Miller. You better get to work. Farley's watching you!"

Mr. Miller handed a note to Bundy. The note read that Frick would bring Commissioner Landis to the post office upon the arrival of the Chicago Special at the Delaware and Hudson station.

No sooner was the note read than they heard another series of train whistle blasts. The blasts were louder than the first time and reverberated between the downtown buildings.

"Hopefully," Farley commented to Bundy, "we'll be seeing the judge and your friend Frick soon?"

"It's likely, sir," replied Bundy, "but it will take them some time to get here. The crowd is thick now, and there'll be plenty of reporters to distract them."

"True enough," Farley responded. "After all, Landis and Frick are the ones bringing the cast of the play."

Bundy furled his eyebrows. "Out of curiosity, sir, why did you refer to Mr. Frick as my *friend*? Did he say something nice about me that I might enjoy hearing?"

Farley chuckled. "He's said nice things about you on more than one occasion and about your people also."

"He likes spending time in this building," Bundy observed. "He says it reminds him of all the time he spent at the post office while he was growing up in Indiana."

Farley wondered, "Frick spent a lot of time as a kid at the post office?"

Bundy replied, "His dad was postmaster of the town where he's from."

"Oh," inquired Farley. "What town was that?"

"I don't recall," Bundy said. "I'm not certain he ever said, and I fear I never asked."

"Well," Farley retorted playfully, "it's good to know he's one of us post-office types!"

Bundy exclaimed, "But I understand you never came through the ranks in the system!"

Farley offered, "We need to get inside shortly, Melvin, but not before I ask a question. It's important to me."

"Whatever you'd like to know," Bundy replied.

"I require your honest opinion," Farley said. "How am I doing?"

"How are you doing? What do you mean, sir?"

"Your point of view is important to me," Farley stated. "However you interpret my inquiry, how am I doing? Be honest. Be critical. Here's your chance to bash the boss!"

Bundy was enthusiastic. "I think you're doing great! Everyone I know in the Postal Service thinks that."

Farley followed up. "Why?"

"Different people, different reasons," Bundy responded.

"Please explain that, Melvin!"

Bundy inquired, "May I first ask you a question, sir?"

"But of course," Farley replied.

"When no one before you could make the post office profitable," Bundy began, "what was the trick in getting the US Postal Service on track?"

"No trick at all," Farley responded. "When FDR took over and brought me on board, he and I both agreed that the US mail was a sacred trust, an important responsibility, and with all the resources the federal government possessed, there was no reason for it not to run securely and efficiently, with the cost of operation to be borne by the users. Without question, both the president and I felt honored to own this important responsibility. The knowledge to improve things was already in the heads of the postal workers. Before us, however, no president had accepted ownership of this public trust, and no one seems to have solicited input from the proverbial *men and women in the trenches*. I just asked some questions of my employees and implemented their ideas. It's not unlike my question to you."

"Three cheers for the little people! Thank you! As for a response to *your* question, people became happier once the [Postal] Service became profitable," Bundy acknowledged. "Customers stopped with the jokes, and the workers take more pride in what they do."

Farley asked, "Which types or groups of employees are *happier*?"

"Everyone," Bundy answered, "as far as I know. Mail carriers and window clerks, men and women, and you're a legend with the nonwhite employees."

Farley looked puzzled. "Legend? I hardly think that!"

"It's true," Bundy retorted. "I heard the nonwhite employees were upset two years ago when FDR broke tradition after Jesse Owens won the Olympics and wasn't invited to the White House. After that, word spread that you would never have done something like rebuke an Olympic athlete for being a man of color. There's a popular story that, when you were in charge of the New York State Athletics Commission, you stopped a boxing match between Dempsey and Tunney for the World Heavyweight Championship because Dempsey refused to fight the number one contender because the man was a Negro. The employees I talked with say they *work for Farley, not Roosevelt*."

Farley smiled and humbly replied, "I recall the headlines—so long ago. Not everyone liked what I did, but it worked."

Bundy chuckled and said, "Maybe I should tell that story to Judge Landis when he comes up here in a few minutes to buy his stamp."

"I don't recommend that, Mr. Bundy. That kind of message is needed, but it needs to be properly planned. Baseball is merely a reflection of this country's populace. The fight should take place soon but at a much higher level and in a much broader fashion!"

Farley placed his large hand on Bundy's shoulder. "Let's go inside, Melvin. Much to do and not much time."

* * *

Farley and Bundy had been at the postal building for fifteen minutes when Baseball Commissioner Kenesaw Mountain Landis arrived. He was accompanied by National League President Ford Frick. Frick, knowing each *player*, made the introductions, after which Landis spoke to Farley.

"I understand from your high-priced messenger," Landis said as he briefly glanced at Frick and then again looked at Farley to continue, "that you wish to speak with me."

Farley mused, "I'm pleased that you have arrived, Mr. Commissioner. I assume you arrived on the Chicago Special."

"I did," Landis replied. "Early in my career on the federal bench in the Chicago District, *The Saturday Evening Post* did an article about me in September of '07 after I handed down a $30,000,000 fine to Standard Oil Company. Albert Spalding, always thinking of his business interests in that town, read the article and subsequently came by to introduce himself to me. He had a thing for chartering special trains, so I thought I might honor him by doing the same."

Farley offered, "Excellent rationale, Mr. Commissioner. I can think of nothing more appropriate on this day!" Pausing briefly, Farley continued. "Mr. Commissioner, Mr. Frick, please step over to the front of this customer line. I would like to sell you the very first of these baseball three-cent commemorative issues."

Landis replied, "My word!" Turning to Frick, he asked, "Did you know about this?" Frick did not reply.

Landis than turned to Farley and confessed, "This is, indeed, a special moment for me to receive such an honor, sir…this stamp on this day by the postmaster general of the United States and, in particular, by a man of your considerable accomplishment."

"The honor is mine," Farley responded. "Your accomplishments are legendary, and you are the first sports figure to ever receive the first of such an issue."

After Landis received the first of the stamps, Frick was next in line. Frick purchased a group of stamps.

Farley inquired, "Sending some letters back home, are you?"

Frick replied, "Different places actually. The first letter is going to Mr. Harry Higgins, Esquire, of Whitewater, Wisconsin. Good guy."

Landis looked at Frick and inquired, "Esquire? You socialize with attorneys?", to wit Frick returned an agreeing nod.

The stamp was printed in a shade of magenta with a picture of a sandlot game of baseball. Aside from the denomination and identifier of *United States Postage* were the following words, *Centennial of Baseball.* On the left side of the envelope was an image of a baseball player swinging a bat in front of a baseball that said *1839* on the left and *1939* on the right side. Beneath the image were the words, *Invented by Abner Doubleday—Cooperstown, NY.* Across the bottom of the envelope were the words, *AMERICA PREFERS BASEBALLS TO CANNONBALLS.*

Farley continued, "Tell me, Mr. Frick, what do you think of the design on the stamp and envelope?"

"It looks perfect," Frick commented. "Nice motto on the bottom too."

Farley laughed. "That's a message straight from the top—of my world."

As Landis and Frick departed, Farley remained to sign autographs. One young lady barely of voting age asked Farley for his autograph. The request and ensuing conversation were overheard by a journalist of the Cooperstown *Freeman's Journal.*

Farley replied, "I can hardly refuse the request of such a beautiful girl."

As Farley signed the envelope, the lady replied, "Yes, and I'm a good Republican too."

Claude Hotaling, a barber competitor of Harry Yule, had to stop by to lament that he didn't get the opportunity to shave Farley in his own shop. "I had to go over to the hotel when I gave Babe Ruth his shave!"

Farley was deluged with autograph seekers and thus remained at the post office until shortly before the ceremonies kicked off as scheduled at 12:15 PM sharp.

* * *

Noon

A half-dozen newsreel cameras were poised in front of the stage located on the sidewalk in front of the National Baseball Hall of Fame. Clusters of microphones were attached near the speakers' podium. They carried familiar broadcasting acronyms: NBC, CBS, ABC, and other national and regional networks. Main Street was packed with people for blocks in either direction. On the stage, seated dignitaries included Commissioner Landis, Ford Frick, American League President William Harridge, National Association President William G. Bramham, former umpire and previous National League president John Heydler, Cooperstown Mayor Roland Spraker, Cooperstown Centennial Corporation Chairman Lettis, and others. The master of ceremonies was Charles *Chili* Doyle, president of the Baseball Writers Association of America, the organization that votes to determine the Hall of Fame inductees. Doyle stood by the speakers' podium.

At noon, the bands began a fifteen-minute medley with "My Country 'Tis of Thee" and concluded by "Take Me Out to the Ball Game" as the crowd boisterously sang the words. The song concluded, and MC Doyle introduced Mayor Spraker. Spraker was the first speaker to give one of several short speeches.

> "We in Cooperstown have been long proud of the fact that baseball originated here. And we are happy that the rest of the United States is being told about it during this centennial year. To those of you present here today, we hope you like our village. We hope the National Baseball Museum and Doubleday Field, which we built in pride,

will be as thrilling to you as it is to us. To those of you listening in, we extend a cordial invitation to visit Cooperstown, the cradle of baseball.

A few hundred yards from the spot where I now stand is a lovely, peaceful lake—Otsego Lake. Just offshore of Otsego Lake is a rock of which, two hundred years ago, the Indian chiefs of the Five Nations used to gather for council. It is known as Otsego Rock and the word *Otsego* is said to be a compound which conveys the idea of a spot at which meetings were held. Today, as Mayor of Cooperstown, I ask you all to remember that word *Otsego, where meetings were held,* and meet with us here in Cooperstown in 1939."

As Spraker returned to his seat amidst applause, Doyle next introduced former National League president Heydler as the *father of the baseball centennial* celebration. After a brief speech, Doyle next introduced Baseball Commissioner Landis. Landis spoke of the special nature of baseball and the museum. He continued, "And nowhere else than at its birthplace could this museum be appropriately situated."

Upon speaking further, Landis added, "I should like to dedicate this museum to all America, to lovers of good sportsmanship, healthy bodies, and keen minds."

Landis then afforded the privilege of cutting the ribbons laid across the entry door to Frick, Harridge, and Bramham. Landis and the other three baseball executives, accompanied by Cooperstown Baseball Centennial Committee Chairman Lettis, proceeded toward the three ceremonial ribbons. Lettis pointed out the symbolism of the colors of the three ribbons in red, white, and blue. Lettis handed a pair of scissors to Frick who cut the red ribbon. Harridge and Bramham cut the white and blue ribbons—with each of the three offering the briefest of statements. Lettis then opened up the door with a key that he subsequently presented to Landis.

Cheers were constant. Along with a drumroll, the thirteen *pioneers of baseball* were named and included such names as Adrian Constantine "Cap" Anson, Alexander Cartwright, Henry Chadwick, Charles "Old Roman" Commiskey, Albert G. Spalding, and George Wright. The first twelve were posthumous honors. Upon announcing the thirteenth name, Cornelius McGillicuddy, the museum door opened, and the man, better known as *Connie Mack*, stepped outside the door to a deafening round of cheers and applause.

Next, Landis called the names of the twelve inductees each to a drumroll. The first five inducted into the Hall in 1936 were Christy Mathewson, Tyrus Raymond Cobb, Walter Johnson, Honus Wagner, and George Herman "Babe" Ruth. The latter four were alive and present and, with the exception of Cobb who had not yet arrived, walked out of the museum after each roll of the drums, with each of the three making a brief statement.

Whenever Ruth was spotted anywhere, he always garnered enthusiastic, favorable crowd reactions. As usual, the *Sultan of Swat* was easily spotted. Today, he was the epitome of men's fashion, donning a well-tailored, comfortably cut summer suit of lightly-shaded Palm Beach fabric. His shoes were covered in white spats. When the Babe appeared somewhere, crowd noise levels typically rose. As Ruth stepped up to the microphone to give his speech, the crowd hushed. Babe Ruth's speech as transcribed from audio by the American Rhetoric Online Speech Bank appears below in its entirety:

> Thank you, ladies and gentlemen.
>
> I hope someday that some of the young fellas that's coming into the game will know how it feels to be picked on the Hall of Fame.
>
> I know the old boys back in there—were just talking it over. Some been here long before my time. They got on it. And I worked hard and got on it.
>
> And I hope that the coming generation, the young boys today—that they'll work hard and also be on it.

And as my old friend Cy Young says, "I hope it goes another hundred years and the next hundred years will be the greatest."

You know, to me, this is just like an anniversary myself, because 25 years ago yesterday I pitched my first baseball game in Boston—for the Boston Red Sox. So it seems like an anniversary for me too, and I'm surely glad, and it's a pleasure for me to come up here and be picked also in the Hall of Fame.

Then, the inductees from the class of 1938 and 1939 also appeared.

The ceremony closed at 1:00 PM with "The Star-Spangled Banner."

Memorable events continued one after another throughout the day and evening hours. Supplementing the local eateries, a variety of casual affairs enabled many to enjoy a meal. Lunch and dinner clambakes, hosted by local Democrats, were held on the lake's edge at *two bucks a head*. Several private parties hosted meal seatings, including a local married couple who, with the assistance of family member and friends, served more than six hundred hungry diners.

2:30 PM EST, Main Street and Doubleday Field

The Cavalcade of Baseball parade began precisely on schedule—and what a parade it was! The procession that began at 2:30 PM offered spiffy high school bands and orchestral groups from various states, military and academy marching units, dignitaries on foot and riding show cars, eye-catching floats and mobile displays, area social clubs showing off historically accurate, brightly colored, and oft humorous uniforms of old-time baseball teams, a comprehensive presence of the greatest baseball stars representing the different major league and other teams from times past and present, clowns, jugglers, and an array of other oddities.

At the tail end of the parade, saving the best for last—the umpires! This tough group of men drew from the crowd a rousing and fun-spirited combination of cheers and boos. The parade was long, loud, colorful, fun, interesting, symbolic, and well-received. There were constant cheers and applause from the thousands of happy onlookers of all ages standing several people deep along the parade route that progressed along Main Street and ended at Doubleday Field ballpark. It was a good show.

An overflow crowd of ten thousand filled the grandstands, sidelines, and standing room areas of Doubleday Field to watch two contests. First, however, the spectators were treated to a fun skit.

In honor of the centennial and dedication ceremonies, there were no officially scheduled games in the major leagues. Rather, baseball fans all over the nation listening on either of three nationwide radio networks were treated to commentaries by broadcast legends Mel Allen and Bill Stern; covering two special baseball contests: an old-timers game with some of history's best veteran ballplayers and an all-star game where people could see the best active players of the day in a contest that pitted the National League against the American League in a seven-inning contest.

It was great fun to watch several of the performances by the old-timers. To the crowd's grand pleasure, Babe Ruth appeared at the bat five years into retirement. Of the two pitches that he swung his bat at, he weakly fouled off the first pitch and then feebly popped up another over home plate. To the dismay of several members of the crowd shouting for the catcher to miss the ball, the pop-up was caught, and the Babe fouled out. A reporter for the Boston Globe thought a ten-year-old boy best summarized most people's feelings: *"Gee,"* he gasped, *"ain't the Babe wonderful?"*

For the All-Star Game, two Hall of Famers were designated as the coaches: Red Sox General Manager Eddie Collins and Pittsburgh Pirates Manager Honus Wagner.

The *Collinses'* starting pitcher was Jerome "Dizzy" Dean. At the time, Dean was best known for frequently raising the ire of umpires by constantly stopping play when pitching because he enjoyed watching planes pass overhead. Nevertheless, Dean's athletic talents did not disappoint anyone on this day. Dean pitched the first two innings and made outs of the six players he faced. Overall, it was a good contest where people witnessed many good plays and performances and a game that was tied going into the bottom of the sixth inning. The *Wagners* won by a score of 4–2 in seven innings.

The only conspicuous absence of living baseball stardom was Lou Gehrig who missed the past six weeks due to *sluggishness*. During the activities at Doubleday Field, Gehrig was playing a charity exhibition game in Detroit. From there, he would take the short jaunt to see some medical doctors at the Mayo Clinic in Rochester, Minnesota, to learn why his timing and coordination had not been up to snuff as of late. The *Iron Man* would never play baseball again and passed away less than two years later.

By any measure, Commissioner Landis, Ford Frick, the people of Cooperstown, and others associated with the centennial celebration must have been pleased at the outcome of the day's activities. Good memories and thoughts of baseball were stirred up from coast to coast without mishap. The various components of baseball were synchronized and in harmony. Although the National Baseball Hall of Fame and Museum has evolved into a world-class institution that has exceeded any reasonable person's expectations over the years, this could not be known at the time. What was known is that the Hall of Fame was off to a great start—something, which in its own small way, paved a route for what, over the years, the Hall of Fame would become.

Although the proper application of logic and historical fact at the proper times may have prevented the Hall of Fame from being located in the village of Cooperstown, New York, that didn't happen. The powers that be pulled it off successfully. The Doubleday legend was *carved in stone* or—at least in brick and mortar.

Thank goodness for this stroke of good fortune! Over the years that followed that spring day in 1939, this community proved its worth. That latter point, however, serves to only supplement the voluminous amount of baseball history that has occurred in Cooperstown since the Hall's dedication to create an immovable anchor for the sport in this place where now, nearly three hundred years ago, leaders of five indigenous American nations, in the words of Mayor Spraker, "used to gather for council."

What of the librarian from the New York City Public Library who also labored at the Racquet and Tennis Club? Robert Henderson's activities after June 12 of 1939 represent the heart of the next chapter of the Doubleday legend.

Facts do not cease to exist
because they are ignored.

—Aldous Huxley

CHAPTER 15

Every Dog Has His Day

Twelve years later...

The librarian would have several significant professional events happen to him over the dozen years that followed the Hall's dedication. Within a year following the centennial celebration, the dream Henderson discussed with David Wagstaff came to fruition. Under the auspices of Manhattan's Grolier Club, Henderson produced a two-month exhibit entitled, "Six Hundred Years of Sport." The production afforded the public an opportunity to see original documents of all sorts relating to various sports—many of which dated back to the sixteenth, fifteenth, and fourteenth centuries.

Three years after the Grolier Club exhibit, Henderson was promoted to what was considered as arguably the most prestigious operational position at the New York Public Library: chief, main reading room. The main reading room is housed at the library's flagship location on Fifth Avenue. The expansive room boasted the largest unsupported ceiling in the world. As the title suggested, his responsibility included directing a staff of fifty employees, including librarians, book pages, security, and other personnel while ensuring the publication inventories remained adequate, current, and comprehensive based on the public's ever-changing demands.

After the passing of another four years, in 1947, Henderson published his landmark work entitled, *Ball, Bat and Bishop*. The well-written volume articulated the evolution of several sports that, in some instances, began 5,000 years earlier with the Egyptians. The book met with modest recognition – far short of its rightful fanfare.

Manhattan, early afternoon, a weekday, January 1951

The desk Henderson sat at was *well-seasoned* when he first began with the library four decades earlier. Henderson always liked the desk, and once he received his last promotion eight years ago, he relocated the desk to his present work space.

Presently, Henderson was teaching a new procedure to three of the many book pages assigned to him. He looked up and, to his surprise, spotted his wife, Lucy; his daughter, Joy; and his oldest grandchild—eleven-year-old Frank. Being the first time the three had jointly visited him, Henderson could not hide the puzzled expression on his face.

One of the book pages said, "Sir, we can get back to the stacks, if you wish, and come back later."

Henderson replied, "Good idea. We'll finish up this afternoon."

The pages promptly departed as the spry Henderson sprung to his feet. The two ladies each gave Henderson a loving peck on the cheek while he placed his hands on the shoulder of his grandson who was leaning against him.

Henderson asked, "What are you three doing here?"

"Sale at Lord & Taylor," replied Lucy as she set a glass of milk on his desk.

Henderson stated softly, "Dear, drinks aren't allowed on desks!"

As if he should have known better, Lucy replied, "It's for your grandson! He's thirsty!"

The two ladies began walking off while little Frank remained at his grandfather's side. Henderson called out, "Where are you two going?"

Without slowing down their departure, Lucy turned back toward him and said, "I told you. We're going to Lord & Taylor. We'll be right back." The ladies were soon out of sight.

A bewildered Henderson pulled an extra chair up to his desk for his grandchild to sit. Before he had a chance to speak to little Frank, Henderson was tapped on his shoulder from behind. He looked back to see two tall male figures in suits with a uniformed security guard standing behind them. Upon quickly standing, Henderson immediately recognized his boss from the Racquet and Tennis Club, Francis "Skiddy" von Stade Sr. The guard was also from the club, and both Henderson and the guard knew one another. Upon locking eyes, the guard and Henderson exchanged nods. Henderson realized the third person was Ralph A. Beals, director of the New York Public Library.

As everyone within the administrative corral was now standing at their desks, Henderson casually lifted the glass of milk, handed it to an associate standing close by, and whispered something, whereby the person took the milk glass and somehow disposed of it.

Director Beals looked at Frank and inquired, "And who might you be?"

The child beamed and responded, "Frank Chapman van Cleef, the Third, sir. Who are you?"

Director Beals replied, "I work here at the New York Public Library with Mr. Henderson, and these two gentlemen," motioning to von Stade and the guard, "work with Mr. Henderson at his other job."

Henderson spoke up. Looking at his grandson, he motioned toward von Stade and said, "This man is my boss at the club."

The child looked unimpressed, and Beals spoke, "They named a giant ocean-going steamship after him." To wit, the child's eyes opened wide.

Motioning to Beals, Henderson continued, "This gentleman is my boss here at the public library. He's in charge of this building and all the other branches around the city too!"

The child's face again displayed an expression of awe.

Turning to his esteemed guests, Henderson boasted, "That's my oldest grandchild, sir. He's never been here before, and frankly,

I'm a bit puzzled as to why he's here now. As a matter of fact, I'm wondering…"

Beals smiled. "You're wondering why we're pestering you too. Right?"

Henderson smiled in return. "I certainly wouldn't put it that way, sir, but I am a bit curious!"

"Wonder no more," Beals said. "I was recently reading the book you wrote four years ago…"

Henderson nodded his head and acknowledged, "*Ball, Bat, and Bishop!*"

"Yes," Director Beals responded. "I was new in my position here at the library when it first came out. I had flipped through it, saw it was interesting and well-written, but only recently read it cover to cover. I apologize it took me so long to pay the work the attention it deserves."

Henderson inquired, "Sorry? I'm honored!"

Beals held up an old set of library bulletins and continued, "From one of the footnotes in your book, I then looked at this library bulletin from ten years ago and—"

Von Stade interrupted and, looking at the guard, stated, "And that bulletin referred to this book."

Wearing white cotton gloves, the guard opened a custom-made container in the style of a cigar box and gingerly removed a little book, held it up, and then replaced the book in its apparent sarcophagus.

Each of the four men standing knew the title of the little book.

Henderson nodded. "*The Boy's Own Book*, Robin Carver, 1834."

Director Beals enthusiastically replied, "That's right!" Then, holding up the eleven-year-old bulletin from July of 1940, Beals stated, "It says in this bulletin that *The Boy's Own Book* is the oldest known publication showing rules that equate to modern-day baseball."

"Yes," Henderson concurred. "At the time I wrote of this in the article you're holding, it was a new discovery. I knew of another book when the bulletin was printed, but that latter book was published one year later—in 1835."

"I discovered that," Beals responded. "I should add that I've been told your piece in the 1939 bulletin caused quite a stir!"

"Yes," Henderson agreed. "In comparison, the bulletin you're holding from 1940 resulted in no heartache for me whatsoever. May I inquire why you have these three publications?"

"But of course," Beals said. "In your book, you referenced the bulletin, and the bulletin referencing *The Boy's Own Book* stating there were two known existing copies—one in the Library of Congress and the other at the Racquet and Tennis Club. I should add, that's quite a little collection of sport books you've amassed over there!"

A smiling von Stade interjected, "It serves the club's purposes well."

"I'm sure," responded Beals. Then, holding up Henderson's book, *Ball, Bat, and Bishop*, the director observed, "I see you give a man, Alexander Cartwright, a great deal of credit for the rules of baseball similar to how we play the game today—referring to him as a *patron saint*."

"I felt he and his teammates who helped codify the rules of the game deserved a good amount of credit," Henderson agreed.

"We also liked the passage you wrote about Abner Doubleday," von Stade added. Then opening a copy of Henderson's book to a passage, he began to read,

> *Undiluted sophistry…why confuse a perfectly good American patriot and historical figure who justly earned distinction during the Civil War with an unhistorical, legendary fame? Doubleday stands in no need of a fame unjustly pinned upon him. To insist upon the baseball legend is not to honor him but to discredit him. Must teachers in our schools perpetuate a legend when they know better?*

Henderson, standing quietly, noticed the crowd already forming loosely around the group. Now appearing close by was Henderson's wife and daughter whose side little Frank decided to return to.

Standing next to little Frank was his father, the Reverend Van Cleef, and next to him was Henderson's son, twenty-nine-year-old Robert L.

Director Beals inquired, "I'm curious, Mr. Henderson. It's been four years since your book came out. Have your theories relating to the origins of our national pastime been accepted by the definitive authorities of baseball?"

"I'm certain there are many respected authorities," Henderson began, "who embrace the findings. There haven't been any loud bands playing music in tribute or fireworks going off in celebration or recognition, however, if that is what you are asking."

"More specifically," Beals asked, "has the *Official Encyclopedia of Baseball blessed* your findings as *gospel?*"

Henderson said in a mildly somber tone, "No. The major publications never chose to acknowledge my book—to the best of my knowledge. I'm uncertain as to what combination of reasons they have for not doing so, but I understand. Nevertheless, I've been pleased with having received quite a bit of good press on what was written!"

Beals asked Henderson, "Hasn't that ever bothered you, not having affirmation from those in a position to acknowledge such things?"

To that question, Henderson's wife stepped forward and responded, "I always wondered that as well. If it does bother him, sir, Robert has never let on. My Robert rarely complains about issues he has little control over. He's driven but not like so many others. His motives are pure. He's quite academic!"

Lucy approached Henderson carrying a good-sized book with a blue ribbon placed upon it.

Director Beals interjected, "I guess worrying about acknowledgment is all moot now."

As Lucy presented the book to Henderson, a large bookmark was placed at the beginning of the book.

Beals began as he held up high for all to see another copy of *The Official Encyclopedia of Baseball*. "Ladies and gentlemen," Beals began, "this is the definitive source on the topic of all things baseball. It was just printed in its jubilee edition. The first thirty-six pages, chapters

1 and 2, are dedicated to and entitled, *Evolution of Baseball.* The first chapter is six pages in length and begins with page 1 within this volume. The first paragraph poses the question, Where did baseball come from? The second paragraph describes the debate surrounding the sport's origins. After that, and up to the discussion regarding the more recent era when a man named Alexander Cartwright formulated rules with his teammates, the chapter is all about Mr. Robert Henderson, his findings on the subject, and his resultant theories as to the origins of this great sport. In all the years that sports scholars and general historians have attempted to discover baseball's origins, only Mr. Henderson succeeded." Pointing to Henderson with his thumb, Beals added, "No one else. Just him. I am going to ask that those of you wishing to applaud his success and the honor it brings to our fine institution hold off until Robert reads the third and fourth paragraphs I am now asking him to read."

Turning to Henderson and pointing to the place where he was to begin, Beals said, "Robert, would you kindly begin reading the two paragraphs that begin here."

With an uncharacteristic level of humility and uncertainty, Henderson began reading the second and third paragraphs.

> "However, most of the unbiased probers have come to accept the version unearthed by Robert William Henderson in his book, *Ball, Bat and Bishop* (Rockport Press, 1947). Henderson, as the librarian of the Racquet and Tennis Club of New York, had an abiding interest in bat-and-ball games. Also, his role as supervisory chief of the main reading room in the New York Public Library and his 35 years of research on game origins come through this volume as clear-cut, complete and convincing.
>
> Quoting eminent anthropologists, Henderson repeatedly proves that all modern ball games are derived from religious rites of ancient times, with fertility (of crops or people) as the

main theme. He places the first recorded "batting contest" in Egypt some 5,000 years ago."

"Congratulations, Robert," Beals and von Stade of the Racquet and Tennis Club began in perfect unison, "you literally rewrote the history books." Beals continued, "Ladies and gentlemen, we proudly bring you Robert William Henderson."

The crowd which was now quite large, broke out in a loud applause—library employees, his family, a couple of friends and fellow members from the Grolier Club, a few members of the Racquet and Tennis Club—and several bystanders he did not know. Though anything but shy, Henderson was characteristically humble and did not speak.

Director Beals asked Lucy, "Mrs. Henderson, can you find something for Mr. Henderson to do this afternoon?"

Henderson interrupted, "I don't think I can leave just yet. There's some unfinished business to conclude."

"No, Robert," Beals retorted. "You're done for the day. This place may become quite a circus with the press and all. Besides, you can't have all the fun. Skiddy and I want in on that action too! For us, it's because we know the guy that figured out what no one else could. He figured out the origin of baseball!"

Continuing with the thought, von Stade noted, "That's right! Ralph and I will enjoy boasting how important we are having a man of your talent working for us."

"Get your coat and hat, dear," Lucy instructed of Henderson.

Henderson half-heartedly inquired, "Are we going to Lord & Taylor?"

"Only if you wish," Lucy replied. "There's so much I like to do when we're in Manhattan, I'm certain you'll pick something with me and all of us in mind. Whatever you decide though, make it fun!"

Henderson turned to his grandson. "Well there, Frank. Fun is your department. You be thinking what we should do!" As Henderson spoke, Lucy firmly clutched the librarian's arm with her two hands and gently tugged Henderson, who seemed trained enough to appreciatively obey.

The applause Henderson received from well-wishers would continue. Newspaper articles giving Henderson credit for determining baseball's origins would appear in publications time and time again. Two years later, applause continued to echo. This time it was in the chambers of the Eighty-Third United States Congress. On June 3, 1953, Congress recognized Robert Henderson and Alexander Cartwright for their contributions to the sport of baseball.

As required, Henderson retired from the public library at age sixty-five. In that same year, 1954, the librarian decided to found the Old Guard in White Plains, a social club for male retirees. In 1972, while at the age of eighty-two, Henderson took on an assistant at the Racquet and Tennis Club. He hired a recent Ivy League graduate by the name of Gerard J. Belliveau Jr. When both Lucy and Robert were eighty-six years of age, Lucy passed away. A couple of years later, Henderson mentioned a personal event to Mr. Belliveau, "The widow down the hall invited me to dinner the other night. I had a glass of white wine. First taste of alcohol I ever had. Lucky I didn't try wine earlier in life."

At the time of Henderson's retirement in 1979, the scholarly Charles Scribner IV, with whom Henderson had known since *Junior* was a child, was now running Charles Scribner's Sons Publishing Company. Scribner had also served for the past eight years as Chairman of the club's Library and Art Committee. Ironically, the history of Scribner and Henderson had similarities to the relationship and closeness between Henry Chadwick and Albert Spalding.

Henderson officially retired on his ninetieth birthday, December 25, serving in his sixty-fifth year with the club. The gruff-but-kind Scribner decided to put on an extraordinary retirement party six days later in Henderson's honor. Although the celebration was on New Year's Eve, it was clear to all present that the affair was produced for the specific purpose of honoring Mr. Henderson. The party was held at the Tennis and Racquet Club and, not unlike the Delmonicos banquet of ninety years earlier, offered a menu that included a limitless number of fine champagnes, caviar, and many other delicacies.

Henderson soon thereafter moved to Hartford, Connecticut, where he would spend the remainder of his life near family. Robert W.

Henderson passed away in Hartford Hospital on August 20, 1985, at the age of ninety-five. The librarian's death was not unheralded. One of the publications covering Henderson's passing was the September 2, 1985, issue of *Time Magazine*. In the publication's "Milestones" section, Mr. Henderson was mentioned along with three other persons: Mikhail Baryshnikov, the Reverend Sun Myung Moon, and Melanie Griffith.

As of this writing, Mr. Belliveau is in his fiftieth year with the club.

Regardless of the acceptance of evidence Henderson found to disprove the Doubleday myth, a survey of the American public would, to this day, indicate that many citizens and fans still believe that Abner Doubleday invented modern-day baseball. Further, and with which the author concurs, the National Baseball Hall of Fame and Museum continues to retain Abner Doubleday as a Hall honoree, and the baseball field by the museum's grounds continues to be named *Doubleday Field*. Thus, despite all evidence to the contrary, the *ball of lies* remains remarkably well preserved.

* * *

This book is dedicated to Howard, husband of my dear sister for sixty years, and a wonderful role model who gave me so much, and never asked for anything in return other than my respect.

BIBLIOGRAPHY

Major Reference Repositories

National Baseball Hall of Fame Library and Giamatti Research Center

The National Baseball Hall of Fame and Museum, Cooperstown, New York. Online at baseballhall.org, inclusive of the Giamatti Online and Reference Library, ABNER Online, and access to other archives, videos, articles, and collections. Some of the many references (photographs separately acknowledged) accessed are listed below:

Jeff Idelson. 'First Installment', *A Shrine is Born in Cooperstown: The Early Innings (1939–'58)*, accessed 2018.
baseballhall.org/hall-of-famers/spalding, "Al Spalding", accessed 2021
The Greatest Team Ever, *Memories and Dreams*, Donor Ed. 2020, pp. 7–8.
National Baseball Hall of Fame and Museum. Giamatti Online Library via link: Menu "In Nine Innings" East Archives Series I, Box 1, Folder 14, Aisle 9, Range A, Shelf 2.
www.collection.baseballhall.org at the National Baseball Hall of Fame and Museum
AG Mills Papers, BA MSS 13, Series I, Volumes 1-8 on microfilm, accessed in 2015 on location

Several documents from the Spalding Scrapbooks referenced within the book and use the following citation:

BA SCR 042 Albert Spalding scrapbooks, 1904–1908, BL-4256-2000, National Baseball Hall of Fame Library, Cooperstown, New York.

Specifically-referenced documents first viewed in 2005 and later years include the following.

Judge W. H. Van Cott, memorandum of witness.

James E. Sullivan as Secretary of the National Base Ball Commission, based on writing by AG Spalding, *Early History of Base Ball.*

Meeting Minutes, Recapitulation of Baseball Centennial Executive Committee, June 1, 1939, Commodore Hotel.

Menu, Testimonial Banquet to Mr. AG Spalding and his Party of Representative American Base Ball Players, April 8, 1889.

AG Spalding, Letter to John A. Lowell, Esq., of Boston, November 5, 1904.

Unsigned, Letter to John Grum of Brooklyn, November 19, 1904.

D. J. McAusean of the US Treasury, Letter to the commission, December 2, 1904.

AG Spalding, Letter to Abraham Mills, February 7, 1905.

AG Mills, Letter to AG Spalding, March 27, 1905.

Abner Graves with introduction by the editor, *Beacon Journal*, Akron, April 3, 1905.

J. E. Sullivan, Letter to Abner Graves of Denver, April 6, 1905.

AG Spalding, Letter to AG Mills, April 13, 1905.

Henry Sargeant, Letter on Jotel Manhattan letterhead to J. E. Sullivan, May 31, 1905.

H. H. Waldo of Rockford, Letter to AG Spalding, July 7, 1905.

J. E. Sullivan, Letter to Philip W. Hudson of Houston, July 27, 1905.

AG Spalding, Letter to James Sullivan, August 13, 1905.

AG Spalding, Letter to Abner Graves, November 10, 1905.

Abner Graves, Letter to AG Spalding at Point Loma, November 17, 1905.

Letter of James Sullivan as "Secretary Special Base Ball Commission," Letter on AAU letterhead to Mills and committee members, October 12, 1907.

Society for American Baseball Research a.k.a. "SABR" (books published by SABR listed separately)

James Mallinson, "AG Mills", *SABR BioProject*, sabr.org/bioproj/person/a-g-mills, accessed 2012.

Bill McMahon, "Al Spalding", SABR BioProject, sabr.org/bioproj/person/al-spalding, accessed 2020.

Bill Nowlin, "Spalding Wins 50th Game of the Season", *SABR GamesProject*, sabr.org/gamesproj/game/october-26-1874-red-stockings-al-spalding.

Brian McKenna, "Fowler", *SABR BioProject*, sabr.org/bioproj/person/fowler/, accessed 2019.

John R. Husman, "August 10, 1883: Cap Anson vs. Fleet Walker", *SABR GamesProject*, sabr.org/gamesproj/game/august-10-1883-cap-anson-vs-fleet-walker.

New York Public Library

Humanities and Social Sciences Library, *Albert G. Spalding Collection*, *NYPL Catalogue*' issued by the New York Public Library.

R. W. Henderson, 'Baseball: The Earliest Known Rules', *The New York Public Library Bulletin*, Vol. 144, Issue no. 7, July 1940, p. 528.

Robert W. Henderson, 'How Baseball Began", *The New York Public Library Bulletin*, Vol. 41 Issue 4, April 1937.

Robert W. Henderson, 'Baseball and Rounders', *The New York Public Library Bulletin*, Vol. 43 Issue 4, April 1939.

Robert W. Henderson, 'Are We Celebrating a Fake "Centennial"?', *The New York Public Library Bulletin*, Vol. 43, Issue 6, June 1939.

The Spalding Collection, Special Collections off the Main Reading Room.

The New York Public Library Archive and Manuscripts "Lyndenberg, Hopper and Beals general correspondence".

The Theosophical Society in America

Online at theosophical.org and in person in Wheaton, Illinois or
   Pasadena, California through the Blavatsky Archives and Blav-
   atsky Study Center.
Henry Steel Olcott, Olcott diary 'Old Diary Leaves', vol. 1, The
   Theosophical Publishing Society, 1900.
Henry Steel Olcott, Olcott diary 'Old Diary Leaves', vol. 3, The
   Theosophical Publishing Society, 1900.
The Theosophical Society. The Lamasery at New York. Interviews
   with Madame Blavatsky, *The Hartford Daily Times*, December
   2, 1878, p. 1, reprinted at www.blavatskyarchives.com/hart-
   ford.htm for the Theosophical Society.
Blavatsky Archives and Blavatsky Study Center, "Who Is Helena
   Petrovna Blavatsky?"
Blavatsky Archives. Online, American Theosophical Society from
   Theosopedia, American Religions, Native, August 16, 2018.
The Blavatsky Study Center with links to: Blavatsky Reading Room;
   Library; Archives; Bookstore; and other article groups.

Magazines and Catalogues

Robert Edwards Auctions, Lot #469: 1907 Henry Chadwick "The
   Graves Fraud Letter" and "Origins of Baseball" Collection.
   Online Auction Catalogue. Lot # 469, Spring 2004, roberted-
   wardauctions.com, retrieved May 17, 2012.
"Six Hundred Years of Sport," *A Catalogue of an Exhibition Held at
   the Grolier Club*, December 12, 1940 to February 4, 1941.
Cover and Index, *Scribners Magazine*, April 1907.
William Hard, "Kenesaw Mountain Landis and His Altitudinous
   Fine" *The Saturday Evening Post*, September 14, 1907.
"Milestones. Died. Robert W. Henderson." *TIME*, September 2,
   1985, p. 45.

Newspapers

Most newspaper sources accessed online at newspapers.com, ancestry.com, nyshistoricnewspapers.org, and nytimes.com.

Nearly all domestic and foreign newspapers were secured online via newspapers.com. Some New York newspapers, e.g. *The freeman's journal*, were accessed via nyshistoricnewspapers.org or via ancestry.com. Some issues of the *New York Times*, available at nytimes.com, were made available via ancestry.com.

The New York Times (New York, New York)

"Died, Doubleday", *The New York Times*. June 13, 1939, p. 9.

Dana Vichon. "The Tao of Skinny-Dipping", *The New York Times*. April 28, 2005.

"Baseball Crowd Causes Forfeit", *The New York Times*. April 12, 1907, p. 10.

Arthur J. Daley, "Baseball Pageant Thrills 10,000 at Game's 100th Birthday Party", *The New York Times*. June 13, 1939, pp. 1, 32.

Wolfgang Saxon, "Robert W. Henderson Dies. Librarian and Sports Expert", *The New York Times*, August 20, 1985.

Guy Gugliotta, "New Estimate Raises Civil War Death Toll", *The New York Times*, Science Section, April 2, 2012.

"Baseball at Delmonico's", *The New York Times*, April 9, 1889, p. 5.

"The Weather", *The New York Times*, July 8, 1878, p. 5.

"Court Notes", *The New York Times*, July 8, 1878.

The Freeman's Journal (Cooperstown, New York)

"Connie Mack Pleased to Bring Athletics", *The Freeman's Journal*, April 5, 1939, p. 2.

"Contributions to Baseball Centennial", *The Freeman's Journal*, April 5, 1939, p. 3.

"Beautiful Effects", *The Freeman's Journal*, April 5, 1939, p. 5.

"Farley Sells Most Popular Commemorative", "Crowd over 10,000", "Many Autographs", "12,000 Throng Village", "Prizes Awarded in Old-Fashioned Parade", and "Letters to the Editor", *The Freeman's Journal*, June 14, 1939, p. 1.

"Baseball Adds Band Music in Colorful Event", *The Freeman's Journal*, June 14, 1939, p. 2.

"The Hall of Fame and Doubleday Field Fittingly Dedicated", *The Freeman's Journal*, June 14, 1939, p. 3.

"100 Years Old", *The Freeman's Journal*, June 14, 1939, p. 8.

Boston Globe and Daily Globe (Boston, Massachusetts)

"Sports, box scores", *The Boston Globe*, August 9, 1877, p. 5.

"Prospects for the Season in the Base Ball Field", *The Boston Globe*, April 14, 1878, p. 8.

"Base Ball", *The Boston Globe—Morning Ed.*, 18 May 18, 1878, p. 4.

"Sports, box scores", *The Boston Globe*, July 6, 1879, p. 1.

"Sports, box scores", The Boston Daily Globe, August 10, 1879, p. 2.

"Globe Trotters Feast at Delmonico's", *The Boston Globe*, April 9, 1889, p. 1.

"Georgia Peach is First of Immortals", *The Boston Globe*, February 3, 1936, p. 8.

"President Roosevelt Pays Baseball Fine Tribute", *The Boston Globe*, February 3, 1936, p. 8.

Associated Press, "Babe Walks Off With Big Show at Cooperstown", *The Boston Globe*, June 13, 1939, p. 18.

Chicago Tribune (Chicago, Illinois)

"Spalding Will Pitch", *Chicago Tribune*, October 20, 1888, p. 6.

"Today We Celebrate", *Chicago Tribune*, July 4, 1863, p. 1.

"Mrs. AG Spalding is Dead", *The Chicago Tribune*, July 10, 1899, p. 5.

"The Rockford Club Victorious by a Score of 29–23", *Chicago Tribune*, July 26, 1867, p. 4.

"Opening of the Dexter Park", *Chicago Tribune*, July 7, 1867, p. 4.

"Weather", *Chicago Tribune*, July 7, 1878, p. 2.

"Base-Ball. Boston, Chicago", *Chicago Tribune*, September 1, 1878, p. 7.

"Their Farewell Game", *Chicago Tribune*, October 21, 1888, p. 11.

"Spalding Will Pitch", *Chicago Tribune*, October 20, 1888, p. 6.

The Inter Ocean (Chicago, Illinois)

"Base Ball", *The Inter Ocean*, October 21, 1888, p. 6.

"The Farewell Game", *The Inter Ocean*, October 21, 1888, p.6.

"Base Ball. The Championship", *The Inter Ocean*, September 2, 1878, p. 4.

"The Farewell Game", *The Inter Ocean*, October 21, 1888, p. 6.

The Brooklyn Daily Eagle (Brooklyn, New York)

"Obituaries—Mary Hewitt Doubleday", *The Brooklyn Daily Eagle*, March 13, 1907, p. 3.

"Surrogate's Court—Henry Chadwick", *The Brooklyn Daily Eagle*, April 29, 1908, p. 3.

"Trade Talks" and "Overseas", *The Brooklyn Daily Eagle*, June 13, 1939, p. 1.

The Philadelphia Inquirer (Philadelphia, Pennsylvania)

"Old-timers" Game", *The Philadelphia Inquirer*, June 13, 1939, p. 20.

"Hitler's Plane", *The Philadelphia Inquirer*, June 13, 1939, p. 2.

"Base Ballists Dine", *The Philadelphia Inquirer*, April 9, 1889, p. 1.

Democrat and Chronicle (Rochester, New York)

"One More Baseball Argument", *Democrat and Chronicle*, May 7, 1939, p. 18.

"Centennial at Cooperstown", *Democrat and Chronicle*, p. 8.

"Wagners Defeat Collins" Team Before 11,000 in Centennial Tilt, 4-2", *Democrat and Chronicle*, p. 20.

The Cincinnati Enquirer (Cincinnati, Ohio)

"Base Ball—The 'Nationals,' of Washington City on Their Western Tour", *The Cincinnati Enquirer*, July 15, 1867, p. 3.
"The Great Base Ball Game", *The Cincinnati Enquirer*, July 16, 1867, p. 2.
"The Closing Game of Base Ball", *The Cincinnati Enquirer*, July 17, 1867, p. 2.

St. Paul Globe, Saint Paul Globe, Daily Globe and St. Paul Daily Globe (St. Paul, Minnesota)

"Anson Annihilated. The Chicago National Team Beaten by the Ruralists of St. Paul", *The Saint Paul Daily Globe*, October 22, 1888, p. 1.
"Laid Low By Long. Anson's Australian Contingent Outplayed at all Points by the Apostles", *The Saint Paul Daily Globe*, October 23, 1888, p. 5.
"Two Players Sold", *The Saint Paul Daily Globe*, October 24, 1888, p. 5.

Other Newspaper Sources

AG Spalding, "The Origin of the Game of Baseball", *Akron Beacon Journal*, April 1, 1905, p.6.
Letter to Editor by Abner Graves, "Abner Doubleday Invented Base Ball", *Akron Beacon Journal*, April 4, 1905, p.5
"Senator Gorman Dead", *The Baltimore Sun*, June 5, 1905, p. 1.
"Obituaries, Frank C. VanCleef Jr.", *The Berkshire Eagle*, July 24, 1996, p. 10.
"Flags Will Be At Half Mast", *The Billings Gazette*, April 23, 1908, p. 5.
Press Reporter Mr. McNeillan, "The National Game" insert, *The Cedar Rapids Evening Gazette*, October 24, 1888, p. 4.
"Cobb Voted Baseball's No. 1 Immortal Player", *The Los Angeles Times*, February 3, 1936, p. 27.

"Base Ball at Cedar Park", *The Louisville Daily Courier*, July 18, 1867, p. 1.

The Age, "News of the Day", Melbourne, January 7, 1889, p. 4.

"Hall of Fame Poll Ranks Ty obb No. 1", *The Miami Herald*, February 3, 1936, p. 16.

"Shanley Suggests that Congress Create a National Baseball Day", *Middletown Times Herald*, February 3, 1939, p. 8.

"The Bulletin", *Nashville Banner*, June 16, 1924, p. 5.

"FDR at West Point", *New York Daily News*, June 13, 1939, p. 1.

"Graves, 90, Shoots Wife", *Denver Post*, June 17, 1924.

"The Base Ball Match", *Daily Ohio Statesman*, July 17, 1867, p. 3.

"The Presidential Election", *Evening Bulletin*, November 25, 1888, pp. 2.

"Baseball Tourists!", *Evening Bulletin*, November 25, 1888, p. 3.

"Obituaries, Henderson, Robert William", *Hartford Courant*, August 20, 1985, p. 26.

"New York Library A Vast Building", *Hartford Courant*, January 21, 1908, p. 18.

"Tyrus Cobb No. 1 Immortal in Baseball's Hall of Fame", *The San Francisco Examiner*, February 3, 1936, p. 19.

"Baseball Needs New Hero Crop", *Spokane Chronicle*, February 3, 1936, p. 14.

"Base Ball", *Daily Blade*, Toledo, August 11, 1883, p. 3.

"Baseball Players" by December 9, 1888, Press Association Telegram, *Press*, Auckland, Vol. 45, Issue 7225, December 10, 1888, p. 5.

"Shipping Telegrams", "Match at Auckland", "Base Ball, An Interview with a Player" by Our Special Reporter, *Press*, Auckland, Vol. 45, Issue 7226, 11 December 1888, pp. 4, 6.

"Football Notes. The Rugby Game", *Liverpool Mercury*, December 10, 1888, p. 7.

News of the Day. Last Aussie Match", *The Age*, Melbourne, January 7, 1889, p. 4.

"Crystal Palace, American Base-Ball", *The Times*, London, March 14, 1889, p. 1.

"The American Baseball Players", *The Times*, London, March 15, 1889, p. 8.

"Cruel Blow Struck Doubleday Legend", *The Windsor Star*, August 16, 1947, p. 12.

"AG Spalding Dies", *The San Diego Weekly Union*, September 16, 1915, p. 1.

"Death Claims AG Spalding at Lomaland; Apoplexy Cause", *The San Diego Union*, September 10, 1915, p. 3.

"AG Spalding Dies, Apoplexy Victim, in Point Loma Home", *The San Diego Union*, September 10, 1915, p. 1.

"Base Ball Match", *Rockford Weekly Register Gazette*, October 7, 1865. "Spaulding" played first team for Pioneers beat Mercantile second nine.

Online References Not Previously Listed

Google at google.com was the primary search engine of choice.

Wikipedia at wikipedia.org was utilized more than any other online resource for both discovery and corroboration of data and information.

Google Maps at google.com was used as a reference in hundreds of instances.

Encyclopedia Britannica Online was also used at multiple times for a variety of subjects at: britannica.com.

"The First Shot of the Civil War: The Surrender of Fort Sumter, 1861", *Eye Witness to History*, eyewitnesstohistory.com, accessed 2006.

John V. Langdale, "The Growth of Long-Distance Telephony in the Bell System: 1875–1907", *Journal of Historical Geography*, Vol. 4, Issue 2, pp. 145–159, April 1978, published by Elsevier Ltd., accessed at www.sciencedirect.com on January 3, 2017.

Baseball Almanac, baseball-almanac.com/teamstats/schedule, retrieved in 2017.

The Lincoln Log, "A Daily Chronology of the Life of Abraham Lincoln," accessed via www.thelincolnlog.org.

American Battlefield Trust, "Vicksburg: Animated Battle Map" and "Gettysburg: Animated Battlefield Map," battlefields.org.

baseball-almanac.com/teamstats, Chicago Area Team statistics for the years 1865–1878, accessed 2020.

baseballhistorydaily.com/tag/ned-williamson, "I was in Sort of a Trembling Condition", accessed 2020.

baseball-almanac.com/teamstats/schedule for the years 1865–1878, accessed 2019.

baseball-reference.com/teams/CHC/1876.

baseball-reference.com/players/s/spaldal01, accessed 2020.

timeanddate.com/sunrise.

Drake Baer and Richard Feloni, 'Fifteen Teddy Roosevelt Quotes on Courage, Leadership, and Success', *Business Week*, February 14, 2016.

Benjamin Hill, "Fowler: A 19th-century pioneer," *MLB.com*, February 9, 2006.

Waymarking.com "US Post Office, Cooperstown, New York."

AmericanRhetoric.com Babe Ruth, National Baseball Hall of Fame Induction Ceremony Speech transribed by Michael E. Eidenmuller.

Baseball-Reference.com var from First National Anthem on May 15, 1862, at Brooklyn's Union Grounds to extreme detail statistics.

www. Grolierclub.org.

The Civil War Trust, civilwar.org/battlefields/fort-sumter by Richard W. Hatcher, III.

civilwar.org/battlefields/fort-sumter "The Civil War Trust, Fort Sumter".

Gjenvick.com Gjenvick-Gjonvik Archives Passenger Lists, Fashion, and Epicurion.

Encyclopedia.chicagohistory Railroad Stations.

Geology.com United Kingdom Map, England, Scotland, Northern Ireland, Wales.

GoogleMaps.com

Mason White, "Elliott, the Tragic Roosevelt", The Hudson Valley Regional Review, Vol. 5 No. 1 via hundsonrivervalley.org., March 1988.

MapWatch.com New York Road Map.

Unit History Project New York Archives dmna.NY.gov 31st Infantry Regiment Civil War.

Amanda Kludt, Remembering Delmonico's, New York's Original Restaurant", NY.eater.com, June 29, 2011.

Albert G. Spalding, "Who Made America?", www.pbs.org/wgbh/theymadeamerica/whomade/spalding_hi.html.

Barbara Schmidt, "Special Feature: Mark Twain and Baseball", twainquotes.com.

Twenty-fourth Annual Reunion…US Military Academy No. 1134 Class of 1842, 9 June 1893, retrievable at Penelope.uh/Thayer/e/gazetteer.

Fergus M. Bordewich, *Smithsonian Magazine*, "Fort Sumter: The War Begins", accessed via smithsonian.com, April 2011.

chipublib.org/archival_post, Chicago Public Library, Archival Collections A-Z online, accessed 2020.

wikiwand.com/en/history_of_the_chicago_cubs, "History of the Chicago Cubs", accessed 2020.

nzhistory.govt.nz/culture, "New Zealand History", last viewed April 2021.

www.loc.gov, Civil War Manuscripts, Manuscript Reading Room, Library of Congress, Washington, DC, accessed 2019.

mendotamuseums.org, "Mendota Railroad History", Mendota Museum and Historical Society, accessed 2020.

chicagology.com/goldenage, "Union Depot—History", accessed 2020.

nationalrrmuseum.org, National Railroad Museum, Green Bay.

usps.com/who-we-are/postal-history, "James A. Farley", accessed 2019.

wikitree.com.

Books Referenced

Albert G. Spalding, *America's National Game*, American Sports Publishing Company, New York and Oxford, 1911.

Peter Levine, *AG Spalding and the Rise of Baseball*, Oxford University Press, Inc., New York, 1985.

David Block, *Baseball Before We Knew It*, University of Nebraska Press, Inc., Lincoln and London, 1944/2005.

Burt Solomon, *The Baseball Timeline*, "A Stonesong Press Book" licensed by Major League Baseball Properties, Inc., 1st American Ed., DK Publishing, Inc., New York, 2001.

Compiled and edited by Dean A. Sullivan, *Early Innings*, University of Nebraska Press, Lincoln, and Bison Books, 1995/1997.

Hy Turkin and C. Thompson, *The Official Encyclopedia of Baseball*, A. S. Barnes and Company, Inc., New York, 1951.

John T. Winterich, *The Grolier Club 1884–1967 An Informal History*, The Grolier Club, New York, 1967.

Robert W, Henderson, *Ball, Bat, and Bishop*, Rockport Press, Inc., New York, 1947.

Edited by Lyle Spatz, *The SABR Baseball List & Record Book*, Society For American Baseball Research, Scribner, Simon & Schuster, Inc., New York, 2007.

Philip J. Lowry, *Green Cathedrals*, Society for American Baseball Research, Walker & Company, New York, 2006.

David S. Neft, Richard M. Cohen, and Michael L. Neft, *The Sports Encyclopedia Baseball*, 20th Ed., St. Martin's Griffin, New York, 2000.

Edited by Craig Carter, *Complete Baseball Record Book*, 2003 Ed., SportingNews Books, The Sporting News, Div. of Vulcan Sports Media, Inc., St. Louis, 2003.

Bernard Grun, *The Timetables of History*, based upon Werner Stein's *Kulturfahrplan*, First Touchstone Ed., Simon & Schuster, Inc., New York, 1982.

Joint Committee on Printing, *Pius Louis Schwert, Memorial Addresses Delivered in Congress*, United States GAO, Washington, 1942.

Stephen Freedman, "The Baseball Fad in Chicago, 1865–1870," *Volume of Sports History*, Vol. 5, No. 2, Summer 1978.

Eric Enders, *100 Years of the World Series*, Sterling Publishing Company, Inc., New York, and Barnes & Noble Publishing, 2005.

Stephen Wong, *Smithsonian Baseball, Inside the World's Finest Private Collections*, Smithsonian Books, HarperCollins Publishers, NYC, 2005.

Henry Chadwick, *Haney's Base Ball Book of Reference*, Haney & Co., Publishers, New York, 1867.

William Doyle, *Inside the Oval Office*, "The Oval Office September 27, 1940, 11:30 A.M.", Kodansha Iternational USA, 1999.

Abner Doubleday, *Reminiscences of Forts Sumter and Moultrie in 1860-'61*, Harper & Brothers, Publishers, New York, 1876.

Helena Blavatsky, *The Collection: Isis Unveiled, The Secret Doctrine, and The Key to Theosophy*, Timeless Wisdom Collection, The American Theosophical Society, Kindle ed., 2015, based on writing from c. 1877.

Miscellaneous Ephemera and Resources

Robert and Lucy Henderson Marriage License, *England and Wales Civil Registration Marriage Index, 1837-1915*, accessed via ancestry.com.

Lucy Henderson Death Certificate, *US Social Security Death Index 07/1976*, accessed via ancestry.com.

Abner Graves Passport Application, retrieved from www.Ancestry.com, film #007545441.

The Illinois Society of the Sons of the American Revolution, "Albert Goodwill Spalding Descendent of Simon Spalding," *US, Sons of the American Revolution Membership Application, 1889–1970*, applied for January 9, 1893, retrieved via ancestry.com in 2018.

Massachusetts Vital Records, "November 15, 1875 married Josephine Keith", *Marriage Index*, West Bridgewater, #239 of 665.

Census, July 17, 1860, taken, Byron (9) with Mary (5) and Walter (3).

Census, June 7, 1900, taken for A. Spalding, 121-5 Madison Ave., Manhattan, New York, New York.

New York State Birth Index.

New Jersey State Census Abraham G Mills accessed via ancestry.com.

Ellis Islands Records and Arhives available at heritage.statueofliberty.org.

ABOUT THE AUTHOR

A good portion of the author's career was spent in leadership positions for a high-tech Fortune 100-size company. At different times, he was in charge of Global Accounting, Corporate Investments, and various departments or high-profile, large-scale government contracts. He subsequently founded a small analytics consulting firm. This business provided market and industry research and analysis, produced bid proposals to administer the operations of government programs, and created and authored strategic planning documents for clients. Dayboch simultaneously founded a CPA practice and maintained a minority interest in an entertainment and hospitality business located across the bay from Atlantic City. Over the years, the author served as volunteer and/or trustee for a variety of charitable and fraternal organizations. Jim is a graduate of the Eller College of Management at the University of Arizona. Prior to college, he was honorably discharged from the US Air Force where he served one tour at Phan Rang in the Republic of Viet Nam.

Jim has been an avid baseball fan since attending in childhood the first ever home game for the Minnesota Twins. He is a member of the Society for American Baseball Research (SABR), The National Baseball Hall of Fame and Museum, and various other museums, libraries, societies, and research centers. The author has a cat named Stormy, resides in a 175 year-old home in Maine and, although a forever Twins fan, roots for the Red Sox and against *you know* who with son, Anthony.

CPSIA information can be obtained
at www.ICGtesting.com
Printed in the USA
BVHW030628260322
632546BV00004B/37